# Lunar Shadows

# Awaken

THREADS OF DESTINY BOOK 1

A PARANORMAL ROMANCE

# Lunar Shadows

# Awaken

D. M. MALONEY

For my husband Ryder, my first
reader and my number one fan.

Thank you for believing in me.

# CONTENT WARNING

This book contains depictions and events that address sensitive topics, such as mental health struggles, sexual assault, explicit language, graphic sex, graphic violence, gore, and death.

Reader discretion is advised.

# CONTENTS

# CONTENTS

# CONTENTS

Unable are the Loved to die,
for Love is Immortality.

—Emily Dickinson

# CHAPTER ONE

## THE ENCOUNTER

### KYRAN

Narrowly avoiding another cart collision, I lean over the packaged beef options with a scowl. I despise being out at this time, there is always an excessive amount of people shopping on a Friday afternoon. At least this is only a monthly trip. I don't think I'd manage more than one busy public outing very well. The general public disconcerts me.

Unfortunately, my drive home will be half an hour longer today because of the weekend special being half-off beef and poultry at the fancy grocery market across town. I should just assign errands to Treyvar since *he* actually enjoys socializing—hell, he *thrives* in it. Although, I suppose I could benefit from the occasional time away from the pack and have some personal space for myself.

With a sigh, I drop my selection of scrumptious ribeye steaks on top of my full cart and move toward the front of the store to checkout. A frown pinches my face as I glimpse two gossipy older women squawking like hens, and my footsteps falter.

I glare at their ignorantly positioned carts in the main aisle preventing my passage. Grimacing, I glance over my shoulder to find an elderly couple behind me hunched over something they pulled off of an end-cap. I'm forced to either turn into the baking aisle filled with the potent scents of detestable chocolate, or face the doom that is a middle-aged woman hellbent on not going home to her loathsome husband. I swiftly decide holding my breath for thirty seconds is the superior choice.

Dragging the full cart around the corner, I walk briskly until halfway down the aisle I notice a petite, curvy woman struggling to reach the top shelf. I pause, briefly considering turning back and finding another route, but the image of the two hens flashes in my mind and I suppress a shudder. *Damn this baking aisle—and this grocery store for that matter—to hell.* I continue down the cursed aisle, finding myself slightly amused with the woman's attempts of climbing the shelf like a squirrel scaling a tree. With each reach her breath puffs out, accompanied by groans of frustration. She mumbles something incoherent with her last attempt at obtaining who-knows-what at the back of the top shelf. As she stretches onto her tiptoes reaching far overhead, the movement accentuates her body in an enticing way, drawing my eyes down over her dips and curves—

*Stop, enough. She is a woman, not a piece of meat to drool over like a dog. You are better than that.*

Momentarily squeezing my eyes shut and pausing my steps, I take a short breath in through my mouth, release it slowly, and inhale deeply to hold once more. Without ogling at her like an animal, I notice how her platinum-blonde hair is twisted into a loose, messy bun atop her head, how she has flour splotches across the front of her baggy gray t-shirt and black leggings. Glancing down, I realize that we are wearing matching tan, fleece-lined moccasins, and the corner of my mouth lifts at the similarity.

*Offer her some assistance, or are you just going to stand here like a fool?*

I should just keep walking and mind my own business, but *something* halts my steps, preventing me from passing her. Clearing my throat as I approach, I remark lightly, "You look like you could use some help."

"Yes, I could," she huffs, pushing stray hairs away from her face with her free hand.

With her feet on the second shelf, we are equal in height, and as she glances over, I am struck by how her eyes are such a piercing crystal blue. I inhale sharply, and my head swims from the overbearing scents filling the aisle.

Scents both odious and intoxicating.

As if transfixed, I cannot bring myself to tear my gaze from hers. This woman has fully captivated me, within just a single moment. She is ethereal with her large, icy eyes, and pale blonde hair framing her delicate jawline. I smirk at the cute upward curve of her dainty nose and her lips part beneath my gaze. Her alabaster skin seems silken, beckoning me for a caress from my fingertips.

She appears ageless, and she is undoubtedly the most beautiful, breathtaking woman I have ever seen in my entire life. *Probably will ever see.* My eyes flutter with the sudden compulsion to inhale deeply through my nose. I nearly become intoxicated from her magnificent scent of rich jasmine combined with the crisp, fresh aroma the air holds after a snowfall. It makes me blissfully unsteady.

*She smells the way moonlight feels. Bright. Free. Like home,* my wolf whispers, his attention stirring at the scent.

A shiver runs down my spine and I blink rapidly, suddenly embarrassed for the unexpected awkward silence. Holding my breath, I break my gaze to reach above this enchanting woman. I grasp the boxed item and gently hand it to her before I hastily grab my cart, rushing out of the aisle. I am immensely grateful that there isn't a line as I head toward the closest empty checkout lane. Quietly groaning, I release the pressure in my chest in a *whoosh* as I scrub my hand over my face.

*Who is she? Why didn't you catch her name? Go back and find her,* Valdr demands, louder this time.

Shaking my head, I promptly stack all the meat packages onto the conveyor belt, glance over my shoulder, toss the bagged ones back into the cart, take another glimpse, and absently swipe my card through the reader. I look back once more, as if by chance I will catch sight of that alluring woman again.

"Sir? Your receipt," the cashier drawls as she stares at me pointedly, holding a long, narrow slip of paper over the register. She raises an eyebrow at me in a silent question.

"Thank you," I murmur while I take the receipt, crumpling it into my pocket.

I make my way out of the busy market and into the fading sunlight, pushing my cart across the cracked asphalt. Tossing the rolled paper bags into the large coolers stowed in the bed of my truck, I snap the lids shut and close the tailgate. More precisely, I unlatch the tailgate and slam it up a second time to ensure it stays closed, knowing how the damned thing pops open with a mean pothole from time to time.

Ol' Bertha is a black 1988 GMC Sierra 1500. She's been everywhere with me since I bought her on a whim during the holidays of '87 off the showroom floor of the fancy dealership out in the city. Pulling open the creaky door, I hop onto the seat, being mindful to avoid the old tear in the edge seam of the cushion and fire up the engine with a thunderous start. Yanking the door shut with a *pop*—the hinge sticks if it's opened too wide—I settle back into the comfortably worn maroon bench seat, shift into first, and head home.

After rolling the window crank down, I rest my arm on the frame to steer while I press up on the radio volume to better hear my favorite tape over the wind. Treyvar insists I take some of our bar earnings and buy myself a brand new, full-size pickup to replace this 'shitbox', but I love this ol' gal. Although she's got some characteristics about her, she runs clean and is in good shape. The way I see it, *'if it ain't broke, don't fix it'*. To me, Ol' Bertha is the best truck I could ever ask for. I smirk as 'This Old Truck' bounces from the crackly speakers.

Rubbing my thumb on the smooth steering wheel, I praise, "Bertha, you know you'll always be my number one gal."

Four times in the hour-long drive home, I catch myself wondering about those icy blue eyes. The desire to gaze into them again is strong, the memory of her intoxicating scent taunting me the whole way.

Cresting the hill at the end of the paved road, I slow my truck to enter my packland's drive. To anyone not aware, the road dead-ends into a small turn around. The path seems overgrown and rough, but it only remains that way for a mile as a deterrent to keep humans away from our homeland. There are several other areas across my entire territory that we use for temporary living, and some of my pack choose to live scattered among these places. I only ask that they maintain security and defense for our territory. My packlands cover approximately one and a half million square miles throughout the Rocky Mountains region. This place has always been, and is what I'll always call, my home.

After threading my truck through low-hanging branches and around bushy shrubs, the glow of my headlights broadens over the lush expanse of one thousand acres filled with rolling valleys, soaring forests, flowing rivers, and small clusters of family homesteads nestled deep into the far northwest corner of Montana. Toward the back region of my homeland are the mountains where my father chose to plant the roots of our pack in the foothills about three hundred years ago. He relocated the pack from the southern part of our territory when human colonizers began moving westward, and his intention was to keep the werewolves guarded. The steep border acts as a protective barrier around the villages fanning outward from the main pack lodge.

Departing the mouth of the passage, my head warrior quickly mindlinks, *Alpha.*

*Good evening, Sigurd,* I mindlink back with a nod in acknowledgment.

Shifting my truck, I pick up speed, cruising through the valleys until the edges of our community appear. Slowing to a safer pace, I smile as I pass through the villages and return the greetings I am given.

"Hello, Alpha!" chirps a young girl's bright voice.

"Good evening, Alpha," an elder voice calls out.

*I'm looking forward to the Convocation, Alpha,* insinuates an old, familiar voice.

I felt that one and with a chuckle I shake my head at Miss Stjarna. She winks at me with a grin from the doorway of her gem shop. That unfortunate woman has spent her entire life of seven hundred twenty-five years searching for her mate.

Mindlinking her back directly with a wink of my own, I jest, *Only in my wildest dreams, Stjarna.*

As I pass her by, she dramatically swoons into the door frame, her thin arm draped over her long, silver-plaited hair. My chuckle turns into a full belly laugh as I pull into my driveway. Even though I've lived my entire life here, the sight of my home never grows old. The main pack lodge is a luxurious, three-story log cabin that was hand-built as a gift for my mother to raise her six children in. My father poured his heart into this home, every detail from the position of the windows to the nature-inspired filigree throughout the home was done with my mother's preferences in mind. Her soul is carved into the very bones of this house. Every time I gaze long enough, I can still see her beaming smile as she opened the front door to call us in for supper. She was my sun, always shining radiant warmth over my life, and every bit of good inside me is because of her.

Swallowing my sudden sorrow, I let the memories fade as I park in the garage and unload the coolers, dragging them into the pantry room. I lift the lid to the closest of four large chest freezers, upend both bins into it, and slap the top shut. Turning around, I find Trey in the doorway gawking at me, completely appalled.

"*Kyran*, seriously dude? Can you not read 'beef', 'poultry', 'pork', and 'fish'?" he chastises me, leaving his mouth agape.

"Nah." I grin, pointing to each of the four chests. "I just see 'fr-ee-z-er'" I turn my shoulder as he halfheartedly throws a punch.

Leaning back against the door jamb, I observe Treyvar as he sorts out the meat haul, once more thinking of our mother, forever seeing her in my brother and sister. Trey is the youngest of my family, and he—as well as his twin Kira—inherited all of our mother's traits. Straight golden hair, gentle jade green eyes, and a warm, charming smile with the personality to match. The only differences being his height at six feet, whereas my mother was petite and lean. Trey is lean as well, with a strength that nearly matches mine. Being my brother and most trusted friend, I chose him as my second in command. I need him to take my place on occasion, and having him as close to my equal as possible, the better.

My mind wanders a bit as he organizes the freezers, my gaze drifting over the stocked shelves and a flash of icy blue draws my eyes closed. Recalling the enticing woman from the store, I clear my throat with a shake of my head. I wait until he finishes with the freezers before asking, "Hey, you up for some training in a bit? I need to let some energy out."

"Yeah, sure. Gym or field?" Trey asks lightly.

"Gym. I need a good workout to clear my head."

Picking up both coolers, Trey nods as he rounds the corner and says over his shoulder, "Sounds good. I'll meet you down there in about ten minutes?"

"Alright. Grab the gloves," I call back, turning into the kitchen.

His voice floats out from the garage, taunting, *"Oof,* that bad, huh?"

Shaking my head, I make my way through the spacious kitchen and head up the stairs two at a time. The second floor holds an open common area with a pool table, bar, poker table, and a couple sets of sofas along the southern, glass-paneled wall at the front of the stairs. Around back, there is an extensive lounge room and multiple bedrooms for the unmated highest-ranking pack members and guests.

Hearing the TV, I round the stairs and find Kira, my younger sister, sprawled on the large sectional. Her left leg is slung across the top cushion, and her right arm dangles over the side as she clicks the remote rapidly, flipping through channels. Hearing my pause, she rolls over, pulls herself up and plops onto the armrest.

Kira flashes me a bright, toothy smile. "Hey, Ky, how was the new store?" She tilts her head slightly, causing her sleek hair to cascade like a golden waterfall over her shoulder.

Kira, being Treyvar's twin, is playful, carefree, and humorous. Though Trey tends to get stuck in the clouds, Kira remains level-headed and keeps the two of us grounded. She is our glue and both of us know we couldn't manage this home—let alone our pack—without her in it. Briefly returning her smile, I just shrug and head up the stairs to my private quarters. Kira flops back onto the couch and recommences her channel surfing unperturbed, knowing not to pry.

Entering my suite, I shut the door with a sigh and lean my head back, closing my eyes in the quiet. These rooms are my sanctuary and no one is allowed inside, including Treyvar and Kira. Most of the third floor is mine, except for a small loft at the top of the stairs for anyone wishing to meet with me while I am inside my rooms. Upon entering from the loft, the bright, luscious atrium is calming, and the gentle scents of the plants help relax my tense mind.

My bedroom takes up most of the left side of the third floor, each room connected by open archways makes for an easy flow, except for the art studio. I boarded up that room long ago. My father built this set of rooms to give my mother her own personal safe haven with the two of them sharing this floor together, excluding the studio. That room was hers and hers alone.

Stepping forward, I breathe in the tropical aroma of the atrium. In the century that I have resided in these rooms, I have kept this garden alive, perhaps even thriving. Various plants hang from the metalwork separating the panes of glass on the ceiling, crawl across the shelving surrounding the windowed walls, and rise from several diverse pots scattered across the floor. Blooms of all colors and scents create a spectacular kaleidoscope, and the earthy soul of the room soothes my restless thoughts.

Gliding my fingers over a soft white star, I lean in and lightly inhale the sweet—and now alluring—jasmine fragrance. I close my eyes, struck again by that mysterious woman from the market. *Who is she? Where could she have come from?* I wonder, recalling her uniqueness.

I have lived in this territory my entire life for just over three hundred years, and never have I encountered someone like her.

Valdr's rough voice curls through my mind. *You must go back. I want to see her again. There is something about her, she is different.*

Straightening, I make my way through to the bathroom, absentmindedly rubbing a hand against my chest. My wolf is restless, he has been since looking into *her* eyes.

*Valdr,* I respond, *the chances of us running into her again are slim. It's a large town. What if she is from the city?* I lean over the sink and place my hands on the counter top, staring at myself in the mirror. *Even if we happen to see her again, what could she possibly want me for?* I wonder despondently.

My amber eyes flash brightly, Valdr's growl rolling through me with his growing agitation. *We are the Alpha of the Rocky Mountains Pack, and a fucking powerful one at that. Get downstairs. I need an outlet for this energy, whatever this feeling is. I don't want to listen to your unwarranted self-depreciation,* he huffs indignantly.

Suppressing a smirk, I cross through my bedroom to quickly change, and make my way to the basement gym for a boxing match with my brother.

An hour into sparring, Valdr distractingly flashes crystal blue eyes across my vision, causing me to falter my block and allowing Treyvar to land a blow to my jaw. Snarling, I glare at him as I chastise my wolf. *Why did you do that? You intentionally caused my mistake.*

*I cannot escape the image and scent of her, it's beginning to consume me,* he grumbles back. *This isn't working. I need to run.*

Rubbing my chest, his unease affects me and I briefly close my eyes, expelling my irritation with a sigh. *Okay, we will. Just wait a bit longer so I can clean up the gym,* I mumble and he recedes a little bit.

Looking up, Trey gawks at me with one red-gloved hand still raised, the other hanging limply at his side. A slow grin spreads across his face and he goads, *'Dude,* I've never landed a full hit before! Looks like someone has lost their game." He taunts me, bouncing on his toes and tapping his gloves together.

"Don't expect it to happen again," I remark shortly, removing my gloves.

Taking a long swig of water, I sit on the matted floor and drape my forearms across my knees. I tilt my head back against the wall, closing my eyes to sort through my thoughts. Trey removes his gloves and takes a seat next to me, giving my shoulder a nudge. I crack an eye open to look sideways at him and he scrunches his brow in return.

In earnest he asks, "Kyran, what's going on? Has something happened? I could tell you were off earlier in the pantry, but didn't feel like you were up for talking. All jokes aside, I know you're more than aware that I have never been able to get a hit on you before. So talk. What's up?" He moves so he is sitting in front of me, mimicking my posture.

*This is useless. Go outside or I'll do it myself,* Valdr demands.

Ignoring him, I momentarily consider how much of the truth to tell Trey, and quickly decide that out of anyone, he is the best person I could confide in. Sighing, I fully open my eyes and look at him levelly. "Alright, I'm going to ask that you stay open-minded with this, okay?"

He nods his head instantly without any humor in his eyes.

Nodding in return, I continue, "I hadn't intended to, but I went to the fancier grocery market across town because I saw an advertised sale in the paper. On my way to the checkout, I had to use the baking aisle and held my breath, because, as you know, I can't stand chocolate." I look pointedly at Trey and he chuckles with a nod.

"Anyway, I noticed this woman climbing the shelf. She was too short to reach something at the top, so I went to help her. When I looked into her eyes…" I pause, swallowing some more water as I vividly recall the intensity of that moment.

"What? What did you see?" Trey interrupts, leaning forward a bit with his brow pinched in interest.

"Her eyes are a bright, striking icy blue. I was almost in a trance. She is the most beautiful woman I have ever met, and with just a glance, she completely captivated me." I avoid his gaze at my admittance.

He leans forward with wide eyes. "Do you feel anything else? Are you sure she wasn't a witch? Maybe we should get one of the healers to assess you. Shit, I'll call Eir now and have her check you over to make sure you aren't under a spell of some kind." Trey rushes as he pulls his phone out and taps the screen, his brows lowering with concern.

To be honest, that thought had never crossed my mind. I consciously focus on my strange encounter, assessing it from a new perspective. Valdr's attention piques, his agitation easing momentarily.

*No,* he denies, *this is not witchcraft. It does not feel the same as what Vala did. It feels…natural. Pure. Not heavy and suffocating.*

Silently agreeing, I rest my palm over Trey's phone and explain, "Yes, I feel something, but it's different than witchcraft. Valdr agrees with me. This is something else."

Nodding slowly, Trey sits back and pockets his phone, waiting for me to continue.

I think aloud, ticking off things I've already considered. "Although her eyes astonish me, it's her *scent* that I cannot shrug off. I'm not certain, but I don't think she is a witch, and she doesn't smell like a human because of how potent her scent is. She is *definitely* not a vampire, it was still daylight outside."

Trey lets out a sigh. "She's not a wolf, or you would've known her as a rogue or part of a pack. Plus, wolves don't have light blue eyes," Trey surmises with a shake of his head. "What else could she be? Wait, faeries aren't real, right? They are just myths the humans tell stories about. Please tell me I haven't been lied to my entire life," he jests, dramatically widening his eyes, trying to lighten my mood.

I silently raise an eyebrow at him, unamused. My other brow arches, suddenly realizing, "She could be a wolf. Maybe I just didn't pay close enough attention? Although, she would have behaved differently, with me being an Alpha, if she was from another pack. Why would another pack have a lone female in my territory anyway? Besides, a rogue wouldn't have even let me walk halfway down the aisle without either bolting or standing ground to fight." Groaning, I drop my head into my hands.

"What did her scent smell like? Could it have been an overbearing perfume, perhaps?" Trey suggests, trying to reason with my thoughts.

Without lifting my head, I immediately describe, "It was overwhelmingly intoxicating. I couldn't function any of my other senses, locked into her gaze and half drunk, my head swimming with her. I wanted to bury my face in the crook of her neck and just *breathe*. Valdr was practically spinning in circles, making me all the more dizzy. Since that encounter, I have not been able to think of anything besides her alluring smell and breathtaking eyes. Nothing else, only *her*."

Treyvar is silent for a moment, the only sound his soft intake and release of breath. In a subdued tone, he reminds me, "Your mate died before you met her. Your fur shows that."

Valdr, who has remained alert, becomes increasingly unsettled once more. Slowly raising my head, I cross my arms over my knees and prop my chin on my forearm. Sighing, I mutter, "I know. That's why this has been bothering me so much. It just does not make *sense* to me, all of it. I cannot explain this."

*Enough with talking. I need to run,* Valdr clips as he pushes at our internal boundaries.

"What does Valdr think about all of this, about her?" Trey asks, peering at me wonderingly.

"He instantly said, that moment in the aisle, *'She smells the way moonlight feels. Bright. Free. Like home.'* I have never heard him refer to anything—let alone *anyone*—like home. Not even here, this house, these woods. Not once," I reply solemnly.

Eyes slightly wide, we both stare reverently at one another for a few heartbeats. With a tight nod, Trey pushes to his feet and I follow suit, gathering my gear and handing it off to him.

With a sly smile, Trey proposes, "Well, hey, maybe you should pick up groceries across town for a while. Give the baking aisle a try every now and then." He gives me an exaggerated wink.

Staring at him blankly, I try to suppress a smirk and fail when Trey waggles his eyebrows. Grinning his victory, I give his shoulder a light shove, heading to the sliding doors to undress. Trey puts away the boxing gear and makes his way over, removing his shirt as well.

"No," I interrupt him, "Valdr needs to let loose. I don't know where we'll go, but I'll be sure to be back home before dawn. I need you at Howler's before opening for an early shipment. If you need anything, just mindlink me."

Trey nods and leans against the door as I turn around. I shift and glance up at the quarter moon. Releasing a deep howl, I receive a few in return across the valleys. Giving Valdr control, he dashes across the lush yard and into the depths of the dark forest.

Whenever Valdr takes over, I can relax and drift in the essence of our woven soul, not really thinking, just observing the outside world through his senses. Valdr is the stronger being between us. It is he who gives me my power and authority as an Alpha, and in his wolf form his power is doubled. Only hearing me when I intend him to, I appreciate this shared form of existence that allows me to have my own personal mental privacy.

Just as when I am in control of the human form of our body—he can hear my every thought, feel every sensation my body encounters—I can do the same with him in physical control of our wolf form. I have the capability to take control over him in this state, as does he with me, if either of us allow it. We could *force* control as well, but out of respect for each other's autonomy, we mutually agree that unless absolutely necessary—in terms of our life at stake or anything related—we will not infringe upon our respected physical forms.

Our thoughts are willingly shared. It helps us to better understand each other, as well as form a solid bond, a companionship. If truly desired, we could completely block the other out, as if walling up our separate consciousness. We tried that once when we were just a pup, and it was a very lonely, cold feeling that neither of us want to experience again. We have since lived cooperatively without much of an issue.

Throughout the night, I scarcely pay attention to his actions and feelings, giving him some privacy and myself some much needed rest. A while back, I noticed slight changes in scenery, but paid no mind, feeling his unsatisfied restless energy coursing through our body.

After some time, I glimpse the bright shine of the moon and stars through sparse branches overhead, and a gentle peacefulness settles over us, allowing sleep to finally take hold.

While my eyes are closed, the alluring scent of jasmine rouses me, and I realize I *still* cannot get that woman off my mind, even with Valdr peacefully resting. A pain scrapes across my bare chest and my eyes snap open to the lightening sky overhead. Belatedly registering that it's daybreak, I find myself lying naked beneath a large blackthorn shrub. I scrub my hands across my face and notice my arm covered in dirt, sweat, and a little bit of blood, assuming Valdr had an unusually rigorous and extended run.

I look down only to come nose to beak with an abnormally large raven perched on my chest. Its beady black eyes stare directly into mine. My eyes widen as I take one swift look around, realizing with horror where I am. I instantly shift into my wolf form, the bird frantically flapping around as I bolt as fast as I can in what *I truly hope* is the direction of home.

Running hard on sore, tired muscles, I mentally cry out, *Valdr! Wake the fuck up!*

My paws pound the earth, heart hammering just as hard and fast. Without a reply, I shout harshly, *VALDR!*

His only response is him stirring slightly.

*What the fuck, Valdr!* I grit my teeth, grunting as I attempt to keep track of the distance and timing it takes me to get home. Panic sets in because I don't have any clue as to how we ended up *there, of all fucking places.* After hurtling through sixteen miles, I cross the borderline to my homelands at breakneck speed. I don't even register the warrior greeting me until I'm halfway across the valleys, and as I blur through the villages, I barely see any of my pack milling about.

I rapidly shift, crashing through the front door of my home and slam directly into Treyvar, Kira hot on his heels. Both look exhausted with bleary eyes and red, puffy faces. With a heaving chest, I collapse onto my hands and knees, weak from pure exhaustion as I surrender completely to unconsciousness.

# CHAPTER TWO

## THE ENCOUNTER

### SELENE

Exasperated, I growl in frustration with my third failed attempt of grabbing this crucial ingredient for Asteria's ridiculous 'healthy' dessert. *As if that is even possible, dessert isn't meant to be healthy.* I take a breath, place my hands on my hips, and contemplate my choices. Either I walk away without the sugar substitute and face the wrath that is my cranky, sugar and carb-deprived sister, or I figure out a way to procure this damned thing and get back home to finish baking before she kills me. Determined to reach this cursed artificial sweetener, I figure that climbing the shelving is my only option.

Wiping my sweaty palms on my leggings, I accidentally rub my hands in flour that *poofed* on me earlier this afternoon. While preparing some decadent chocolate chunk cookies, I may have been a tad overzealous with mixing the dry ingredients to the beat of 'Blue Monday'.

Clapping my hands together, I grin with resolution. *This might actually help.* I glance down the aisle, and seeing how nobody is around to assist me, there aren't any scolding eyes to chastise me either.

*Fuck it, I don't have the time to chase down an employee anyway.*

Gritting my teeth, I grip the edge of the top shelf and wedge my foot between two sacks of flour. Stretching my arm up and over, my wiggling fingers barely graze the box I need, pushing it further back. Straining on my tiptoes with one leg kicked out, I grunt loudly in frustration, yet again inching the damned box completely out of reach.

I contemplate risking a jump to grab it, but instantly picture my clumsy ass sprawled humiliatingly across the tile floor and think better of it. Sighing in resignation, I hang my head, mentally preparing myself to call Asteria and let her know she won't be eating her cardboard hockey pucks tonight. This way, she can rage about it without me there and the flames will settle before I get home. *At least, I seriously hope so.*

Feet scuff the floor nearby and an amused husky voice comments, "You look like you could use some help."

With one hand still holding onto the shelf, I shove my messy hair off my sweaty forehead and respond on an exhale, "Yes, I could."

Glancing up, I am startled to see a tall, ruggedly handsome man smiling at me. He's burly, but he has a kind and playful lopsided grin. Standing level with me, his piercing, wild amber eyes stun me, and my mouth pops open beneath his intense gaze. Never before have I seen such mesmerizing eyes. *I want to paint them, their color and infinite depths that lure me in.*

I can't help but gawk at him as my gaze drifts over his features. He has shoulder length, unruly midnight black hair with a scruffy beard to match, a straight nose that slightly hooks right at the tip, a mischievous, sultry mouth, and clear sun-kissed skin conveying his time spent outdoors. My eyes involuntarily drift downward, absorbing how his broad shoulders stretch the black t-shirt across his thick chest and equally powerful, tattoo covered arms.

My cheeks flush and I snap my mouth shut, forcing myself to look elsewhere. I notice he has a shopping cart chock full of...*meat?* Scrunching my brow, I glance back at him as he reaches up and grabs the box of elusive sweetener. *What a peculiar man,* I muse, eyes following his movements.

When he carefully draws his arm downward, I catch a whiff of his cologne, oddly compelled to inhale it as deeply as I can. Closing my eyes, I *feel* him the way sunshine warms a forest after a rainstorm; his scent is earthy and slightly musky, but in a comforting, pleasant way.

*Wow, he smells incredible,* I breathe the thought with a sigh. Feeling more than a bit flustered, I blink stupidly as he gently hands me the small box. Before I can even attempt to voice my gratitude, he snags his cart and promptly disappears around the corner without a word.

Stumbling down off the shelf and grabbing my basket from the floor, I rush to grab the last few items on my list. Hurrying to the checkout lanes, I hope to see that mysterious, captivating man again to give him my thanks. Searching around, I realize that he is gone, nowhere to be found, as if he was only a figment of my imagination. *Tch, like I could conjure up something as wonderful as him.*

I frown, feeling oddly disappointed and choose a lane at random. I absentmindedly place my items on the conveyor belt before paying with exact cash. Thanking the cashier and bagger before trudging out of the market, I sling my canvas bag onto my shoulder and head toward my sister's powder blue Prius. I slide in, gently closing the door. Pressing the power button to start the car, I hear the little *beep* and sigh, wishing for my own vehicle again. Not that I have anything against her Eco-friendly car, but Asteria's idea of practicality is a bit too *blah* for me. I prefer something with a bit more…character.

*Damn you, Bolvi, for wrecking not just my car, but my life.* The intrusive thought pops into my mind as I stare at the wheel. My ex-boyfriend—if he could even be called that—was abusive, controlling, manipulative, and really just an all-around piece of shit. I didn't spend much time with him, less than three months to be exact, but he still managed to dismantle so much of my life. He would belittle me and make me believe that I wasn't worth anything to anyone if I wasn't *'the fun girl'*. Going out with his friends, any chance he got he would shame me into drinking more alcohol than I was capable of handling, and I would always become embarrassingly drunk. I never fully remembered what happened during the nights we would go out, but I always felt like shit the next morning, and regretted it every time.

Bolvi became threatening, almost to the point of physical violence when I told him I did not want to spend my time with him anymore. Thankfully, he does not know where my home is, and I am still super grateful it isn't near the city. It took quite an effort to get him to leave me alone; I had to change my phone number twice in two months. I left the city, moved back in with my mother and sister to evade him. He saw me out with Ria and our friends once, about two weeks ago at what was our usual lounge in the city. In a complete psychotic rage, he stole my car and totaled it beyond repair. That was the last time I had seen him, and I truly hope to never set my eyes on that foul, pathetic excuse of a man again.

Asteria had offered to help me purchase a new vehicle, but I adamantly refused, feeling like this is something I need to heal from and resolve on my own. She respected my choice and has kindly given me free use of her car in the meantime. Smiling to myself as I think of my sister, I make my way home to our cozy cottage in the woods to bake her 'dessert' as my way of showing my gratitude. She allowed me my autonomy and I, in turn, respectfully cater to her unique lifestyle, even if I find it sacrilegious.

Halfway home, the golden sun sinks below the horizon, igniting the sky in an amber glow with a striking new familiarity. Wistfully, I daydream about seeing that mysterious meat-cart guy once more.

By the time the headlights illuminate our ornate wrought iron gate, the sun had long-since sunk beneath the horizon, making way for a clear night sky. I wait as the bars lazily swing open at my arrival, then ease the Prius onto the winding dirt driveway.

Nestled in the center of one hundred acres rests our splendid yet quaint cottage, surrounded by what I can only describe as a natural paradise full of every flower, herb, tree, and shrub imaginable. Approximately thirty acres around our home are luscious open fields dotted with varying fruit bearing trees, soaring pines that whisper to the clouds, smooth pebbled pathways curling around mossy boulders, assorted flower beds, and two glittering creeks leading to a vast, two-acre wide pond. My favorite spot, the small, weathered white-painted gazebo rests behind the picturesque pond, caressing the edge of the forest. Shading the gazebo is an enormous, ancient willow whose branches cascade down, sweeping the shore. Off the left side of the cottage, my second story bedroom and cozy balcony overlook the spectacular view.

Behind our home is the largest fruit, vegetable, and medicinal garden I have ever laid eyes on. In the exact center of the garden sprouts a prodigious, circular three-tiered fountain with a large gazing ball on top resembling a sparkling full moon. Surrounding the exquisite fountain in quarters is a breathtaking moon garden, shaped by tiers of semi-circle beds filled with glowing moonflowers, stars of jasmine, supple gardenia, and evening rain lilies. I have spent endless nights laying on the edge of the fountain beneath the moon and stars, basking in the glorious aroma of the blooms. More than enough times to count I have asked my mother how these flowers stay alive—being native to warm climates—and she always just gives me a small smile, answering, *'With love, dear,'* and leaves it at that.

My mother's only request is that we keep out of the forest. She has always been averse to the woods, ever since I moved here fifteen years ago as a teenager. To enhance her *request*, she lined the three edges of the fields with spiky blackthorn shrubs which tangle together to create an impenetrable makeshift fence. The visual effect is beautiful when in bloom, but it's slightly intimidating when it is just the bare thorny branches.

Pulling up the rest of the driveway, I gaze at my beautiful home in the moonlight. Our cottage consists only of wood, stones, and metal, except for the furniture and decor filling each room. Potted plants live in every nook and cranny, and more books than any library I've ever been in are stacked, scattered, and displayed anywhere there is a flat surface throughout the house.

The cottage is spacious but practical, giving the three of us and our two dogs plenty of room to live, yet not be wasteful with utilities. We have electricity, though it is only used for sparse modern luxuries. Except lights. I have no idea *why* the aversion to light bulbs, of all things, but have never questioned it out loud.

A grand, antique candle chandelier drapes over the center of the first floor, dripping with glittering crystals, and it emits enough light for the entire floor. Torch-like sconces are dotted throughout the home, and every evening we light the candles with the flame from the large hearth in the living room. As far as I can remember, there has always been firelight in our house, and never have I seen it without the warm glow.

Parking my sister's Prius under the carport, I loop my bags over my shoulder and walk around to the front veranda. Two large caged torches burn brightly on the stone pillars, warming me as I skip up the steps and into the foyer. I carry the groceries into the kitchen, placing the bag on the wide island. I discreetly stash my prized pint of fudge brownie and cookie dough ice cream deep into the back underneath bags of frozen diced veggies.

Quietly closing the freezer and padding to the living room, I find Asteria sitting cross-legged on the floor in front of the TV. She's wearing a black sweatshirt with the hood pulled up and fuzzy purple flannel pants, carefully painting her pointed nails blood-red while watching *Hocus Pocus*.

"Hey, Selene," Asteria greets me without looking up from her nails, being mindful not to smudge the polish. "Were you able to find the sweetener for my keto cookies?"

Sitting back in the corner seat of our small leather sectional, I tuck my feet under me and softly reply, "Yes, I did, though not without difficulty." I pick at the hem of my old t-shirt, remembering the help I was given.

*Specifically the helper.* I smirk at the memory.

Dipping the little wand into the bottle of polish, my sister grins over her shoulder and teases, "It isn't necessary to hide your ice cream from me, regardless of the poorly chosen, conspicuous place. I am willingly choosing to forgo all that is carb-loaded and sweet. Day three and my headache from hell is finally receding. I'm already feeling clearer, and who needs all that extra sugar anyway when you're as sweet as me?" She tosses me a sly wink.

My only response is a flat stare, not at all amused when for the past few days she has been nothing but totally *sour*. Asteria has been absolutely intolerable to be around, resulting in me scouring the Internet for hours to find some damned fake cookie recipe to 'satiate the cravings without caving'. *Speaking of cravings, I wonder if meat-cart guy is a local? How would I even ask that, though, without sounding too eager?* I wonder, trying not to smile.

"Okay, okay. I apologize, I know I haven't been the most pleasant person to spend time with this week, and I'm sorry for that. I did not expect this to be such a difficult task for me. Not all of us can eat whatever we want with no consequences like you," she lightheartedly jests, turning back around to screw the nail polish bottle closed.

Ria lithely rises from the floor and plops next to me on our worn couch. Pulling down her hood, her long, shiny auburn waves spill over her shoulders, making her eerie violet, almond-shaped eyes stand out in contrast. Though her hair color is artificial—her natural tone being a soft black—it is still strikingly beautiful. I examine my sister in comparison to me. Where I am petite, she is lanky. The roads of my body take a more scenic route, whereas hers are direct and streamline. Her rich, olive skin contrasts my pallor tone. In a sense, we are like opposite polarities, and perhaps that is why we fit together like two puzzle pieces.

By no means do I feel inferior to Asteria; on the contrary, I think we make a pair of uniquely beautiful women. However, I do not find myself to be extraordinary, if anything I am just a bit different than the average woman around my age. More than a few times I have been asked if I have albinism because of my complexion and hair, and the answer is no.

The mystery man crosses my mind again. *He didn't seem perturbed, though, earlier today. If I'm not mistaken, he might have been interested in me, based on the prolonged look he gave me. But, why would he suddenly disappear?*

Completely lost in my thoughts, I almost miss Ria's question. "So are you up for making the cookies, or what?"

Halfheartedly replying, *"Mm-hmm,"* I replay the expression on Mr. Amber-eyes' face, concluding that he was definitely more than impartial to me. *Why didn't I act on it? Ugh, this is why I'm still single at thirty-one. He probably thought I wasn't interested.* I shake my head ruefully.

Ria's hand lightly grips my shoulder, and I turn to face her as she asks, "Hey, Sel, are you okay? I did not mean that joke about eating stuff, you are the most beaut—"

"Ria, *shh*, you're fine. I'm not upset, I know you were joking," I interrupt, reassuring her with a small smile. "I…met someone today at the market, and I can't help but keep thinking about them," I hedge with a slight grimace.

Her lavender eyes immediately round, doubling their size. "Who is he? What does he look like? What happened? Tell me *everything*. I need *details*," she demands, quickly turning to pull her legs up and crosses them, propping her elbows on her knees with clasped hands.

Stalling for time, I pull the clip from my hair and stick it in my mouth, slowly twisting my hair and refastening it while composing the events in my head.

*"Selene, I swear—"*

*"Ugh, alright!"* I throw my hands up with surrender. "I didn't catch his name, but he was huge and wild and kind and *ugh*, he smelled delicious and—" I take a deep breath, "and he was the most beautiful man I have ever seen in my *entire life*." My cheeks flush at the admission.

Stunned speechless, Asteria blinks at me, having never heard me speak so rashly before. Her owlish eyes narrow to a squint as she orders, "Explain, and don't you *dare* leave anything out."

Taking a slow breath, I nod with a small smile. "In the store, I was failing miserably at getting your sweetener. It was on the top shelf and every attempt I made to grab it pushed it further back out of reach. Having no other option, I climbed the shelves and *still* could not get a hold of it. Just as I was nearly giving up, this tall, burly man with incredible amber eyes offered to get it for me and I immediately accepted, grateful for the assistance. The weird thing is, when we looked at each other, it was as if I could not move, breathe, *think*. All I could see was him, and there is *a lot* of him, if you catch my drift." I enhance my words with a wide hand gesture.

Ria raises her eyebrows with a quick nod and I continue my encounter. "I felt so embarrassed, hanging on the shelf and ogling him like an imbecile, so I forced myself to find something else to look at. Get this, he had an *entire shopping cart* full of raw meats! It was so peculiar that whenever I think of this moment, I call him meat-cart guy." I giggle at the nickname and glance up, Asteria's face rapidly shifting from humor to pinched skepticism.

Sensing the doubt, I quickly reassure her. "He was a kind man, really. He grabbed the sweetener for me and even handed it to me gently, then left without a word. I'll admit, I was a bit disappointed to not get his name. I wanted to ask you, does he sound like anyone you know from around here? Or perhaps one of your friends might know? It's a long shot, but I was hoping to maybe see him again," I admit shyly, my voice growing quiet.

Ria remains silent for a few heartbeats, seeming to digest my story. Wringing my hands, I bite my lower lip and wait for her reply.

Giving me a small smile, she simply says, "I don't know personally, but I'm sure I could ask around."

As if manifesting from thin air, our mother sits on the coffee table and leans in between us. "Hello, dear, how was the market?" she asks with a smile, swiping a stray hair behind my ear.

Before I can answer, Asteria chimes in, "Sel met an interesting man today." She grins wickedly as she hops off the couch and scampers away into the kitchen.

Glaring over my shoulder at her, I shift uncomfortably as my mother takes Ria's vacant seat. Groaning internally, I briefly squeeze my eyes shut before turning back to face my mother. Trying to buy extra time before she questions me, I comment, "Your hair looks lovely this way, you should wear it short more often. It suits you." I give her a bright smile, hoping she will focus on herself and not my inactive love life.

My mother enjoys changing her hair the way some women use clothes. She must have an entire closet full of an assortment of wigs in all lengths and styles to fit her mood for the day. Yesterday, she wore her hair pin-straight down the length of her back. The day before that, it was choppy layers with blunt bangs. She is partial to the color, though, her hair always being raven black. Like Asteria, they have identical, ethereal eyes and a pretty olive skin tone. She is a reserved woman, and she especially values her privacy above all else. Her private quarters are off-limits, and she extends this preference to our property in general, having it fully fenced and gated to keep unwanted guests away. Regardless of her peculiar ways, I wouldn't trade her for any other mother.

Sixteen years ago, I was adopted by Kat who had rescued me from a tragic accident. I was in a coma for an extended period of time, resulting in prolonged amnesia. To this day, I have been unable to access memories of my past before waking up in the hospital. I have no painful associations—and therefore no grief—over what was perhaps lost, only a mere curiosity; I was told that there was nobody for me to return to.

I moved here when I was fifteen years old and have lived a peaceful life, besides my botched 'relationship' with that piece of shit

Bolvi. With my mother being more than well-aware of *that* ordeal, she tends to be a bit protective of me when it comes to men. She and my sister are the two most important people in my life, and I have had my fair share of relationships in the decade away from home, but nothing has ever been serious enough to have introduced anyone to my family.

Giving me a wan smile, my mother sighs and folds her hands in her lap. "Selene, I would love to hear about your encounter, it has been some time since you met anyone *decent*. However, do not feel pressured to share anything that you are uncomfortable with. Just know I am always here for you and your sister, no matter what, okay?"

My brow scrunches, caught off guard by her solemn tone. I was expecting another harping lecture on *'taking the time to find the right partner, save myself for someone worthy'*, and am taken by surprise with her previous archaic views not being present at the moment. I rest my hand over my mother's and genuinely tell her, "Yes, I know. Thank you."

She holds my gaze for a moment and narrows her eyes, giving me a sly smirk. "Let's go bake some desserts, yeah?"

We find Asteria at the kitchen island with all the ingredients needed for her no carb, no sugar cookie recipe, and together we bake and dance to some folk music crackling from the record player. At the *ding* of the timer, I remove a tray of sad, crispy, thin cookies from the oven. With a frown, I place the baking sheet on the island, giving them a look of disdain.

Cackling, Asteria picks one up and turns it around, stating, "Well, this is completely unappetizing."

Her teeth crunch into the cookie, crumbles crashing onto the tray. About three chews in, her mouth twists down into a scowl as she hurries over to the trash bin to spit out the bite.

Chuckling, I take a seat and the creaking oven door betrays my mother's sneaky attempt of sliding in her own tray of white chocolate macadamia nut cookies. She gives me a silent wink over her shoulder. Amused, I watch Asteria promptly grab the tray of our failed experiment and upend them into the trash bin. Plopping back down onto her stool, she rests chin in her hands and jokingly pouts.

Knowing that despite the drama, she is genuinely disappointed, and I consider the recipes I have. *I might be able to create something that fits her diet plan.* I lean forward, catching her attention. "Hey, let's both go to the store tomorrow morning to get some almond flour and anything else you might think would work for you, and we can give this another try in the afternoon, okay? I have an idea that might work," I add with a supportive smile.

The timer *dings* again. We both look up and smell the decadent aroma of our mother's cookies as she places the scrumptious tray in front of us.

Staring hard at the tray, Ria groans. "Fuck it," she mutters as she caves and snatches a cookie, shoving it in her mouth. Her eyes roll closed with another groan. *"Mmmf, thith ith tho goof!"* she exclaims around a mouthful, pulling laughter from both myself and our mother.

Grinning, I quickly get up and scurry over to the freezer, pulling out my ice cream. I turn and place the pint on the island, holding out three spoons. The three of us dive in greedily. I take two golden cookies and squish a scoop of ice cream between them, making a scrumptious little sandwich.

Before taking a bite, I look at Asteria and ask, "Hey, Ria, do you think Hazel and Melody would like to meet up next Friday? It's been a little while, you know?" I scrunch my nose, remembering the last time I'd seen our friends was when I had the blowout with Bolvi. We all used to get together weekly before *the incident.*

Ria eagerly nods with a big smile. She's more than likely going to be whining tomorrow about breaking her diet three days in, but I plan to create at least a *semi-decently* flavored recipe for her as long as she wants to continue it. She's been a solid support for me through all of this and I intend to fully reciprocate that as best I can.

After gorging on sweets and giving my mother the rundown of my strange encounter at the store, she gives me a silent, long look then just nods once, leaving it without any comments or questions. Glancing over at Ria, she busies herself with intently examining one of the last remaining cookies. Unperturbed, I wash our spoons and toss the empty pint into the trash bin. My family isn't the most normal, they both behave quite odd at times and with them being related, I always just assumed it was a trait they shared.

"I'm going to wash up and go to bed. Goodnight Mother," I give her a squeeze, "and I'll see you in the morning," I add with a smile at Asteria as she wipes the counter tops clean.

Making my way upstairs to my bedroom suite, I have the thought that we are not a typical household. Most women my age have long-ago left and planted themselves in a home or apartment of their own, many of which are even married and have families. I was one of those women, but years passed and I never felt *at home* anywhere I went. I've always been drawn back here, back to this town, and my mother said she felt most comfortable with her daughters under her roof.

Not to mention my horrible experience of a 'relationship' that could have ended *way* differently had I remained by myself. Asteria and I agreed that we would move in here, on the terms of the three of us sharing the home as equals. We pay our share of costs, split duties around the home and property, and take care of each other in general. In simple terms, we are all very tightly knit.

After a quick shower, I squeeze my hair with a towel, pulling the curtains open wide over my balcony door. I gaze at the clear moon shining through the glass, admiring its beauty.

Shuffling to bed, I can't help but replay what I felt when looking into that mysterious man's eyes. He was captivating, kind, charming, and just as delicious as the dessert was earlier. *Who buys that much meat, though? Maybe he was hosting a large cookout or something. I'd like to see him again, even just once. I want to thank him for his help.* I yawn tiredly, smiling at the prospect.

Rolling onto my side and yanking the covers over my head, I slowly fade into a restless sleep.

*Racing through the forest, I weave around trees and under branches, feeling as free and light as the wind. A soft glow emanates around me, illuminating my invisible path. The tiny hairs at the nape of my neck raise, sending shivers down my spine, though not from fear. Pure joy and warmth radiate within me, feeling the chase coming to an end. Breaking through the tree line, I dash across lush, tall grass dancing in the midnight air. Spinning around, I slowly prowl back the way I came, crouching low to the ground. Raising my head above the soft blades, two glowing amber orbs pierce into my soul, beckoning me to follow into the depths of the woods. Stepping forward—*

I bump into something solid, my hands flying out into thin air. As my eyes tear open, I distressingly find myself at the edge of my balcony, reaching out over the railing. I instinctively throw myself backward and trip over my own feet, plopping painfully onto my ass. With my legs sprawled out in front of me, I gawk at the lightening sky, completely bewildered and disoriented.

*What the hell? Why am I out here, at dawn?*

The chill of early morning pushes me to my feet, and I wrap my arms around my torso, quickly shutting the doors. I slowly sit down at the edge of my bed, unsure of how I ended up on the balcony in my sleep, and wonder what that dream was or even meant. *Maybe I should ask Ria, she has a profound knowledge on the dream realm and its interpretations,* I consider as I stare at the glass doors.

Nodding to myself, I shake off the sleepiness and get dressed for the day in an oversized light gray hoodie and comfy black leggings, haphazardly brushing my hair and twisting it up into a claw clip. I head downstairs, deciding to share my dream and odd sleepwalking with Ria later this morning on our ride to the market.

# CHAPTER THREE

## MORE THAN COINCIDENCE

### KYRAN

*Kyran, wake up. Please don't leave us. Wake up, we need to know you're okay,* a distant voice pleads in the dark.

Gasping, my eyes fly open to a view of my loft railings. Groggily sitting up, I rub my face and groan, my body aching all over. Looking around, I realize that I'm wrapped in a blanket on the sectional with Trey and Kira hovering over me. My brow pinches at the tears streaming down my sister's face. Trey, however, is livid.

"Where the *fuck* have you been? What happened, why couldn't I mindlink you? There was no connection, like you just fucking vanished from existence!" His chest heaves, face flushed and mottled.

"I went out to run and I guess I lost track of ti—"

*"All night!* You are *never* out for more than three hours unplanned," he seethes through clenched teeth, hands fisted at his sides.

"Trey, relax. I will explain in—"

*"Relax?!"* he shouts, spittle flying. "Kyran, I thought you *fucking died!* I had to tell Kira my fears after *six hours* had passed because our connection was vacant. We were about to gather the fucking pack before you busted through the door!"

There's a glint in his bright jade eyes and it registers how awful this must have been for him, and for Kira. I understand why he couldn't contact me, but to him it must have felt terrifying to reach for our bond and it not be there. Clutching the blanket, I slowly stand and grasp Treyvar's shoulder.

Holding his gaze, I sincerely apologize, "I did not intend to cause you distress. I truly lost track of the time and where Valdr was going. I will explain to you the cause for our disconnection, but I need to take a shower. I regret the pain this has brought upon you. Both of you," I add, looking over his shoulder at my sister, feeling sorrowful.

Trey slightly relaxes, and I release him to briefly hug Kira. She tightly squeezes my middle with a sniffle and gives me a wan smile. Climbing my stairs, I turn halfway up and ask Kira, "Would you mind taking over duties today? I will meet with you momentarily in the kitchen to answer your questions," I add, switching my gaze to Trey. They both nod once and I continue up the stairs, closing my door a bit more forcefully than intended.

*What the fuck is wrong with you, Valdr? Do you have a death wish?* I snarl mentally, dropping the blanket on the bathroom floor as I crank the shower handle to the hottest setting. Whipping around, I stalk to the sink and glare at my reflection, grimacing at my tangled mess of hair and the gross smears all over my face. *What fucking reason would you have for going there, of all places?*

Eyes flashing brightly in the mirror, his indignation rolls through my chest and releases in a low growl.

*You're annoyed, with me? Are you fucking serious? You almost got us killed! We shouldn't be here right now!* I berate him with narrowed eyes.

The sink creaks and I release my death grip with a huff. Clenching my jaw, I briefly close my eyes and inhale through my nose before exhaling slowly out my mouth. Not bothering to close the shower door, I stand under the scalding water, washing away both the grime on my skin and the lingering trepidation from earlier this morning. Leaning forward, I place my palms against the tiles and drop my head, letting the water run cold.

Once I am dressed in my black work shirt and light jeans, I leave my room and slump down the stairs. Feeling exhausted, the thought of fixing a meal seems too big of a task to accomplish at the moment, and I appreciate the aroma of breakfast wafting from the kitchen. Shuffling in, I find Trey at the stovetop flipping eggs onto a platter filled with bacon, sausage, home fries, and a tall stack of fluffy pancakes.

Plopping myself onto a stool at the large island, I yawn and grin as Trey places the platter in front of me. "Thank you. For this, and for giving me some space earlier. I appreciate it," I say quietly, holding his gaze for a moment.

He silently nods and tosses me a fork. I shovel the food in as fast as I can chew and swallow. Trey takes a seat next to me with a slightly smaller plate, casting me a sidelong look. "What happened, Kyran? I don't ever want to experience that again." His voice is low with concern etched onto his face.

Raising a finger, I quickly scoop up the last few bites and turn on my stool to face him. "Valdr had been insisting on running for most of the day, so when I headed out last night I left him to it, not really paying much attention to what he was doing or where he was going. I barely even noticed the length of time either, and that's my fault. The entire time out running, I could feel his restlessness and didn't think much of it, not really noticing where he chose to finally rest. It was daybreak when I awoke, and I was lying beneath a blackthorn out past the western border. I ran back to our territory as hard as I could the moment I realized where I was." .

Treyvar's fork clatters onto his half-eaten plate, his hand still held up to his mouth. Eyes wide, he gravely whispers, "Were you seen?"

Swallowing hard, I nod silently, recalling the intense gaze of the raven. Trey presses the back of his raised hand to his mouth, his wide eyes boring into my solemn ones. "Are you *sure*? Don't you think she would have contacted by now? *Done* something? You aren't enchanted or cursed...I had Eir assess you while you were unconscious," Trey informs me, his face a bit pale.

"I'm unsure what to think about it altogether. Valdr won't even respond to me. He has not answered any of my questions about why the fuck he ended up there in the first place," I growl, still feeling extremely frustrated with him.

Trey clasps his hands and leans forward on his elbows, deep in thought. An image of the baking aisle at the grocery store across town—more specifically, *who* I saw in that aisle—flashes through my mind.

*Valdr, talk to me. Do you think she's connected? Neither of us felt magic from her. I need to understand why you went to rest in those woods. Were you compelled?* It is an effort to ask with a calm tone.

His response is curt. *I cannot answer your questions because I do not have the answers.*

Perplexed, I scrunch my brow and try to remember getting there. The only thing I can recall was glancing up at the moon numerous times throughout the night. *Why did you choose that shrub?* I ask with subdued confusion.

Sensing apprehension, I patiently wait for his reply. *I found her scent on the wind, and could not resist following it. I went as far as the barrier and no further, fearing the consequences,* he quietly admits.

*Whose scent? The witch's?* I clarify with a pinched brow.

Bright eyes of icy blue envelop my vision, causing my breath to falter. Trey notices and rests a hand on my shoulder. "Hey, are you alright?" he asks, brow creased with worry.

"Yeah, I just—I think—maybe I need to go back to the store," I stammer stupidly, gazing down toward the floor.

Perturbed, he asks, "Uh, *now?* Why?"

"Um, meat sale? You know, gotta stock up, can't pass an opportunity as it arises," I halfheartedly reply, rubbing the back of my neck.

He raises his eyebrow. I sigh, admitting in a mumble, "I'm hoping I can somehow run across that woman again."

A mischievous smile spreads across his face, crinkling his eyes. "Well, if you're feeling alright, I say go for it. Nothing ventured, nothing gained, am I right?" Trey winks, lightly pushing my shoulder.

I can't help but smirk at my brother. Even when in a bad spot, he finds a way to lighten the mood. The both of us stand and Trey takes our plates to the dishwasher before turning to me with a sly look. "Well, go on then. Get going," he demands and waves his hand, gesturing at the garage door.

I give him a small smile as I walk away, Valdr's anticipation rising as I enter the garage. Firing up Bertha, I keep the radio off with the window down, enjoying the white noise of the wind as I drive.

Pulling a cart from the stack, I meander around the store, glancing down each aisle in a pitiful attempt at finding her here. Realizing how unlikely it is for her to come here two days in a row, I give up after a full pass through the store and head toward the back wall. Figuring I should at least take advantage of the sale while I'm here, I reload what is essentially the same cart that I filled yesterday. Turning into the chip aisle, I hunt for something to snack on during the drive home. Pursing my lips, I grab two bags of chips—Doritos and sour cream and cheddar—unable to choose between them. Shrugging, I toss both bags atop the mounding cart, and continue down the aisle toward the checkout lanes.

I nearly stop dead in my tracks.

*No way, how is this possible?* I ask myself incredulously.

Seeing *her* again, here of all places, feels surreal. She is with another woman her age, staring up at the top shelf with a frown. A strange flutter in my chest snags my breath when her friend taps her shoulder and she quickly looks my way. I walk as casually as possible, careful not to betray my hidden elation as I step closer.

Although hushed, I clearly hear them whisper, "Who is *that?*" and "Holy shit, it's *meat-cart guy!*"

My sudden amused laugh drowns out whatever is said next.

## SELENE

With our heads bent close together, Ria murmurs, "*Mmm-mmm, look at him. He's so beefy, I'd throw away my diet just to take a bite outta his juicy—*"

"*Asteria! Shut the fu—*" I cut myself off as *he* approaches. Straightening, I raise my voice to greet him. "Hey, funny seeing you in here again, like this. Um, would you mind lending another hand?" I sheepishly ask, pointing to the organic dried cranberries on the top shelf.

Leaning forward, he quips, "Maybe you should keep a step ladder in your car. It seems that would come in handy." He smirks, easily grabbing a bag and passing it to me.

Rolling my lips into my mouth, I bite back a grin. Asteria nudges my shoulder as she turns around, announcing, "I just realized I forgot something. I'll be back in a couple of minutes." She slyly winks at me before rounding the corner.

My cheeks heat from her blatant behavior. Glancing back at the alluring man, I notice a catchy logo on the breast pocket of his black t-shirt, reading '*Howler's Bar & Nightclub*' in two arcs around an image of a full moon. "Is this where you work? I've never heard of it before," I murmur curiously, indicating his shirt with my hand.

Briefly looking down, he shrugs a rounded shoulder. "Yes, I, uh—" He clears his throat. "I actually own the place with my brother, Treyvar. We opened it earlier this year in the springtime, so it's still fairly new," he murmurs.

Wanting to hear his husky voice some more, a shy smile pulls at the corner of my mouth as I prompt, "Oh, that's awesome. Where is it?"

"Just past the town line, across from the city park on the corner. You can't miss it," he replies instantly. Rubbing his hand on the back of his neck, he offers, "You, uh, you should drop by sometime. I work the main bar. You can have any drink you'd like, on the house," he quickly adds and flashes a charming grin.

*I gotta tell Ria, we should change our plans for Friday with Hazel and Melody to check out his bar instead of the lame lounge we always go to.* The idea flits through my mind with a smile.

Blushing, I swipe a lock of hair behind my ear as I glance at my shoes. Peeking up at him through my lashes, I murmur, "I will keep that in mind. Thank you for your help, *again*." Taking a step back, I turn toward the end of the aisle.

*Shit, his name! I forgot to ask for his name!* I abruptly realize my mistake and pause my steps. Spinning on my heel, I gasp as I bump against him. My eyes flick to his, cheeks flushing from my hands splayed on his firm chest. He seems surprised as well, as if not expecting me to turn back around. Flustered, I stammer, "I-I, your na—I forgot—"

A squeak escapes me as he leans in close to my ear, another amused smirk tugging at his lips.

In a low voice, he murmurs, "Kyran, but *meat-cart guy* works just as well." He chuckles, grabbing the end of his grocery cart and drags it behind him as he leaves the aisle.

My mouth drops wide-open, face on fire. I momentarily forget how to breathe as I twist around, watching his wide back disappear. Ria crests the corner moments later, her face identical to mine and we grab hands, silently squealing like schoolgirls.

"Okay, Sel, I *totally* get why you were acting so weird yesterday!" she exclaims with a huge grin.

"*Shh!* He might still be nearby," I scold, grinning just as wide as my sister. Peering around the corner, I spot *Kyran* at the checkout. Pulling back before he notices, I round my eyes at Ria, still feeling a bit flushed. "Did you catch any of that?"

She snorts, rolling her eyes. "Duh, I was in the next aisle over. I heard *everything*." She waggles her eyebrows suggestively.

Smirking, I roll my eyes at her. "So you know about his bar, then. I thought maybe we should ask the girls if they'd like to slightly change the plans for Friday night?" I hedge, biting my lip.

"Sel, I'm way ahead of you." She holds up her phone, showing me the group text with Hazel and Melody already informing them where we're going on Friday.

I lightly swat her shoulder as I grin, picking up our basket and make my way to the checkout. Once we stop to wait in a short line, I glance at the exit and catch Kyran looking over his shoulder. He smiles warmly and gives me a small wave. With my stomach slightly flopping, I smile and shyly wave back at him before he walks out.

Ria plops her ingredients on the counter and pays for the groceries while I watch Kyran through the large windows overlooking the parking lot. As he leaves, I notice his truck, getting a little glimpse at his character. *He has plenty of money to spend hundreds of dollars on two shopping carts of meat, yet he chooses to keep an old truck.*

Tilting my head, I consider that to be an admirable trait, financially stable enough to not have to be frugal with groceries, but not being boastfully ostentatious about it either. *Although, a cart full of meat is still quite peculiar,* I wonder as he drives out of view.

Giving me a slight nudge, Ria leads me out of the store and we cross the lot to her Prius. As she drives, I can't help daydreaming about the way Kyran's voice sounded so close to my ear, deep and enticing with his gravelly tone.

A small shiver traces my spine as I close my hands, remembering the brief contact with his broad, firm chest. *He certainly takes care of himself,* I muse, smiling as I bite my lip.

Attempting to distract myself, I absently discuss the muffin recipe with Ria during our long drive home.

I retire to my room and sit on a floor cushion in front of my open balcony doors after a successful day of baking and taste-testing muffins. Peering through the slats of the railing, I watch the draping branches of the massive willow dance in the moonlight as the crickets' songs float through the night, lulling me into a peaceful drowsiness. Stretching my arms overhead, I rise to latch my doors closed and climb into the middle of my plush bed. My last thought before gently falling asleep is the playful glint of Kyran's alluring gaze.

# KYRAN

After I returned from the grocery store, I spent many useless hours attempting to catch up on office work and sitting through a drawn-out pack meeting—one that definitely wasn't given the best of my attention. Restlessly laying in my bed and staring through the skylights recessed in the vaulted ceiling, I watch the moon leisurely crawl across the stars. Sighing irritably, I throw the covers off and resume pacing my bedroom, trying to think of a way to get me to sleep. It's impossible when silvery strands of moonlight hair, flashes of azure, and the sweet scent of jasmine have taken residence in every aspect of my conscious thought.

*Take to the woods. This is becoming unbearable,* Valdr grumbles with irritation.

With a lack of any better alternatives, I concede and descend the stairs quietly, not wanting to disturb anyone from sleep. Stepping into the gardens, I mindlink Trey about taking a run alone and not to expect me for a few hours. Removing my clothes, I allow Valdr to take control and remind him, *Stay to the south, keep to the prairie lands and valleys tonight.*

Receiving only a glance to the moon and a snort in reply, I wait until Valdr bounds into the forest. After keeping watch to ensure he heeds my words, I grow tired of Valdr running relentlessly without direction and let my mind wander once more. Hours pass until I notice he's come to a peaceful place to rest and we both drift off to sleep.

A sharp peck to my nose jolts me awake, an accusing squawk echoing from that damned raven perched on my bare chest again. My breath turns to concrete in my lungs as I am immediately reminded of the unmasked threat from long ago.

*'Your kind are not welcome here, not anymore. I need not give you my reasons. You stay away from me and mine, and I shall stay away from you and yours. Leave my woods and my home alone. If you absolutely have need of me, you know how to contact me. If any one of you shows yourselves around here, I will kill you without hesitation'.*

That was two centuries ago, and no questions have been asked as to *why* the sudden change, nor has any challenge been made to the declaration since. She is not one to be crossed. Only a complete moron would dare provoke *her* power. I was just a boy when I watched my father unequivocally agree with her, here in these very woods I lay in now.

*So why am I here, in her forest, two nights in a row?* I wonder with growing apprehension.

Shaking my head, I quickly rise to my feet, sending the annoying bird flying and swiftly shift, making a beeline toward home. Icy fingers of fear grip my heart the entire way back as I imagine her following through on her grave threat.

# Chapter Four

## THE PARK

### SELENE

*Spinning around, I prowl slowly back the way I came, crouching low to the ground. Raising my head above the soft blades, two glowing amber orbs pierce my soul, beckoning me to follow into the depths of the woods. I cautiously place my weight on my front foot, pausing slightly, unsure if I should continue. A sudden snap of a twig sends my eyes flying upward as a black shadow emerges—*

Gasping awake, cold air rushes into my lungs as my eyes fly open, gripping the balcony railing. Heart thumping heavily in my chest, a cold sweat dampens my neck as I realize where I am. *Again? How can this be? I don't recall ever getting out of bed, let alone opening these doors. And the dream, how bizarre. It felt as if I was looking through someone else's eyes.* I rub my forehead with unease.

Closing my balcony doors, I cross my room to gingerly sit at the edge of my bed. Plucking my phone off the nightstand, I open the notepad app and tap out a description of the dream the way Ria instructed me to do yesterday morning.

Fully awake, I decide to get dressed and make my way downstairs to prepare an early breakfast before heading out. Quickly eating scrambled eggs and toast with homemade strawberry jam, I pluck one of the few remaining muffins out of the breadbox and scribble a note saying I'll be back later this morning after a walk in the park.

Slinging my purse over my shoulder and taking a bite out of the muffin, I close the front door behind me and am instantly shoved back by two massive, fluffy bodies. Phylax and Machitís, our two Tibetan Mastiffs, greet me enthusiastically with whines and butt wiggles. They are both entirely black, except where Phylax has brown patchwork along his underside that peeks out near his chest. Both boys stand two feet tall at the shoulder and weigh no less than one hundred and fifty pounds of muscle, fluff, and drool.

Crouching, I split the muffin in half and hold it out, each of them taking their piece gingerly. Rubbing their heads, I notice their furs are covered in dry mud with leaves and twigs sticking out everywhere.

"Boys, *where* have you been? Looks like today's going to be bath day, isn't that right, we get to play with the hose!" I croon, receiving slobbering licks to my face. "*Ugh,* okay, okay! Enough." Chuckling, I rise to my feet and make my way down the porch toward Ria's car, wiping my cheeks with my sleeve.

Phylax and Machitís are known to disappear for a day or two at a time, most often returning a complete mess. They spend the majority of their time roaming the property, doing who-knows-what. Occasionally, their booming barks and howls can be heard off in the distance deep within the woods. I like to take them on a weekly walk in the town park, it helps keep them at least *semi*-domesticated. Today, however, I leave them behind due to their filthy state and head off to the park alone.

# KYRAN

*Trey, meet me in the gardens. I'll be there in five minutes,* I mindlink while dashing through the fields on the outskirts of the villages.

Keeping a wide berth, I lope through the woods along the backside and stay out of sight. Just as daybreak pushes through the branches, I emerge into the gardens at my home. After shifting, I check in with Valdr. *Are you okay? If something happened, please let me know.*

He has remained silent since I awoke to the raven and has not responded to any of my questions. Stepping around a large rose bush, I find Treyvar sitting on a worn, old oak bench and instantly recognize it as one of Mom's favorites. He glances up and wordlessly holds out some clothes, giving me a chance to get dressed before his brow quirks in silent question.

I groan, dropping my face into my hands as I plop down next to Trey. "It happened again, just as before. I awoke under the same blackthorn shrub, right at the edge of the boundary, with the same damned raven pecking me."

He takes a slow, measured breath. "Why? Why now, why you? Does it feel intentional? As if you're being compelled or ensnared magically?" He speaks lowly, mindful to not be accidentally overheard.

"No."

*Yes,* Valdr responds at the same time.

*What? Valdr, you have not mentioned this!* I hiss at him, and my face must reflect my confusion and anger because Trey looks at me with worry.

Extremely irritated, I drag a hand down my face. "Valdr believes so, *apparently,*" I grumble between clenched teeth.

"Have him explain and reiterate back to me, please," Treyvar says with earnest concern.

*Valdr, why haven't you said—*

*I have not spoken because it did not make sense to me until now. I do not bring us there on purpose. If anything, while running, I only think of not going there,* he explains with a terse voice. *During both runs—specifically at midnight—I feel almost pulled, as if my chest is attached to an invisible line and the tension increases until I go in the direction it tugs. Only when the tightness is gone do I lay down to rest from exhaustion. The closer I am to it, the more difficult it is to pull away. It becomes painful to try.*

I repeat the words to Trey as Valdr speaks them, both of us staring at each other with wide eyes. When I finish, Trey gives a slight shake of his head in disbelief. I am very confused, aggravated, and even a bit fearful.

Trey knits his brow. "Could the witch have need of you? But if that was the case, why not just speak with you or send a message? Maybe it's a spell, one designed to trick you into breaking the unspoken vow. What for, though? Has someone pissed her off?" He grimaces with trepidation, staring out into the woods.

I speak firmly, holding his gaze to solidify my seriousness. "Arrange a meeting with the elders and see what they know of her, but do not disclose *any* of this to anyone. We do not know enough at the moment, and I would rather keep it between us for now."

Trey drops his eyes with a stiff nod and solemnly replies, "I will find as much information as I can. I do not want to cause you more distress."

Standing, I rest a hand on Treyvar's shoulder. "Thank you. I'm going to head to the park, then take a drive after. I need some time to sort my thoughts without pack-life interfering. I will let you know when I'm back and we can discuss your meeting with the elders," I say quietly, turning to walk toward my home.

Entering the kitchen, I fill a water bottle and swipe my truck keys from the dish Kira placed on a small table near the garage door. Grabbing my running shoes off the overfilled rack, I stoop to lace them and silently hope today brings me some clarity.

The town park is frequented by many people exercising, walking their dogs, and relaxing under trees or on benches on a daily basis. With summer solstice not too far in the future, more people have been spending time outdoors, apparently even on early Sunday mornings. The dirt lot seems fuller than usual, and the warming weather is probably to blame.

Sighing, I shut off the engine. *Well, at least I won't have pack interruptions here,* I consider, giving a slight shrug and roll my neck as I set off onto my favorite path.

Spring blooms have been fully open for a few days, filling the park with cloying aromas. I try not to breathe too deeply as I jog, the scents here can easily become overbearing at times. Autumn is my favorite time by far, less people tend to stay around with crisper air and I like how the earth settles in preparation for winter. The flaming trees and migrating birds give for beautiful scenery to run in as well.

Though currently, I focus on weaving between people and their either growling or cowering canines along the pathways instead of watching the park around me. Rounding a corner, I approach a group of middle-aged women power-walking and gossiping loudly. They are oblivious to me and nearly block the entire trail, causing me to hurdle over the log border and stumble a bit on the suddenly uneven terrain. Leaping back onto the path, I glare over my shoulder at their sheer ignorance and shove hair out of my eyes as I face forward again. I immediately collide with a small woman, a slight shriek of surprise escaping her as her face smacks into my chest. I carefully grab hold of her shoulders to prevent her from falling backward and take a step back myself.

"I am so sorry," we both blurt at the same time.

*Oh my fucking g—*

*"Kyran?"* she gasps, gazing up at me with wide, bright eyes.

I can't breathe as I stare at the woman from the store. The beautiful, mysterious woman whom I cannot get off my mind. *This is insane, this must look so bad to her. I hope she doesn't think I'm a creep or anything.* I cringe as I swallow thickly, taking a ragged breath.

She reaches up and twists the end of her silky ponytail, looking toward the lake. "I apologize, I wasn't paying as much attention as I should have been. I can get carried away at times when lost in thought." She wrinkles her nose with a small smile. It's cute as hell and I can't stop the smile from tugging my lips upward.

"Are you alright? Did I hurt you?" I ask with genuine concern, my smile falling as I look her over.

She seems stricken at my words. Glancing down, she replies quietly, "Um, no. I'm alright, you didn't hurt me. I've had much worse, *ha*." Her eyes briefly flick to mine before darting away.

*That was odd.* My brow creases and I am about to ask if she is sure when she softly clears her throat.

"Ahem, I didn't get the chance to introduce myself before. My name is Selene, and I'm sure we're bound to meet again, so at least now we can say hello properly," she jokes lightly and extends her hand with a warm smile, the previous shadow over her gone.

I can't help but grin and gently take her hand in mine. "It is a pleasure to meet you, sweetheart," I murmur as I bend, brushing a kiss across her knuckles.

My chest constricts as Valdr's elation blooms at the contact. *Why the fuck did I just say and do that?* I cringe again, keeping my face downward for a moment longer. Straightening, I release Selene's hand, watching her fair skin flush into a rosy pink shade.

*Dammit.*

She presses her hand against her chest, blinking her eyes a few times. "Likewise," she replies breathlessly, grinning.

I couldn't stop the responding grin if I wanted to. *I feel like an idiot. Have her meet you here tomorrow. If not, then when she can,* Valdr eagerly insists.

I give her a purposeful hint so I don't come off as too direct. "I always run here early, every morning. I like to start my days in the sun. It shines particularly bright today," I add softly, unable to remove my gaze from hers.

She chews the corner of her lip as if in thought, glancing up at the clouded sky. Peering back at me, I raise my eyebrow with a growing smirk. "Until next time, Selene," I murmur, taking a step back and then around her, resuming my jog.

Glancing over my shoulder, her hand covers her mouth when she turns to look back at me. Laughing, I continue on the path, not seeing anyone else as my smile carries me all the way back to my truck and stays with me the entire way home.

## SELENE

Standing dumbfounded in the middle of the walkway with my mouth gaping wide—*again*—my brain struggles to process what Kyran just said. I excitedly realize that *he wants to see me again.* My flytrap pulls into a grin as I hurry back to the parking lot, feeling giddy. Rushing past a knot of teenagers riding bicycles, I hear a faint thrum of an engine and glimpse what I believe is Kyran's old pickup pulling onto the main road. I notice he takes a left toward downtown, wondering if perhaps he lives there. *He doesn't strike me as a city guy. But there aren't any country homes out that way for dozens of miles, just vast forests and prairies,* I ponder as I get into the Prius.

Taking a right from the park, I smile at the idea of coming back early tomorrow morning. Easing into the entrance of our long drive, I wait for the gates to swing open. When the iron creaks loudly, two booming bellows echo in response, followed by Ria's shriek of annoyance. Smiling, I pull up to our cottage, finding Phylax and Machitís both sopping wet and bounding toward the car.

As I park, I roll up the window, cracking the door open enough to command, "Halt! Sit!" at the dogs before they make a mess of me. Getting out, I give them praise and receive thumping tail wags in return.

"*Ugh,* I do not know how you manage to do this and stay clean at the same time," Ria scoffs, rounding the corner of the cottage.

Stifling a laugh, I press my hand to my mouth at seeing Ria's auburn hair plastered to her face and neck, her black t-shirt clinging to her body. A snort manages to slip out and with her puckered expression, I can't help but burst with laughter. Ria swipes at her face with a huff and cracks a grin, chuckling with me.

"What happened? It looks as if you took their bath for them," I tease, glad she isn't genuinely angry.

"Well, I woke up, brought tea out to the porch like always and was greeted by those bush monsters." She rolls her eyes, nodding her head in the dogs' direction. "With you nowhere to be found, I decided to clean them up. I thought, *'how hard could it be?'* Well, it's safe to say I will *not* be doing that again." She laughs, shaking her dripping head.

"*Mm-hmm,*" I intone sarcastically, "you just want me to do the dirty work." I wink and stick my tongue out at Ria.

Getting an identical face in response, I giggle as I turn toward the side yard with a sharp whistle. Phylax and Machitís bounce past me, knowing where to go as I find the hose and twist the spigot, turning to my boys. "Stand. Stay," I say seriously, and they follow my command immediately, remaining still as statues. "Good boys," I murmur, starting with Phylax.

Ria hands me the shampoo and just shakes her head, wringing out her hair. "I truly do not get it. They both weigh more than you, yet behave like robots at your command. What's your secret?" Ria grumbles before she suddenly purses her lips and glances away.

I notice the very peculiar expression on her face, but decide not to make a comment. After rinsing Phylax, I move on to Machitís. "We have an understanding," I reply as I work, "I respect them and they respect me. I've always felt a connection with them since we moved here and they became part of our family." I smile as I rub Machitís on his snout.

Ria is quiet and her focus is on the gardens out beyond our home. I wrap the hose around the reel and pick up the supplies, placing them in the tote bin on the porch. Ria disappears inside, returning shortly with some towels and hands me one, giving me a wan smile.

As she squeezes her hair dry, I prompt, "Hey, would you like to take the boys to the park with me in the morning? I would've brought them with me today, but I didn't want them making a mess in your car." I nibble on my lip, hoping my smile doesn't betray me.

"Sure, that sounds nice." She nods in agreement and turns toward the stairs. "I'm going to get changed. I have some errands to run, I'm meeting Mother…out in town. You'll have the house to yourself for most of the day, but we should be back in time for dinner."

"Okay, see you then." I smile, not letting on that I'm aware of her mood shift.

Asteria can be volatile at times, her emotions changing quickly with unspoken thoughts. Most of the time I leave her be, I'd learned the hard way when we were younger not to prod her. One time, I was annoyed with her for becoming moody and she lashed out at me in the living room, singeing my hair with the match she was using to light the hearth. She apologized profusely right away, feeling awful about it for weeks. Then there was the time in the garden I told her she is like a light switch, flipping on and off randomly around me, and she drenched me with the watering can in anger. Again, she felt terrible for her actions and worked hard at keeping control of her emotions. I'd never blamed her or held anything against Ria, but simply came to understand that I needed to be mindful of the things I say to her.

I'm glad that she agreed to come tomorrow and the possibility of seeing Kyran again has me smiling once more. I spend most of the day doing chores, cleaning and dancing to music, folding laundry, and mulling over what to start for dinner. As evening rolls around, I lift the lid off the pot of veggie soup and ladle some into a bowl, add the roasted chicken into my dish and snag a roll from the breadbox on the counter.

Once I've finished, my mother and Ria have yet to return. I decide to close up the kitchen, leaving a note about the soup in the fridge and if Ria is still up for going to the park to be ready at dawn.

After I shower, I make my way to bed, glimpsing the moon peeking through the clouds over my balcony. Checking that the doors are latched, I pull the curtains closed and climb into bed. Grinning like a fool, I replay my chance meeting this morning and find myself hoping I'll be lucky enough to catch him again tomorrow.

Gasping awake, I find myself once again on the balcony at twilight. Crouching shakily, I sit on the deck floor and take slow, deep breaths to ease my racing heart.

*That's three nights now I've had the exact same dream, causing me to sleepwalk and wake here at the exact same time. This is weird, too weird. I've got to talk to Ria or Mother about this, they might have advice for me.*

I scrub my hands over my eyes and look out between the railings. Golden hues of dawn illuminate the shadows around the property. Noticing movement in the luscious field below, I watch my mother making her way toward a path at the edge of the forest. Gathering ingredients for today's cooking, I assume.

Remembering this morning, I eagerly bound through my room, showering quickly to wash the night's sweat off. I decide to brush on some light copper eyeshadow and black mascara, nothing much, but just enough to brighten my tired eyes.

Stepping off the stairs, I find my sister in the kitchen glaring at a large, round cast iron pot with slightly burnt contents boiled over the side. *Well, that answers my thoughts of seeing Mother earlier,* I muse with a smirk.

"Wow Ria, you've definitely perfected your domestic skills of a doting housewife," I drawl teasingly.

"*Ha-ha,* you are *hilarious,*" she responds dryly.

Grasping the handles, she walks backward out the side door and upturns the pot over the porch railing. She places it in the sink basin, scrunching her nose at it. I laugh and she walks over to me with a smile tugging at the corners of her mouth.

"Are you coming with?" I ask over my shoulder, taking the keys off the hook in the entryway.

She's dressed in all black, wearing a lacy blouse with billowing sleeves, a flowy maxi skirt, combat boots, and has chunky silver jewelry adorning her neck and hands. I raise an eyebrow, unsure if she wants to walk in the park.

"Yeah, but I'm driving." She snags the keys from my hand and pulls the door open, shooting me a sly grin. "Have you seen the dogs—"

A jarring bark causes Ria to twitch, her expression going flat. "Never mind," she mutters, giving Phylax a *look*.

I laugh again and close the door behind us, scratching both dogs' ears before stepping off the porch. Opening the back door of the Prius, I give a short whistle and the two beasts come loping around the corner, piling into the tiny car. I have to push on Phylax's bum to get the door shut. Ria starts the car and fully rolls down both back windows, each of the dogs shoving their massive heads out, their tongues lolling in the wind during our short drive to the park.

After we park in the dirt lot, I let the dogs out and they wait patiently as I fasten their collars, holding one leash in each hand. "Let's go, boys!" I chirp as we set off onto the paved pathway.

Due to their sheer size, many people keep a wide berth when passing us and are weary of my dogs, even though they have never once given a reason to be truly feared. There are a few regulars who say hi as we walk, some waving and smiling, and some call out to the dogs in greeting as well. Both of their leashes hang loosely, swaying from my wrists as we walk.

We cross a small footbridge and take the long path that leads around the pond, Ria following my lead. I chose to take the path I had yesterday with the hope that Kyran would do the same. I'm about to mention this detail to Ria, but she nudges me with her elbow, nodding toward the lake at two brawny, shirtless men running alongside one another. It only takes a moment for me to register that one of them is most definitely Kyran. I abruptly feel sheepish, blood rushing to my face. I've stopped walking and Ria notices, turning around curiously.

"What's up?" She quirks her eyebrow.

"I, uh, I think I left something in the car," I flounder, trying to turn around and tug on the leashes.

*Total. Chicken-shit.*

I glance up to smile at Ria, but it feels like a grimace instead. She looks at me oddly, then turns her head back toward the path and my eyes involuntarily follow. I catch Kyran's gaze and he grins in return. He is much closer than before.

*He knew! He totally knew that I would be here and this is definitely intentional.* My heart flutters at the idea of him wanting my attention.

Ria quickly looks back at me with wide eyes, pursing her lips in a mischievous smile. My sudden nerves prevent my feet from moving so I straighten, heeling both dogs beside me. As Kyran and his friend approach, Phylax immediately shoves himself against my legs, bodily pushing me backward with a deep growl. Machitís launches to his feet with his hackles raised and he snarls menacingly, pulling his leash taut. Startled, I glance at Asteria and find her brow creased in concern. I rest my hand atop Phylax's head, shushing him.

"Enough," Kyran lowly states, staring directly at Machitís. He doesn't break eye contact and gently commands, "Lay down."

To my complete astonishment, Machitís swiftly obeys, contentedly laying on the walkway in stark contrast to his demeanor seconds ago. Phylax follows suit behind him, neither of them looking away from Kyran. My eyes flit between them a couple times before peering up at Kyran. He gives me a crooked smile.

"They don't listen to anyone but me. Not even my sister," I mumble, glancing over at Ria who looks even more concerned.

She's blatantly staring at Kyran's friend, a tall blonde man, slightly shorter and a bit younger than Kyran. They kind of resemble each other with some features. *A brother, perhaps?* I wonder as I glance at Ria, noticing her eyes traveling down and back up again, obviously checking him out. Smirking, I turn my attention back to Kyran.

"Are you a trainer? Do you work with dogs? I have to admit, that was quite impressive." I give him a small smile.

His friend—*brother?*—abruptly barks a laugh and scratches his nose, glancing away as he clears his throat.

Kyran smirks, shrugging his shoulder. "Something like that."

At the movement, my eyes are drawn downward and I cannot help ogling at him. His body is thick with defined muscle, his tanned skin marked by numerous tattoos and scars. One in particular curves up the back of his neck from his left shoulder in two jagged parallel lines. I trace it with my eyes, wondering what the story is behind that vicious scar.

Ria chats quietly with the other man, but I pay no mind to what they discuss. Peering up at Kyran, I realize he is staring at me intently and I blush at being caught. Instead of looking away, however, I give him a slight smirk and boldly continue observing the details of this man. His unruly black hair drifts past his face on a breeze and I impulsively reach up to brush it away, resting my fingertips on his cheek.

"You shouldn't hide behind all this hair. You are a very handsome man," I murmur, my hand lingering against his warm skin.

Quickly pulling my hand away, my face lights on fire, stunned by my boldness.

His amber eyes are bright as they bore into me, and his brow draws inward, as if in disbelief. He moves suddenly and his hand meets mine, pressing palm to palm, splaying my fingers against his. I look down from his gaze at our hands, liking how his dwarfs mine. A radiant heat smolders between our palms, pervading its way up my arm and throughout my entire body.

My body erupts in tiny tingles, a gentle current of electricity flowing beneath my skin. *What is this? What's going on?*

With wide eyes and parted lips, I glance up at Kyran. He looks just as surprised as I feel.

An iron grip clenches around my wrist and a sharp jerk sends me backward, pulling my hand out of Kyran's gentle grasp. Startled, I twist around to find Asteria moving in front of me, hand extended.

"Asteria, and you might be?" she aggressively intercedes, glaring at Kyran.

"I'm Kyran," he says slowly, looking equally confused as me and takes her hand in his.

Pure hostility infects Asteria in both her face and her posture as her body tenses, poised as if she were about to physically attack him. She wrenches her hand free of his, and Kyran simultaneously takes two steps backward with a sharp intake of breath.

"Selene," my sister hisses without looking at me. "Go to the car. Now."

"Asteria, what—"

*"Now!"* she seethes, whipping her head around and glaring at me.

I am too horrified to scream. My entire body tenses with fear, rooted to the spot and I cannot bring myself to run.

Her eyes are inhuman, flooded pitch black, the irises a pure white with slits for pupils like a cat. My body abruptly registers what my brain is processing and I nearly fall over as I turn to run away, desperately yanking on the leashes until the dogs come with me.

My feet pound the pavement as I take the turns on the walkways faster than ever. People give me weird looks, but I don't stop until we reach the Prius.

Throwing the door open, I shove the dogs inside and a sudden gust of wind blows the door shut. I frantically open my door and fall into the seat before my door is blown shut, too. My entire body quivers like a leaf in October about to fall from a branch.

Asteria manifests in the driver's seat, cold wind swirling viciously in the car. My chest is too tight to scream with fright. She solemnly looks at my stricken face and presses her fingers to my forehead, whispering, *"Somnum."*

My eyes roll upwards, blackness swallowing me whole.

I wake to bright light streaming into my room and by the looks of it, I've *definitely* overslept. Rolling over, I check my phone, my bleary eyes seeing 10:47 a.m. Groaning, I rub my face, remembering the vivid, wild dreams I had.

*I must have gone back to sleep after waking at dawn again. It felt so real, being at the park and seeing Kyran again. Why would something so intense and bizarre interrupt what started out so well?*

I press my hands together lightly, recalling the warmth emanating from Kyran. A flash of Asteria's wicked eyes makes me suck in a breath, and I release it slowly, beginning to feel concerned about these bizarre dreams. Deciding to discuss my sleep issues with my family, I get dressed before making my way downstairs. My mother and Ria speak in hushed tones in the living room, sitting close on the couch. They look up simultaneously, ceasing their conversation.

"Hey, good morning. I guess I needed some extra sleep today." I yawn, taking a seat in an armchair. "I, um, would like to talk with you both about some perplexing dreams I've been having," I say quietly as I look between them.

My mother draws her burgundy robe around her and gives me a tight smile, but Ria looks concerned and pats the cushion next to her. I sit with them on the couch and explain in detail my dreams from the past few nights.

# CHAPTER FIVE

## LAID BARE

### KYRAN

*W*e *must take after her, do not let her disappear!* Valdr insists in an extremely agitated tone, trying to force a shift.

I stand paralyzed in the center of the pathway, unable to breathe or blink. It is as if I have turned to stone, glaring into the eyes of one seriously pissed off witch. Only when she vanishes on a gust of wind am I returned to normal. My skin crawls, suppressing the intense urge to shift into my wolf form.

Clenching my fists, I grit my teeth as her threatening words echo in my mind.

*'If I find you anywhere around her, if she so much as speaks of seeing you again, you can kiss your balls goodbye before I cut them off and choke you with them. If I find you outside my home again, I will hunt you down and savor your slow, miserable death as I hand you over to my mother. Let this be your only warning.'*

A tumultuous swarm of emotions drown me with a mix of rage, fear, confusion, disbelief, and—*unbelievably*—blinding white euphoria. My entire being vibrates as I shove everything down deep, barely able to maintain control until I focus solely on that one impossible feeling of pure joy. Even Valdr pauses at the heat and tension blooming within my chest.

*"What the actual fuck was that!"* Trey shrieks, swinging his arms wildly and whips around to face me.

He's sweaty and breathing heavily, no doubt fighting the urge to shift as well. Glancing at the humans in the park, he takes a shaky breath and exhales slowly. "Kyran, I need help understanding this. I was just standing here, fascinated by Asteria, then she's suddenly spitting venom at you and *turning us into statues!"* he hisses in a harsh whisper.

*We must find her. Whatever the cost, we have to get to her,* Valdr insists again.

"What was she cursing at you? It was hard to hear over the screaming in my head," Trey mutters when I don't respond.

I cannot remove my gaze from the bend in the path where I last saw Selene.

*Take to the woods, we can run faster than the vehicle. We will cut them off.*

*"Hello?* Are you lis—"

*"Enough!"* I growl through my teeth, directing the command to both of them. "Just…give me a moment."

Trey scrunches his brow in thought. "What would a witch be doing with a human?" he asks, speaking lowly as we turn to step off the path and sit on a log, facing the woods with our backs to the park.

"She isn't a human," I mutter.

"Well, she certainly isn't a vampire, seeing how it's daylight. Was her scent masked? Perhaps the witch keeps her as a pet," he jests, nudging my shoulder, trying to lighten the air.

Selene's intoxicating jasmine aroma wafts from my hand, pulling me back to her touch. My face still burns wonderfully from her fingertips, and my palm lightly pulsates. *Definitely not masked. I can't believe I didn't see this before,* I wonder in disbelief.

"Wait, she isn't also a witch, is she? Dude, you're trying to get with *a witch?* Are you *insane?"* Trey leans forward incredulously.

Glaring at my brother and teetering on the precipice of losing all control, I only shake my head in response. Treyvar, sensing my turmoil, remains silent. Breathing raggedly, I manage to inform him, "Selene is not a witch, but she resides with Asteria and *her mother,* in the *forbidden woods."*

Trey's eyes bulge and he nearly chokes on air. "You can't be serious," he whispers harshly.

"I need to speak with the elders *immediately*," I say between clenched teeth, roughly pushing to my feet and breaking into a run toward my truck with Trey close behind.

"I told you earlier, they didn't have much to say. Nobody has seen or heard anything within the last few centuries. Why do you need to speak with them?" he asks incredulously, his voice bouncing with his quick steps.

Yanking the door open, I stare into my brother's eyes. He is confused and slightly frightened by what he must see on my face. Trey crosses in front of the truck and sits in the passenger seat, looking at me expectantly. I get in and my truck roars to life as I say the words that I never thought would leave my lips.

"I believe—no, I *know*," I growl through clenched teeth, "Selene is my mate."

Entering the Great Hall, I find our elders talking quietly among one another, my ears ringing from my hour-long drive listening to Trey's incessant squawking. I asked my brother to wait outside the door and told him that I'd call on him if I felt I needed his input on things, disregarding his protest.

Walking slowly toward the large wooden banquet table at the head of the Hall, I consider the best way to begin this conversation. This news will undoubtedly cause excitement and celebration throughout my pack, but that does not negate the problems surrounding my newfound knowledge.

Raising my gaze, Stjarna squints one eye at me and purses her lips. When I mindlinked each of the four elders to meet me here immediately, I did not give reason as to why. The elders slowly rise as I come to my place at the center of the table. I briefly dip my head in respect to the group, receiving equal recognition back. Many alphas would claim they bow to no one, however I know that I would not be where I am today if it weren't for the experience and wisdom shared from these four people, and I respect each of them deeply.

# LUNAR SHADOWS: AWAKEN

Drawing my wingback chair toward the edge of the dais, I gesture for the others to follow suit and create a circle. Once seated, I take a moment and regard each elder individually. Stjarna has known me my entire life, she had even been present at my birth and was very close with my mother for most of her life as well. Stjarna had taken her in as a stray pup without hesitation and raised my mother as her own, considering she'd never found her mate and didn't have any children. She has always been someone I greatly care about and consider to be family.

Seated to her left are Eirene and Chrestotes, a mated pair bonded as soon as they came of age. They came to my father seeking refuge from their warring Grecian packs, both wounded and with quite a story to tell. After they'd become mated, each had been held captive in the other's pack lands when they were found together. They were torn apart for centuries before escaping and fleeing to North America. My father had told me that it was my mother's tears of sorrow for the pair that compelled him to admit them into his pack. Their loyalty has never once wavered.

Lastly, on my left sits Tomur, a stony man who sparsely speaks and when he chooses to, his words are blunt. He is my father's uncle and served him as his second in command until I became Alpha. He lost his mate, as did my father, on the same day the vampires attacked our pack. It is commendable how he is still here today. I do not know of anyone else who has lived a long life after their mate died. When Tomur speaks, I heed him unquestionably.

"I appreciate you all for meeting with me and allowing me the time to compose myself before you. I have asked you here for your honest thoughts and opinions, specifically for advice on matters that I do not fully comprehend at the moment. Please refrain from interrupting, and you can speak freely once I am through." I exhale heavily, leaning forward and placing my elbows on my knees.

Rubbing my face, I explain the past few mornings, why I had Trey speak with them yesterday, the encounter with the witch Asteria, and ending with my experiences with Selene. Stjarna is silently delighted, Tomur seems troubled, and Eirene and Chrestotes clasp hands with mixed expressions of concern and hope.

"Neither Valdr nor I could understand why Selene felt different to us, why she smelled so strongly or looked so strikingly distinctive from other people. I didn't notice the heat between our fingers the first time we touched, I was too distracted by her to pay much attention. It wasn't until I fully pressed my hand to hers did I know that *somehow*, this woman is my true soulmate. I do not understand it, but there is absolutely *no doubt* she is mine. I feel it in every fiber of my being. The hollow part of my soul that I thought was from my unmet mate dying has not stopped aching since I met her. Please, help me make sense of all this," I plead quietly, sitting back in my chair and flicking my gaze between them all.

When my eyes meet Stjarna's, she throws her arms around my neck and squeezes tightly. Pulling back, unshed tears sparkle in her crinkled green eyes as she smiles broadly at me. "Oh, Kyran. I was damned sure we were destined," she teases with a laugh, a few tears spilling over.

With a chuckle, I smile helplessly and wipe a tear from her cheek.

"Why would a female wolf be with a witch, let alone *them?* Why would they hide her wolf, not to mention protect her so blatantly from her own kind?" Tomur asks gruffly as he leans forward, looking me dead in the eyes. "This doesn't happen, you have the mark on your chest as proof. It could very well be a spell or a trap, for whatever reason. Mates don't come back from the dead," he states gravely.

I nod in acknowledgment. I had these thoughts myself on the drive back here, but it does not convince me, not with what I *feel*.

"To clarify, you have not crossed the boundary, correct?" Eirene asks softly, her brow creased with worry.

"No, I have not," I verify with a shake of my head.

The mated pair look at one another, clearly speaking through their bond. Chrestotes turns to me solemnly, his voice like gravel as he murmurs, "There were stories of her, in our packs. Passed down through alphas and elders of ancient Greece. My only advice to you is this, you would be unwise to test her, to challenge her in any form. If she has your soulmate, perhaps there is more for you to learn than what you have been shown." His eyes narrow slightly with his last words.

I lean forward, furrowing my brow. "What do you mean by that, exactly?"

"It is not our place to speak of it further," he replies with a slight shake of his head.

I clench my teeth, becoming agitated. Nothing is making any sense, speaking out loud just makes it seem more insane, and nobody has any clear answers. The elders discuss things among themselves quietly, their voices soon increasing with intensity and speaking over one another. I drop my head into my hands, at a loss for what I should do next.

A light brush glides against my mental barrier—something only Trey, Kira and few select warriors have permission to do. I look up, my gaze meeting Eirene's weathered yet clear, brown eyes, and question if I was imagining things. Her brow pulls upward in the middle in a silent plea. With a slight nod, I allow her to speak to me through mindlink.

Her quiet voice murmurs, *Go to her boundary and request to confer with her. I implore you to take care with each word spoken and action performed.*

*Now?* I ask hesitantly, my spine straightening with anticipation.

Eirene's face slackens a bit, her eyes becoming unfocused. Sharply, she looks at me and hisses in my mind, *Yes, now. Immediately. I will explain what I can to the others, now go!* She flashes me a warm smile before quickly composing herself.

With a curt nod, I abruptly push to my feet, sending my chair toppling backward. I've shifted and am bounding toward the doors before it hits the floor.

*Are you sure of this?* Valdr asks warily.

I stop at the door, swinging my head behind me with my ears pulled flat.

*Please trust in me, Alpha Kyran, I would not send you to your demise,* Eirene reassures me as I meet her gaze.

With that being said, I burst through the heavy wooden doors, startling Treyvar. He shifts into his sandy wolf as he hastily runs after me.

*Do not follow me. I will reach out to you when it is safe to do so,* I demand as I run.

He skids in the dirt, a low whine trailing after me.

*Go speak with the elders,* I say in a kinder tone as I briefly glance behind me, meeting his wary gaze. I quickly head west, my paws pounding the earth in tune with my heartbeat the entire way.

# SELENE

Breathless, I glance between my mother and Ria, the both of them looking very uncomfortable. After I finished explaining my recent recurring dream and sleepwalking episodes, I described what felt like a nightmare earlier this morning. I wanted to know what my subconscious might be telling me, but they have both remained silent since I stopped speaking.

"Should I be worried?" I hesitantly ask, pulling my sleeves over my hands.

"No, dear. Dreams have a way of speaking, even if you do not know their language," my mother assures me. "Listen to your feelings within each dream, and you may hear the message being spoken."

Nodding, I stand and shuffle into the kitchen, reflecting on each night. *I've felt curious and drawn to go someplace, toward something unknown. Perhaps I need to get out for a while, experience something new. Only this morning did I feel anything negative, and coming from Ria, I might just be projecting fears about meeting a new man.* Shuddering at a fleeting memory of Bolvi, I sharply shake my head and focus on making something to eat.

"Hey, would either of you like—"

Both of them jump to their feet. Startled, I whirl around and my mother storms across the floor with her face twisted in anger.

"What's wrong?" I ask with concern, but she swiftly leaves the cottage, slamming the door behind her.

Ria is at my side, pulling me up the stairs and into my room. Phylax and Machitís nearly trip me as they push past us and lay in front of my balcony doors, staring outward.

"*What the hell?* Asteria, what's going on?" I demand in a high voice, alarmed.

She doesn't answer right away, also looking outside, as if she's searching for something. Turning to look at me, she softly replies, "Mother said she thought she saw a wolf and wants us to remain inside." Her lavender eyes narrow with worry.

"*A wolf?* Here? What would she be able to do? Why would she go outside?" I ask incredulously, suddenly worried.

"She has experience with them," Ria murmurs, her focus back out the windows.

Perplexed by this information, I peer out the glass doors. I don't see anything amiss and I'm not even sure where my mother had gone. A few minutes pass without anything happening until I hear a *thump-thump,* and look down to find Machitís' tail wagging happily against the floor.

Glancing outside once more, I notice my mother emerging from the woods. Her mouth is drawn in a hard line. Right before disappearing from view, she looks up at me with furrowed brows.

*What could be so concerning?* I wonder, turning to ask Ria, but she is no longer standing beside me. Spinning around, I see the hem of her skirt float through the doorway. It catches my attention, the flowy black material, and I narrow my eyes in thought. *That looks familiar, is it new? Maybe I saw it while we were shopping?*

Following my sister downstairs, I step into the living room as our mother comes through the door. "Is everything alright?" I ask hesitantly, unsure of what she could do about a wolf.

She sweeps her wavy ebony hair into a bun, brushing wispy pieces away from her angular face. Her violet eyes are wary, but she pulls me into a hug and presses a hand to the back of my head. Drawing backward, she gently lays her palm on my cheek, whispering, "I sincerely hope so," and turns away to climb the stairs.

Scrunching my face in confusion, I look sideways at Ria, silently mouthing, *"What the fuck?"* as I scrunch my face in confusion. She just raises her eyebrows and shrugs her shoulders, plopping down onto the couch.

I wait a moment to see if she'll say anything more, but when she remains silent staring at the dark TV screen, I turn around with a shake of my head and walk toward the kitchen, pulling out ingredients to make a sandwich. Sighing, I glare at the expired meats and dump the packages into the trash bin.

"Hey, Ria, I've got to run to the store real quick, do you want me to get you anything?" I ask as I make my way toward the door.

"I'll go!" She hops off the couch, already halfway to the door. "You stay here, I'll be back in a flash," she breathes out quickly.

"But you don't know—"

"Turkey and roast beef, half-pound each." She flashes me a grin over her shoulder.

With a jangle of keys and scuffle of shoes, the door bangs closed, leaving me standing between the kitchen and living room completely bewildered. *Today is a very weird day. Ugh, I didn't mention I wanted chips or a snack. Oh well, I'll just go out later by myself.* I groan softly, rubbing my forehead.

I pick up the remote and curl onto the couch, deciding that a mindless reality show should help pass the time. Clicking around aimlessly, I sigh and choose *The Bachelorette*.

Ria returns a little over halfway through the episode, pushing open the door with a few bags slung over her arms. Hopping off the couch, I follow her into the kitchen, finding that she picked up sour cream and cheddar chips—*my favorite*—along with the sandwich meats, some peanut M&Ms, and a few things for herself. Smiling, I hug her around the waist.

"Thank you. How did you know I wanted these?" I murmur into her soft hair.

She shrugs dismissively, mumbling, "I just know you."

I grin at her and we prepare an early lunch together before watching garbage TV for a few hours, laughing and scoffing at the drama that unfolds.

## KYRAN

Trotting to a stop next to the newly-familiar blackthorn, I assess the woods around me. It is eerily silent, there aren't any birds chirping or squirrels flitting through branches. Taking a few slow steps forward, the barrier tingles like electricity and I crouch low, lying tense on my belly, ready to run if necessary. Earlier this morning as I was hastily leaving, I definitely saw a figure at the edge of the woods standing mere meters away from where I had been resting beneath this scraggly shrub. I am unsure if I had been seen, but I didn't dare wait around to find out.

*Are you ready?* I ask Valdr with trepidation creeping up my spine.

*Yes,* he brusquely replies.

Releasing a breath, I crawl forward, forcefully pushing my snout through the barrier and holding it there as long as I can withstand. Magic burns and zaps around me viciously. I snarl and withdraw, shaking my head vigorously.

*If that doesn't get her attention, we'll have to run through,* I mumble with a snort.

*I'd rather go to the groomers,* Valdr's dry voice mutters back.

Rolling my eyes as my muzzle quickly heals, the faintest brush of dry grass catches my ear. Snapping my gaze upward, I lock eyes with the one being I am *certain* I would not prevail against standing directly in front of me. Launching to my feet, I instinctively bare my teeth and growl lowly, my hackles rising with the threat of her presence.

*Control!* I demand to Valdr, and together we forcibly lie down once more, finding it nearly impossible for us to be willingly submissive.

I never take my eyes off her, however. She crouches down, her willowy body folding gracefully until we are face to face. With her head slightly tilted, her deep violet eyes bore into me and searing agony rips through my skull.

I instantly can't hear, can't see, think, or breathe. My paws scrabble at the earth as a keening wail tears from my throat before turning into a deep, rumbling growl.

With every ounce of energy in me, I will my mind to shield against the onslaught of painful magic. Focusing hard, I push her out, away from my mind and seal my mental barrier, snuffing the inferno of pain radiating throughout my body. With my chest heaving, I hold her gaze once more, making no move against her in retaliation and remain lying on the ground. She slightly narrows her eyes, the ghost of a smile softening her sharp features.

"You are strong, and capable of more than you are aware," she murmurs in a cool tone, rising to her feet and lifting her palm in a gesture for me to stand.

Warily pushing off the ground, my head levels with her chest and I take a couple steps back to maintain better eye contact.

"I've gleaned all there is to know of you. However, I wish to hear you speak for yourself. *Transmuto,*" she intones sharply, forcing me to shift into my human body.

*It is beyond unnerving, her having absolute control over our kind,* Valdr mutters and my bare chest rumbles with our joined displeasure.

Drawing to my full height, I bow my head deeply before looking into her eyes. "Hekate," I acknowledge respectfully, firmly holding her sharp gaze.

"Kyran, *Valdr*," she greets in return, nodding her head ever so slightly. "You have come here, three nights now, only to leave at the break of dawn. No disturbances or challenges have been presented, yet here we stand." She turns her hands over before lightly clasping them together.

My insides feel prickly, like tiny bugs are gnawing their way through me, and I shift my weight in discomfort. Although she did not ask a question, I answer her anyway. "Thank you for receiving me. Hear me out, if you please," I request, pausing, and she gives a slight nod. "Valdr explained to me what felt like a calling, or an urge of sorts, to follow the pull to this very place. He respected your boundary and would go no farther, always resting just outside it and finding comfort enough to sleep. I would wake here unknowingly, immediately returning to my lands fearing you would assume I've broken the treaty and seek retribution." I take a breath, running a hand through my hair before I continue.

"It wasn't until earlier this morning that I realized the reason. *She* lives here. Selene. I only met her three days ago, at the market on Friday. I know in my heart she is my soulmate. I do not understand though, *how can this be?*" I thump my palm to my chest twice, then shift to my wolf form and raise my head, showing the small patch of pale fur on my chest.

The mark of a deceased mate.

Hekate's brow lowers, and her violet eyes darken when her gaze dips to my mark.

Shifting back to my human form, I plead, "*Please,* I need to know if this is true, that I am not going insane. I cannot bear the thought—" I clench my jaw, rethinking my words. "I just want to know that she is free to be with me, if she so chooses," I murmur, flicking my gaze between her eyes.

I have a thousand questions, plenty of speculations, and even some accusations pertaining to this whole mess of a situation, though none of which I dare voice aloud. We stare in silence for a few heartbeats as neither of us moves. Suddenly something shifts in her face, just a minuscule pinch of her brow and my heartbeat falters in anticipation.

"She is not ready yet," Hekate murmurs softly, shaking her head.

Her words are unexpected. "What do you mean? Ready for what, exactly?"

Hekate's mouth draws into a thin line as she exhales through her nose. "Selene is unaware of what you are, what *she* is. That part of her remains dormant, in stasis, unable to be broken by outside force. She is awakening, however, and I believe it is because of *you*. When the time comes, great change will be upon you, upon your kind." Her voice grows distant and quiet as she looks past me into the woods.

Shocked, I wonder, "How can that be? What changes do you speak of?"

"She once roamed freely, as a child, many centuries ago. Things became…volatile when she grew into adulthood. For her safety, I had to enspell her and wipe her memory of that life and anything supernatural. Not long ago did she wake, but it was only with her human half. I beseech you, do not force this upon her, it will only cause harm," Hekate quietly explains with a grave voice and clasps her hands.

I notice her avoidance of my questioning the changes she'd mentioned and decide against pushing the subject, choosing instead to nod my head once in silent agreement. Hekate reaches a hand out, placing it on my shoulder. I cannot suppress the flinch that jumps at her touch.

Her eyes pierce mine for a few painful heartbeats, and it feels like she is looking at my soul, deciding whether or not to extirpate it from my body. Releasing me with a nod, she steps backward until she reaches the edge of the woods.

"Farewell, *Custos*," she murmurs, gesturing in a wide arc.

My entire reality explodes in a kaleidoscope of bursting lights and colors, twisting and pulling me in every direction at once with wind ripping the air from my lungs. On the verge of passing out, I find myself abruptly deposited on my front doorstep, crashing into my extremely distraught brother. My gut clenches and I twist sideways, retching over the hedges lining the walkway.

*"Kyran?* What the *fuck!* How did you—where did you—*are you okay?"* Trey cries out as he grabs my face in his hands, his eyes bulging wide with alarm.

Wiping my mouth with the back of my hand, I push him away with a grimace, my nerves completely shot. "I just met our maker, lived, *and* came to a sort of understanding with one another, I think?" I mumble, staring bewildered at nothing as my mind flashes over everything that just happened.

Stumbling through the open door, I leave Trey there picking his jaw up off the ground and head to my bedroom to take a long, *long,* hot shower.

# CHAPTER SIX

## UNEXPECTED

### SELENE

The week passes in a blur, each day blending into the next, with every night resulting in the same dream but never progressing much further. Asteria has been acting strange, continuously having reasons for me to stay home. Being cooped up for three days has left me feeling restless.

My mother has been scarce as well, only showing herself around dinner and eating mostly in silence. I don't like to pry into people's affairs, but both of them have been acting almost cagey lately. I've wondered if the wolf sighting has anything to do with the tension these past few days, though I haven't seen one here myself. I've glimpsed a few out in the distance while driving through the deep countryside, but only a small handful of times.

Standing with my closet doors pulled wide, I sift through my clothes, debating on what to wear tonight when we go to the new club. *Kyran's nightclub. Ugh, I don't have anything that feels good enough, he's only seen me in my scrubby house clothes and I want to make a lasting impression.* I groan at the thought and bite my lip, deciding to go to the mall to find an entirely new outfit for the occasion. I eagerly turn on my heel, about to head over to Ria's room and ask if she'd like to come with me, when she bursts through my door with a grin.

"Let's go shopping!" she chirps and claps her hands, bouncing on the balls of her feet.

"Girl, you read my mind. I can't find anything to wear!" I laugh, grabbing my purse and follow her out to the car.

On our drive to the mall, Ria and I talk about her distance this week, how she feels bad about it, and she lets me know that there had been some misunderstandings, but everything should be okay. As cryptic as she can be, I think I understand what she means, for the most part. Ria hopes that going out tonight will *'spark some energy'*, as she put it, which I'm assuming means she's looking forward to it as well.

Glancing over with a smile, she tells me, "Hazel and Melody are psyched for tonight, they've called me twice for input on outfits and their hair. They are also really excited to see you again. It's been a while since we've all gone out together."

"Yeah, since leaving that ass-hat didn't go so well, I thought it'd be best if I stayed out of the city nightlife for a bit. I feel ready though, he's in my past. I fully intend to keep him there for good," I say under my breath, looking out the window.

A few months ago when I had broken up with Bolvi, he'd grabbed me so hard that I had bruises on my arms for almost two weeks. He kept shaking me, screaming that no one would love me as much as him. How if I tried to go to any of the bars, everyone would know I was just a dumb whore looking for money. How if he ever saw me, that I would regret it. Three weeks ago was the result of that threat, leaving me with my wrecked car. Asteria had never met him, and did not know the details of what I'd endured until it was too late. She was the reason I had the strength to leave.

Unwillingly, I recall the trauma he caused me as unwelcome flashes of memories flit through my mind. *'You're pathetic'. Liquor and vomit. Migraines. Screaming. Falling backward, 'Get up, bitch.' Pain. 'No, please,' sobbing. 'Nobody loves you as much as I do,' slap. Violation. Sleepless fear. Hollow darkness. Alone. Empty.*

Flinching when Ria's hand firmly squeezes my knee, I'm gratefully pulled back from the depths of despair. I only spoke about my experiences out loud once, and it was with her. I felt that I did not want to give life to any of it by speaking it into existence, and only talked about it because she had confronted me. She didn't agree with my choice not to address it further, but has respected and supported me in healing, being with me through all of it.

It has taken me a while to work through everything mentally, meditating and finding healthy outlets to release the negative energy that resided in me, some of which still lingers heavily. Even with the efforts to expel the trauma, it is all too easy to drown in the pain and darkness I had been suffering in for too long, and I can't bring myself to fully face it.

*I wish these memories would just fly away like ashes of fire in the wind.* I sigh as I watch the woods pass by in a blur.

Glancing over at Ria, I take her hand in mine and give her a small smile, which she returns brightly. As we park at the mall, I take a slow, measured breath and release it gradually, fully expelling the air. As Ria rounds the car, I genuinely grin with my excitement for the night ahead.

*Each day is new. I will not let the woes of my yesterdays bring fear to my tomorrows.*

We spent the majority of the day in the mall, going through every store and trying on dozens of clothes, piecing together the perfect outfit head to toe. Ria bought herself an armful of bags filled with all sorts of items from blouses, skirts, dresses and accessories, using today as an excuse to '*revamp her wardrobe*'. Oppositely, I only have three bags for a jacket, dress and shoes, deciding today was only for my outfit and not my closet.

I eagerly sit at my vanity, unwrapping the towel from my head to comb through the tangles in my hair and do my makeup. After drying and styling my hair, I shimmy into my new, ruched, figure hugging black dress. It has a deep v-neck, full-length lace sleeves, and is cut above the knee. Sitting at the edge of my bed, I step into my new, black leather ankle boots with a tapered heel, zipping them up the back. Standing, I slide into a black leather jacket, deciding to leave it open.

Turning toward the antique full length mirror, I am floored by my own appearance and mumble, *"Damn,"* as I give myself a grin, feeling better than I have in a very long time.

*"Damn* is right," Ria startles me with a low whistle, and I find her in the reflection leaning against my door.

Laughing, I turn around. "You look amazing! Are you ready to go?"

Ria twirls around, sending her wavy auburn hair flying with the sparkly, corseted purple and black dress. The high-low hem shows off her spiky heeled combat boots. "Question is, are they ready for me?" she drawls with a wink.

Rolling my eyes, I check my purse for my phone, wallet, and other miscellaneous things that are always randomly needed. *Couple of hair ties, lip balm, lotion, a few band-aids, tissues, nail file, and pepper spray because you just never know. Better to have it and not need it,* I muse as I snap the bag closed.

With a satisfied nod, we make our way downstairs, our heels clomping loudly on the hardwood floor. My mother looks up from a large book on the couch, her eyebrows rising in approval. "You two look incredible. Oh, Selene, come here a moment," she murmurs as she stands, rummaging in her robe slung over the couch.

I step toward her curiously and wait with a small smile. Straightening, she holds out a long, shiny silver chain with a gleaming diamond encrusted crescent moon charm. I gasp, pressing my hand to my mouth.

"For you, dear. May it protect you in your transition into new beginnings," she whispers, pulling me into a hug.

My mother is always saying odd things that half the time don't fully make sense, but I take her words as an endearment. Grateful for my beautiful gift, I squeeze her back, thanking her with a grin. She slides it over my head, the pendant resting on the center of my chest. Fluffing out my hair, her violet eyes crinkle with her smile as she pulls back and gives my shoulder a pat.

"We'll be out late, but hopefully we'll be back before dawn," Ria jokes, grabbing the car keys and heading out the door.

With a shake of her head, my mother puts a hand to my face. "Be careful, but have fun. I remember my days spent reveling," she says wistfully, pushing me toward the door.

Being thirty, you'd think it would be weird living at home with a sibling and parent. But I had lived on my own, and look how that turned out. I have grown to appreciate the close bond we've formed, the three of us living together as if we're best friends.

Looking over my shoulder, I wave to my mother in the window and get in the car with Ria.

"Alright, let's go get the girls and have ourselves one hell of a night," she declares with a grin, and we make our way toward the city.

## KYRAN

Every night this week, the compulsion to run to Selene grew stronger as each day passed. I'd keep to the woods, knowing that the sight of me would undoubtedly cause distress. She'd pace her balcony at dawn, seeming to be unaware or almost as if she were in a trance, repeating it daily like a routine. It wasn't until today that I realized *that* moment is also when I would wake underneath the blackthorn shrub, which stands a few feet from the edge of the woods in front of her balcony.

As I was leaving this morning, Hekate and Asteria manifested in front of me. We had discussed Selene's situation and how they believe it is best for her safety that we spend time with one another. Asteria lightly apologized for her threats the last time we spoke, saying that she *'Renounces any and all vows she may have made against me,'* and hopes we can have an amicable friendship. I voiced that I understood where she was coming from and harbor no ill will toward her, and that I would have acted worse if I were her. We three came to an agreement that Selene's awakening is of utmost importance. I left feeling good about everything that has transpired, my trepidation melting away into a blooming hope that our collective efforts would help bring Selene's wolf out of stasis.

Having just returned from Hekate's woods, I need to shower and tend to a few pack matters before working tonight. Standing in my bathroom, I stare at myself in the mirror with Selene's last words echoing in my mind, *'You shouldn't hide behind all this hair. You are a very handsome man.'* Brushing my hair out of my face, my fingers lightly trace the spot where hers had invisibly branded me. Impulsively, I stride through my bedroom to my desk, rifling through the drawers until I find scissors.

*What are you doing?* Valdr inquires, mildly curious.

Ignoring him, I face myself in the bathroom mirror, grabbing ahold of my unruly hair. Without hesitation, I shear off a handful at the back of my head. Taking another chunk, I snip that just as quickly, black strands fluttering around the sink to the floor. Clumsily, I continue until all my length is gone. Stepping back, I realize how terrible it looks, as if I let a pup hack into my hair with a pair of hedge trimmers.

Groaning, I lean on the sink in defeat.

*Well, that's definitely one way to get Selene's attention,* Valdr drawls dryly.

*Shut it,* I growl at him. Thinking about it, I know just the person to call on for help. *Kira,* I mindlink, *meet me at my door, please. I need a favor.*

She instantly chirps back, *Oh, this ought to be good. I'll be right up!*

Kira's light footsteps echo on the stairs and I walk over to my door, opening it just before she knocks. I give her a sheepish smile, running my hand through the mess of my hair. She stares at me for a moment, her green eyes going wide and rolls her lips inward before releasing them with a *pop.*

"Come with me," she says flippantly, turning on her heel and jogging down the staircase.

Not really wanting to be seen, I follow her closely into her room and head straight for the bathroom. Kira drags a stool over from her vanity and I sit, watching her collect shears, a comb, and clippers from a cabinet. She assesses my head, turning me every which way with pursed lips. Choosing a guard for the clippers, she clicks it on and gets to work, humming quietly.

As the time goes by, I think of the tasks I need to straighten out for the weekend, some orders that need processing at Howler's, and what I want for lunch. Kira shuts off the clippers and combs through my hair, snipping a few times before patting my shoulder.

"Alright, you're all set. Go jump in the shower, you stink," she mutters, putting away her tools.

Pushing to my feet, I glance in the mirror. She gave me a tapered cut, pushing the front of my hair to the side with some layering just long enough to run my fingers through. "Wow Kira, I would've expected you to just buzz it short," I jest as I grin at her. "It looks great, thank you so much for your help. I don't know what I was thinking. Next time I'll come straight to you."

Smiling wide, she pushes me toward her door. Opening it, I turn and pull her into a hug. She ruffles my hair, murmuring, "Whoever she is, she'll be stunned speechless." A sly smile pulls at her lips. "Now go, I've got things to do, places to be. *Muah.*" She kisses my cheek before shutting the door in my face.

Laughing with a shake of my head, I make my way back to my room, deciding to give myself a shave. I use a beard trimmer that's been buried under my sink for a while now, going down to just stubble and clean up the edges.

*Wow, I look a hundred years younger.* I give myself a smile, but it fades quickly. I sweep up the mess I made before taking a quick shower. As I'm drying off, Trey's urgent mindlink crashes through my mind.

*Kyran, I've just got word from Sigurd. We need you in your office. Immediately.* My brow pinches with concern at the tightness in his voice.

I rush out of my room, clutching the towel around my waist. Leaping down both sets of stairs, I burst through my office door seconds after Trey finished speaking in my mind. Around my desk hovers Treyvar, Sigurd, my head warrior, Jeger, the best tracker in my pack, and Vala, the lead hybrid warrior, who also happens to be my ex-girlfriend. We had a rough falling out due to her despicable actions, but I chose to set my personal issues aside and allow her to remain in position for the betterment of my pack. I notice her eyeballing my towel and I glare at her.

Focusing on the matter at hand, I wait as they finish greeting me. "What's happened? Speak freely," I say sternly, crossing my arms.

Sigurd steps forward and announces, "I had been alerted to vamps crossing into our territory. A few wolves chased—"

"Two females have been abducted and four of our men were slain in defense of the attack," Trey interrupts Sigurd, cutting him a sideways glare.

My gaze flits between them. *What the hell is that about?*

"I tracked them a few miles past our eastern lands, but they seemed to have vanished mid-stride. I discerned at least five separate scents, all vampire," Jeger explains quickly. "I mindlinked Vala to come to the place where the trail ended to see if she could sense anything."

Vala, being a wolf-witch hybrid, has some magical abilities, one of which is seeing magical footprints or auras. It is a very useful tool with traps or spells unseen to the normal eye, especially if someone had been enspelled with a charm or curse.

She clears her throat but doesn't meet my gaze, her eyes roaming my shaved face when she elaborates, "I saw that a form of transport spell had been cast, but could not detect if it was performed at the location or remotely. I can confidently say that the vampires are working with at least one witch, though." Her sharp voice cuts the air with anger.

Witches are not known to side with either werewolf or vampire, always choosing to remain impartial to our skirmishes. They neither help nor hinder, generally keeping to themselves and are hardly ever seen. However, if they do decide to become involved in any way, it drastically tips the scales in favor of whoever is within her good graces.

Sitting in my chair, I lean forward and rest my elbows on the desktop, pressing my fingers together. "That makes it six women now, this year. Over a dozen last year, and that's just from our pack.," I growl through my clenched jaw. "Not long ago, I spoke with the other alphas and they confirmed the same is happening to them."

Sigurd steps forward again, glancing narrowly at Trey. "I noticed that they've been—"

"The vampires are not selecting our females at random. A pattern has been discovered, each woman being under four hundred years old and having blonde hair," Trey cuts off Sigurd again, his eyes boring into mine.

Immediately sensing what he means, I undoubtedly know we are thinking the same thing. *Our mother was taken by the vampires, and dad ended up going berserk. He died because of it. Because of me.* My thoughts darken and I curl my hands into fists, dragging my gaze away from my brother's.

*They are looking for someone,* Valdr realizes abruptly. *The vampires have been taking our women, the females of all packs, for centuries now. It's a search, but for who?*

*"Fuck!"* I snarl, slamming my fists on the desk and startling everyone. "The vamps are searching for someone specific. They have been for centuries."

My mother's disappearance sent a shock wave through our entire pack, and it was amplified by the death of my father. Although it was necessary, he was still—*somehow*—revered as a good leader, and the aftermath of their deaths gravely impacted everyone here.

Rising to my feet, I bark out orders. "I must contact the other packs. Trey, get the victims' families into the Great Hall. Let them know that I will meet with them shortly. Vala, find every female of *any* age who has blonde hair—natural or dyed—and color their hair dark, preferably with a spell or charm if you can. I cannot have this happen again, especially now that we have this knowledge. Jeger, do a sweep of our immediate perimeters around the villages and see if you can find traces from *anyone* not of this pack. Sigurd, stay here."

Waiting as they quickly nod and depart, I turn my focus to the head warrior. "What exactly happened, Sigurd? Last I checked, you were patrolling the eastern fields and woodlands yourself. Explain." I cross my arms, watching him closely.

He looks at me warily with regret in his eyes. "I was ambushed during one of my patrol runs. A few of them crossed my path, distracting me while more came upon me from behind. Before I had time to alert anyone else, I had been thrown against a tree and was momentarily knocked unconscious. When I woke up, I mindlinked the warriors about vampires in our territory, but it was too late. I was being overwhelmed with distress calls about our females' capture, and the vamps left without a trace," he admits morosely and lets out a breath, dropping his head in defeat.

Valdr bristles. *Something does not feel right. Do not let on your suspicion, but be mindful of him. He is not outright lying, but he is not speaking the full truth, either.*

Nodding my head once, I meet his gaze. "Take the rest of today to settle yourself. I will meet with you and the other warriors tomorrow," I say brusquely, gesturing toward the door.

"Yes, Alpha," he mutters, leaving my office.

I'm dialing the phone on my desk before the door clicks shut, calling my only friend outside of my pack, Alpha Felagi of the Northeast Region pack. We could speak through mindlink, but out of respect we use the phone lines with the intention of not intruding on one another unless under dire circumstances.

After three rings, my friend's booming voice greets me brightly. "Kyran, my boy! It's been some time, how the hell are ya'?"

"Felagi, I have pressing matters you must be made aware of. I'd like nothing more than to catch up, but let's leave that for the approaching Convocation. I've had another vamp attack, they've abducted more females from my pack. What I need you to know is that every single woman who has been taken is no older than four hundred, and *all* have blonde hair. They are searching for someone in particular, and we have no way of knowing who or why. Now that a pattern has been recognized, we can protect any potential victims," I bite out, anger making my voice tense.

"Shit. *Shit.* I'll let the others know immediately. Thank ya', Kyran. I've lost women recently, and thinkin' back on it, they've *all* been light-haired. Every one of 'em. How could I not *see* this?" His voice trails off, undoubtedly thinking of his mate.

Shortly after my mother's capture, Felagi called my father completely distraught with the news of the same thing happening to him with his mate. He was not at home when his pack was attacked, or else he surely would have been bitten as well, suffering the same fate as my father. I remain silent, unsure of what to say at the moment, and think about anything else that could be connected to this long-sustained issue.

His hushed voice crackles over the line. "She's still out there, I can feel her. She cut me off shortly after her disappearance, but I *know* she's alive. I can't bear the thought of it at times, my mind imagining the most *horrid* things possible." He sucks in a breath and the line goes quiet.

I feel great sorrow for this man. His mate's death would have been an easier thing for him to get past than this. He'd spent many years searching the earth for her, never being able to pinpoint where his broken bond led him, saying it was as if she wasn't exactly on our plane of existence.

"Let me know if you find anything more about this. I'm always here for you, remember that," I say sincerely, waiting for a response.

When the line remains silent, I deposit the phone on the receiver and drop my head into my hands with a sigh. Feeling my short hair,

I am abruptly reminded of Selene. Guilt washes over me, feeling responsible for my distractions this past week. *If only I had been paying better attention to my duties, this wouldn't have happened,* I berate myself.

*Do not think this way. They would have figured out a way regardless, you are not to hold sole blame,* Valdr admonishes me.

I sit at my desk reflecting on everything that has transpired in such a short amount of time. I take a few moments to collect myself before setting out to the Great Hall. I spend a while speaking with the families who'd been directly affected by the vampire attack, consoling them and reassuring them that I will do everything in my power to find the ones responsible and seek retribution. I let them know to come to me directly for anything, at any time of day. A few hours pass by quickly as I have meetings with my warriors, holding lengthy conversations to form a concrete timeline and compare recollections.

I briefly check in with Vala, and with the help of the other hybrids, they created bracelets charmed to glamour the wearer into having dark hair. Made with elastic material that withstands a shift, the bracelets maintain the glamour in wolf-form. I commend her for her ingenuity and instruct her to notify Treyvar once every blonde female was wearing one, making certain she stresses the importance to never remove it.

Feeling a bit worn out, I trek up to my bedroom and lie on my bed with my hands behind my head, staring at the clouds passing by through the skylights. I have a few hours left before opening Howler's and take the time to rest. Friday and Saturday are always the busiest nights, the bar is constantly full from open to close and I usually don't mind the mundane work. Treyvar enjoys working at the busier club bar, whereas I generally run the lounge bar.

Vala occasionally acts as a waitress, mostly on the bigger income nights such as weekends or when events take place, and she always puts the money she earns in tips toward our community in the form of clothing or food supplies. It's an appreciated gesture, but I suspect she only started doing it to get my attention after we broke up.

Closing my eyes with a sigh, I catch myself smiling as I imagine the chance of Selene coming to my bar, hoping she'd remember our brief discussion. I huff a dry laugh and shake my head at the thought.

*Psh, I don't have that kind of luck.*

# CHAPTER SEVEN

## HOWLER'S

### KYRAN

Waking from my nap, I stretch in bed and check the time. With a couple hours to spare, I get dressed, pulling on my black work shirt and faded jeans before heading down to the kitchen to make a quick dinner. As I round the corner, the *clank* of dishes echoes through the hall and I find my siblings setting plates and silverware on the island.

Kira smiles at me warmly, admiring her work as her eyes graze over my hair.

"Hey, there was too much going on earlier to say anything, but you look like a whole new man," Treyvar comments with a grin, turning over his shoulder at the stove top. "I'm willing to bet a certain *someone* is—"

I snatch a stray dish towel and throw it at his head. Trey pulls it off with a laugh, giving me a goofy grin. I can't help the smirk that pulls at my lips in response and I just shake my head.

Gasping, Kira rushes over and perches on the stool beside me, her eyes wide. *"Please* tell me he isn't just being an ass," she begs, taking hold of my arm.

"He's always being an ass." The towel smacks the side of my face.

"*Eek!* Oh, *Kyran*, I am so excited for you!" she squeals and throws her arms around my neck, nearly choking me. Her voice is shrill with her sudden excitement. "What is her name? How'd you meet? What does she look like? When can I meet her?"

Prying my sister off me, she bounces in her seat with her hands clasped to her chest. She resembles our mother so much, it's often disconcerting. Recalling what happened earlier today, I suddenly panic. "Kira, please tell me you've spoken with Vala today?" I ask her desperately, grasping her arm.

"Kyran, don't you dare tell me that you've gotten back together with her," she chastises me, her face pinching with disappointment.

"No." I let out a frustrated sigh. "Kira, listen to me. I need you to meet with Vala, *now*, get the bracelet from her and *never remove it*, do you understand?" My voice is grave, and her face goes slack.

"What is this about, Kyran? I just got back to pack lands about an hour ago, what happened?" she asks quietly, concern etched on her face.

*Vala, meet me in the lodge kitchen with a bracelet, immediately,* I mindlink her directly. *Actually, make it two,* I add, thinking it's best to be extra cautious.

*I'm on my way,* Vala replies shortly.

Treyvar explains today's events for our sister while I pile a plate with spaghetti and meatballs, snagging a couple slices of garlic bread. Just as I'm sitting back down, Vala opens the front door, breathing heavily.

"Give them to Kira," I say over a mouthful, pointing with my fork. "One on each wrist."

Kira looks stricken, but she holds her arms out as Vala clasps the bracelets for her. Instantly, my sister's honey skin darkens into a deep bronze, and her hair shifts from golden to chestnut. It's a stunning glamour, and looks completely natural to anyone not aware of the bracelet's power.

Looking down at her hands, Kira gasps, running into the hall bathroom and gasping louder a second time. "Vala, this is *incredible!* We could improve these into changing an entire appearance, use them as full disguises if necessary. Wow, this looks so beautiful! I'm in awe," she trills, smiling wide as she comes back into the kitchen.

Turning toward me, Vala explains, "A few women volunteered for us to model the glamours after them. Each bracelet slightly differs from the next with skin tone and shades of hair colors, helping to create a natural effect, especially in a group. We are still handing out some bracelets, but the majority of the pack who needs it has one. Most women responded similarly to Kira and were joyous at the results, thinking they may continue to use them once the threat to their safety has disappeared, enjoying the change. A few even asked for us to make some to change like outfits," she mentions offhandedly, glancing at my sister with a small smile.

I nod in understanding, noticing how her indigo gaze lingers over me, no doubt because of my haircut and shave. Staring at her blankly until she averts her eyes, I continue eating my dinner. Before meeting Selene, Vala was the most attractive woman I'd spoken to. Her dark copper hair caught my attention and the deep purple tone in her eyes was striking in contrast. Now, though, I only see her as a formidable wolf in my pack. Any attraction I'd had for her was wiped away after her mistreatment toward me.

My sister grabs Vala's arm, pulling her out of the kitchen. "That would be so amazing! I can see it now, going on a trip to the beach wearing the 'summertime' bracelet and putting on an instant, glowing tan with sun-kissed, highlighted hair. Oh, or maybe a 'nightlife bracelet' where my skin gets all glittery, and strands of hair glow in the dark! How about…" Kira's bright voice fades away as they climb the stairs toward the lounge.

Finishing my plate, I bring it to the dishwasher and reach for Trey's as well. He gives me a confused look as he turns back from over his shoulder and I just shrug. I don't quite get any of what our sister was going on about, and by the looks of it, Trey feels the same. We both laugh as we head into the garage to leave for our bar.

## SELENE

We pick up Hazel and Melody at their loft on the outskirts of the city, which happens to be close to where I walk in the park, and apparently, also Kyran's bar. It was only a five minute drive once we left their place. We all hurry out of the car, excited for the night ahead. Hazel bounds over, her tight black pleather pants squeaking as she pulls me into a hug.

"I'm glad you're here!" she exclaims, grinning. "Oops, I'm so sorry. Here, let me help," she mumbles as we pull apart, my hair caught in her gaudy necklace.

I laugh, separating some strands. "Well, this is why I wear it up most of the time," I joke sarcastically. Tugging sharply, I free myself, rubbing at a little sore spot on my head where some hair pulled out and Hazel apologizes again.

"It's okay, no worries," I reassure her, grabbing my purse off the floor of the car.

The four of us make our way to the street, the clatter of our heels clacking along the pavement echoing into the night. Hazel and Melody are twin sisters who Ria met when she graduated high school. They have matching light brown hair with copper highlights, but Hazel wears hers in a sleek bob, and Melody keeps hers long and wavy. They have pretty purple-toned gray eyes, sharp facial features, and tall, slender bodies, similar to how supermodels look.

Peering at our group as we walk, I suddenly feel like a shrub in a forest of redwoods. Cute, but not incredible. *It doesn't do any good to feel self-conscious. I'm unique, comparatively. That can be a good thing,* I think to myself, smiling. All of us are beautiful, in our own ways, and we *definitely* put in the effort to show that off tonight.

Ria at me smiles over her shoulder as we wait for the light, standing across the street from the growing line. At the signal, we scurry over and take our place at the end with a few more people coming up after me. Hazel digs in her purse, pulling out a compact and checks her reflection. Glancing around, I admire the bright neon sign on the side of the building that reads *Howler's Bar and Nightclub,* illuminating everyone in blue, pink, and yellow as the script gradually shifts colors. We're less than halfway in line toward the door when I notice the quickly growing number of people behind us.

"Hey, what time did this place open? It's getting really busy," I remark quietly, impressed.

"Um, at nine o'clock, I believe," Ria answers, pulling out her phone. "Yup, at nine. It's only nine-thirty now, it'll probably get quite rowdy tonight," she says with a sly smirk.

Holding out my hand, I silently raise my eyebrow at her. Fishing in her purse, she rolls her eyes and hands me the keys, being melodramatic, as usual. "Thank you," I say dryly, knowing very well *that* would've been quite a challenge toward the end of the night.

At the front of the line, I stuff the keys in my purse and Hazel glances over her shoulder, her red lips pursed in a smirk. "Ready? Let's have some *fun*." She snickers, catching my eye then turns back toward the two bouncers.

The men give the four of us a long appraisal, one of them even raising his brows. "Ladies," he greets with a smirk, holding one of the doors open for us. "Welcome to Howler's." His rough voice slides away as the noise emanating from within pours out of the doorway.

Upon entering, there is a wide staircase that descends below street level. The walls are painted a deep burgundy color, bare of decoration, and are illuminated with warm, old-fashioned wall sconces. At the foot of the stairs, heavy bass thunders out from a second set of double doors. We spill into Howler's, finding the bar filled with a wide variety of people of all ages and styles. As rock music rolls out of the record player, a cacophony fills the air of voices mixed with laughter and shouts, glasses clinking in the distance, muffled sportscaster jargon buzzing from the TVs, and the sharp *clack* of pool balls spinning onto a table.

Gazing around in awe, I observe the vaulted ceilings, my eyes trailing up to the large skylights and I notice a lofted lounge area with luxurious leather sofas, decorative furnishings, and small tables lining the railing. The staircase handrail is gorgeous, the smooth wood delicately carved with vines and leaves trailing down the iron balustrades. Three pool tables with forest green felted tops and intricate filigree woodwork line the left half of the bar. My eyes drift past a group of men clustered around a dart board in the corner, near the entrance.

To my right, there is a stage area for a live band, and beyond that is a wide entryway. Watching a few people wander through, I glimpse a tunnel-like passage leading into the nightclub. A large, retro record player sits on the other side of the arch, a new song floating out of it.

Abstract painted art and various photographs of landscapes hang along the walls. I gaze at the beautiful pictures, and a portrait of a black wolf in the woods catches my eye specifically.

Handmade wooden furniture is dotted around the booth-style tables lining the walls, carved with filigree matching the pool tables. A spacious, black marble floor leads from the entrance to the large, horseshoe-style bar situated in the back of the main room. The bartop is made of the same shiny, smooth black marble as the floor, and is also adorned with ornamental wood, tying the whole room together.

*This place is absolutely incredible,* I wonder in awe, smiling at the magnificent sight.

I find myself searching for Kyran with the hope that he'd be working tonight. My eyes drift across the full lounge, skimming the faces of patrons and flitting over a few men working behind the bar. Quickly backtracking, my breath catches, captured by Kyran's amber eyes from across the room. He is unrecognizable at first, with his short hair and stubble in place of the unruly hair and beard I'm used to seeing. But it's his warm eyes that I could never overlook.

A slow, wolfish grin spreads across his handsome face.

My heart skip a beat, cheeks heating beneath his gaze. *Okay, scratch that,* he *looks absolutely incredible.*

## KYRAN

Trey and I got to Howler's an hour before opening to help prep in the kitchen and set up the bar. The moment I gave the go ahead, my bouncers opened the doors to a flood of people, an endless stream pouring in that even now, half an hour later, hasn't subsided. Busy drying glasses, I chat with a few customers as I overhear some lewd obscenities float around the lounge. Glancing up to find the source of the salacious comments, I notice a pair of attractive, willowy women enter the lounge and haughtily take in the crowd around them.

*Witches,* Valdr grumbles lowly.

*All are welcome here. I intend to keep this place a neutral zone for all walks of life,* I remind him, returning my attention back to the glasses. I place them on a rack beneath the bar, peering at my brother seated in front of me.

"Shouldn't you be tending the bar in the club?" I mutter, resting my hands against the bartop.

Grinning, he holds up his cup of ice water, shaking the cubes. "I'm finishing my break. I've been working *such* long hours, you know, slaving away for my master," he drawls languidly.

"It's nine-thirty," I say flatly. "Get your ass over there! It's swamped in here, I can only imagine what the club is like," I grumble at him, suppressing a smirk.

Throwing his water back like a shot, Trey turns in his stool to leave. I take his glass and wash it, reaching for the towel to dry the water spots. My brother whistles lowly and I glance up, following his line of sight to the entrance.

My chest constricts, eyes falling on Selene gently letting the door shut behind her, looking around with wonder at my bar. She is absolutely *breathtaking*. My gaze traces the flow of her hair cascading over her beautiful face, down along the length of the black dress hugging her amazing curves. Clenching my jaw, I press my palms against the bartop to steady myself. Her appearance completely throws me off guard. A low, rumbling growl rolls through my chest as I watch her move.

"*Damn*. Aren't they all a sight for sore eyes," Treyvar murmurs, turning back to me with a sly smile pulling at his mouth. "Tonight's gonna be a *good night*," he insinuates, raising his brows.

Planting my hand on the side of his head, I shove him off of the stool without taking my gaze from Selene. "Get back to work, asshole," I mutter halfheartedly, my mouth pulling up at the corner.

Trey's laughter follows him through the bar and he disappears within the passage leading to the club room. Leaning on the bartop, I watch Selene as her gaze roams the main room, taking her time absorbing the details of my bar.

Her beauty is ethereal, a beam of light in the dim lounge. Completely unaware that more than a few sets of eyes follow her as she slowly walks in from the entrance, she admires the decorations and turns to look at each wall as she passes.

Selene's gaze drifts over the bartop, her bright eyes looking past the patrons and passing over me briefly until they dart back, locking onto mine. I slowly grin when she notices me watching her. Even from back here I can see the flush of her pale skin, and it only makes my smile grow wider.

*Out of all the men in here, she stares at me,* I wonder in disbelief.

Feeling bold, I straighten and gesture for her to come sit at the stool in front of me. She hesitates for a moment and I raise my brow in a teasing challenge. Selene purses her full lips before she turns toward Asteria, saying something in her ear. A rogue wolf plops down in the vacant stool, blocking my view. I glare at him with a snarl. He leaps off the seat as if his ass was on fire and he hurries toward the end of the bar.

I glance across the room and find Selene walking toward me, her hips swaying distractingly. Dragging my eyes up to hers, I catch the coy smile and quirk of her brow as she changes her stride, lengthening her steps and exaggerating the seductive way her body flows. Clenching my jaw, I flex my arms as I fold them across my chest, cocking a brow in return.

Her eyes drift downward and the corner of my mouth lifts with amusement. *Two can play at that game.*

## SELENE

I try—*and fail miserably*—to not stare at Kyran's body. It doesn't help that he's wearing a tight black t-shirt that defines his thick muscles, *especially* his bare tattooed arms. Biting the corner of my lip, I drop my gaze to the bartop as I take the seat in front of him. He slides his arms across the dark marble of the bar, leaning on his elbows.

Peeking up, his face is close to mine, amber eyes burning into me. "What'll it be, beautiful?" he murmurs, smirking.

*You.*

Blushing, my breath catches and I clear my throat.

"Two daiquiris served up, and a gimlet on the rocks, please." I tuck some hair behind my ear. "I, um, also have kind of an odd request for myself," I say a little softer, scrunching my nose.

Kyran smiles with a nod and pulls out three cocktail glasses, clinking them on the bar. "What do you mean?" he asks lightly, raising his brow.

"Could you make me a drink that isn't alcoholic, but looks like one? I, um, I'll be driving tonight," I mumble, not wanting to divulge the true reason behind abstaining.

His eyes squint in thought, and he nods with a lopsided smile. "Sure, I've got an idea. Just give me a few moments," he murmurs as he busies himself, expertly preparing the drinks.

"Where is the restroom?" I ask, feeling slightly awkward just sitting here, watching him in silence.

"Just before the pool tables, there's a hallway on the right. Take the second door." He gestures with a free hand. "Around the corner is my office, as well as the alleyway exit. The bathroom is hard to miss." He flashes me a crooked smile.

"Okay, thank you." I slide off the stool, patting my hand on the seat. "Could you keep this open for me?"

"Of course." Kyran grins, shaking the daiquiris.

Blushing, I maneuver through the busy bar and stop to wait in a short line. Once inside, I anxiously fix my hair and makeup in the mirror. I let out a nervous breath, feeling slightly self-conscious. A woman washes her hands beside me, and smiles brightly at me in the mirror when my gaze meets hers.

"You are stunning. Whoever he is, he's a lucky man." She grins widely, winking, and shakes the water off her hands before disappearing into the crowded hall.

The stranger's compliment makes me smile, and I carry it with me as I make my way through the line of women, skirting around a pair of men stumbling into the hallway. Passing the pool tables, I accidentally bump into someone bending over to shoot. I begin to apologize, but instantly choke on my breath as I look back at him.

Spinning away, I rush straight to the bar, shouldering people out of the way as I go. I risk glancing over my shoulder for a moment, feeling uneasy.

*He didn't see me, he barely even looked up. Bolvi, here, of all places! Why? Fuck! Fuck fuck fuck!* My mind reels as panic rises, unsteadily gripping the edge of the bartop and staring hard at the reflection of the lights.

*Breathe. Slowly. Nose, mouth, repeat. Just breathe.*

Kyran appears in front of me, his easy smile shifting rapidly to concern as I shakily take my seat, feeling a bit on edge. He sets the finished gimlet aside, gesturing for a waitress and instructing her to bring the drinks to my sister's table.

I sneak a look over my shoulder, glancing back toward the pool tables. My gaze flits around the lounge.

*Where is he? Did he see me?*

"Selene," Kyran says lowly, pulling my attention back to him. "Are you alright? Did something happen?" He softly lays his hand over my shaking one.

His voice is direct but gentle, and I glance up into his concerned eyes. Leaning toward me, his eyebrows pinch, posture tensing. He lightly glides his thumb over my hand, comforting me.

Relaxing slightly, I mutter, "I unfortunately bumped into my ex, by accident. It caught me off guard. We, um, didn't exactly leave on good terms." I scrunch my face, grimacing.

"I don't mean to overstep, but the way you look right now is not typically how someone reacts to simply running into their ex." He holds my gaze intensely.

Twisting my lips, I glance away to the side, unsure of what to say.

"Selene, do you not feel safe?" he asks seriously, giving my hand a light squeeze.

Kyran's strong presence is calming, and my nerves ease with him here. His gentle touch is warm and comfortable, making me feel safe.

"I do now," I murmur honestly, peering up into his eyes.

His mouth draws into a flat line and he lowers his head, asking tersely, "Could you point him out to me? Just so I can keep an eye on him for you. I will not let *anything* happen to you, Selene."

The sincerity in his voice makes me smile. "Thank you, but...I can't find him anywhere. I might have just imagined it. I don't know." I shake my head, squinting my eyes. "Um, if I do see him again, I will let you know right away," I murmur, feeling embarrassed.

My hand grows warm and tingly beneath his. Blood rushes to my face as I realize that I turned it over at some point. I clasp his fingers briefly before pulling away.

A clear drink sits forgotten on the bartop in front of him, garnished with mint.

"So, what fancy drink will be my go-to tonight?" I gesture toward the glass, hoping to lighten the mood.

Kyran takes a moment to respond, his eyes sharply roaming the room. Glancing down, he picks up the drink, announcing, "May I present the Nojito, all the fun without the headache." He hands it to me with a tight smile.

I chuckle, placing it down to dig my wallet out of my purse. As I go to give him my card, he puts his hand up with a shake of his head. "On the house, it's my pleasure."

"Thank you." I smile, rising to my feet. "I'm sure I'll be back soon," I murmur and give him a wink, receiving a grin in return.

Kyran straightens as I turn around, my cheeks hot. Asteria, Hazel, and Melody are openly gawking at me from the side of the room. Ria just *happened* to find a booth within direct line of sight to the bar. Rolling my eyes, I can't help the grin that spreads across my face as I make my way to our table, sitting beside Ria. She roughly nudges my shoulder. Glancing down at the napkin she's holding, I raise a confused eyebrow.

"For the river of drool pouring out of your mouth," Ria says dryly, grinning with a waggle of her eyebrows.

Everyone cackles and I laugh along earnestly, peeking over at Kyran who quickly turns away.

*Was he listening? But it's so loud in here, he couldn't hear her.*

"Am I *that* obvious?" I ask, looking around the table.

"Well, not as obvious as *him,* that's for sure," Melody remarks flatly, finishing her daiquiri.

Several minutes pass as we talk about the bar and catch up with one another. I stand and gather the empty glasses, brightly asking, "Another round?"

Everyone cheerfully voices their agreement. I grab my purse and hurry over to the bar, finding a gap between groups of people. As I place the empty glasses on the bartop, Kyran nudges the bartender aside in front of me.

He smirks, gesturing at the glasses. "You didn't have to bring those with you."

I scrunch my nose. "I like to help where I can. Would you make another round, please?"

He lifts a shaker with one hand and places three more cocktail glasses on the bar. "Already on it," he says slyly, giving me a wink.

Holding his gaze, I intentionally shift my attention to his short black hair, taking my time looking at him. "You're really handsome," I murmur appreciatively. "Not that you weren't before, it's just that I think this style suits you better," I hastily add, returning my focus to his eyes with a blush.

"You should've seen me before my sister fixed it. All credit goes to her." He laughs a little sheepishly, running a hand through his hair.

Finished with our drinks, he slides them over and Ria leans past me, placing a twenty dollar bill on the bartop. "We snagged a pool table. Come play if you get the chance." She grins at me, picking up the cocktails with ease and leaving without a backward glance.

Kyran slides the bill back toward me with a mischievous smile. "Keep it. Save it for a rainy day."

Narrowing my eyes, I grab the money and catch the attention of an attractive red-haired waitress, beckoning her over. "Excuse me, would you kindly accept this tip? Service has been great tonight," I chirp, handing her the twenty.

"Oh, sure! Thank you," she smiles hesitantly, her indigo eyes flitting over Kyran before she turns around and places the money in a bucket on the shelf of liquor bottles.

Pursing my lips, I raise my brows at him in challenge. My resolve is short lived when I crack a smile. He laughs loudly, his eyes crinkling in the corners. I pick up my glass with a grin and push off the bar, turning to head toward the pool tables. Taking my hand, Kyran gently tugs me back around, leaning over the bartop to reach me.

"Listen to the music. The next song is for you," he murmurs and releases me with a crooked smile.

Flustered, I just nod silently. As I make my way across the busy lounge, I automatically look around for Bolvi, feeling slightly paranoid. After pushing through the crowded floor, I find Melody alone at a pool table, chalking a cue stick.

"Ria and Hazel went to check out the club and will be back in a bit. Wanna play a round?" She holds out a second stick for me to take.

Our game moves fast, mostly in part because I totally suck at playing billiards. I have fun anyway, laughing at all my mistakes and not taking it seriously. As Melody is lining up for a shot, the music changes to a punchy drum beat with a plucky guitar, and I recognize the classic hit "Oh, Pretty Woman".

As the lyrics bounce from the record player, my eyes round and as my cheeks flush hotly. *I can't believe this man!* My heart beats rapidly as I stare down at my feet, feeling flustered again. I peek up at Melody. She is completely oblivious to what is happening as she focuses on finishing the table.

The end of the second verse passes and I steel myself, knowing what's coming. I sweep my gaze through the bar to find Kyran. Leaning against the wall by the record player, I meet his eyes just as he mouths the growl part from across the room and laughs. *If my face was any hotter, I'd combust into a pile of ashes.* I groan internally, rolling my lips between my teeth. A wolfish smile spreads across his face and I return the wide grin, slightly shaking my head in disbelief. I hurry to clear the table, putting our sticks back on the wall and re-racking the balls neatly.

Feeling brazen, I intentionally avert my eyes from Kyran and keep my back to him until the end of the song nears. Slinging my purse over my shoulder, I turn around and catch his gaze. I mimic the second half of the last verse, beginning to cross the floor toward him with a sly smile as the words *'But wait,'* ring out. Watching Kyran full out laugh—the way his eyes crinkle with amusement—makes me giggle a little bit, a warm, electric feeling washing over me.

Melody grabs my arm, quickly turning me around. Ria and Hazel rush up to us, flushed and laughing. They grab my hands, pulling me toward the club. Glancing over my shoulder, I scrunch my nose and stick my tongue out playfully, making Kyran smile again as he leans forward, watching me disappear through the archway.

The booming bass drowns out my thoughts as we enter. Moving through the club is difficult, the floor tightly packed with gyrating bodies. Multi-colored strobe lights flash in the hazy air, illuminating the shiny poles on the stage to my right, showcasing a number of lithe dancers. The club floor is huge with a sea of people stretching on further than my height allows me to see. The girls pull me up to a large, straight bar at the back wall, ordering drinks from a handsome blonde man. The three of them make a show of giggles and flirting, behaving like teenagers.

*Why does he look familiar, have I met him before?*

Laughing, I roll my eyes at the girls. After they get their drinks, we make our way to the center of the dance floor and I find that walking is impossible. The only way to traverse the crowd is with shakes and shimmying steps. Letting the joy of the evening take over, I dance with my sister and friends to the thumping beat of the house music. As time passes, I catch myself thinking about Kyran.

*He is so different. Very hands off, yet completely unapologetic with his flirting. That was one hell of a move he pulled with the song, and it definitely worked.* I smile warmly at the thought.

Steeling myself, I decide to go back and seek him out. I turn toward the hallway between the bar and nightclub, only to come to an abrupt stop as I slam into a slim, firm chest. The smell of him makes me instantly sick.

I take one swift glance at Bolvi, his sneer and rusty eyes boring into me, before bolting for the tunnel. Shoving harshly against the throng of gyrating bodies, the mass of people becomes impenetrable and I hastily change direction toward the raised dais.

I scramble over a sofa between two entwined couples, startling them as I launch myself onto the platform. Trying to avoid contact with blurry bodies, I run as fast as my heels will let me, my heart pounding in my throat. Without looking, I leap off the edge of the stage and dart behind some tall side tables, squirming past a group of boisterous women coming out of the passageway and hurry through.

A sob threatens to escape me as I frantically dig around in my purse, wrapping my fingers around the pepper spray. My purse tears from my shoulder and I let it go, gasping and trying not to cry. I whirl around with a shout swallowed by the thumping bass, spraying a stream directly into Bolvi's face. He swipes at his eyes with a snarl and knocks the small can from my grasp. I kick him in the crotch with the tip of my boot, not waiting around to see if it worked.

I hurdle into the lounge, barely seeing Kyran crouched by the bar sweeping up glass. Panic sets in. My only thought is to *get away.*

Dashing across the floor and into the hallway beneath the stairs, I cut the line and shove through the women's bathroom door. Going to the furthest stall, I crawl under the door and the woman occupying it shrieks at me. Seeing my distraught face, she hastily leaves.

Locking the stall, I fall back onto the toilet, pulling my feet up and stifle a sob with the back of my hand, trying desperately to calm my erratic heart.

I wait for a few minutes to get my breathing under control before going to the sink to compose myself. *Nothing happened, it's okay. Text Ria, tell her you're ready to go home and to meet you outside.* Reaching for my purse, I abruptly remember losing it in the passageway.

*"Fuck,"* I groan, putting my hands to my face.

*Breathe. In, out.* I try to calm down as I clean the smudges from my makeup and adjust my hair, but nothing I do takes the fear out of my eyes. With shaking legs, I cross the bathroom and cautiously open the door, peering out into the hallway. Finding it empty, I sigh in relief and take a few steps before a sharp pain burns at the back of my scalp, yanking me off my feet.

My hands fly to my head and I yelp as my back slams into the wall. Tears spring in my eyes and pour freely down my face from both terror and pain. Not thinking, I drop my bodyweight and am repaid with a gut wrenching knee to my stomach, pinning me to the wall. Openly crying, I fear what Bolvi will do to me.

"Stop, *please!"* I squeak breathlessly, sobbing.

Wild, flat, burnt umber eyes glare at me as he leans in. His rough voice grates through clenched teeth, hissing, "I got you now, *you little bitch.* I've been waiting for you." His sour breath washes over me, making me gag.

With one hand still fisted in my hair, Bolvi gives my head a harsh shake and slams the other into my throat, cutting off my air. I claw at his arms, his face, desperate to find purchase anywhere—

*Snap!*

The relentless pressure vanishes and I gasp, choking on a cough as an agonized yell tears from Bolvi's mouth. His weight is thrown off of me, his grip ripping out a chunk of my hair as he flies down the hall. I let out a hiss of pain, pressing my hand to the back of my head. Falling to my knees, I glare through my tears at Bolvi's slumped body in the corner of the hall.

A shadow moves past and I jump with a cry, startled and afraid.

Kyran slowly kneels down in front of me. His face is twisted with rage, his chest heaving with every breath. Seeing him brings a flood of fresh tears as a feeling of relief washes over me.

Without hesitation, I collapse forward into his warm embrace, and my tension abates as his strong arms envelop me. After a moment, he pulls back and his warm fingers gently lift my chin. His amber eyes are bright, gazing intensely at me.

"I am *so sorry,* Selene. Are you hurt? Are you alright?" His deep voice is laced with concern, sounding rougher than usual.

Sucking in my lip, I start to nod, but end up swiveling my head around and shake it a few times. "*No,* I'm not alright," I say on a sob.

He cups my face in his hand, stroking my cheek with his thumb.

I stare into his burning eyes and lean into his warm palm.

*I am now, with you. You feel safe.*

# CHAPTER EIGHT

## TAKE CARE

### KYRAN

Kneeling in the hallway, I angrily mindlink my brother. *Treyvar, office hall, now. Selene has been attacked. I need you to remove the body.*

*Shit,* he responds instantly, *I'm on it.*

Forcing myself to release Selene, she reaches up and rubs at the back of her head with a wince. When she withdraws her hand, I notice how her fingertips are coated in her blood and mine immediately boils at the sight. Whipping my head around to glare at the bastard responsible, I find the hall empty.

*"Fuck,"* I groan through clenched teeth, balling my hands into fists.

*Find him! He cannot be allowed to roam free,* Valdr demands with rage.

Heavy footfalls echo into the hallway as Trey comes barreling around the corner. He takes a moment, looking around noticing only Selene and myself, and his brow pinches as he meets my gaze.

I mindlink Trey, hot ire coursing through me. *Fucker's gone, must've left out the alleyway exit. He looked familiar, but I can't place him. His eyes betray him, though. Bastard is about to become fully berserk.*

Trey's face hardens. *Must've been a rogue, then, to behave this way here. I'll get Jeger and let you know what we find. What happened?* He glances down toward Selene, nodding at the blood on her hand.

*We can talk about it later, I need to tend to her. Go find Asteria and inform her of this, but assure her that Selene is safe with me. We'll be in the office,* I tell him tersely.

"I'll be right back," Trey blurts out loud, turning on his heel and hurrying away.

"Can you stand?" I ask quietly, gently taking her hands in mine.

Meeting my gaze, Selene nods and I help pull her slowly to her feet. I notice the way she discreetly presses a hand to her stomach and grimaces, my anger flashing again at the sight of her pain.

Clenching my jaw, I swallow harshly against the growl bubbling up my throat. "Come with me, I'll help you with your wound." I raise my arm, guiding her down the hall.

Opening my office, I flick on the light and have her sit in an armchair as I dig through the closet, pulling out a first-aid kit. Turning toward Selene, I meet her gaze and ask, "Is it okay for me to check the wound on your head?" I wait for her permission before moving.

Her brows pull together and up, as if in disbelief. "Yes," she whispers, her crystal eyes gleaming with unshed tears.

Rounding the back of the chair with clenched teeth, I stretch gloves over my hands and gently sift through her stained hair, searching for the wound. Lifting a section, I find a small bare patch wet with blood. Leaning over the armrest, I tell her softly, "I need to flush this out to get a better look at it. I'm going to use sterile water, but it might hurt a little. I just want you to be prepared for it, okay?"

"Okay, thank you," she replies with a small smile.

Taking an irrigation syringe out of the packaging, I prep it along with some gauze and antiseptic spray, setting everything beside me on a disposable towel. Closing my eyes, I resist the urge to just imbue my healing ability into her, to wash away any wounds she may have. *It would cause problems, I can't do that.*

Suppressing another frustrated growl, I lift the syringe and separate her hair. "Ready?" I ask, waiting once more for her confirmation.

"Yes," she replies quietly.

Flushing the wound, her head twitches from the contact and I look closely to see if it needs stitching. Only seeing a small circle of missing skin, I'm relieved it isn't a gash as I set the syringe down and grab the spray. "I am going to spray antiseptic on the wound, to kill any possible bacteria. It will sting," I tell her, pausing again for her reply.

She just nods slightly in response. I quickly spray and take some gauze, pressing it to her head. "Hold this firmly for me, please," I instruct, gently placing her hand over the pad. Removing the gloves, I discard them in the trash can by my desk and kneel in front of Selene.

"You're missing a small patch of hair and scalp, though I didn't find a deep gash or split. You don't need stitches, but it's going to be sore for a while, so be mindful when showering or brushing your hair," I quietly advise her and she nods, her eyes not meeting my gaze.

"Selene, *what happened?* A woman came rushing up to me, frantic about some crazy lady climbing into her bathroom stall, so I went to check it out. *Finding him like that with you—*" I cut myself off as my voice hardens from my rising anger and I close my eyes, exhaling harshly. "I just about lost all control, seeing you like that," I murmur, sitting down on the floor and her eyes flick to mine.

*You should've. I would love nothing more than to rip him apart,* Valdr seethes in my mind.

For a moment she just sits there, silently holding her head and staring at me. Glancing to the side, she releases a shaky breath. "That was my ex, Bolvi. I had only seen him that one time, earlier in the night, when I had been acting weird at the bar. I kept looking for him, but I never saw him again, not until I was dancing with my friends and…" She pauses, her eyes meeting mine with a blush. "I went to find you again. Except I crashed into *him,* unexpectedly. I don't know where he came from or how he found me. I immediately ran, trying to escape. *Ugh,* my purse." She groans, pressing her free hand to her face.

I can only quirk my brow in response, my jaw clenched too tightly for me to speak out loud, fearing a harsh growl would tear free if I did.

"He tried pulling me back into the club but I dropped it. Someone's probably made off with it by now. At least I pepper sprayed the bastard, and kicked his nuts into his stomach." She sighs, dropping her hand.

Looking intently at me, she leans forward, pressing her soft palm to my cheek. *"Thank you,* Kyran," she whispers as a tear wells and spills down her face.

As I reach up to wipe it away, a knock rattles the door before Treyvar pushes it open. Behind him is Asteria with both fury and fear clear on her face. Trey lifts his arm, a black purse dangling from his hand.

"I believe this is yours?" he offers, smiling at Selene.

When she rises from the chair, I stand with her and gently take the gauze from her head, seeing that the bleeding has stopped. She takes her purse, checking its contents briefly before slinging it over her shoulder.

*We have a problem,* I mindlink Trey, giving him a hard look.

With his mouth going flat, he glances at Asteria, then at Selene, and back to me. *Should we make sure they get home safely?* he asks in a serious tone.

I nod imperceptibly, noticing the pinch of Selene's brow and slight frown of her lips. I watch as she taps her phone, an idea forming. Stepping in front of her, I hold my hand out and ask quietly, "May I have this for a moment?"

She obliges, placing her phone in my palm. Peering down at the cracked screen, I open her contacts and add my information. Smirking, I silently hand the phone back to her. As she glances at her phone, a tinkling laugh like that of a bell chimes from her mouth. Grinning up at me, she swats my arm playfully.

*"You weren't supposed to hear that,"* she whispers, giggling as Ria lightly takes her arm.

"Sel, let's head home. I already texted the girls to meet us at the car. That is, if you're okay to drive?" she asks, concerned.

"I'm fine. Just mostly shaken up, and a bit sore, but I can drive." Selene turns back to me, biting her lip as her eyes grow watery once more. "Thank you, again. I really don't want to think about what would have happened if you hadn't been there." The raw emotion in her voice grips my heart with fiery fingers.

Before I can respond, she wraps her arms around my middle, squeezing firmly. She releases me quickly and heads into the hallway, glancing over her shoulder with a small smile. I take a step toward her, intending to see them to their car when Asteria looks back at me.

"We'll be okay from here. Thank you," she says tightly, her eyes flashing black.

I nod, watching them round the corner. I close my eyes, run my hand through my hair and bow my head a moment, taking a slow breath. Scenting jasmine, my chest quietly rumbles and I inhale deeply.

*She smells incredible,* Valdr mumbles.

*"Dude,* did you just sniff your shirt?" Trey scoffs, grinning.

Glaring at him, I grab the back of his neck and toss him into the hallway, pulling the office door closed behind me.

Running stealthily through the woods along the road, Treyvar and I discuss everything that had happened. After meeting with Jeger in the alleyway, he confirmed my suspicions and took off after the scent trail, letting me know he'd give me an update if he found anything new.

My brother and I decided to keep watch as Selene and Asteria made their way home, in case they were being followed. When Selene had told me it was her ex who attacked her, I recognized his name immediately. Bolvi was once in my pack. He is a lesser ranked wolf with no special skills or ability. There had been claims he was involved with the abduction of my mother, that he had been directly in contact with the vampires for some time and used their venom as a drug to get high. My father had exiled him after exerting his will as Alpha, discovering the truths buried in lies, stripping him of any ties to us, and branding him as a traitor, deeming him a rogue never to be part of a pack again. Seeing his eyes tonight showed me the vamps must've gotten sick of his shit, too.

*Maybe he'd been tracking her, followed her and found an opportunity to attack. But why, though? Just because someone dumps you doesn't give you reason to go psychotic,* Trey mindlinks me, dodging around a tree.

Glancing at the tail lights of the Prius, I am reminded of running into Selene at the park. Her dark words echo in my mind. *'I'm alright, you didn't hurt me. I've had much worse, ha.'* I didn't fully understand then that she meant those words *literally.*

*This is not the first time that he's hurt her. It was not a coincidence.* Valdr snarls angrily.

Trey and I both growl in response to Valdr's realization. Women are treated highly within our race, and only a weak, pathetic excuse of a man would harm a female. If one is ever exposed for their despicable actions, he would be brutally beaten, tortured to near death and exiled from the pack. He would be physically branded with a vampire fang, scarring him beyond healing abilities, forever being known as an abuser.

*Why at Howler's, though? Why would he wait to attack there, where risks of being caught are very high, rather than at the park or the store?* I ask Valdr and Trey, ducking beneath a fallen oak.

*My only thought is maybe she caught him by surprise, that maybe he didn't know where to find her,* Trey offers, coming to a stop beside me.

Satisfied to see her safely pull into her driveway, I drop the small sports bag I'd carried in my mouth, and wait for the large iron gates to fully close before shifting.

"Whatever the reasoning is, he escaped, and Jeger hasn't contacted me since following his trail. He's almost fully berserk, I am certain of that. His eyes had a red tinge and it's only a matter of time before he's fully out of control. I cannot have him roaming about freely. He needs to be dealt with, and soon." I sigh, running a hand through my hair.

Trey kicks a branch with a pinched brow. In the distance, the car doors slam shut, followed shortly by the house door. Releasing a breath, I tip my head back and gaze at the stars, readying myself for what I need to do.

"You can head back, I'll meet you at home in a little while. Could you bring my things with you?" I glance over at Trey and he nods once before shifting.

He opens his jaws and I place the strap of my bag between his teeth, waiting until he lopes away into the woods.

Bracing myself for the onslaught of pain, I inhale deeply and shove my hand through the barrier around Hekate's lands. Nothing happens as only empty air greets my hand, though it has a slight pressure to it. Perplexed, I swish my arm around and reach a bit farther, feeling the barrier going past my elbow.

Still nothing.

Narrowing my eyes, I tense before I leap through, planting my feet on the other side and drop into a crouch.

*Can I help you, Kyran?* Hekate's sharp voice rattles my mind.

I launch to my feet like a startled cat, twisting in every direction in search of the witch goddess.

*I am elsewhere, a bit indisposed at the moment. Why have you come?* she asks with a clipped tone.

Hearing the rustling of feathers, I sweep my gaze around the dark woods and locate a raven intently staring at me from a nearby tree. I bow my head, acknowledging her presence.

*Hekate,* I address the raven, *Selene had been attacked by a rogue wolf tonight. He's a berserker, and also her ex boyfriend. I intervened, but being mindful of Selene, I unintentionally allowed him to escape. He is currently being tracked and I fully intend on eradicating him myself. I wanted to make you aware, in case extra protection is needed.*

The raven eerily cocks its head, silently watching me with beady eyes. *If it's any consolation, you're the only thing that has come in contact with my barrier and lived,* her voice states chillingly.

Whipping its head to the side, the raven *caws,* and moments later, a bat flies directly into the barrier. Magic snaps, flashing brightly like a bug zapper on a porch and disintegrates the bat before it even fully makes contact with the force field.

Frowning, I glance down at the pile of ashes and swallow thickly.

*You are safe to cross now that the magic knows you. You are welcome on my lands, however only when absolutely necessary. Thank you for informing me of the threat. Would you like a transport?* she asks lightly, a hint of humor in her voice.

My eyes round as I quickly shake my head and shift, promptly running toward my lands. The raven soars above me for a moment before veering off into the sky with a *caw.*

*Take care, Custos,* Hekate's ghostly voice calls out, following me through the night.

Having slept like shit, I roll out of bed and take a quick shower. I couldn't get the witch's voice out of my head and kept thinking about what she had said to me twice now.

# LUNAR SHADOWS: AWAKEN

As I'm getting dressed, I mindlink Elder Eirene, though it takes a moment to locate her pack-bond. *Could you meet with me this morning? I need help understanding something involving what I believe is Latin.*

I wait a moment, feeling only an empty silence. As I'm about to contact Elder Chrestotes in concern, Eirene's quiet voice replies, *Alpha Kyran, I am not on our lands and expect to return in a few days. Is it of high importance? I can't speak long, this distance is quite taxing on my old mind.*

*No, it's alright, thank you. I will speak with you once you have returned. Safe travels, Elder.*

Sighing, I shut my door behind me and trot down the stairs to the lounge. At the last step, my phone buzzes in my pocket, and I read a text from an unknown number.

**Hey meat-cart guy ;)**

Grinning widely, I reply,

**Good morning, sweetheart ;)
I hope you slept well**

While waiting for her response, I add Selene to my contacts as 'sweetheart' and lean against the wall next to the stairs.

**I was thinking about last
night...
How does a do-over sound?**

**What do you mean?**

**Well...since the night didn't go
as planned, I thought maybe
you could show me how fun
your bar can be**

**That is, if the owner will let
you take some time off on a
Sat night ;p**

Narrowing my eyes, I think about what she could mean by that. Realization strikes me and I bark out a laugh as Kira walks down the hallway.

"Kyran? Why are you smiling at your phone like a—*omigosh!*" She gasps, her hand flying to her mouth. *"Gimme* that!"

She snags my phone out of my hand, bounding down the stairs.

"Kira!" I yell after her, taking the steps two at a time.

Her laughter floats through the house as she flits around, typing on my phone. I catch her around the waist and haul her off her feet with one arm, snatching my phone out of her hand. Dropping my sister on her ass, I look at the screen and groan.

> hmm…idk…if u
> think u can handle it
>
> meet me tonite & I will show
> u just how much fun I can be
> ;)

*"Kira!"* I growl, glaring at her.

She just grins at me as she turns toward the kitchen, and I move to follow when my phone buzzes again. I quickly swipe the screen, smiling like an idiot at Selene's message.

> **Hahah**
> **Sounds like a challenge ;)**
>
> I'm sorry, that was my sister…
> She can be a real pain lol
>
> I would like to see you again,
> I'm sure I can work something
> out with the owner ;)

Glancing up, I notice Trey laughing with Kira at the stove and get an idea, tapping out a couple of texts.

> Bring your sister, too, if
> she'd like to come again.

**I think I know someone
who'd be happy to see her**

**Okay I will!**

**I'll see you tonight :)**

**Sounds good
:)**

Grinning, I turn toward the garage and close the door behind me, heading to the park for my morning run. *I hope the day passes quickly,* I muse, smiling the whole way there.

## SELENE

I spent the day milling around the property, texting with Kyran and asking a ton of questions about one another. We talked about what our hobbies are, the music we listen to, favorite things to eat, and a lot of our dislikes as well. Hours passed quickly with laughter and surprises, discovering that he and I are quite similar, except where he lives a busy life and mine is more laid back.

Kyran admitted to playing guitar, but he hasn't touched one in a long time, and I confided in him, telling him I love to sing, although nobody has ever heard me because I'm afraid of the vulnerability it brings. He let me know he understands, sharing that he would only sing around his family while playing his guitar. We both messaged that we'd like to hear each other sometime, and it made me smile warmly.

Ria had come out to the gardens to sit with me in the sunlight. We talked about last night and she was very upset that she wasn't there when it happened. She felt angry and guilty about how she should have done something to help me. I reassured her that in no way was it her fault, telling her how impossible that was since everything happened so quickly, and with the bar being so busy, she couldn't see.

I mentioned going out again tonight, to try to make a better experience out of it, and she lightheartedly teased me about Kyran. I offered for her to invite the girls again, since she's closer with them than I am. She agreed, leaving me here to call them.

My phone vibrates in my hand and I check the screen with a smile, reading Kyran's latest question.

> **What is one food you could eat for the rest of your life and never get sick of? Mine would have to be pizza**

Quickly tapping, I send my answer without hesitation.

> **Easy, ice cream! :) Ooh, put ours together and we'd have the best forever food combo! Sweet and savory, yumm**

Glancing up with a grin, I notice the sky has turned a deep gold, making me abruptly aware of the time. Feeling giddy, I hurry into the cottage, making my way up to my room.

Leaving my door open, I call out into the hallway, "Hey! What should I wear tonight? I need ideas." I turn on the shower and brush out my hair.

"Check your bed!" Ria's distant voice reaches me.

Glancing over, I notice she's left me a new outfit and I grin, picking up the clothes. Ria got me a pair of light denim distressed skinny jeans and a long-sleeved, white v-neck bodysuit made from stretchy, glittery fabric. *Of course she got the shimmery one.* I laugh with a shake of my head.

"Thank you! This looks really pretty, Ria," I call out to her with a smile.

Tossing my jacket on my bed, I hastily take a shower, eager to get ready and go to the bar. In my bathroom, mindful of the sore spot on my head, I dry and style my hair straight. Checking the mirror, I make sure the little bald patch isn't visible. Sitting down at my vanity, I do the same makeup as last night, except I use concealer on the bruise that bloomed on my cheek overnight.

Getting dressed in my second new outfit, I slide into black ankle boots to match my leather jacket. I take a look in my mirror as Ria knocks on my door, entering with a whistle.

"Oh yeah, I'm totally digging the *naughty and nice* look you've got going," she drawls, waggling her eyebrows.

"How the hell do you pee in that thing?" I ask incredulously, eyeing her tight black pleather jumpsuit with a laugh.

"Very carefully." She winks with a grin in return. "Oh, hold on a sec." She crosses my room, her black stilettos *clicking* as she shimmies up to me. Holding out my moon necklace, she drapes it over my head and murmurs, "There, perfect."

Stepping around me, she smacks my ass with a bright, "Let's go!" tossed over her shoulder and sashays out of my room.

Blinking a few times, I shake my head with a laugh and follow her downstairs. "You're *ridiculous,* you know that, right?" I mutter toward her.

As I step off the stairs, I head for the door and snag the car keys before Ria does. She turns toward a wall mirror, messily pulling up her auburn waves.

"Up, or down?" she asks, releasing her hair.

"Down, definitely. You look like if Poison Ivy and Catwoman morphed together." I grin at her, opening the door.

"That is *the* best compliment, ever." She grins back wickedly and hands me my purse.

I smile excitedly, checking the time as we get in the car, feeling anxious to see Kyran again.

# CHAPTER NINE

## TENSION

### KYRAN

Wiping down the bartop with an easy smile, I think about my ongoing conversation with Selene. She's got a great sense of humor, is witty, intelligent, and has a silly side that is very carefree. I sense a darkness within her, however. It clouds the bright light that is her soul, and I found myself often wondering today how to help her break through it.

One of my bouncers pokes his head into the bar, bringing me back to the present. I give him a nod to open and the door swings closed behind him as he disappears. Within moments, the eerie stillness of the lounge washes away to the din of excitement, music, and glasses clinking. Clicking the remote over my shoulder, I turn on the TVs to play the sports channels.

Every time the entrance doors swing open, I find myself eagerly searching for Selene, wanting to see her icy blue eyes again. Feeling anxious, I methodically roll my sleeves up to my elbows. Rather than my work shirt, I decided to wear a plain black tee underneath a deep green and black flannel, leaving it unbuttoned. It is an old, comfortable favorite, given to me as a birthday gift from Kira a few years back.

She had told me, *'It contrasts your eyes nicely,'* whatever the hell that is supposed to mean.

A hand rests on my shoulder and my chest tightens momentarily as I look up, only to deflate upon seeing my brother.

"You alright? You look kind of lost," he chuckles, leaning against the back of the bar.

"Yeah, I'm good. I kinda feel like a teenager again," I mumble, glancing around the lounge.

"Huh? Why would you—*no way!*" Trey grins widely as he pushes upright. "You're expecting to see Selene again, aren't you? Aw, are you guys having a *date?*" he says mockingly, making a kissy face at me.

"You're such an *ass.*" I roll my eyes, hiding my smirk. "Why don't you worry about your own interests, *hmm?*" I add, giving him a slight shove out from behind the bar.

"What?" he asks confused, turning back toward me.

I just give him a toothy grin, pushing him bodily toward the club passageway. Stopping at the record player, I browse some music, trying to keep myself distracted. A sharp elbow jabs my side and I glare at Treyvar, about to tell him to get to work when I notice his smirk.

I whirl around toward the entrance. My chest tightens, finding Selene holding the door open and letting Ria in behind her. I glance at Trey, laughing at his expression as he gawks at the door, his face going slack before he scurries through the tunnel like a rat.

*"Coward!"* I teasingly call after him, laughing again.

Meeting Selene's gaze, she smiles and gives a little wave. I grin widely and wave in return, making my way back to the bar to get her drink order prepared. She waves at her two friends from last night sitting in a nearby booth. Glancing at their table, I take out two cocktail glasses and make a couple of daiquiris for them as well.

Adding a slice of lime to each glass, I place them on a tray and carry them over to their table when Vala steps in front of me, grasping my forearm. I silently glare down at her hand. Flicking my eyes up to hers, she quickly removes it. Worry pulls her brow down and she steps around the tray, leaning in to speak quietly.

"A group of vamps just entered, at least seven of them." Her voice is unusually tense.

Narrowing my eyes, I respond lowly, "This is a neutral area, they have the freedom to be here as long as they don't cause problems. You know this. Go out back and dust off the mixers we have saved, but let them know we have low stock," I mutter, moving toward Selene's table.

She grabs me again. "Ky—"

*"Don't touch me, Vala.* You know I don't like it." I growl and she withdraws again, her eyes slightly round.

*"Caedes is here,"* she hisses with a mix of fear and anger.

Whipping my head toward the doors, I lock eyes with him, surrounded by his eerie group of the undead.

*What the fuck is that bastard doing here?* Valdr snarls, sending a rumble through my chest.

Pushing the tray of drinks into Vala's hands, I direct her to Selene's table and stalk toward the entrance. Caedes is their leader— *the* vampire king—and he's at least two thousand years old, though his appearance suggests otherwise. He has a narrow face with sharp features, unblemished, smooth milky skin, and short ebony hair. His lanky body belies the extreme strength he is capable of, as well as speed. To humans, if his blood red eyes are glamoured, he looks to be in his mid-twenties, and his alluring, nearly-too-perfect features is what makes him—*all of them*—so dangerous.

All vampires have the same eyes, body type, strength, and speed. Most have some magic and psychic abilities, all of which vary in intensity and are what they primarily use to catch their prey. Their powers are useless against other supernatural beings except for their physical traits, putting them on even ground with us werewolves.

*What the hell are they doing here? I haven't seen him since Mother's disappearance, over a hundred and fifty years ago.* I growl as I cross the floor through the parting crowd.

Valdr reminds me of a distant memory, bristling at the vampires' proximity. *There was that one time in the Underground, he was pissed you ripped his henchman in half during one of the fights. Remember how he bared his fangs at you from the stands?*

Growling as I approach, Caedes steps out of the creepy group, each one of them staring at me. It always weirds me out how they never seem to blink.

*"Ah, Kyran.* You've grown, though not out of that nasty temper of yours, I see," he taunts, his red eyes gleaming.

I glare at them all. "Glamour your eyes, all of you. I won't have this shit ruin my business."

Their leader nods and they comply, their eyes becoming muted shades of brown. I turn my attention back to Caedes. "You are not welcome, Caedes. Not here, not after what you did to my pack. *Leave, before I force you out,"* I snarl, feeling the energy of my pack's attention around me.

*"Hmm,* yes, I know, I know. I am just stopping by to speak with a *friend.* I heard about this little place and wanted to *take a look around.* No bother from me," he drones, his eyes darting around the bar. His sharp gaze abruptly comes to a halt, a smug smile tugging on his thin lips.

Quickly turning sideways so I don't put my back to him, I follow his gaze to Selene's table. *Thankfully her back is to us, she's completely unaware of what's happening.* Lashing my hand out, I clench Caedes's throat, lifting him off his feet as I shove him through the door.

His parasites to *hiss* behind me.

Snarling, I slam him against the concrete wall, cracking it with the force of his impact. Caedes glares at me with a wicked grin, not bothering to move against me. Lifting his hand, he points a sharp finger at my chest.

"Looks like you have a weakness, *dog,"* he taunts, running his tongue over his teeth gleefully.

My control slips and I smash my fist into his face, shattering his nose and cheek, then launch him halfway up the stairs. Before his body hits the concrete, he twists into a crouch and his head snaps up, baring his fangs at me. A low *hiss* escapes him and his leeches rush into the stairwell, their wind lightly billowing my unbuttoned shirt. In a blur, they're on the street within a heartbeat.

Caedes spits a mouthful of blood at my feet then darts away, leaving his dry laughter echoing around me. With untethered rage, I slam my fist into the place his face was moments ago. Clenching my jaw, my hand heals and I wipe the blood on the inside of my flannel, turning at the sound of the door swinging closed. Trey and Vala come through wearing mirrored expressions of concern.

"I didn't hear anything from you and wanted to see if you'd need backup. Why the hell were they here?" Trey looks baffled, putting a hand to the back of his head.

"What did he say to you? I haven't seen you that angry in a *long time*," Vala says quietly, eyeing the broken wall.

She steps through the door with a shake of her head, briefly returning with a tall painting and hangs it over the smashed area with magic. Glancing at the blood on the floor, Vala waves her hand over the wet stain and it turns to dust. Looking back at me, she silently raises an eyebrow.

"He didn't say much, just that he was meeting a friend and wanted to look around here because he'd heard about it," I mutter, running my hand over my face.

*I can't be so reactive, not anymore. I have too many people depending on me to behave rashly.* I take a measured breath and sigh, grateful that it didn't turn into a bloodbath.

Pushing the door aside, I hold it open for Vala and Trey to walk through. I turn to follow them and abruptly stop, nearly colliding with one of Selene's friends making her way outside. I step back and let her through, giving her a small smile. She doesn't even acknowledge me, pushing past and hurrying up the stairs without a glance.

*Bitch,* Valdr grumbles irritably.

*Enough,* I reply, suppressing a chuckle at his grumpy tone and step into the lounge.

"Hey, Kyran," Selene's soft voice calls out, and a wave of calmness washes over me at the sight of her.

She's setting up a billiards game with Asteria. My eyes involuntarily run over her, appreciating her beauty, feeling as if every time I see her it's like the first time all over again. I smile genuinely, snatching Treyvar's shoulder before he gets too far ahead of me and drag him over to their table.

*Did he just whimper?* Valdr teases, making me huff out a laugh.

"Selene, Asteria, this is my brother, Treyvar," I announce with a grin, sensing the tension rippling through his body.

"Hey," Selene greets with a smile, placing the balls onto the table.

*"Mmm, we've met,* officially. Last night," Asteria drawls out with a smirk, conspicuously unzipping her bawdy clothing a few inches lower.

I glance at Trey incredulously. His eyes bulge as he stares at the floor, swallowing thickly.

*Dude, I gotta hear about this,* I mindlink him with a laugh.

A shake of his head is his only response and Asteria laughs, rolling her eyes. Selene hands me a cue stick with a wink, and I grin widely, eager to enjoy the night with her.

## SELENE

"You're very beautiful, Selene," Kyran murmurs, leaning in to take the cue stick from me.

I blush, tucking some hair behind my ear. "Thank you." *It's disorienting, hearing him say that. I'm used to the crass compliments men usually hand out, but never something so simple and truthful, the way he says it.*

I turn away awkwardly, racking the balls. "Hazel left her wallet in her car and will be back in a moment. We can play a quick game. I'll take it easy on you guys, don't worry," I banter sarcastically, grinning.

*"Ha!"* Ria barks a laugh, tipping back the last of her drink.

Laughing, I set my stick against the table and take her glass from her, grabbing my empty one as well. "I'll be right back," I say over my shoulder, stepping toward the bar.

Kyran's gentle hand brushes against my lower back and his warmth blooms over my skin, sending tingles along my spine as he leans toward me. "I'll make them, so you can trust that your *request* is done properly," he says quietly, giving me a small smile.

Grateful for his attentiveness, I smile warmly as I hand him the glasses, watching him cross the floor and duck behind the bar. Turning back toward the pool table, I narrow my eyes between Ria and Treyvar, sensing some tension.

Noticing my sister's smirk, I ask curiously, "Hey, Treyvar, how'd you meet Ria?"

He scuffles his shoe against the floor, glancing at Ria then quickly averting his gaze to me. "I, uh, she—*ahem,*" he coughs dryly, "I work the bar in the club, she ordered a couple of drinks from me." His words come out in a rush with flushed cheeks.

I raise my brow at Ria and she shrugs her shoulders with a sly smirk. "He's scared of *wi—*" she clears her throat. "Ah, *women.* Confident, *powerful women.*" Ria flashes a grin at Treyvar, waggling her brows.

I roll my eyes with a laugh, knowing damn well how imperious Asteria can be. Kyran returns, handing me my Nojito and gives Ria a pretty looking purple cocktail. I curiously point to her drink. "Ooh, what's that?"

"It's called Purple Rain, I figured it suits Asteria. If you don't like it, I will make you a different drink," Kyran offers as he turns to her, running his hand through his dark hair.

"Thank you, and no worries. This is *delicious,*" she responds brightly, already a quarter of the way through her drink.

Placing my glass on a small table against the wall, I pick up my cue stick and chalk it. "Alright, you guys ready to get your asses handed to you?" I jest with a grin, bending down to line up my shot.

Jamming my stick into the cue ball, I barely make the break and laugh as I scratch immediately, my humor joined by everyone else. Straightening, I notice Kyran's amber eyes narrowing as he smirks, easily pocketing a few balls in succession. When he meets my gaze again, I scrunch my nose at him playfully, making him laugh.

Treyvar excuses himself, mumbling something about work and scurries across the lounge toward the club. Ria laughs loudly, watching him go before clearing the table of a few more balls.

*I've gotta talk to her about this. Something is up, I just know it.* I take a sip of my sweet drink, peeking over the rim at Kyran as he lines up for a shot across the table. Smiling mischievously, I turn sideways and sit on the edge of the table, directly in front of the ball he is aiming at. Watching the cue ball bounce off the cushion, I grin when Kyran's warm gaze flicks up to mine. His eyes narrow slightly and I pout innocently, pretending not to notice the twitch at the corner of his mouth.

Hopping off the table, I try earnestly to line up a shot straight down the side of the table. As I aim, Kyran's arms fold over the edge, his muscles contracting as he leans forward. Focusing and biting back a smile, I take my shot, sinking our last ball in the corner pocket. With a wide grin, I gasp in surprise and Ria *whoops* loudly, finishing her drink. Kyran gives me a crooked smile and gestures at the eight ball near the center of the table.

As I move toward the cue ball, I brush past Kyran and his hand lightly squeezes my hip, sending tingles down my leg. My ears grow hot, feeling a bit flustered.

*He's very respectful, but I want to show him how he makes me feel,* I wonder, enjoying his gentle touch.

As I turn to look back at Kyran, I notice Hazel coming back into the bar. Once she reaches our table, Melody appears from the club entrance, smiling broadly. "You guys, you gotta get in here!" she calls over, waving at us excitedly. "This crowd is *wild.*"

Hazel glances at Ria for a moment before her gaze shifts to Kyran, then lands on me. A sly grin spreads on her face as she takes my hand, pulling me toward the club. "C'mon, let's go," she eagerly says over her shoulder.

"Hold on a second," I murmur, tugging my hand back. I remove my jacket and fold it over my purse, looking at Kyran. "Is there somewhere safe I can put these?" I ask, smiling a little awkwardly.

Kyran takes off his flannel, my gaze lingering on the way his thick arms flex with the movement. He holds his hand out for my things and I give them to him, waiting while he bundles them up inside his shirt.

Leaning down near my ear, he murmurs, "They'll be in my office. I keep the door locked."

He straightens and takes a few steps back, nodding his head past my shoulder for me to follow Ria and Hazel. I smirk, turning and slowly walk toward them, knowing he's watching me go. Hazel firmly grabs my hand again in her heated palm as we disappear into the booming club.

*"Let's go get some drinks,"* she yells over the music, pulling me along toward the bar.

Ria takes the lead, easily carving a path through the mass of gyrating bodies. In the flashing lights, I can barely see Treyvar behind the bar as he turns toward us from the far end. Melody squeezes in between Ria and I, giving him a wide smile as he approaches.

"Ladies," he greets with an easy smile, his earlier awkward demeanor completely erased. "What can I get for you?"

Each of the girls order their drinks, laughing and flirting with him as he works. I watch how they take the glasses, all three of them being borderline obnoxious as they lean too far over the bar, pushing their chests out, gliding their hands over his arms. Treyvar looks disheveled when he gets to me. The girls step back and form a small group, laughing together.

"How about you, what can I do for you?" he asks, straightening his shirt and smoothing a hand over his sandy hair.

I hold up my hand and slightly shake my head. "Nothing for me, thank you," I say politely. "Oh, Kyran has my purse, could you open a tab?"

Glancing at the girls, Treyvar just shakes his head. "Don't worry about it," he mutters, moving toward another customer.

*"Come on, Sel, let's dance!"* Ria cheers, disappearing into the crowded floor.

Hazel and Melody each grab my hands, chasing after Ria. As the swarm of bodies swallows me whole, a wave of anxiety hits me, remembering last night. With my chest constricting, I breathe shallowly for a moment, wondering if Kyran is going to find me in here. *I honestly cannot picture him in this club.* I give a little laugh at the thought, my tension easing a bit. Glancing up, Ria whirls around with her drink held high, her hair flying around her while she dances. We catch up to her shortly, but the twins don't let go of my hands.

*"Dance,* Selene. Have some *fun,"* Hazel says lowly, holding my gaze with a grin.

My anxiety washes away, and laughter bubbles up from my chest. I dance, the bass of the music thrumming beneath my skin. I can't stop the euphoric feeling from taking me over. Time seems to melt away with the hypnotic energy coursing around the club and my body feels like it's floating with my movements. Tilting my head back, the colors of the lights swirl in a kaleidoscope of changing shapes. I laugh at the mesmerizing sight, spinning around and around until they blur into glittery streams.

Warm hands gently caress my shoulders, making me shiver with pleasure. Rolling my head to the side, Kyran stands close behind me, his mouth moving but I can't hear what he says. I step backward into him, taking his hands and slowly drawing them down my sides. Placing his palms on the front of my hips, I dance to the music, threading my fingers through his. The heat of his body is heady, making me feel as if I am weightless.

Closing my eyes, I tip my head back against his firm chest as we move. He bends forward, resting his forehead on my temple as his nose brushes my cheek and sends tingles down my spine. Smiling wide, I slide my hand up his arm and over his broad shoulder, gripping the back of his neck. Kyran pushes lightly against my hips, turning me around.

I snake my other arm up and around him, pulling him close. His hands press on my lower back as he gazes down at me, his amber eyes glowing in the neon lights. Kyran's brow lowers and he dips his head toward mine.

"Hey, you look a little flushed. Would you like me to get you some water?" His husky voice tickles my ear.

I breathe heavily, blinking up at him. "Yeah, I am really thirsty..."

He slowly pulls away with a nod and disappears into the blurry crowd.

Feeling a little hazy, I lick my dry lips as I look around for Ria, but she's nowhere to be found. My gaze drifts past Melody, however, and I wiggle my way toward her. My head swims a bit with my movements.

Leaning over with a slanted smile, I yell over the music, *"Hey, I gotta go to the bathroom. Be right back!"*

Not knowing where the bathroom is in here, I turn toward the passageway and push through the worming bodies, starting to feel a little uneasy. The dark wall comes up fast and I smack my hand against it, using it to support some of my body weight.

*Wow, she wasn't kidding when she said it's wild in here.*

As I stumble across the lounge on shaky legs, I bump into the pretty red-headed waitress by accident.

"Oh, oops. I'm so sorry," I apologize, putting a hand to my forehead as sudden queasiness washes over me.

Her indigo eyes bore into mine, staring at me intently. Grabbing my wrist, she harshly asks, *"Are you feeling alright?"*

I'm instantly overcome with severe dizziness at her touch. The room spins, making me feel off kilter. I pull out of her grasp and stumble backward, placing my hand flat against a wall, taking deep breaths. My stomach twists a little, and with another slow breath, things settle slightly. Opening my eyes, the waitress is gone, as if she was never there to begin with.

Standing upright, I unsteadily cross the bar toward the bathroom, waiting in line. Once it's my turn, I carefully make my way into a stall and sit on the toilet with my head between my knees. Squeezing my eyes shut, it takes a few moments for the dizziness to fade and I let out a breath of relief for not getting sick. I do a mental check over my body. Feeling mostly normal, I push to my feet and step out of the stall. My body careens slightly to the side and I let out a nervous laugh as I reach a hand out to steady myself against the sink.

A young pair of women give me knowing looks as they throw paper towels into the trash and giggle on their way through the door, one of them raising her beer bottle in salute toward me. My brow pinches with worry at how unsteady I feel, and I turn to fix my makeup in the mirror, running my fingers through my hair. I smile at myself a little, thinking about Kyran and the way his body felt against mine as I smooth my hands over my clothes.

Carefully making my way back across the lounge, I notice my sister and our friends coming through the club entrance. They're laughing loudly, with Kyran and Treyvar following behind them. I turn toward an empty table and drop into a seat as they all make their way over.

"I couldn't find you in there." His voice sounds far away. "I'll be back with some more water, don't go anywhere," Kyran murmurs beside me, winking. "Would anyone else like another drink?" he asks lightly, glancing at the others.

His words are difficult to process. My head swims as I look around and blink a few times, disconcerted. Treyvar follows Kyran to the bar as the girls take their seats around the table. Melody and Ria are chatting animatedly about something I can't focus on, their voices blending together incoherently. Hazel quickly gets up, going to the bar to grab the drinks. She returns to hand them out and places mine in front of me with a *clunk*.

"Drink up," she murmurs, "you must be feeling quite thirsty." Her eyes narrow, mouth lifting at the corner.

Suddenly feeling really parched, I snatch the glass of water and gulp it down greedily. Finishing the entire drink, I belatedly taste something off, something bitter. Scrunching my brow, I hold the glass in front of me, trying to smell if anything was in the drink. My vision blurs slightly after a few heavy heartbeats.

*What the hell? Am I drunk?*

Suddenly pissed off, I push to my feet and glare at Kyran as I unsteadily cross the floor. He notices me coming and smiles broadly, leaning over the bar on his elbows. Wobbling on my feet, I sneer at him and the glass slips from my slack fingers. It crashes on the bartop, sending shards flying everywhere.

"Selene?" Kyran asks, alarmed. "Are you alright?"

*"How could you? I trusted you,"* I slur, chest constricting with my wild emotions.

I bite back a wave of sadness at feeling betrayed and grip the edge of the bar to steady myself.

"What? What do you mean?" he asks quickly, his wide eyes searching mine.

I lose focus on him as he doubles, my vision blurring again.

"Selene? *Selene, look at me.*" Kyran's voice is hard, his bright eyes tight with his intense gaze.

He firmly takes my hand, giving a slight tug. I close my eyes when his skin presses against mine. Warmth embraces me at his touch and my stomach drops to the floor. I gasp, my eyes flying to his concerned gaze in a scarce moment of clarity.

*I know I didn't have any alcohol. Kyran didn't*—wouldn't—*do this to me. Only a monster*—

*"Ky, I don't know*—*I can't*—*"* I stammer as my hand slips from his grasp, my body rapidly growing heavy. *"Help me,"* I beg on a whisper, slumping forward against my will.

I barely register my head hitting the bartop as my body crumples to the floor.

## KYRAN

The moment her hand slips from mine, everything moves in slow motion, as if time was freezing. Just as Selene collapses, I vault over the bar and pull her limp body into my arms. Her heart beats sluggishly, her shallow breath coming in uneven pants. I can hardly breathe through the fury flooding my veins.

*"Psh,* lightweight," Treyvar teases jokingly.

I launch to my feet, cradling Selene close. Rage ignites an inferno inside me. "She didn't drink any alcohol you fucking bastard," I snap, glaring at him. "*What the fuck did you give her in there?*" Seething, my chest heaves harder with each breath.

"Sh—I—she didn't have anything," Trey stammers, his eyes rounding with fear as he lifts his hands placatingly.

Sensing his truth, my skin crawls hotly at my next words. "She has been *drugged,* Trey. Someone in here dosed her with venom, I can *smell* it on her breath. Make sure her sister gets home safely and bring her things back to my room when you get home," I order him tersely.

Turning sharply on my heel, the murmuring crowd quickly parts as I push my way toward the alley exit, holding Selene tightly to my chest. Shouldering the door open, I hurry to my truck, pouring my healing magic into her body to no avail. Shifting her weight to one arm, I pull the door open, gently laying Selene on the bench seat as I hurry around to climb in behind the wheel.

Carefully setting her head and shoulders in my lap, I brush silky strands of hair away from her beautiful face, clenching my jaw so tightly I fear my teeth may crack. My truck roars to life and I take off toward home, driving faster than I ever have before.

I mindlink our best healer while tearing out of town. *Eir, meet me in my bedroom, immediately. Find and take whatever you need to help treat venom ingestion. I will be there soon.*

*Has someone been bitten?* her soft voice responds hesitantly. *There isn't much I can do except comfort and sedate.*

*No. She drank it, unknowingly. Someone intentionally drugged her at Howler's. Please tell me you can heal her,* I plead, glancing down at Selene's unresponsive body.

*Yes, Kyran, I believe I can, as long as no blood came in contact with her,* she immediately responds, her voice strong. *I will be prepared and waiting by your door.*

I cup Selene's slack jaw in my hand and swallow thickly against the trepidation crawling up my spine.

*Who would do something like this? Please hang on, sweetheart. I need you to be okay.*

Kicking the garage door open, the knob shatters as I burst through, racing up the stairs. Eir waits at the threshold, her face pinched with concern, and I nod my head at the door. She quickly opens it, stepping aside for me to hurry through.

"Put her in the shower, this is going to be messy," she calls behind me in a tight voice.

Kneeling on the cold tile with Selene, I gently lay her beside me and helplessly look up at Eir. She sets a basket down on the floor and kneels next to me, placing her hands over Selene's stomach. A soft, warm glow emanates from her palms and her brow pinches in concentration. Pulling her hands back, she hastily takes vials out of the basket and uncorks them.

"This is the strongest venom I've ever felt," she murmurs under her breath with a worried expression. "Sit her up, but be prepared to turn her sideways. First, I'm going to purge her, then I'll evaluate the toxin level, and I may need to do it a second time. Afterward, I will need to purify her blood. We *have* to move fast for this to be successful. Do not hesitate with any command I give you. *Please trust me, Kyran,*" she says sternly, taking my hands in hers, her golden eyes burning into mine.

Squeezing her hands tightly, I whisper, "I trust you."

Taking a measured breath, she nods once and releases me. "Are you ready?"

I move behind Selene, gently lifting her and resting her back against my chest. Nodding at Eir, I confirm, "I'm ready."

She opens Selene's slack mouth, tipping her head back slightly and pouring a cloudy vile down her throat. Dropping her hands, she motions around Selene's abdomen a few times then hastily circles her hands upward, following a line toward Selene's mouth.

"Quickly now, turn her over," Eir directs me and I twist away from her, holding Selene's chest and head in my arms.

Her body convulses and heaves as she violently vomits. Selene falls still, her body becoming listless once more. Rolling us back and sitting upright, I watch anxiously as Eir's hands glow over Selene again, assessing her. Shaking her head, she pours another vial into Selene's mouth and we repeat the process, but this time a low moan leaves Selene afterward.

"Selene? Can you hear me?" I search her face for any sign of awareness, seeing no change. *"Please stay with me, sweetheart,"* I murmur into her hair, pressing a kiss to the top of her head.

Eir removes Selene's shoes and unbuttons her pants. I lift her body to help as Eir pulls her jeans down her legs, leaving her in the white bodysuit. My brow draws tight at the scalpel Eir pulls out of the basket, but I remain silent, trusting her and waiting for direction.

Looking at me with hard eyes, Eir speaks firmly. "When I cut her, hold her tightly. Restrain her limbs and *do not let go*, no matter what. I am going to use an immense amount of magic and I will need to siphon your energy to complete her healing. When I touch you, please do not resist me. I will not harm you, Kyran," she adds quietly with gentleness in her bright gaze.

I wrap my arms around Selene, pinning her arms to her body and grasp her hands in mine. Lifting my feet, I hook them over her knees and press my legs firmly down atop hers, using just enough pressure to immobilize her. Nodding at Eir, she nods back and readies herself, lifting her open hand with her fingers splayed above Selene's leg. The air around her hand blurs with the magic she draws forth.

The moment Eir presses the blade to Selene's inner thigh, her blood pulls upward and streams into the air, pooling into a swirling sphere suspended by Eir's magic. I stare completely mesmerized as Eir keeps the shape with one hand and raises the other, glowing bright with her warm healing light. She shoves her hand into the globe of blood, illuminating it like a macabre bulb as her healing magic purifies it of the venom.

"Take the blade and cut a vein, anywhere you can reach without letting her go," Eir directs in a strained voice as she concentrates.

Grasping Selene's wrists with my right hand, I hold on to her firmly and take the scalpel, quickly dragging it along a vein at the back of her hand. A thin rivulet of glowing blood flows into her hand and my gaze follows it up to Eir as she guides the stream of purified blood, performing magical dialysis. I've never heard of or seen *anything* like this in my entire life.

Selene's body bursts with blinding light. Her limbs strain against me as her back arches and she throws her head into my chest. A keening wail—nearly a howl—rips from her throat and pierces straight into my heart.

Valdr bristles, whining softly in my mind.

She remains like this, her body taught and writhing, the bright, white light emitting from her pulsing like a heartbeat. Selene's endless cry echoes around us as Eir keeps the flow of her blood steady until the glow streams out from her leg.

Removing her hand from the suspended orb, Eir guides both of her hands toward each cut, returning the blood into Selene's body. With labored breaths, Eir slumps to the floor on shaky arms. She stares hauntingly at Selene, as if she's seen a ghost. Straining against Selene's thrashing, I glance down at her, noticing the blood seeping out of her leg. My eyes widen with alarm.

"Eir, her leg. Eir? *Eir!*" I sharply shout, snapping her out of her trance.

She abruptly grips my arm with both hands and I instinctively brace myself at the sensation, fighting against the invasion. Her fingernails dig into my arm and I relent, allowing my energy to drain into her, fueling her healing power. I shiver against the shower tiles, clinging to Selene who writhes against me unconsciously. A few more seconds pass and I begin to feel faint—the same sensation as if I've lost too much blood—before Eir pulls away with warmly flushed skin.

She presses her hands to Selene's gash and the bleeding slowly abates, taking longer than it should to stop. I lift my leg to make contact with Eir, pushing the rest of my healing power into her and closing Selene's wound. Eir carefully removes her hands, our collective energies totally spent.

Selene falls limp once more, and Eir leans forward to examine her.

The white light emitting from Selene diminishes, the glow barely perceptible as she lies still. The cut on her hand is gone, but there is a small pink scar on her inner thigh, unable to be fully healed from the lack of magic. Her breathing is slow and even, as if she's in a deep sleep.

I carefully release my hold on her, letting my limbs flop to the floor and glance at Eir. Sitting beside us, she hugs her knees with her thin legs folded close to her body. Bloody smears cover her arms and face, blending into her coppery hair. I watch her as she stares at Selene, her ageless face expressing the consternation she feels.

"That has never happened before," she murmurs, not taking her eyes off Selene. "The thrashing, yes, but not that light." Her voice drifts off as she sits frozen in place, staring blankly.

I glance down at Selene and her illuminated skin, then lift my gaze back to Eir, feeling completely exhausted. I'm at a loss for words with everything that has happened.

"Where—*how* did you find her?" she whispers, her gilded eyes flicking over to mine.

"The grocery store," I say distantly, feeling quite displaced at the moment.

"The gro—*ha.*" Eir scoffs, wiping a bloody palm down her face. Dropping her hand, she looks sideways at me and her mouth pulls into a thin line. "What do you know of this woman, Kyran?" she asks me seriously.

"In what way?" I hesitantly ask.

"As in, where she comes from? Where does she live?"

"Oh, yeah, about that. She, ah, lives with Hekate and her daughter, actually," I gingerly reply with a wince.

Eir's eyes immediately round and she barks out a laugh, looking toward the ceiling. *"Hekate. Ugh,* yes, I should have known," she mumbles, dropping her head with a shake.

Taking a deep breath, she rises to her feet and swiftly gathers her supplies into the basket before placing her hands on her narrow hips. "Alright. First, I need to get her cleaned up, then she needs to rest. Could you find some clothing for me to change her into? Also, she'll need these in the morning," Eir mutters as she hands me a small glass container.

Glancing down at the ibuprofen pills, I look up at her, bewildered. I open my mouth to ask her to explain herself, but she raises a hand with a shake of her head. "It is not my place, Kyran, but you should go and speak with Hekate sooner rather than later. Some clothing, please." She sighs and gestures toward the door, turning to tend to Selene once more.

Stiffly pushing off the bloody floor, my gaze drifts over Selene and I realize that her clothes are ruined in a bloody mess. I woodenly cross my bedroom, placing the pills on my nightstand and head to my closet. Grabbing the first t-shirt I see and pulling open some drawers until I find some sweatpants, I make my way back to the bathroom.

"Where is your wolf, *ithildin*?" Eir's voice softly mumbles. "*What happened to you?*"

As I enter, I find Eir undressing Selene. I abruptly turn on my heel, not intending to intrude on her privacy and place the clothes on the counter, quietly returning to my bedroom. Running my bloody hands through my hair, I abruptly realize how badly I need a shower. Grabbing a change of clothes for myself, I make my way to the door, averting my gaze as I cross through my bathroom.

I speak quietly, not waiting for a response. "I'll be downstairs. If you need me, don't hesitate to call for me, I'll be here right away."

Knowing he isn't home yet, I head down to Trey's room. I turn the shower to its hottest setting and peel my clothes off, tossing them in the trash. Stepping under the steaming water, I let it run over me as I tip my head into the spray, thinking back on how quickly the night flipped from amazing to terrifying.

*How could this have happened? Who the fuck would do something like this to her? I made damn sure the rogues were not in my bar tonight because of her attack last night. I was surprised she even wanted to come back at all, let alone so soon. No vampires remained at my bar after Caedes's strange appearance, and he himself barely set foot in the bar to begin with. I was the only one to make her anything to drink tonight, and she only had juice and water. Treyvar swore she didn't have anything in the club, and I didn't smell anything on her while I was in there, either. How could this have happened?* An agitated growl vibrates through my chest.

Replaying the events over again, I cannot understand this. I angrily scrub at my skin until the water runs clean, shutting off the flow and harshly rubbing a towel over my body. Tugging on my clothes, I leave Trey's room, flipping through memories of everyone who came into contact with Selene tonight. It just *does not* make sense.

*Wait,* Valdr demands at the same time the realization hits me, recalling something off about the bar.

Clenching my jaw and fists, I stalk down the hallway and shove open the door to a dark bedroom. Valdr and I growl simultaneously.

*Where the fuck is Vala?*

# CHAPTER TEN

## THE AFTERMATH

### KYRAN

Pacing the lounge at the foot of my stairs, I mindlink Trey. *Where are you? We need to talk.*

Exhaustion creeps up my body, my limbs growing heavy with each step I take, but I cannot calm down enough to rest. I have attempted to reach Vala multiple times, both mentally and over the phone, receiving no response either way. Nobody has seen her since leaving for work early in the evening, either.

*I'll be there in ten, is everything alright?* Trey's voice echoes in my mind, a sharp headache forming from the stress.

"Kyran?" Eir's voice distantly calls.

I launch up the stairs, barreling through the door and into the bathroom. My eyes widen at Selene lying still on the floor, and I drop to my knees, the breath leaving my lungs in a harsh rush.

"She's okay, she's fine," Eir quickly reassures me. "I've kept her asleep to heal and she'll wake in a few hours. I need you to carry her to the bed for me. Cleaning and dressing her took everything I had, unfortunately," she says softly.

Shuffling forward on my knees, I carefully lift Selene, trying not to jostle her as I walk into my bedroom. Gently laying her on my bed, Eir pulls the covers up to Selene's chest and gives her a little pat. Turning to me, she clasps her hands and speaks quietly.

"The last thing she'll remember is passing out, wherever that may have been. I can assure you, waking up in a man's clothes—*in his bed*—is going to be extremely distressing for her, *especially* with her last thought being that she fell unconscious. Please be mindful of her, of your words. I need to rest now, and I suggest you do the same." She sighs tiredly, rubbing a hand over her face.

Giving me a wan smile, Eir pats my shoulder before leaving my room, and her footfalls echo down the stairs. Standing beside my bed, I observe Selene for a moment, getting an idea that might help her. I rummage through some drawers, finding a pad of paper and a pen to write a note for her to read once she wakes up. I let her know where she is, how she is safe, that the pills are ibuprofen if she wants to use them, and for her to open my door when she is ready to talk with me. I snag a bottle of water from the bathroom cabinet, as well as the moon necklace from the counter, but it gives a warm zap of energy when my hand touches it.

I frown at the shiny jewelry, holding it up to my eye-level to take a better look at it. Turning the moon charm in the light, a ripple of reflection emits from the gemstones and remains constant, even when the light no longer bounces off it. My mouth pulls into a flat line, recognizing the necklace for what it is.

A magical artifact.

Understanding it contains either Hekate's or Asteria's magic, I gingerly grasp the chain between two fingers and take care *not* to touch the charm, fearing the repercussions. Padding across my room, I set the unopened bottle on the nightstand, along with her peculiar necklace and the note signed with my name.

I busy myself with cleaning the bathroom, making sure to place her clothes in a plastic bag rather than just tossing them in the trash. As gory as it may seem, I feel that maybe she could inspect them to verify what I told her had happened. *What the hell can I tell her? She's completely unaware of the supernatural shit going on around her. Fuck.* I groan, tipping my head back.

*She needs to be made aware,* Valdr mumbles. *It is not safe for her to be in the dark without knowledge.*

Agreeing with him, I leave the bathroom light on as I quietly close my door behind me and descend to the lounge. Pulling an armchair around to sit in front of the staircase, I lean back and close my eyes, feeling extremely worn out both physically and mentally.

Footsteps rush up the stairs, startling me awake. Glancing over, Trey's golden head bobs toward the lounge with Kira right behind him. As they round the corner, they both give me an odd look, no doubt wondering why the hell I'm sitting here.

"Kira, where's your bracelet?" I ask harshly, glaring at her natural complexion.

"Relax. I only take them off in the house, don't worry." She crosses her arms, raising her eyebrow at me. "What are you doing, sitting down here like this?"

"Is she alright?" Trey asks with worry clear on his face. "Ria was a complete mess. She was very upset and demanded to speak with you as soon as possible." He sighs heavily, sitting on the lower step in front of me.

Valdr's sudden agitation sends a harsh growl through my chest and Trey pops to his feet, alarmed. I run my hands over my face and lean my elbow on the armrest, propping my head up with a fist. "I'm sorry. She's upstairs, resting. I'm feeling a bit on edge at the moment," I explain curtly.

"She?" Kira's brow pinches in confusion. "What's going on?" she whispers, glancing between Trey and me.

Stifling a yawn, I mumble my response as I sink lower into the chair. "I'll explain in the morning, I need to rest. Have either of you seen Vala?" I ask suddenly, my eyes opening wider at the thought.

They both shake their heads, watching me warily. Trey silently holds out my bundled flannel and I place it in my lap, resting my arm over it.

"The last time I saw her was before the girls came into the club. She didn't look happy, but that doesn't really say much," he jokes flatly, and his smirk quickly falls when I don't react.

I just nod and close my eyes dismissively, mumbling, "Wake me if anything changes."

The soft swish of a blanket drapes over me and Kira lightly kisses the top of my head before going to her room. Trey falls onto the couch behind me with a heavy *thump*.

"Rest. I'll stay awake until you need to get up," he says quietly and I nod, slipping into unconsciousness.

## SELENE

I wake to warm sunlight shining over me and I shield my eyes against the brightness, my head throbbing in pain.

*Ugh, what happened last night?*

I groan, reaching down to grab the comforter—

*Black?! What the fuck?*

I gasp and fling it off of me, bolting upright in the foreign bed. Glancing down at myself, I discover with horror that I am wearing an enormous dark gray t-shirt and equally large black sweatpants. My hand flies to my mouth, stifling the sob that bubbles out.

*Where am I?!*

I panic as I take in my surroundings. My eyes flit around the neat, rustic room, over the few guitars hanging on the wall among some nature paintings and photographs, matching dark wooden furniture, and abruptly stop on the nightstand beside me. There is a water bottle, a little glass jar holding some white pills, and a folded paper on the table.

With a shaking hand, I open the note.

*Selene, I brought you here to my home after you collapsed in my bar last night. You're in my bedroom on a private floor, which no one has access to except me. You are safe here. I have left some ibuprofen and water for when you get up, but please take your time. I needed our healer to help you and you are undoubtedly feeling unwell after everything that has happened. I will answer your questions and explain what I can, when you are ready. I am just outside the door. –Kyran*

Setting the paper down, I grab the water, twist the cap off with a *crack* and take a long swig. Eyeing the pills, I decide I'd rather deal with the headache than take them, not quite trusting what they are at the moment. Noticing my necklace, I reach over and pluck it off the table.

The moment I hold the moon charm in my hand, blurry flashes of the night come crashing down. Overwhelming images of the club lights, my friends' faces, red hair and indigo eyes, drinks at a table, Kyran's wide amber eyes across the bar before everything went black. Tears stream down my face as more memories assault me. Cold shower tiles, vomiting, blood flying around, blinding light, pain everywhere inside me, tearing my mind in half.

The water bottle drops from my slack hand, spilling onto the hardwood floor and I fling my necklace away with a cry. I pull my knees to my chest, rocking slightly as I try to make sense of everything. My eyes catch on eerily familiar tiles peeking through an archway and I scramble off the bed. My upper leg pulses sorely as I take a shaky step. Glancing down, I pull the sweatpants low, finding a small pink scar on my inner thigh and my stomach heaves. Clamping my hand around my mouth, I stumble into the bathroom and fall to my hands and knees as I vomit all over the gleaming floor.

Sobbing, I shuffle backward until my back presses against a tall cabinet, my elbow brushing a plastic bag. A thin wail escapes me at the sight of my bloody clothes from last night. I kick the bag away, dropping my head into my hands and rock back and forth.

*"No no no!"* I cry, over and over.

A knock sounds from somewhere, a door clicking open. I am frozen in place with fear, on the verge of having a full-blown panic attack.

"Selene?" a deep voice calls out, "I heard a scream, and I just—" Kyran enters the bathroom, his face tight with alarm at seeing me and walks quickly across the floor. *"Are you alright?"*

"S-stay aw-way from m-me!" I stammer, scared and confused, my entire body shaking uncontrollably.

He stops immediately, slowly raising his hands. Glancing around, he looks at the mess on the floor, then into the bedroom, and meets my eyes as he kneels on the floor in front of me. He reaches a hand out toward me and I whimper involuntarily, pulling my arms around myself tighter. Withdrawing his arm, Kyran drags both his hands through his hair, gripping the back of his head.

"Selene, I know you're scared. What happened to you was horrible, and I am *so sorry*. Please believe me when I tell you that you are safe here. You are safe with me. *Trust me, sweetheart, please. I would never harm you.*" His voice breaks, tears welling in his eyes.

As I stare into his mournful gaze, something inside me eases and I just *know* he didn't bring me any harm. I feel the truth just as easily as I can feel my heart beating, trusting that *I truly am safe* with him. Sobbing, I crawl forward and wrap my arms around him, burying my face into his chest. His strong arms envelop me, holding me tight as he smooths my hair and pulls me into his lap. My headache noticeably lessens to a mild pressure with his comforting warmth and presence. We stay like this for a while until I can get my emotions in check, and Kyran never moves or makes a sound as he lets me collect myself.

I lean back and sit on the floor in front of him, wiping my face. He rises and holds out his hand, taking mine in his and gently pulls me to my feet. Guiding me into his bedroom, he brings me over to a small leather sofa and hands me a fleece blanket.

"I'll be right back. Do you need anything?" Kyran quietly asks.

I just silently shake my head and pull my feet under me, bunching the blanket in my lap. I watch as he goes back into the bathroom and returns with a towel, picking up my forgotten water bottle and mops up the spill. He places my necklace on the nightstand, crossing into the bathroom again to clean up my vomit and I grimace, feeling a bit embarrassed. Once finished, he leaves the bathroom and disappears around the corner, returning momentarily with a bundle of clothing.

My mind flashes back to the bar, remembering him wrapping my purse and jacket in his flannel before I went into the club. *Shit, Ria. She's got to be so worried.* I groan, rubbing a hand over my face. Kyran hands me my purse and sits on the other end of the sofa, giving me some space. I appreciate his attentiveness and give him a small smile. Fishing around in my purse, I pull out my phone and find that the battery died. I drop it back in with a sigh. Turning to Kyran, I take a deep breath and release it slowly.

"What happened, Kyran?" I ask timidly, chewing on my lip.

"You were drugged," he answers tightly, narrowing his eyes. "You hit your head and went unconscious as you fell. I brought you straight here and had my healer treat you. It's hard to explain at the moment, but she needed to…access your blood to effectively remove the toxin." He grimaces and gestures toward my thigh, explaining the scar I found.

"Your clothes were soiled in the process, and I was unsure whether or not I should discard them. I thought it could maybe help you understand better." He sighs heavily. "Anyway, Eir, my healer, she cleaned you up and dressed you in my clothes afterward. I, uh, was not present for that part of the night," he mumbles, rubbing the back of his neck.

*Healer? Does he mean doctor? Why not just bring me to the hospital?* I scrunch my eyebrows, trying to follow along. Confused, I look to Kyran again as he continues explaining.

"I laid you in my bed since you remained unconscious and, well, here we are. I do not know who did this, or how, but I am having people look into it as we speak. I *will* find out, and they will be...*punished* accordingly," he says darkly, his eyes roaming over my forehead and cheek. "I am truly sorry for these past couple of nights, Selene. I wish I could go back and prevent them from happening." His voice grows soft as he casts his eyes to the floor.

Pressing a hand to my cheek, I remember the bruises Bolvi left me with and I'm assuming another one has formed from last night, as well. *Gee, I must look delightful.* I sigh, pulling my tangled hair over my shoulder. Laying my hand on Kyran's knee, he glances over at me and I give him a small smile.

"I don't," I say lightly.

His brow pinches. "What?"

"I don't wish these past two nights didn't happen. Besides the, um, *accidents*, I've really enjoyed being at your bar," I say shyly, glancing to the side. "And being around you," I add quietly, blushing.

Not hearing a reply, I peek up at Kyran. He's grinning widely. I can't help but grin back, his smile is infectious. Wondering at the time, I realize I should probably go home and talk with Asteria, not wanting to keep her worrying.

"Hey, what ti—"

"I'm glad I met you," he blurts, and his cheeks flush. He clears his throat with a cough. "I'm sorry, what were you going to say?"

I respond distantly, distracted by his words. "I was going to ask what time it is. I'm glad I met you, too," I whisper, smiling warmly.

We sit in a comfortable silence for a moment until his phone buzzes, breaking the spell that shrouds us. My eyes roam his face while he checks his phone. *You're different, unlike anyone I've ever met. I like you, Kyran, more than I think I should. But I like you, a lot.*

His head snaps up and he looks me in the eyes with parted lips. "What did you say?" he whispers, his brow pinching upward.

I rub a hand over my mouth, mortified. *Did I just say that out loud?* "Um, I—"

Kyran abruptly stands and walks over to the nightstand, grabbing my necklace. He stalks back and holds it out toward me. As my fingers brush his, a small electric zap shocks me and I drop the necklace, quickly pulling my hand to my chest.

"I'm sorry," I murmur as I lean over, carefully pinching the chain, not wanting to touch the moon again and drop it into my purse.

"I should take you home. You need to speak with your family," Kyran grumbles, heading toward the bathroom.

Slowly rising to my feet, I sling my purse over my shoulder and follow his path, walking to the far side of the bathroom. Kyran bends over to pick up the bag of bloody clothes and I put my hand up. "You can throw those out, I don't want them. I believe what you've told me, even though it's hard for me to wrap my head around it all at the moment." I sigh, absently rubbing my forehead.

Silently nodding, he leaves the bag on the floor and trots back into his room, returning shortly with my jacket. I smile, reaching out to take it from him and drape it over my arm. He steps past me and beckons me to follow into another room. My mouth pops open, gazing around in amazement at the unexpected sight of a large atrium full of magnificent flowers and plants. The beautiful glass panel walls let in so much warm sunlight that it feels like a mild sauna, comfortable and relaxing. Trailing my fingers over leaves as I walk, I sneak a glance at Kyran's back as he opens a door.

*You're just full of surprises. Is there a catch? There's gotta be. Maybe you're a really shitty cook or something,* I wonder humorously, following him out onto a small loft.

With a smirk, Kyran turns to close the door behind me. Giving him a questioning look, he just smiles crookedly and gestures for me to go down the stairs. As we descend, he mildly speaks about his home and points out a few things, but I can't focus on his words with the sudden ringing in my ears, my head throbbing again. I just concentrate on my bare feet padding across the floors, suddenly realizing I'm standing on cold concrete.

Glancing up, we're in a large garage, in front of his old truck with the passenger door hanging open. I smile thinly at Kyran, slowly climb in and click the seat belt in place. He closes my door and is soon sitting beside me with a look of deep concern on his face.

"Selene, are you alright? You look unwell." He frowns, leaning over to look into my eyes.

"My head really hurts and I can't hear that well. I'm just exhausted, I guess." I sigh, resting my head against the cool window. After he starts his truck, I give him directions to my home and he nods silently. I close my eyes as we roll out of the garage.

# KYRAN

Before I turn out of my drive, I mindlink my entire pack. *I need everyone to remain in human form, and for any wolves to stay out of sight. No magic is to be performed until I am off our lands. I have a human with me,* I add quickly to ease any questions or concerns to such a bizarre request.

Glancing at Selene, I notice she is asleep and I drive in silence through the empty villages. The look of horror on her face at seeing me this morning replays in my mind, fists tightly clenching the wheel. I can only begin to imagine the thoughts she must have had, waking up the way she did. Eir had said she wouldn't remember anything, but her eyes said otherwise. She has no reasonable explanation for what she may have seen last night in the bathroom, and her ignorance only hinders her.

*This needs to change. She is clearly in danger,* I mutter with rising frustration.

*She is awakening,* Valdr murmurs.

Peeking at Selene, I furrow my brow at her closed eyes, mouth slack from deep sleep.

*Her wolf, can't you feel her?* Valdr asks incredulously.

*I heard Selene's thoughts while leaving my room, as if she was thinking them at me, unintentionally. So, yes, I suppose that means I can feel her as well.* I smile as warmth pools in my chest.

*I want to see her, hear her name, her voice. Smell her. I want to run and—*
*Enough.* I chuckle, slightly shaking my head at Valdr's eagerness.

Selene's cottage is a half an hour away by road, and I'm glad she gave me directions because if I drove her there without her telling me, that would've been extremely awkward and uncomfortable to explain. *Especially* after this morning.

I spend the rest of the drive thinking about her wolf, how eerily beautiful she'd be with platinum blonde fur and bright, icy blue eyes. She'd be damn hard to camouflage in the forests, but her fur would be excellent during the winter. We don't have too many blonde wolves, most of them being closer to either warm honey, sandy, or ashy tones when shifted, so hers will be exceptional to see.

*Why is she hidden, locked away and inaccessible? I've never heard of anything like it before, to this extent. Some punishments have been doled out with a witch's magic to prevent a shift from happening for a set time, but never an entirely dormant wolf. Some pups don't emerge for a few delayed years, sure, but a full-grown adult? It just…does not seem right. I'd feel so hollow,* I solemnly wonder to Valdr, only getting a grunt in response.

Rolling my eyes at his aloofness, I turn onto Selene's road, finding the gate to Hekate's cottage already open. Grimacing, I slowly drive toward their home, preparing myself for *any* kind of response from her. I roll to a stop and turn off the engine, giving Selene's shoulder a gentle rub.

"Hey, sweetheart, we're at your house," I murmur and she inhales deeply, squinting her eyes.

Asteria manifests just outside Selene's window, frowning deeply. As the hairs on the back of my neck raise, I momentarily close my eyes before turning around to face Hekate's glare. Her eerie eyes are flooded entirely black with a halo of white around her pupils.

*Get. Out. Now,* she furiously demands in my mind.

*I did not harm her. I saved her fucking life. She was intentionally dosed with vampire venom, Hekate. There was no time to contact you. She nearly died!* I snarl, baring my teeth through the window. *Tell that to your reckless daughter, who'd rather get fucking wasted than protect her sister. She alone could have easily—*

My door wrenches open and I am dragged through the air, slamming into the ground completely immobilized. Chest crushing in a vice, my throat constricts painfully as Hekate's face twists with rage above me.

"You know *nothing* of what Asteria has done for her. She, too, was drugged last night. Someone gave her fae blood, temporarily impairing her magic. *Who did this?*" she seethes, her voice thick with power.

*I don't know, I'm trying to figure it out!* I harshly mindlink in response since I'm slowly suffocating. *Caedes was there, albeit briefly, but I suspect he has something to do with this. Eir said she had never felt venom so strong before and it would make sense for it to be his. But I don't know how.* I groan into the dirt, the pressure building achingly in my face.

"*Ugh, Eir,*" Hekate scoffs, releasing me with a slash of her hand.

Coughing, I wipe a hand over my face as I push to my feet and search for Selene, finding her still asleep in the truck. Asteria scowls at me beside her. Looking sideways at Hekate, I mutter, "Yeah, well, the feeling is mutual, *apparently.*"

I turn away from her to spit, grains of sand still stuck in my teeth.

She throws her head back and barks a laugh, reaching out to clasp my shoulder. I go rigid at her touch, feeling extremely on edge around this woman. Turning her now-violet eyes to me, she grins for a moment before her face goes somber.

"Thank you, for saving her. I cannot express how...*dire* that may have been," she says cryptically. Sighing, she gestures toward Selene. "I guess she needs to learn the truth, now. What does she know of last night?"

"Eir had said she would not remember, but I believe she does, somehow. All I have told her is that she was drugged and needed her blood cleaned of the toxin, but I left out the *how.*"

Hekate nods knowingly. "Her necklace, was she wearing it?" she asks suddenly.

"Yes, until Eir cleaned and changed her."

Hekate's eyes narrow as she mutters, "She'll remember."

The necklace must be a charm of sorts, perhaps protective or warding. I recall the shock it gave me when I first touched it, and also when I handed it to Selene. *Maybe that was the reason for her glowing skin last night?*

*Tell her about this morning,* Valdr urges me.

"Tell me about what?" Hekate asks, raising a brow.

I give her a disturbed look, not liking how she can hear Valdr speaking to me.

She rolls her eyes. "I can hear *everything*. Now tell me, what?"

Eyeing her with unease curdling my blood, I quietly answer, "I heard Selene's thoughts, as if they were directed at me, when we were leaving to come here. I believe that her wolf is awakening."

She nods her head slowly, thinking. "What else do you feel, with her?"

"Warmth. Peace. I also become strengthened, in a sense, as if she brings me power? I'm not entirely sure, it's hard to place. If I concentrate hard enough, I can almost *feel* her presence within me," I murmur, rubbing a hand over my chest.

A small smile tugs at Hekate's mouth and she sighs. "Your bond is strong already. Just wait until she's whole, fully herself once more." Her voice trails off as she looks toward Selene. "I am going to inform her of her identity—her *true* self—tonight, of me and Asteria, even of *you* and your kind. She may not take it in stride, she's a stubborn woman. Please have patience, *Custos*. You will have the answers you seek soon enough." Hekate speaks softly, giving me a tired smile.

Before I can respond, she waves her hand and the three of them vanish, leaving me with her sharp swirling wind. I stand dumbfounded for a moment, blinking at the empty space she'd occupied less than a breath ago. With a shake of my head, I get into my truck and hastily make my way home, eager to see if Elder Eirene has returned yet. I decide to gather the elders again to confer with them about this weekend's events.

A thought nags at me the entire way home, my irritation growing. *Why does she keep calling me that?*

# CHAPTER ELEVEN

## EXPOSURE

### KYRAN

While on my way home, Elder Eirene let me know that she had only just returned and required some rest before meeting, so I asked for everyone to gather later this evening in respect to her needs. Pulling into my driveway, Treyvar stands at the front door with his arms crossed and a grim look on his face.

Quickly parking my truck, I hop out and jog up to him. "What is it, what's happened?"

"We found Vala," he responds lowly and pushes the door open for me.

Stepping into the foyer, I carefully listen to the voices below me. Trotting down the hall, I descend the stairs into my basement, finding Jeger, Sigurd, and Kira standing around Vala. She's bound to an armchair with her mouth taped shut and a pissed off look in her eyes. Brow furrowing at the sight, I take a step forward to ask what's going on, but Trey grabs my arm and pulls me around.

*Don't listen to Sigurd. He said Vala is innocent, but we know that to be untrue. Hear Jeger first.* Trey holds my gaze intently.

I narrow my eyes, remembering his hostility the other day toward Sigurd and ask quickly, *After here, are you available? I'd like to discuss something I forgot to address the other day.*

He nods once and I return the gesture, circling back to the group. Glancing briefly at Sigurd, I decide to heed Trey's warning and instead focus on Jeger.

"Explain," I demand in a clipped tone.

"I followed your command to track the rogues two nights ago, and I came upon an abandoned house in the suburbs, finding the place reeking of vamps. There were too many scents to determine exactly how many there were. I estimated at least twenty, though, as well as over a dozen rogues. The only one inside was the guy who attacked the female, from what I could tell. It was nearly dawn by the time I had searched as much of the building as I could without being detected. I chose to sleep for the day in the nearby woods, in case anyone showed up in the evening.

"Late last night, I am *certain*—" he glares at Sigurd, "that Caedes arrived among a group of his sycophants. I cannot say what went on in the house because I could not get close enough to see, but I did hear them arguing. Specifically, I heard things about a small blonde woman, her blood being tracked, magic being used to enspell her, and dosing her with venom. It was a plan of attack, I am sure of it." Jeger stares at me with a stony expression, his gray gaze unwavering.

I can't hold back my growl as the picture behind the mystery clouding Selene's attack grows clearer. Jeger pauses, waiting for me to speak. I just nod for him to continue, clenching my jaw against the anger spiking with this information.

"I watched as Caedes and a few leeches left the house, leaving the rest of the group behind to stay inside with the rogue. I remained where I was on the chance I'd glean more information, and had planned on leaving at dawn. A few hours had passed since Caedes left and moments after he arrived again, none other than *Vala* appeared, creeping around the house." He sneers at her, and she shakes her head with a muffled exclamation behind her gag.

"I was instantly suspicious of her, how could I not be? We fought a bit and I knocked her out, bringing her back here for you to decide how to handle her," he says tiredly, rubbing a hand over his face.

"You did well, Jeger," I say sincerely, clasping his shoulder. "Go and rest. You *did* see Caedes, he was at my bar last night, if only for a short moment. What is he doing here, why *her?*" I mumble, stepping in front of Vala and crouching down.

Before I speak to her, Kira taps my shoulder and holds out her phone. "Here, you might want to take a look at this," she says quietly, concern pulling her face tight.

Taking her phone, I press play on the video she has ready. It's a recording from a security camera in my bar, zoomed in on Selene entering from the club. She looks a little uneasy with her hand pressed to her forehead before she walks straight into Vala. Vala grasps her wrist and leans in, saying something to her. Selene immediately braces herself against the wall, looking extremely unwell. Vala quickly looks around then darts through the tunnel to the club, returning shortly after Selene stumbles out of view. I watch as she hastily leaves the bar from the front entrance, which is not normal for anyone who works there since we all park out back.

Silently handing Kira her phone, I glare at Vala as my rage grows, clenching my jaw and fists with my breath coming in short, fast bursts. Reaching up, I rip the tape off her mouth and force my alpha will over her. A quiet whimper escapes her beneath my furious gaze.

*"You will speak the truth,"* I command sharply, and she flinches. "What did you say to her, to Selene, in the bar?"

"I asked if she was feeling alright," she immediately replies, eyes wide.

"Why did she react to you the way she did?" I demand harshly.

Vala scrunches her brow with a shake of her head.

"Answer me!" I shout, making her jump.

"I—I don't know!" she says shrilly, straining against her binds.

*"Did you use magic on her?"* I grind out between my teeth.

"Y-yes, but—"

With a vicious snarl, I bare my teeth and lean in close to her face. "At the vamp nest, were you there to see Caedes?" My voice is dangerously low.

"Kyran, you don't—"

*"Were you there to see Caedes!"* I bellow and Vala winces away from me.

"Yes," she whispers dejectedly, her eyes filling with tears.

A coldness creeps down my spine at her admission and I rise to my feet, livid. Turning sharply, I cross the basement and unlock the safe room, yanking the thick door open. At the back of the room, I shove a tall safe aside with a loud scrape and unlock the secret one recessed in the wall. I pull out a tiny vial containing glimmering, iridescent blood and uncork it with extreme care. Taking a small glass pipette, I pull a single drop out and cork the vial, replacing it in its holder and locking the safe. I drag the large safe back into its place and exit the room, slamming the door behind me.

Stalking across the basement, Vala starts thrashing in the chair, desperate to break her bonds when she sees what I'm holding. "Kyran, no!" she yells, her voice going hoarse with despair. "Please, no! *You don't understand!*"

Stepping behind her, I grip her jaw and force it open as I tip her head back. She struggles in my hold and screams a garbled protest. I suspend the pipette above her mouth and squeeze, watching the droplet of blood sizzle on her tongue before evaporating.

"Sigurd, take her to one of the oubliettes and bring me the key. Go with him." I look sharply at Trey, raising my voice over Vala's sobs. "Meet with me in my office when you're back."

Brushing past Kira, she silently places her hand over her open mouth, shocked at what I'd just done.

Vala screams raggedly at my back as I stalk up the stairs. "Kyran! Kyran, *please!* Don't do this to me! You have to listen to me, you don't understand! *Kyran!*"

I don't turn around and my steps don't falter, not when she's betrayed me after everything that I've forgiven her for.

Pacing in the gardens, I try to make sense of why Vala would do such a thing. *How could she betray me like that? Why work with the vampires—their fucking king—and still act loyal to me? Is she plotting to go against me? Did she attack Selene out of jealousy? Was killing her the goal? Why?* I grit my teeth in irritation as I round the same tree for the hundredth time.

Anger bubbles hotly in my chest, turning my thoughts over, never finding answers. A growl of frustration leaves my lips and I blindly grab a wooden bench, hurling it against a tree. The satisfying *crunch* of splintering wood does nothing to salve my temper. A distant *knock-knock* echoes and I pause my pacing, listening.

"Kyran, you in there?" Trey calls out from inside the house.

Cutting through some bushes, I trudge inside and push past Trey into my office. Silently, he steps in and closes the door behind us. I drop down onto a small sofa, resting my elbows on my knees and grip my hands together, waiting for Trey to sit. Handing me a rusty key, he pulls an armchair around, staring at me warily.

"Can I ask you a question?" he asks quietly.

I tightly nod in response.

"What was that, what you put in Vala's mouth? I've never seen anything like it before."

"Faerie blood," I say flatly, holding his gaze.

Trey blinks once, slowly. His eyes twitch before doubling in size and his mouth pops into a small circle. *"You've gotta be shitting me,"* he gasps.

I let out a dry huff of a laugh, slouching back against the sofa. Holding up a hand, I explain, "Before you ask me a thousand questions, yes, they are real, no, you won't find one they are extremely rare, yes, they have supernatural abilities, yes, they can use magic and their blood absorbs it, no, I won't tell you where or how I got their blood. Most werewolves are unaware of their existence because they have no use for us. Only humans and witches keep their interest. Be thankful for *that*, trust me." I rub my forehead, feeling worn out.

Trey just gapes at me incredulously. A tiny squeak leaves his mouth and he gestures wildly around him. My tension eases a bit as I laugh at his ridiculousness.

"No way. No fucking way! That's…that's just…*wow.*" He raises his eyebrows and shakes his head, blowing out air. "Alright, sure. Faeries are fucking real. But, why did you give the blood to Vala?"

I speak lowly, my irritation with making my voice rough. "Faerie blood disables magic, and as long as it is in her body, she will be powerless. I needed her to be without magic to keep her imprisoned."

"Can it be undone?" he asks hesitantly.

"Yeah, but only from a faerie."

I hold his gaze as the realization dawns on him.

*"Shit,"* he whispers, falling back into his chair.

"I only intend to keep her there until I can get this mess figured out. There's still a lot of pieces that don't fit yet. It doesn't quite make sense to me and I need to find out why. I'll deal with Vala once I can fully understand what's going on. Until then, nobody is to visit her, and only you or Kira will bring her food and water, understood?" I speak to my brother in a way I have never before with a hard, cold tone.

"Yes, I understand. I get it, everything you've done and said. But…Kyran, try to not let your rage swallow you again, okay? It feels like we've barely had you back, and I know we—me and Kira— would be devastated if it happens to you again. Not to mention Stjarna, or even the whole pack for that matter," Trey says quietly and pulls his eyebrows up, the worry clear on his face.

Sighing, I close my eyes and tip my head back on the cushion. "As would I," I mumble, my brow knitting with the unwanted memories.

*Screams of agony and elation jumbled together, the crack and crunch of bodies breaking, flashes of fangs, claws, and cameras, blinding rage in a hunger that could never be satiated, and blood, so much blood.* Decades upon decades of living in that hell with no sense of humanity, no life outside of brutal torture, maiming, and slaughter. So much death. It was all I knew, from the moment I first shifted until *far* past becoming Alpha.

*The Underground made me into a man I don't want to be, not anymore. I thought I'd laid this fury to rest, but knowing that Selene had been targeted twice now is dragging everything back to the surface. With Vala's betrayal on top of it, this energy inside me has resurrected, and I fear I'm not strong enough to overcome it this time. I can't tell Trey, it'll only cause him to worry and fret over me.* I force myself to rein in the ire that arises as I swallow down my darkness.

Valdr feels restless, remaining silent.

I absently rub my hand over my chest, the tension in me coiling deep. Opening my eyes, I peer at my brother, watching him type a message on his phone. When he finishes, I sit up and hold his gaze.

"What's going on between you and Sigurd? I noticed when we met to discuss the abductions how you looked pissed at him, and then earlier, you told me not to listen to him. Why?" I try to keep my voice calm, holding back the simmer in my tone.

"His story didn't quite add up with the accounts of the other warriors on the night of the abductions. He was acting sketchy, as if he was almost hiding something or not telling the truth. I confronted him about the gaps in the reporting, how his explanation didn't match fully with the others. He got defensive, borderline aggressive. With everything that had been going on, I did not want to expend my energy fighting him, so whatever it was you sensed was residual from that.

"As for this morning, he was adamant that Vala is innocent and should not be punished. Without him physically *being there* with Jeger, how could he know that for certain? Jeger informed me he mindlinked some of the other warriors about the situation, and they went out to help bring her back here. Sigurd had shown up half an hour before them and nobody could understand how. He was *supposedly* running guard watch when he heard about it, and said he was close to the border near the suburbs.

"Now, I don't know *for sure* what's true or not, but he feels off to me. I don't trust him or what he says, and I cannot give you a specific reason why. I just don't." Trey exhales sharply, flopping back against the chair.

Thinking about what he's said, I nod and rise to my feet. I cross my office toward an ornate mahogany hutch, my father's handcrafted liquor cabinet. Selecting one of his favorites, I take a glass off the shelf and hold it up to Trey in question. His brows raise as he nods and I grab another glass, pouring us both a hefty serving of Stagg bourbon. As I watch the amber liquid swirl, I reflect on seeing my father standing here when I was a child, pouring glasses for himself and Tomur. Walking over to Trey, I hand him his drink and lean against my desk, taking a long sip.

"I like how you replace the bottles over time, in his honor," Trey mentions quietly, nodding his head toward the hutch. "He always smelled nice, like warm bourbon and the metallic tang of his forge."

I just grunt in response, taking another sip. My brother's memory of our father vastly differs from mine. *He smelled of sour breath and blood to me,* I mutter to myself as I avert my gaze. Shaking my head to dispel my thoughts, I throw back the last of my drink and move to pour another when icy spiders crawl down my neck.

My back goes rigid with the unexpected sensation.

*Come to me at once. At my cottage, our revelation has not been easy. Selene is unwell, she needs to see the truth to believe it. She must see you, Custos. Now.*

Shuddering at Hekate's voice in my head, I slam my glass onto my desk and hurry to the door. Trey jumps to his feet, alarmed.

*"What the hell!* What's going on?" he demands behind me, following me down the hallway.

Wrenching the door open, I hastily shift and burst through my clothes, the tattered fabric floating to the ground around my paws. Bounding through the gardens, I pause for a moment to look back at Trey rushing to undress.

His face pinches with worry and I mindlink him, *Stay here, I'm going to Selene. There's no danger.*

At his silent nod, I take off through the woods with Valdr sharing the thrill of the run. As I lope through the trees, I can't help but think of how she'll react to seeing us, seeing *me* emerge from my wolf form. *Will she be scared? Amazed? Angry?* I wonder, feeling a mix of apprehension and excitement.

*Maybe it will pull her wolf out of stasis and we get to meet her.* Valdr's eagerness bleeds into me, pushing my legs faster.

Imagination takes over, distracting my mind until I reach the edge of Hekate's boundary. Selene's distant voice tightens my chest with anticipation. I've never shown myself to a human before. Selene is not a human, but her perception has been altered to the life of one, and I am anxious about revealing myself to her. Especially since I had not planned on it going like this.

*I wanted to tell her first, to talk about this part of me before showing her. What will she think?*

I worry, slowing to a stop at the edge of the woods. Pacing nervously, I wait by the familiar blackthorn shrub for the right time to reveal myself and silently watch the cottage.

## SELENE

I wake to distant voices, first sounding like murmurs then growing clearer as the fog lifts from my brain. Cracking my eyes open, I rub the side of my head, the pounding pain hurting worse than before. I'm lying on the living room couch, squinting at the bright sunlight filtering through the lace curtains billowing over the open window. The voices grow louder, my mother and sister arguing in stressed tones.

Ria hisses from somewhere behind me. "She has to know *everything*. It's for her own safety!"

"I am afraid she will react negatively and won't understand my reasoning," my mother responds lowly.

"She almost *died* because of how grossly unaware she is! *None of this* would be a concern if she had just fully awakened." Ria's voice cracks, her footsteps clomping loudly on the porch, and the door bangs open with a *thwack*.

"Asteria, this is not your fault." My mother's voice is calm and quiet, sounding closer.

Rubbing my face, I slowly sit up and stare at my chest, confused. I'm wearing my necklace over my favorite blue hoodie and black leggings, definitely *not* what I arrived here in. Glancing at the kitchen, Ria meets my gaze with tears in her eyes.

"Selene, are you alright? How do you feel?" she asks in a rush, coming to sit beside me.

I put my hand up and take a deep breath. Catching my mother's gaze, she warily takes a seat in the armchair next to the couch and gives me a tight smile.

"Honestly? I feel like shit," I say dryly, falling back into the cushions.

"Do you need anything? What can I get you?" Ria's voice is pitched higher than normal, a wild look in her eyes.

"What I *need* is for someone to tell me exactly *what the fuck is going on!*" I snap, breathing heavily.

Pinching the bridge of my nose, I take a few breaths and turn to Asteria. "Last night, I felt…high, in the club. As if everything was heightened, euphoric. Kyran had said I looked flushed and left to get me some water, but I suddenly felt ill and went searching for the bathroom. I ran into a woman whose eyes were like *yours*, and as she grabbed me, I became violently sick and dizzy. It was the same feeling of being extremely intoxicated and the world is spinning around you," I add with a scrunch of my nose, and Ria nods her head, chewing on her lip as she listens.

"Before I could register what the hell was happening to me, she was gone, as if I imagined the whole thing. When you and the girls came out of the club…everything is a bit fuzzy from here for me to remember." I sigh, narrowing my gaze as I try to focus. "I recall sitting at a table, drowning myself in cold water, and becoming sluggish and heavy. I don't know what I did or said as I went to the bar, I just know that's when I passed out.

"This is where I cannot separate drugged haze from reality, and I am beginning to believe none of it was my imagination. I have flashes of a beautiful, fair, red-haired woman with glowing hands hovering over me, blood floating in the air, immeasurable pain throughout every fiber of my being, and my own skin ablaze with light. A splitting migraine has stayed with me since, and the only time it abated was in Kyran's arms." My voice grows quiet with the memory, and Ria looks at my mother with concern. I take a few calming breaths before I continue my explanation.

"I don't recall what happened afterward, except for waking in a room that was not mine, wearing someone else's clothes, with barely any recollection of *what the fuck I went through* until I grasped *this*." I yank at the necklace around my throat, shaking it at my mother. "*Somehow,* I saw and felt everything that had happened to me like there were movie frames flashing through my mind. *How is that possible?* I was so beyond terrified that when I saw Kyran again, I thought he had done something awful to me. I know now that is not the case, I just *know* in my soul he wouldn't do that. He said I need to speak with you," I glance from my mother to Asteria, "the both of you. Here I am, I don't want to eat, or bathe, or sleep. I want the truth. *Now*. So speak," I demand as I breathe harshly through my teeth, tightly clenching my jaw.

Silence. Nobody moves or speaks for a few moments as my eyes bounce back and forth between them. Ria lets out a long breath, raising her eyebrows at our mother who rubs her hand over her mouth before dropping it into her lap.

"Alright," she sighs, straightening her skirts and firmly holding my gaze. "The words I speak are nothing but the truth, Selene. Believe me when I say you will want to reject everything you are about to hear. I need you to truly listen. *Trust* me, and your sister as well, understand? Our days of secrecy are behind us." Her voice is clipped and I can feel the seriousness in her words.

Pulling my legs underneath me, I look into her eyes and nod my head once.

"Asteria and I are goddesses. To be more precise, my real name is Hekate and I am the goddess of witchcraft and magic, among other things that aren't important at this moment," she mumbles, waving her hand flippantly. "Anyway, what you experienced last night was healing magic from the elven goddess Eir, although I believe she is keeping her identity undisclosed at the moment, for whatever reason. She saved your life by cleansing your blood of the vampire venom coursing through your veins.

"The source of which, we are still trying to understand, and we do not know exactly *how* it happened to you, unfortunately. The *why*, however, I do know. Had you been human, the venom would have killed you quickly, drastically thinning your blood and eventually stopping your heart. It's truly because of Kyran that you're alive, he could smell the venom in you. This is due to his nature of being a werewolf…as are you." Her voice trails off, watching me warily.

I just stare flatly at her for a moment, then burst out laughing. I turn to Ria, expecting her to be laughing along with me, but she isn't. She is serious, looking extremely concerned. My laughter falters along with my smile as I look between Ria and our mother. "You're joking, right? Please tell me you're joking," I say highly, my voice pulling tight.

"No, Selene, I most certainly am not." Her response is intense, mouth pulling into a tight line.

*"You're serious,"* I whisper, my heart racing.

Abruptly pushing to my feet, I take a few quick steps away, shaking my head. "No, no. That's *impossible*. How could I not know that? No. A *werewolf?* Me? *Ha!* I think I'd know if I was a *fucking shape-shifting creature of mythology!"* I shriek, turning on them. "What is this, a candid camera prank or something? I can't believe this!"

"Selene, *please*, I am not lying to you or pranking you, nothing like that. *I am telling you the truth,"* my mother pleads as she rises to her feet, clutching her hands.

"*Right*, because you're a goddess and Dracula tried to kill me last night. *Oh*, I almost forgot, I want to date *Wolverine*, and my sister is a *witch*," I sneer angrily, throwing my arms up.

"I'm technically a goddess," Asteria says quietly with a tight smile, slowly walking toward me.

Crossing my arms, I snap back, "Yeah? Then prove it, if it's *really* true."

Glaring at me, her eyes flood black, the irises flashing white. She slashes her hands out to the sides, fire blazing to life in her palms. A blast of wind whips her hair around as it billows through the house, and all of the candles ignite at once. The floor beneath my feet tremors, shaking the leaves of the plants hanging around me. Water droplets materialize from nothing, suspending in midair like diamonds.

I stumble to my ass in shock, shuffling backward until I am pressed against the wall with wide eyes. Asteria immediately returns to normal, the house quieting and going still as if nothing happened.

Short, fast breaths puff out of my gaping mouth. *"Holy shit."*

Glancing over at my mother, she remains in the chair and rubs her forehead, watching me warily. I silently raise my eyebrow at her. Rolling her eyes, she disappears, just *vanishing* into thin air. I blink, completely stunned.

My body jolts at a tap on my shoulder.

Whipping my head around, I find myself nose to nose with my mother and I clap my hands over my mouth with a shriek. She and Ria laugh loudly as I sit there gawking at the both of them.

I burst to my feet, outraged. "What the *fuck!* This isn't funny! How could I not know, all this time? Everything I believed to be *fantasy* is *real?* I...I can't do this." I hastily cross the room and wrench the front door open.

Going as fast as my shaky legs will carry me, I stumble off the porch, not really seeing where I'm going. I push through some bushes and stalk away from the house, away from the madness that threatens to consume me.

*This can't be real. I must be dreaming. Last night, all of it. I need to wake up.* I pinch my arm hard, wincing at the bite of pain.

"Selene! Wait!" Ria calls out, running behind me.

I stop beneath my favorite willow just outside my bedroom and glance at the balcony, half expecting to see myself sleepwalking. Ria catches up to me with my mother close behind her.

"Sel, I'll answer any question you ask me," she pleads, reaching her hand out.

"This isn't real. This can't be real," I deny harshly, shaking my head.

Branches rustle near the edge of the woods and I expect Phylax or Machitis to appear, but they never show. Turning back to Ria, I am startled to see the dogs sitting on either side of my mother, watching me intently.

"W-what—how…" I stammer, unable to finish my question.

The rustling grows louder and I feel compelled to move toward the sound, as if being pulled by a line in my center. Placing my feet one in front of the other, I slowly step across the soft grass, my heart beating frantically. A branch snaps, sending my gaze flying upward and a black shadow creeps out from the tree line. I freeze in place, my breath catching in my throat at what I'm seeing.

An *enormous* wolf—easily twice the size of my dogs put together—emerges cautiously, its head low and ears pulled flat. It takes a few slow steps toward me, looking up at me with bright amber eyes.

*Amber?* My brow pinches in disbelief, and I shoot a glance over my shoulder. Ria gives me a small smile, and my mother just slightly nods her head. Turning my attention back to the wolf, I narrow my eyes, observing the thick, shiny midnight-black fur coat and notice a tiny patch of white on its chest. When our eyes meet again, the wolf crouches low and lays its head on its massive paws, waiting.

I tentatively step forward, coming to a stop an arm's length away from the wolf. Its tail twitches side to side, *swishing* the grass, and its pointy ears swivel forward. Crouching, I peer at the wolf and it raises its head until we're eye level with one another.

"You're so beautiful," I murmur, brazenly stretching my hand out to hover just above its muzzle.

The wolf tips its head, gently pressing its nose into my palm. A warm thrum radiates up my arm and throughout my body, washing away the headache and all of the trepidation coiled inside me. I gasp a shuddering breath, my eyes flying wide.

"*Kyran,*" I breathe in disbelief, staring into his familiar warm gaze.

Ria appears beside me, silently holding out a pair of pants.

*The gray sweatpants I was in earlier.*

Confused, I look up at her but she just nods her head at the wolf, guiding my attention back to him. When I meet his eyes once more, his face blurs and seamlessly shifts into the one I recognize, his entire body following suit.

*His entire naked body.*

I gawk, belatedly understanding the pants. I can't help but watch as he pulls them on, unable to take my eyes off of him.

Kyran holds out a hand for me and I shakily grab it, allowing him to pull me to my feet. I feel disconnected, as if I am watching this happen to myself rather than experiencing it directly. Swallowing hard, I blink a few times, trying to process everything that has happened since opening my eyes. I silently look over to my mother and sister, then slide my gaze back to Kyran, grimacing as darkness suddenly clouds my vision and pulls me into unconsciousness.

# CHAPTER TWELVE

## ORIGINS

### KYRAN

Lunging forward, I catch Selene as she falls, lifting her into my arms and cradle her against my chest. I share a look of concern with Hekate and Asteria, and follow them as they turn to make their way toward the cottage. Their dogs bound ahead of them, oddly unaffected by my presence. Padding across the porch, Selene groans softly, her eyes fluttering open as I step through the open door.

I glance around and find the home to look exactly the way I'd imagine the witch goddess to live. Dark and eerie. Hekate gestures toward a small leather sectional before she disappears without a word and I cross the dimly lit home, laying Selene down gently. I sit in an armchair beside the couch to give her some space.

"Would you like some tea?" Asteria asks quietly, carrying a tray with an ornate porcelain tea set into the living room.

"Yes, thank you." I give her a small smile as I take a cup.

Sniffing it, I sense lavender, chamomile, and mint, among a few other scents I can't quite place. Taking a tentative sip, I find the tea to be very pleasant and soothing, bringing me immediate relaxation.

Narrowing my eyes over the rim at Asteria, I state dryly, "There's more than just herbs in here."

A sly smile pulls at her mouth and she looks sideways at me, setting the tray on the coffee table. "Indeed," she replies candidly, pouring herself a cup and sitting at the end of the couch by Selene.

"Care to enlighten me?" I ask in a dry voice, raising my cup. "What's in this?"

"Now, Kyran, a witch never reveals her brew," she intones sarcastically, giving me a wide grin.

I stare at her flatly, her demeanor reminding me of my brother in a way. Before I can say anything else, Selene slowly sits up, rubbing her forehead. Asteria sets her cup down and looks back at me with a smile.

"No need to fret. There isn't anything debilitating in it, just natural herbs to help calm the nerves and a little magic to boost it a bit. I wouldn't give you anything harmful, not intentionally," she adds lowly, looking toward the floor.

"Hey, it's alright. I would've sensed anything bad before drinking it, and I trust you." I smile when she looks up at me with surprise.

Selene drops her hands to her lap with a *thump*, silently looking between Asteria and me. Her wary eyes flicker to me and flutter around my bare torso. Her brows draw together, a small frown pulling the corners of her mouth down. As she glances back at Asteria, her frown deepens further and she lets out a sigh. Selene stands slowly and I quickly rise to my feet, sending my cup clattering on its saucer.

"I need a moment alone, please. Excuse me." She swiftly steps around the low table, past me, and up the wooden staircase.

After her feet disappear, I sink back down into the armchair, feeling unsure what to do with myself. As I sip the tea, I notice Asteria staring at me with an arched brow. I raise mine back in silent question.

"What's it like, for you? Did you know when you met her who she was? How does it feel to know that your bond is a real possibility for you?" She murmurs her questions, crossing her legs and leaning forward curiously.

"Honestly? It feels extremely...foreign." I let out a sigh and explain, "I don't really know *how* to process anything I've felt since meeting her. I just know that she feels *right*. I did not know what she was at first. I was confused for a while, until we pressed our hands together that day at the park. Even then, I was totally thrown off because of my mark. Since it appeared, I've had a...*challenging* time accepting it. After meeting Selene, I feel both hopeful and afraid about my bond, but mostly confused still. There's a lot I don't understand right now," I mumble, leaning forward to set my cup and saucer on the table.

Asteria has a wistful look on her face as she thinks about what I've said. Her eyes narrow sharply. "That's nice to hear, but you didn't answer one of my questions."

I scrunch my brow, unsure what she means. "Which question?"

"*If you knew who she was when you met her,*" she says tightly, glaring at me with growing intensity.

"What—"

"Asteria, enough." Hekate's sharp voice cuts behind me, making the hairs on my neck raise.

Turning my head, I find both her and Selene making their way down the stairs. As they come into the living room, Hekate sits beside Asteria and Selene stops beside my chair, shyly meeting my gaze. I rise to my feet as she silently holds out my gray t-shirt and I take it, pulling it on over my head.

"Now I can listen properly. You're very distracting," she murmurs, giving me a smirk.

My eyes crinkle from the wide smile that spreads on my face and she blushes, turning quickly to take her seat on the couch. I meet her gaze and then Asteria's, and the three of us look at Hekate. I sit down and lean my elbows on my knees, waiting patiently in the tense silence.

With a sigh, Hekate turns to Selene. "Are you sure you are ready?"

"Yes. I understand I didn't accept what you both were saying and kinda had a freak out, but I want to know the truth. All of it," Selene replies firmly.

"You actually did much better than I anticipated," Asteria says with a small laugh, leaning over and giving Selene's knee a pat.

She rolls her eyes but smiles back, shoving Asteria's hand away. I can't help the small smile tugging at my lips when I watch her and I try not to stare for too long.

"Well, take it from my perspective, how hard it is for me to wrap my head around all...*this.*" Selene gestures vaguely around with her hand at the lot of us, making everyone chuckle. "It does feel right, though, almost familiar? I don't know how to place it at the moment, but I believe and trust my instinct with everything I've been told. And shown," she adds quietly, glancing at me for a moment.

"I understand that, we all do. I, for one, wanted to have this discussion with you under better circumstances." Hekate sighs. "For your safety and well being, however, it is best you know everything about who you are and the life you're destined to live. If you truly feel ready, I have a lot to go over with you and the three of us here can answer any question you have at any time." She assures Selene with a strong, clear voice.

Hekate turns to address me. "Kyran, I am sure you're well aware about a lot of what will be discussed, and most will be previously learned knowledge. However, what you uncover here today with us *must not* be spoken about with *anyone else,* do you understand?" she sternly asks me.

I immediately nod, responding in a serious tone, "Yes, of course. I vow to never speak, write, or communicate in any form what we discuss today with anyone outside of this room, unless you grant your approval." I hold out my hand to her and when she clasps it, our magic flashes as it seals the vow, binding me to it.

She mindlinks me, her gaze hard. *I will leave the matter of mates to you, for when you decide it is best to speak about it with her. I trust that you will handle it delicately.* I silently nod once in acknowledgment, firmly holding her gaze.

Nodding her head, Hekate adjusts herself momentarily before turning to Selene again. Her eyes are wide as she stares at my hands, then flickers her gaze over to Hekate and blinks a couple times before giving us an uneasy smile.

"Okay, well, it'd be best to start at the beginning, *hmm?*" Hekate says lightly, folding her hands in her lap.

Settling back into the chair, I keep my attention on Selene as Hekate begins the story of our origins.

## SELENE

*Was that magic, just now? There is so much I want to know,* I wonder as

I wait for my mother to begin speaking once more. My chest is tight with an anxiety I can't quite tell is good or bad. I chew on my lip in anticipation.

"Selene, if at any point you are unsure of something or want me to stop, please interrupt me. I want you to have as best of an understanding as possible, but I want you to be comfortable at the same time, okay?" My mother's voice is gentle as she gives me a look of concern.

"I will, thank you." I take a calming breath before nodding. "Okay, I'm ready." I give her a small smile and glance at Asteria, finding her smiling at me as well.

Kyran's heavy gaze weighs on me and although it isn't uncomfortable, I can't bring myself to look at him as I listen to my mother speak.

"Do you recall the mythologies I had you study when you were younger?" she asks lightly, and I silently nod before she continues. "Good. Much of what you read was written as tales. However, everything holds truth, although most of the events had taken place amongst realms and planes of existence surrounding the one we currently live in."

My eyes widen, a question already forming. "Does this include *every* cultures' mythology?"

"Yes, certainly. A lot of cultures held awareness of the same beings and entities, and through time they had developed separate languages and stories. This altered some depictions and names, but I can assure you they all connect if you really look at them. I can explain realms and levels of existence to you on another day, if you wish to learn about those?" she offers with a raised brow, and I nod enthusiastically, smiling wide.

*That would be so crazy. Realms?! I'm going to need a notebook. Or a few.* I catch my mind beginning to run off track and take a steadying breath. "Please continue," I mumble, focusing back on the explanation of my current situation.

"I told you that you are—what you believe to be only supernatural—a werewolf. They are more than just fantasy stories in books and movies. As you saw with Kyran, they are *real beings*. I'd like to start with the creation of werewolves, but to do that, you need to understand me and a few other powerful beings that are interwoven with this creation."

I just stare, wide-eyed and silent, and wave my hand for her to continue.

"As I said before, I am Hekate, goddess of magic and witchcraft, and I created the race of werewolves. The reasoning behind their existence is due to Nyx, the goddess of night. She created the vampires. Being the daughter of Chaos, there really isn't much question as to *why* she made them, I suppose." Her voice trails off for a moment, her eyes staring distantly and she shakes her head.

"Vampires resemble some of her attributes. They're creatures of the dark with telekinetic powers, insurmountable strength, and are virtually invulnerable, which gives them eternal life, in a sense. Nyx created the vampires by mixing her soul's essence with humans to bring herself power through their existence. The more of them there are, the stronger she would become. As you can guess, this wreaked havoc within the mortal realm, disrupting the balances that had carefully been put in place.

"Your namesake, the goddess Selene, had watched the horrors the vampires would commit during the night and felt it was unjust for Nyx to empower herself at the humans' detriment. She came to me, requesting my help in creating a race that can balance the power of the vampires." My mother pauses her explanation when she notices my scrunched face.

"Hold on a moment, I don't fully remember…who is she?" I ask, feeling unsure of my studies.

"Selene is the moon, my dear. With her, myself, and Artemis, we three are close in our duties and work well with one another. I'll save that story for another time, though." She smiles softly before clearing her throat. "Now, at Selene's request, I came up with the idea of warriors, in a sense, to combat the destruction caused by the vampires. Being partial to canines myself, I chose to intertwine them with humans to create a new race of beings. Having formed my plan, I sought out Fenrir to make a deal with him."

"Is this Nordic? As in, Odin and Ragnarok?" I ask, fascinated.

My mother nods her head, smiling. "Yes, exactly. Being that he was essentially helpless, bound and imprisoned unfairly, I offered to weaken his bindings in exchange for some of his essence, his…*soul,* you could say. He agreed, seeing how the Fates decided that one day he would break free and seek his revenge on those who imprisoned him.

"Taking his essence and my idea, I met with Selene to explain my thoughts. She happily agreed, and offered to mix in her magic so the werewolves would have virtual immortality along with the vampires. I concocted an elixir with Selene's magic, my own, and some of Fenrir's essence, and gathered willing mortals to take it. Both men and women were transformed into the race of werewolves, having super speed, strength, heightened senses, night vision, the ability to heal from wounds and shape-shift. I personally added in the ability to speak telepathically with one another to aid in their efforts with battling the vampires. There was a discovery, though, of the werewolves sharing bodies with another soul, the human-half and wolf-half respectively having a mind of their own. The complexities behind that is what Kyran can explain to you when you have the time to delve deeper into it with him." She pauses again, flashing a glance at Kyran before adjusting herself in her seat.

"Selene had asked these first werewolves if they would agree to bind their lives to her, aiding in her empowerment as a deity, which they accepted honorably. She had felt it would be necessary in case Nyx needed to be checked, and thankfully has yet to ever pull from that pool of power. Very quickly, our race of wolves began to succeed in culling the vampire numbers into a manageable amount, keeping them in line without eradicating them fully. Many had come to an agreement of sorts, only keeping willing mortals and not endlessly slaughtering villages upon villages of people.

"As a show of gratitude for my success in the werewolves' creation, Selene had proposed a gift of sorts. A second daughter for me, on one condition." My mother's voice grows quiet as she warily looks at me.

Sitting there with my mouth hanging open, I snap my jaw shut and take a deep breath through my nose. Glancing over at Kyran, I find him watching me carefully while I think about everything I just learned. *If I'm a werewolf, then he should be able to hear me, telepathically, right?* I wonder, feeling a bit insane. Staring at him harder, I concentrate on speaking to him in my mind. *If you can hear me, answer this question out loud. What do clouds wear beneath their clothes?* I roll my lips inward, suppressing a laugh.

Kyran grins widely, a deep laugh escaping him. "Thunderwear," he says aloud with another laugh, and my eyes widen into saucers.

My mother chuckles and Ria looks at him completely confused before she turns her head back to me.

Slightly dizzy and astonished, I gape at Kyran. *"Y-you can hear me?"* I breathe in amazement.

"Ah, that must mean your stasis is wearing thin. This is great news!" my mother chirps excitedly, sharing a smile with Ria.

"My what?" My shock turns to confusion as I look from Kyran's fading smile to my family.

"If you don't mind, I will circle back to this in a moment, okay? I'd like to continue again, if that's alright." She gives me a small smile.

"Alright, I've only got about a million questions, but go ahead," I respond dryly with a chuckle, giving her my attention once more.

"As I was saying, Selene wanted to give me a gift of sorts, on a condition which I easily agreed to. She gave me a piece of her pure soul to entwine with Fenrir's, and with my magic, we created a powerful werewolf to unite the race as one and keep them in line with one another. This wolf would be above all hierarchy, with abilities far greater than the others, and would essentially be the personification of Selene, bearing her name. Thus, *you* were created." She smiles warmly at me as she drops a bomb on my reality.

"I—*what?*" I gasp, not comprehending.

"The white wolf," Kyran whispers with rounded eyes. "It—*she*— is supposed to only be a legend," he says quietly, looking toward my mother in disbelief.

"Yes, I know. That would be my fault," she admits with a wan smile.

"Both of our faults," Asteria adds quietly.

"Wait, *wait*," I plead, trying to understand. "How, um, *old* am I, exactly?" I ask in a high voice, my throat closing tight with rapidly growing distress.

Asteria scrunches her nose before replying. "Technically? About a couple millennia." She tries to smile, but it just looks like a cringe.

*"T-technically?"* I stammer, completely shocked.

She grins, trying to ease my tension. "If it makes you feel any better, I'm a bit older than you."

"I don't—um—I am not sure I can fully grasp all of this. I think I need a break, for a moment, if that's alright," I say on a breath, feeling overwhelmed as I stare at nothing.

"Of course. Take all the time you need, I know this must feel like a lot right now. I'll be here when you're ready." My mother smiles gently and pours herself a cup of tea.

Slowly rising to my feet, I cross the room to the kitchen and fill a cup with ice water. Shakily, I raise the glass, needing both hands to take a sip. I make my way to the back porch, carefully lowering myself onto the bench swing. Staring out at the gardens, I reflect on what my mother has told me so far.

*Everything sounds like pure insanity, but deep inside, somehow I know it to be true. Why do I not remember any of this? How do I not know myself? What did Kyran mean by the white wolf and how it is supposed to be a legend? There is so much I still need to learn.*

Groaning, I let out a heavy sigh at the questions buzzing in my mind.

I sit in silence, gently swinging and turning my thoughts over as I watch the clouds drift by until my nerves settle.

A gentle knock pulls me from my thoughts. I turn to find Kyran leaning in the open doorway and give him a small smile.

"Hey, are you alright?" he asks quietly, standing upright and stepping onto the porch. "I just wanted to see if you needed anything."

I slowly rise from the bench. "I have a ton of questions, feel a little lost, and my head hurts a bit, but I'm alright. I think."

"If you're feeling up to it, we can talk afterwards and I can help to better explain the wolf side of things. I'll answer any questions you have," he offers lightly, running a hand through his hair.

When he drops his arm, I find myself distracted by the messy way his hair sticks out, making me want to comb my fingers through it and I quickly avert my gaze. My cheeks heat with a blush and I awkwardly smile up at him, nodding my head.

"Yeah, I think I'd like that. There's definitely *a lot* I do not fully grasp yet," I mumble, turning to go back inside.

"Same here," he murmurs behind me.

I curiously glance at him over my shoulder. "What do you mean?"

"Let's just finish listening to Hekate first." He gestures down the hall, sighing. "I have a feeling the answers to my questions will be found, and I will explain what I mean in a little while, okay?" He gives me a crooked smile and my heart thumps at our close proximity.

Nodding silently, I turn toward the living room where Ria has pulled out some snacks. I eagerly grab a couple chocolate chip muffins, taking a bite of one and handing the other to Kyran. He takes it from me and his nose scrunches slightly, but he smiles at me with quiet appreciation.

Curious, I ask, "Do you not like muffins?"

"Oh, I do. I, ah, I'm not a big fan of chocolate," he murmurs his admission, rubbing the back of his neck.

"Oh, no! Is it because you're a wolf? Does it make you sick, like how dogs can't digest it well? N-not that I'm calling you a *dog*. Ugh, I'm sorry, I wasn't even thinking," I ramble, slightly embarrassed, and I scrunch my face uncomfortably.

He huffs out a laugh, and both my mother and Ria laugh too.

My face flushes hotly.

"Ah, no, it doesn't bother me at all. I just…don't really care for the smell of it, so I've never bothered to eat it. I'm not much of a sweets guy, I guess?" He smiles crookedly, making my stomach flutter.

Ria steps over, holding out a banana walnut muffin with a grin. "Here, try this. It's more savory than sweet, but there are a few chocolate chips in it."

Kyran accepts it with a smile and takes a bite, his eyes rounding slightly. *"Mmf,"* he swallows, "this is delicious." He stuffs half of the muffin in his mouth, chewing quickly. "Where did you get this?" he asks before devouring the rest of it.

*Well, I guess I can see why it's called 'wolfing down your food'.* I grin as I watch him.

"Selene baked them," Ria says simply, shooting me a wink.

Blushing, I turn to take my seat again in the corner of the couch and pull my feet up beside me. My mother silently sips her tea as she watches us, the ghost of a smile pulling up the corners of her mouth. Kyran snags two more muffins before sitting down with a gleeful expression on his handsome face.

"Really? Well, then I just might be a sweets guy after all," he jokes with a smirk, taking another bite and causing us all to laugh.

My mother places her cup on the table and leans toward me. "Selene, do you feel ready to continue? Is there anything you are unsure about or need me to expand upon?"

"I think so. I have a lot of questions, but I will wait until you've explained things further before asking any, in case you answer them along the way," I respond with a small smile.

"Alright then, I will pick up where we left off." She sits back and folds her hands in her lap. "After your creation, I introduced you to the werewolves and explained who you were. They immediately took you in and guided you through your childhood years as teachers, in a way, taking you during the daytime so you could learn their ways. Asteria helped me raise you as we would any child, though your wolf emerged much sooner than that of the normal werewolves. Generally, they don't emerge until around the age that a human child experiences puberty, but you were what would equal a five year old human at the time you first shifted."

I lean forward, interested. "Hold on, what do you mean by 'what would equal'?"

"Kyran, would you help me explain this properly?" she asks, giving him a timid smile.

"Of course," he responds over a mouthful, quickly swallowing and brushing muffin crumbs off his shirt as he sits forward. "While young wolves—pups is what we call them—are developing, they appear like regular human children. However, werewolf growth is much different than that of humans. When a pup is born, their growth rate is twice as fast as a human child's until they reach five or six years of living age, meaning their body is equivalent to that of a ten or twelve year old human. This is when their wolves generally emerge and they experience their first shift. Once this takes place, their growth slows tremendously, to ten times slower than humans, to be exact." He pauses for a moment as he narrows his eyes in thought.

"For example, let's say a werewolf first shifted at the age of five during the year that a human turned ten. That werewolf would appear to be only around the age of fifteen themselves when the ten year old human reaches the age of fifty. As we grow into adulthood, our appearance hardly changes until we reach about five or six hundred years, and then our hair and skin begins to alter, the hair slowly graying and skin softening into wrinkles. But even then, many wolves at these ages are hard to determine *exactly* how old they are by just looking at them. Is this making any sense to you? I know it is an extreme concept, and I guess it would be a little weird to envision." He gazes warmly at me, giving me a sympathetic smile.

Absorbing that information, I find I do understand it, though it seems entirely bizarre. I observe him, noting the smooth, tanned skin of his face. If I didn't know any better, I'd say he was maybe late twenties or early thirties, judging off his general appearance.

Pursing my lips, I narrow my eyes at him, wondering aloud, "How old *are you?*"

"I'm around three hundred and fifty years old, but it gets tough to keep track of the exact years as time passes," he murmurs, his sharp eyes watching me carefully.

"*Wow,*" I whisper and sit back against the couch, staring at him. I want to ask a bunch of questions, but I suppress the urge. Looking to my mother once more, I gesture for her to continue.

"Since your first shift, your wolf quickly became noticeably different, and not just in appearance. She possesses abilities far greater than any wolf in existence, and no one could force her will through commands. As time went on and you grew into adulthood, the werewolf race spread far and wide, creating their own factions with alpha leaders and forming loyalties known as packs. This helped to ensure easier control over the vampire race seeing how they don't particularly *like* to follow any set of rules. They *do* adhere to their king's rule, however. He is what I know to be the first created vampire. His name is Caedes, and once he discovered your existence, absolute turmoil erupted between the two races.

"Caedes began to hunt for you. He learned that their venom could inflict severe damage on werewolves and cause them to entirely lose control. This would be where the lore of werewolves originated from with humans, depicting a shape-shifting man with no sanity slaughtering innocent people. These werewolves are deemed as berserkers, their wolf-side fully taking over, and essentially becoming rabid beasts with their human side gone. Caedes intended to use these werewolves against you, to cause chaos amongst your race. When you had first encountered one, you and I discovered that your wolf holds the ability to *heal them,* to rid them of the infection the vampire venom causes."

Kyran sucks in a breath, rubbing his hand over his mouth. He flicks his fingers to Hekate, signaling her to continue explaining.

"We managed to keep this ability a secret, with only the alphas of the separated packs knowing the truth. During a gathering with them, Caedes had sent a few of his best servants to try and kill you, murdering many of these leaders. In a fit of rage, I released my magic into the remaining alphas, transforming them into the Guardians. They are elite shifters with the ability to morph their human bodies with the attributes of their wolf, giving them the upper hand when combating the vampires. Your wolf had given each of them her blood, allowing them to share your immortality, powers, and granting them immunity to a vampire's venom. The Guardians' purpose is to protect you, to ensure the safety of the werewolf race. If you were to be slain, the entirety of the race would perish due to Selene's soul essentially binding each life to yours. Without your life, the werewolf race would be severely weakened and vulnerable, and Caedes somehow figured that out." My mother clears her throat, taking a sip of her tea.

I blink slowly, trying hard to process everything I am hearing. Kyran slumps back into the chair with his eyebrows drawn low.

"I—we, my entire pack, *every wolf I've ever known*—thought that the white wolf and Guardians were just a tale of long lost history. The only thing I truly know about them was their disappearance, supposedly over a thousand years ago. The legend has been told to pups as bedtime stories and from elders around campfires. I'm now going to assume that the stories are completely true and real, and from what you've told us, the disappearance was *not* a coincidence," Kyran states in a serious tone and leans forward on one knee, pressing a hand to his mouth again.

My mother nods once. "Yes, that is correct. Most everything that has been spoken throughout time about Selene's wolf and her Guardians holds truth, though I'm sure some embellishments have been woven through here and there. I have good reason to believe that when her wolf fully awakens from stasis, her Guardians will as well." She sips her tea, watching Kyran over the rim of her cup.

I glance between them and then at Ria, finding her violet eyes observing me carefully. She gives me a gentle smile as she rubs my knee and I return a smile of my own. Turning my gaze to my mother once more, I curiously ask, "Could you explain what you mean by awakening and stasis? I don't fully understand what that means."

"Ah, yes, I apologize." She sets her cup down again, turning to me. "Some time after Caedes's attack and the rise of the Guardians, we—Asteria and I—noticed an alarming amount of berserk werewolves and lone wolves, called rogues, growing in numbers along with the vampires. It was clear Caedes was building the masses to work against us, to find you. There had even been some entire *packs* of wolves out searching for you, to hand you over to him in the hopes that it would end the chaos between races.

"The three of us had been constantly changing home locations throughout the years, to keep our trails unclear. When we had realized it was going to amount to either an all-out war or you and Caedes fighting to the death, Asteria and I decided to propose we place you and your wolf into stasis. That means you are enspelled into a sleep-like state, ultimately freezing in time neither alive nor dead, indefinitely. Think of the tale of *Sleeping Beauty*, it is much the same. In your case, we had to hold you in stasis for over a thousand years. We wanted to wait until any wolf alive at the time you were in existence had been long dead. Asteria offered to enter stasis with you, to use her magic to fuel the spell. I begrudgingly agreed.

I pulled her out first, around six or seven hundred years later, but somehow you had remained in stasis for a few hundred years past that. Our intentions were to reintroduce you and your wolf to the werewolves once nobody knew who you were, when the issue of Caedes' small army had passed.

"Unfortunately, he has been hunting *any* young, blonde female, both from werewolves and humans, for a thousand years. I know his intent is to uncover one of them to be you. I'll give it to him that he's intelligent, and I know that he has not abated in the slightest with his search. You nearly encountered him last night, at Kyran's bar. And before you jump to any conclusions, Kyran was completely unaware of this potential catastrophe." She breathes out a tired sigh and rubs at her forehead, sitting back in her chair.

Kyran's sharp intake of breath drags my rapt attention to him, fury, confusion, and fear warring on his face. He clenches his hands and his brow pulls tightly, deep in thought.

"He's been aggressive with his abductions recently, and he even had taken women whose wolves were obviously undisguised. He took my mother," he mumbles, looking down at the floor. "It all makes sense now, the abductions, the reasoning, all of it. There's got to be a way to stop him. Wait, when did Selene—*our* Selene—emerge from stasis?" he asks suddenly, looking up at my mother with a tight expression.

I can't help the warm fuzziness that blankets me when I hear his use of *our*. Chewing on my lip, I watch my mother for her answer. "Roughly one hundred and fifty years ago," she says quietly, glancing at me.

My mouth hangs open, dumbfounded. *What? How?*

Kyran abruptly stands to his feet and runs his hands through his hair, pacing between the living room and kitchen. "He knows," he mutters, flopping his hands to his sides.

"Pardon me?" my mother asks, her brow knitted with concern.

"Caedes, *he knows*. He has to. My mother, along with hundreds of other blonde women, had been abducted by groups of hostile vampires across the country *a hundred and fifty years ago*." Kyran growls between clenched teeth. "He knows Selene is here, somewhere, there's no other explanation."

"*Shit,*" both my mother and sister hiss at the same time.

Still reeling from discovering I've supposedly been *awake for over a century without any recollection,* I take a deep breath and drop my head in my hands, my headache pounding painfully.

"I get the dire circumstances of being hunted by a psycho vampire and all, but could we rewind a moment, please?" I mumble, rubbing my temples.

"What do you need to know, Selene?" Ria's voice asks nearby.

"How the fuck do I not remember being alive for over two lifetimes?" I ask seriously, lifting my head and catching the guilty twist of her mouth as she glances away from me. "*Ria?*"

"*Ugh, fine!* When you woke from stasis, your wolf did not, and she stayed dormant long enough for us to realize we had a problem. So, I crafted a brew that erased all memories involving magic and put a spell on you to alter your perception of time." Her voice lowers quickly as she speaks, ending with a mumble.

*"Hold the fuck on,"* I breathe incredulously. "Everything I know is a lie. What I thought was *fifteen years* has been *a hundred and fifty?* Is the story of being adopted and moving here fake? My pretend amnesia was from a make-believe car crash, I presume? Why the lies, the deceit? Why not just *tell me the truth when I woke up!"* I yell shrilly, launching to my feet.

*"I am sorry, Selene,"* she says desperately, wringing her hands. "Truly, I am. It was a choice I hastily made without regarding mother, and to reverse that and *then* disclose everything else to you was just…too much. It was the wrong choice, I know that now, and I really am sorry for it, for all of it. I've tried *tirelessly* to bring your wolf out of stasis, for your memories to restore, but I just *can't* make it happen!" Her voice breaks as tears spring in her eyes.

My anger deflates and I let out a long breath, giving her a wan smile when she meets my gaze again. "It's alright, I think I understand. I'm just a bit overwhelmed at the moment, with all of this. I just…wish we could have skipped the whole keeping me in the dark part," I mutter with a grimace, pressing my fingers to my temple in soothing circles.

"Hekate, could I speak with you for a moment, please?" Kyran's deep voice rumbles from the kitchen.

As our eyes meet, the amber color in his flashes brightly, sending a sharp pain radiating through my head.

*"Ah!"* I gasp, clutching my head with both hands and squeeze my eyes shut, doubling over.

"Selene! What's wrong?" My mother's alarmed voice is immediately beside me and her cool hands press over mine.

"It feels—*argh*—like my head is…*splitting in half,"* I grit out as my breathing intensifies, my chest heavily rising and falling from the force of the pain.

"Asteria, help me. I can't pull the pain from her body," my mother commands and Ria's hands press down on the top of my head.

The pressure becomes unbearable and I bite my lip hard to stop myself from crying out. A small whimper escapes me, though, my eyes filling with hot tears.

"It's her wolf. I can *feel* her," Kyran's husky voice softly murmurs close by. "Let me try."

The cold touch of their hands disappear and an incredible warmth envelopes me, the agony fading away like dust in the wind. Opening my eyes, I find Kyran crouched in front of me, his hands cupping my face gently with a hopeful look in his bright gaze. Sighing with relief, I press my cheek into his palm, feeling beyond exhausted.

"How—" My voice cracks and I clear my throat, but Kyran answers me anyway.

He speaks quietly, searching my eyes. "I remembered that moment in my bathroom, how you responded to my touch when you were distraught. I noticed the way you instantly relaxed, and just now I felt the urge to reach out to calm you. I think your wolf is fighting to break free and it's causing you this pain."

We stay like this for a moment, gazing at each other in peaceful silence until a deep weariness washes over me. Reaching up, I lightly grasp Kyran's wrist and pull one of his hands into mine. "Thank you," I whisper, giving him a small smile and shyly lean my face into his other cupped hand.

"Always, sweetheart," he murmurs, his thumb lightly stroking my cheek.

Tingles race from his touch like an electric shock and I shiver when he slowly withdraws his hands. A *pull* lurches from within and I quickly rise to my feet, reaching out to grasp his hand again.

*Mate,* an ethereal voice whispers in my mind, like the echo of a crystal bell.

Kyran's eyes fly wide open as he gasps, clutching my hand firmly between both of his. From the corner of my eye, I see my mother press her hand to her chest and take a deep breath.

"Was—was that *her?*" I whisper, blinking owlishly, and Kyran silently nods. "What did she mean by that?" I ask, searching his warm gaze.

"Selene, I think you should rest. You're looking a bit faint, dear," my mother says in a quiet, tight voice.

Nodding, I don't remove my gaze from Kyran's as I murmur, "I think I need to lie down. Ria?" I ask, glancing over my shoulder.

"Would you, um, put me to sleep? If that's something you can do? *We* need to talk later, by the way." I scrunch my nose at her.

She lets out a tight laugh and nods, stepping toward me. I turn back to Kyran and place my palm on his cheek.

"Please stay," I whisper.

"Of course," he whispers back, pulling my arm around his neck.

He bends down and lifts me off my feet, gently holding me in his strong arms.

Resting my head against his shoulder, I give Ria a tired smile. "Thank you," I mumble.

She smiles warmly and reaches up, pressing her finger against my forehead as she whispers, *"Somnum."*

I blissfully fall into unconsciousness.

# CHAPTER THIRTEEN

## CONNECTION

### KYRAN

Taking a deep breath, I relax in Selene's calming jasmine scent and slowly sit on the couch. I gently lay her in my lap, holding her close. Glancing over at Hekate, I catch her gaze as she finishes speaking with Asteria and takes my place in the armchair.

"You heard that, right? Her wolf spoke to me. She recognizes me," I say quietly in disbelief.

"Yes, I did, and it almost made me cry. I haven't heard that voice in *so long*. She—" Hekate clears her throat. "She is a beautiful soul, Kyran." She looks past me, shaking her head slowly.

"I wanted to ask you about my bond. How is this possible? I'm trying to understand. Who she is and the story behind her makes sense, but it still isn't clear to me. My mark appeared a few years before my mother was taken, and it seems to be around the time you say Selene woke from stasis," I tell her, pulling my brow up in confusion.

Hekate narrows her eyes at me. "I know, I haven't been able to find a clear answer or reason for this as well. I've thought about it since you first started coming here, and especially when you showed me your mark. The only explanation I can find is perhaps when she awoke and her wolf did not, due to the nature of the stasis, the mate bond became broken without her wolf's presence to accept it. I'm guessing the magic was disrupted by Selene's human-half resurrecting alone, so to speak," she wonders aloud, looking past me in thought.

I nod slowly, her words making sense. There is no way to fully understand since Selene's wolf is different from the rest of us. I look down at her peaceful, sleeping face. *How am I her mate? There could have been thousands of better options for her, why me?*

Hekate rests her hand on my knee, and I look up to see her smiling sadly at me. "I could not understand why Selene did not wake when I pulled Asteria from the stasis. She remained there for hundreds of years, regardless of our attempts to remove her. Now, I feel that I *do* understand, at least a part of it." She speaks softly, giving my knee a pat before withdrawing her hand.

Puzzled, I look at her curiously and she gives me a wide grin. "It's because of *you*, Kyran. Her soul was waiting for you."

Astounded, my lips part slightly as I stare at her before gazing down at Selene once more. "But, why?" I whisper. *She doesn't deserve to be with someone like me. I'm not worthy of her.* I sternly reject the idea as my eyes trace her beautiful face.

*Enough. She is our mate, and you will prove to her our worth so she chooses to accept our bond,* Valdr demands, his indignation hotly rolling through me.

"Crazy how things are all connected, *hmm?*" Hekate murmurs, her gaze distant once more. With a slight shake of her head, she pulls her eyes back to me and smiles warmly.

Resolving myself, a thought occurs to me clearly and my chest tightens with anticipation. "I think I can awaken her wolf. I'm not exactly sure how to do that, but I feel her pull growing stronger the more time I've spent around Selene," I say firmly, feeling the truth behind my words.

"I concur. You will need to discuss this bond with her soon. Who knows, she may even show you the path without either of you knowing it." Hekate raises her eyebrows in thought and shrugs a shoulder.

"Could I ask you something?" I murmur, my thoughts swirling with the new information I'd absorbed from earlier.

She nods once, patiently holding my gaze.

"The Guardians, the ones you created with your rage in retaliation to the vampires, you said they were immortal because of Selene's wolf. Does that mean that Selene is immortal? And what happened to the Guardians once she was placed into stasis?" I ask hesitantly, unsure if I truly want the answers or not.

"Ah, yes, I suppose I didn't clarify that, did I? To answer your first question, yes, Selene is technically immortal. Her soul is a direct piece of the goddess's, thus tying her existence to every werewolf. When she roamed about, wolves in her vicinity would become more empowered, naturally drawn to her like moths to a flame. Her immortality only lies in her lifespan, however. She can be killed like any of you, although with her full abilities, that would be one *hell* of an achievement to accomplish.

"As for the Guardians, they continued on for a time after she went into stasis, and one by one, Caedes had managed to eradicate them. However, their bloodlines live on, though their magic lies dormant. As I said earlier, I believe once Selene's wolf awakens, the Guardians will awaken as well. Only through an Alpha's blood can the Guardian powers be passed." She looks at me knowingly, sitting back in her chair.

A few moments pass as I think about what she has said, her past words echoing in my mind. My head snaps up and I gape at her as realization crashes over me like a tidal wave. "You kept Eirene from meeting with me, didn't you?" I accuse her hotly, and she smirks in response. "*That's* why you kept referring to me as *'Custos'*. I have Guardian blood, don't I? How did you know?" I ask incredulously.

She closes her eyes briefly, and when they open, there's a softness in them I haven't seen before. "I met your father's spirit as he crossed realms. I meet each one of you as you die and make your way to the underworld. As he was passing my crossroads, I sensed the dormant Guardian spirit within him, and he surprised me by asking me to look after his son before he moved on. Curious, I followed his essence first to your younger brother. Not sensing the spirit in him, I searched until I found you.

"I was saddened to find a young wolf covered in gore in the fighting pits, recognizing his rage as my own. The reason you feel that intensely is from your ancestral lineage, unbeknownst to you. The way your father abused that trait was despicable, and I commend you for pulling yourself through it, even though you feel as if you have not. I am sure that upon his death, your father had come to realize the mistakes he had made concerning you and he wanted me to rectify that. I have not intervened in any aspect of your life, though. I have simply observed you from afar," Hekate quietly informs me with a small, sad smile.

"I remember seeing you, when I was very young. You severed connection with our pack that day, after meeting with my father in the woods. That was when Selene awoke, wasn't it?" I mumble, lifting my gaze to hers. As she nods her head in confirmation, I ask, "How come you didn't sense my father's Guardian spirit then, in person?"

"I cannot sense the Guardian spirit because their magic is dormant in this realm. Only once the essence of your wolf separates from your human side at death can it be found. I try to assess each werewolf that passes through to the underground for this spirit and trace them the way I found you, but sometimes your kind dies in droves and it's difficult to find," she mutters with a shake of her head.

"My grandfather. I never met him, but my father told me he died in a great battle between wolves and vampires. You don't suppose—" Hekate's sly smile catches me off guard and I falter, pinching my brow. *No shit, huh?* I say on a breath. "My grandfather lived over fifteen hundred years ago, and he was one of the original Guardians?"

*Makes sense, no wonder why we're so badass,* Valdr says arrogantly, making me snort.

Hekate laughs loudly, her voice resembling the caw of a crow. "Like I said, crazy, *hmm?*" She waggles her eyebrows with a grin.

Selene stirs a little, burying her face into my neck as she sleeps. "I'm going to bring her to her bed," I say quietly, getting to my feet and carefully cradling her to my chest.

Walking over to the stairs, I glance back at Hekate. "Thank you for including me here, today. I have a much better understanding of things, especially with myself and aspects of my life. I will do my best to help Selene and her wolf in any way I can." Hekate bows her head briefly in acknowledgment. "Once I lay her down to rest, I'll be outside if you need me," I add, placing my foot on the first step.

"No need, *Custos.* She did ask for you to stay, no?" She grins widely before vanishing with a light breeze.

Blinking a few times, Asteria's sharp laugh echoes from the kitchen and I smile as I carry Selene up to her room, following the trail of her sweet scent. Stepping over the threshold, I take in her airy room, the walls painted a soft pastel green with a light pine wood ceiling and matching trim, a plush white carpet, and her small bed with a cozy white comforter. Leaning down, I pull the blanket back and gently lay her in the center of her bed, covering her carefully. Selene rolls over with a sigh and nestles into her pillow, remaining asleep.

Mindlinking Trey, I tell him, *Hey, I won't be home until some time tomorrow. I'm fine, so you don't need to worry.*

*Thanks for letting me know,* he replies immediately, his voice relieved.

Noticing the moon rising high outside, I rub my hand over my face, feeling worn out. Crossing her room, I sit by the balcony doors and lean back against the wall, facing Selene's bed. With her calming scent surrounding me and the sound of her steady breathing, I tip my head back, quickly drifting off to sleep.

## SELENE

I wake with a yawn, peeling my eyes open to soft, early morning light streaming in through my balcony windows. Immediately remembering yesterday, my eyes fly wide and I abruptly sit up, glancing around my room. I slump back against my pillows with a frown, staring at my ceiling fan as I wonder how long Kyran stayed after I had Ria put me to sleep.

*There's so many things I want to ask him. I want to see his wolf again, too,* I wonder wistfully, recalling his eerily beautiful form.

Sighing, I roll over, reaching for my phone on the nightstand and stifle a gasp when I find Kyran asleep on the floor beside my bed. I watch the way his broad chest slowly rises and falls, noticing how soft he looks while sleeping. There's no hardness to his features, no rigidity in his posture. Smiling, I carefully lift my phone and roll onto my back, snapping a photo of me and him. Opening the editor on my phone, I draw on the photo, making cute little clouds and stars surround him. Intending to send it to him as a joke, I open our text conversation with a grin, typing out a sarcastic message.

"Were you gonna stick my hand in a bowl of warm water, too?" Kyran's voice rumbles softly close by, startling me.

Hitting send, I accidentally drop my phone on my face, groaning. He chuckles and I turn to glare at him playfully. "You're *really quiet*. I'm sorry if I woke you," I say softly, placing my phone back on the nightstand.

Kyran pushes to his feet and stretches languidly. "I was already awake, I just…didn't want to seem like a creep, just sitting there staring," he mumbles, rubbing his neck.

I laugh and wiggle backward, patting the bed beside me. I slide the extra pillow over and fluff it up as Kyran carefully lays down beside me. Propping my head up on my elbow, I hesitantly smile. "I have some questions, if you don't mind answering some for me?"

Lying on his back, he pulls his arm up, resting his head on his hand and turns to look at me. "Sure, ask me anything," he quietly replies with a small smile.

I take a moment to think about where to begin. Deciding on what I last heard before needing to rest, I ask, "What is meant by 'mate'? Could you explain this, please? I don't believe my mother had mentioned that. Maybe she did, there was *a lot* to process yesterday," I mumble, thinking back on our conversations.

"No, she did not discuss that. You are correct. There's a lot involved with this, if you're ready to learn more," Kyran murmurs, giving me a questioning look.

I nod and he clears his throat, turning his head to look at the ceiling. "When Hekate created the werewolf race, she tied in the magic of what we call a mating bond, a spell that connects soulmates. This is the only way our race can reproduce. No pups are born outside of a mate bond. The only exception to this is if a witch lays with a wolf—bearing what we call a hybrid—but witches seldom choose to do so, for whatever reasons. Unmated wolves are virtually sterile, and I have never heard of one having a human parent.

"Humans also cannot hold the mate bond, meaning they mostly remain separate from our lives. Werewolves and humans only interact with each other in aspects of general living. Werewolf mate pairs, or soulmates, are usually born close in age from one another. This allows for a higher chance to meet. If one was born a few hundred years before their mate, they'd likely die without their mate ever being old enough to search for each other. It's clever, really, the way Hekate designed this magic. Sadly, though, there are wolves who spend their entire lives never finding their mate. I know of one, her name is Stjarna. She is just over seven hundred years old, still hopeful she'll find him someday." Kyran's voice grows quiet for a moment before he turns to look at me once more.

"Once a wolf's mate dies, regardless if they have bonded or never met, a patch of their fur color appears on the living mate's chest over their heart and is shown in wolf form. With mated wolves, due to the nature of the bond, the devastation that a death can cause most often results in the death of the living mate as well. The pain of it either drives them to seek reckless behaviors that kill them, such as fighting or thrill seeking, or they take their own life to cease the endless suffering. I personally know one wolf whose mate has passed and he still lives, though he carries the weight of it every day. His strength is very commendable." He stops speaking as he clenches his jaw, turning his head away toward the windows.

I ponder this for a moment, finding it romantic in a way. Knowing my mother created this bond doesn't surprise me. She has always held a soft spot for love, as far as I'm aware. My brow suddenly pinches as a thought occurs to me. "Kyran, when I saw your wolf, he had a light colored spot on his chest. I don't recall seeing any other coloring, he was completely black like a shadow. Did you lose your mate?" I whisper, my chest constricting at the thought of his pain.

He takes a deep breath and releases it slowly, looking back toward the ceiling. "I had not yet met her when my mark appeared," he replies quietly.

I exhale heavily and whisper, "The grief you must have felt— must *feel*—for the bond you never had." I shake my head sadly. "Oh, Kyran, that is so awful. I can only begin to imagine the anger, the *sadness* it must have brought with it when there should have been joy and love," I murmur, tears welling in my eyes at the thought of experiencing something like that.

His only response is a grunt and I realize this must *not* be something he'd like to discuss. "I-I'm sorry, Kyran. I shouldn't have asked," I whisper, gently placing my hand on his arm.

At my touch, he quickly turns his head, looking at me with a creased brow. He pushes himself up and leans back against my headboard. I get up as well, turning to sit cross legged in front of him, trying to understand his confused expression. *Did I misinterpret something?* I wonder worriedly as my eyes flick between his.

"Selene, there is nothing for you to apologize for, everything you said is true. It was devastating to one day see my reflection in the water and find that mark on my chest. I felt destroyed inside, my only hope of ever feeling something, *anything*, other than—" He abruptly cuts himself off, rubbing his hand over his face with a heavy sigh before meeting my gaze again.

"It is not a feeling I would wish upon anyone. But, I don't think you fully understand everything, Selene. My mark appeared roughly a hundred and fifty years ago, which I now know was the time you woke from stasis," he murmurs, watching me carefully.

Connecting the dots, I press my hand to my mouth, perplexed. "Last night, I—you—*we* heard...her. She said *'mate'*. Was she speaking *to you?*" I breathe out, and my eyes widen when he slowly nods. "But, your mark...this doesn't make sense at all. How could—but I'm not even sure—*ugh*." I drop my head into my hands, feeling frustrated as my mind races.

"I spoke with Hekate for a while about this last night," he murmurs, holding my gaze intently. "She thinks because you awoke but your wolf did not, it might have disrupted the magic that forms the mate bond. It could have triggered my end of it as if she had died, since she wasn't *technically* living, at the time. We both still don't quite understand it, but that's the only explanation we can come up with."

"Wait, *wait*. Hold on, my mother knows? Did you know about this, before?" I ask incredulously.

He sighs, nodding slightly. "Yes, I did, but *please* hear me out first, okay?" He leans forward with his brows raised pleadingly.

I narrow my eyes at him, a million thoughts and accusations crossing my mind before I silently nod, waiting for his explanation.

"When I first met you, in the store, I had no idea. It wasn't until the second day at the park that I felt it, when I pressed my hand to yours," he says quickly, pulling his eyebrows together.

Remembering that moment, my breath leaves me in a *huff*. "That wasn't a dream," I whisper, looking past Kyran as I recall my foggy memory. *"Ugh, Ria,"* I mutter, shaking my head.

"Definitely *not* a dream." He smiles crookedly before his mouth falls into a frown. "Selene, I don't want you to get the wrong impression. Before I was even *aware* of this bond, I...was drawn to you. I wanted to see you again, I couldn't get you out of my head. You captivated me that day I saw you in the store. Once I felt your touch in the park, I was extremely confused because I had my mark, and I couldn't make sense of anything I was feeling. Still, I wanted to keep seeing you, to get to know you. I'm glad we've connected, I truly enjoyed spending an entire day and night texting like a fucking teenager." He lets out a laugh, smiling boyishly at me, and I can't help but smile back.

"I *want* to get to know you more. I had fun talking about each other that day. I haven't spoken with someone like that in, well, forever," he murmurs, his cheeks flushing. "My point is, Selene, regardless of the bond magic, I like *you*, for who *you* are. And I'd like to know more of you, all of you, if you'll have me," he says quietly, running his hand through his hair.

My entire body relaxes beneath a blanket of heavy, comforting warmth as I stare into his amber eyes. No butterflies, no nerves or giddiness, just a simple, sure feeling enveloping me. I feel *safe*. I feel his truth, and I believe him.

Gently nodding, I smile warmly at him and take his hand in mine. "I feel the same way," I murmur in response.

Kyran smiles in disbelief at me, giving my hand a gentle squeeze and running his thumb over my knuckles. "There's more to understand, Selene, about mates. We—werewolves, that is—hold women with high regard. They bring us our life, and they hold the choice to either accept or deny the mate bond when it is presented. It isn't just an immediate binding that happens, when a mate-pair meets. The woman has the option to accept the man or deny him, permanently severing the bond magic.

"This differs from a death, however. Both man and woman then have another opportunity with a new mate bond, but the chances of that happening are beyond slim. Not impossible, but unlikely." He shakes his head, clearing his throat as he sits up straighter.

"Upon meeting, some wolves will offer their spirit to be assessed by the woman. Her wolf can glean who they are without the potential lies and deceits that words can bring. It is raw and vulnerable to offer oneself that way, though it shows the sincerity the wolf holds. Once a mate bond is formed, the only way it breaks is through death." Kyran sighs, holding my gaze intently.

I slowly exhale, amazed. "Wow, this is so fascinating. Humans are *so boring*," I say with a laugh. "How is the bond recognized?"

He smiles with a nod. "Through touch, in either human or wolf form. It's what makes it so rare to happen. Someone could walk past their mate and not even realize it unless they accidentally brush past one another, or help them reach something off a tall shelf in the grocery store," Kyran murmurs, looking down at our entwined hands.

I laugh, squeezing his fingers. Eager to learn as much as I can, I ask, "How many werewolves are there, do you know?"

He twists his mouth, thinking for a moment. "I'm not exactly sure. In my pack, I have just over three thousand wolves ranging from infant pups to elders, and it's is the largest pack in North America. With the other packs, there's roughly around, oh I don't know, maybe ten thousand or so, in our country? This does not include the rogues. They're werewolves who either refuse to swear allegiance with a pack or had been exiled from one. I'm not sure how many there are of them. It's somewhere in the thousands, though. As for the entire world, your guess is as good as mine." He laughs lightly, his eyes crinkling in the corners.

"I can see why the mate bond is considered a rare happenstance," I mumble, trying to wrap my head around it all.

"Yeah," he murmurs with a nod, raising his eyebrows. "That's why we hold the Convocation each year, to help encourage unmated wolves with an opportunity to potentially meet their mates."

"What happens there, at the Convocation?" I ask curiously, propping up my chin with my free hand, happy to watch him as he talks.

"The six packs of our country meet in an enormous, week-long gathering filled with celebrations, dancing, hunts, and, ah, well, lots of willing, unmated wolves," he smirks. "Their alpha's are present as well in case newly mated pairs are from different packs and want to join the other's.

"Each alpha hosts the Convocation respectably, to divvy up the responsibilities and the traveling required every year. This is actually my year to host the Convocation, and it's held on the week of the summer solstice, which isn't long from now. I would—what, what's wrong?" he abruptly asks, looking concerned as his gaze drifts back to my astonished face.

Stunned, I lean backward and my hand falls from his as I stare at him. "*You're an alpha?* Like, a leader? Top-dog, I—I mean top-wolf?" I stammer as sudden understanding dawns on me.

He nods, laughing. "Yeah, I guess I forgot to mention that. I don't really know *how* I could have told that to you though, you know?" He clears his throat, sitting up straight and holds his hand out. "Hi, nice to meet you. My name is Kyran Gennaíos, and I am the Alpha werewolf of the Rocky Mountain Region pack," he says mockingly with a toothy grin.

Giggling, I agree, "Yeah, I guess you're right. I would've turned and ran faster than The Flash." I grin and we both laugh.

In the pause after our humor fades, my stomach rumbles loudly. Kyran rises to his feet, smiling broadly. As I shuffle out of bed, he holds out his hand and I place mine in his. "So, what's your favorite thing to eat for breakfast?"

"*Hmm*, do you have any more of those muffins?" he jests, and we laugh together as we make our way downstairs.

While I make us breakfast, Kyran tells me about his brother and sister, a few of the people he is close with in his pack, and describes what his daily life is normally like. It is really interesting to learn how he and his people are very similar to regular humans, besides the magical ability to transform into wolves. Everyone has a job, skill, or purpose in his community, and most people get along well with one another. He says fighting does happen, but it's part of their nature to settle matters that way rather than through talking, which makes sense when I listen to his reasons. He let me know that rarely do these skirmishes result in serious injuries and if they do, werewolves have the ability to immediately heal most wounds. When necessary, a healer's magic is called upon. He reminds me of his healer, Eir, who had taken care of me after being poisoned with venom at his bar. Apparently, she wields special magic and there hasn't been anything other than the berserk wolves that she cannot heal.

As I finish the last bite of my breakfast, Kyran stands from the table and takes my plate to the sink, beginning to wash our dishes. I hurry over and try to pull him away.

"Oh, no, you don't need to—"

"Of course I do, you made me food. Which was delicious, by the way. I won't let you cook *and* clean for me. What am I, some kind of animal?" He flashes a wolfish grin at me over his shoulder.

My mouth twists up into a smile and I lean against the counter beside him, watching as he methodically scrubs and rinses our plates. I can't resist trailing my eyes up his arm, curious about his tattoos. I peer closer, my eyes following the intricate designs and shading, wondering how old they are. My gaze drifts, sweeping across his broad chest pulling his gray t-shirt taut and I admire his strength. I peek up at his face, finding him staring at me. He smirks when our eyes meet. I blush furiously, but I hold his gaze and smile cheekily back at him, making him laugh.

Pushing off the counter, I make my way toward the porch door, sighing dramatically. "Like I said last night, you're very distracting." I give him a wink over my shoulder.

"You have no idea, sweetheart," he murmurs, drying his hands on a towel and follows me.

I grin at him and head outside into the late morning sunshine, a thought nagging at me. Crossing through the lush grass, I meander toward the willow tree and take a seat on the bench beneath the sweeping branches. Kyran sits next to me a moment later, admiring the tree. When he glances at me, I chew on my lip, unsure how to ask him what I want.

"What is it, Selene?" he asks easily, throwing his arm across the back of the bench.

"Um, I was wondering…if you'd show me your wolf again?" I ask shyly, tucking some hair behind my ear.

A slow, wide smile grows on his face, eyes flashing brightly. My mind gives a dull throb in response at the sight. "He's eager to meet you again," Kyran says huskily, his voice rougher than before.

Unsure what to say, I swallow thickly as I gesture to the grass in front of us, watching nervously as he stands. Taking a few steps backward, Kyran removes his shirt, my eyes following his hands moving toward his sweatpants. My cheeks flush warmly and he gives me a devilish grin before his entire body shimmers, blurring for a moment as he shifts into his wolf.

Long, sleek black legs step out of the pants pooled on the ground.

Astonished, I press a hand to my mouth and gasp as the enormous wolf shakes his midnight fur, watching me with those stunning eyes. His head is higher than mine while I sit, and carefully rising to my feet, I find I'm not much taller than him.

*He's massive. This is amazing! He looks so soft.*

I stare in wonder as my eyes flit over his body. His paws are huge, the same width as my outspread hand and tipped with sharp claws. Slowly walking around him, it takes a few steps for me to reach his tail, and I realize exactly *how big* he is.

As I make my way up toward his head again, I reach my hand out, tentatively pushing my fingers into his heated black fur. A light vibration rumbles through his body, similar to a cat's purr, and it makes me smile. Stepping in front of him, I scratch my fingers along his neck and he lifts his head, clearly enjoying it. Raising my other hand, I reach up to rub his ears and laugh when his rumbling intensifies. He drops his head, jaws parting, and I stare wide-eyed at his menacing teeth.

Swallowing thickly, I glance into his amber eyes and murmur, "Well, I can see why they call it a *wolfish* grin."

His eyes narrow with humor and I smirk at him, scratching his chin lightly. A tingling sensation trickles down my neck, drifting throughout my body as I hold his gaze. Leaning forward, I slowly press my forehead to his. Our eyes close upon contact and a comforting warmth accompanies the tingling as I remain connected with his wolf.

*What is your name?* I ask in my mind, intentionally pushing my thoughts toward him.

*Valdr,* a gravelly, rough voice responds, giving me goosebumps.

*Diko mou,* the crystalline, ethereal voice resonates deep within me once more, this time louder than before.

Gasping, my eyes fly open and a soft growl emanates from Valdr.

*Drottning min,* he responds immediately, pushing gently against me and nuzzles my neck with his nose.

Stumbling backward, I fall onto the bench and absently rub my forehead. "What was that? What did she say? What did *you* say?" I whisper, shocked.

*She said 'mine' in Greek, and he said 'my queen' in Old Norse, their respective origin languages. Valdr's soul is connected to his ancestors of the first werewolves, and yours is…well, the original soul,* Kyran's familiar deep voice caresses my mind, helping me understand.

Smiling at the sensation of hearing him this way, I nod and close my eyes. Focusing inwardly, I ask, *What is your name? I cannot remember anything of my…our past. If you're unaware, it's been a very, very long time.*

I am only met with silence for a moment, then a slight pressure builds in my head, similar to a headache, but without the pain. Scrunching my brow, I open my eyes and glance at Valdr. "I can't hear her, but I think I can feel her energy?"

He steps forward and pushes his head beneath my hands, resting his chin on my lap. The moment we touch, her voice bursts into my mind in a rush.

*I can hear you, Selene, but when I try to communicate with you, it is as if I'm speaking underwater. Luna, my name is Luna. The last thing I remember was agreeing to let Hekate place us under stasis, to protect us from the vampires. It feels as if I've been deeply asleep, only to suddenly wake to a warm, enticing pull toward sunshine and cedar trees. To what feels like where I belong, to my home. Him. It feels like flying in sunlight when we touch him. Don't ever let go, I don't want to go back into the darkness. I don't know how to get out, I feel stuck, immobile. Selene, get me out! I can't stay like this—*

Reeling from her tumultuous emotions, I lift Valdr's head from my lap and hurry away from the bench with hot tears pouring down my face. Feeling overwhelmed, I keep walking and take a few uneven deep breaths, trying to process everything as best I can. My head feels like a balloon has inflated inside me, threatening to burst.

"Hey, hey, it's alright," Kyran's voice hushes from behind me. His warm hands gently grasp my shoulders, turning me as he pulls me into his chest. "This is a lot, I know. I heard her too, she sounds scared beneath her excitement. We will do whatever we can to help you, *both of you*, okay? Take all the time you need though, Selene, the past few days have been tremendous," he murmurs comfortingly, stroking my hair and holding me close.

Sniffling, I nod and tightly wrap my arms around his thick torso. The pressure in my head eases, but Luna's voice does not reappear. She seems comforted as well, thankfully. We stay like this for a few minutes, Kyran never wavering and giving me time to collect myself. Pulling away, I wipe my face with the backs of my hands and look up at him with a small smile.

"Thank you, for not being upset," I say quietly.

His brow pinches. "About what? I understand her distress, and *yours*, for that matter. I honestly don't think I'd be handling any of this remotely close to okay if I were you."

"N-no, I mean, for giving me space to *feel* all of this. I've never…had that," I admit with embarrassment, glancing away.

"Selene." He reaches out, brushing his fingertips over my chin and gently turns my face towards his. "You can say, do, or show me *anything,* and I will not judge you or berate you for a single part of it. I know from personal experience just how awful it can be to shove shit down inside, to let it fester and rot. To have someone hurt you with your own feelings is a terrible thing to experience, and I am sorry for that, truly. Trust me, I will *never* be that person to you. I promise," he says seriously, intently holding my gaze.

Stunned, my eyebrows pull upward with a genuine smile. I take his hand in mine and squeeze it tightly. "Thank you, Kyran. As will I, for you, if you ever need me," I whisper, watching his warm smile grow.

Tugging his hand, I walk toward the cottage with Kyran. "I want to get Luna free, whatever it takes," I say softly after a few quiet moments.

"We will," he assures me, gently rubbing his thumb over my knuckles. "I'm not entirely sure how, but we will."

Thinking back on what Luna had said, I pause my steps. "I might have an idea of something we could try, if you're up for it?" I grin mischievously at Kyran and he nods right away without hesitation, giving me a bright smile.

"I'm up for anything with you, sweetheart," he murmurs, his amber eyes flashing brightly.

I smile and pull Kyran toward the woods, my heart fluttering faster with each step.

# CHAPTER FOURTEEN

## FLARING

### KYRAN

Selene's laughter rings out melodically, echoing around the forest as I bound through the trees with her on my back. My spirit feels free with her like this, as if I'm soaring instead of running and I've never felt anything like it before. The warm sun filters through the branches, casting everything in a hazy glow. The only sounds are my paws thumping a beat on the earth to the song that is Selene's joy.

*"Faster!"* she calls on a laugh, giving my sides a little squeeze with her legs.

*Hold on,* I mindlink her, and her hands grip into the fur at my shoulders.

I launch us forward with a burst of power. She squeals delightfully, her arms wrapping around my neck, not quite making a full circle. I growl lightly in amusement. Careful not to accidentally lose Selene, I don't run at my fastest speed, but I push my legs hard enough to give her a thrill. Trees *whoosh* by in a blur as I dodge around them, choosing my path at random as I go, running aimlessly through the forest. A few moments pass before I notice a brightness up ahead and make my way toward it, hoping it'll be a field.

With my wish granted no sooner than I thought it, we burst from the shadowy woods into an open field of wildflowers, dozens of acres wide. With glee, I quickly mindlink Selene, *Want to see how fast I can run?*

Her limbs tighten in response and I push my body into a flat out sprint. Small grunts leave my chest with each exhale, and a pealing scream mixed with excitement and fear tears from Selene, followed by wild, bubbling laughter. Wind whips past as we fly across the field until I gradually slow my stride, loping around in a wide circle before coming to a stop. Crouching low, I flop onto my belly and Selene slides sideways off my back, falling into the grass beside me.

I've never felt more alive.

Chest heaving rapidly, I glance at Selene, enjoying the wide grin she has plastered on her face. Her hair is billowed around her in a silvery cloud, icy eyes shining brightly, creamy skin glowing like starlight. She's the most amazing woman I have ever seen.

*You are breathtaking, Selene. So beautiful,* I mindlink her admirably, liking the way her cheeks flush a rosy pink.

She sits up and reaches toward me, brushing her hand against the side of my face. "You are too, like this *and* in your human form. You have a beautiful soul, and I see it in you as much as it shows outwardly," she murmurs, smiling brightly.

Impulsively, I lean down and lick the side of her face. She laughs and playfully pushes at my muzzle. Completely unfamiliar feelings consume me. Warmth and fuzziness, light, airy joy, and *freedom.* For so long I've always felt weighed down by my suffocating darkness, suffering endlessly while pretending I'm fine on the outside. But I don't *need* to pretend, with her. She gives me the peace I didn't realize I've been silently screaming for all my life.

Closing my eyes, a heated tear slips free and Selene's gentle hand presses to my face.

"Kyran? What's wrong?" she quickly asks, her soft voice concerned as she pushes her fingers into my fur.

A quiet, low growl rumbles through my chest at her touch. I open my eyes, and Selene stares at me with worry.

*Nothing is wrong,* I mindlink quietly. *I'm very happy. You make me feel free, Selene, and I can't express to you what that is like, for me. I am very grateful to have met you.* I gently press my snout to her belly.

She laughs lightly, pushing her hands beneath my chin. I raise my head, gazing into her gleaming, crystal eyes that sparkle with unshed tears. "I understand that more than you know," she whispers and leans forward, kissing the tip of my nose.

My tail *thumps* softly against the ground. Selene grins with a chuckle and leans back to remove her sweatshirt, baring her small torso as she lifts her arms. I can't help but yearn to run my hands along her smooth skin, to follow the curves of her body. Resting my head on my paws, I blink lazily at her, watching as she runs her fingers through her hair. She smiles adorably when she notices me staring.

*I like when you scrunch your nose. It's cute,* I tell her, earning a laugh as she blushes and intentionally scrunches her nose at me.

"Shift back. I want to ask you some more questions about wolves," she demands, giving me a smirk.

*Mmm, yes ma'am,* I respond with a light growl, making her snort a laugh as I shift to my human form.

Selene holds out her sweatshirt for me, mumbling, "Here, you can, um, cover yourself with this. Because, you know, *distracting*." She waves her hand around the air with another blush.

I chuckle and take her sweatshirt, placing it in my lap as I sit up. Selene rests her elbows on her knees, propping her chin up in her hands with an eager expression. Ready to answer any question she has, I lean back on my hands with an easy smile.

"What would you like to know?"

## SELENE

I lose track of my thoughts as my gaze drifts down Kyran's bare body, over his tanned skin glowing warmly in the sun, his thick muscles on full display. I so badly *wish* I was bold enough to keep my sweatshirt from him, but I don't think I could bring myself to actually *do that,* and I wouldn't want to possibly make him feel uncomfortable, either. He clears his throat, tearing my attention back to his face and my heartbeat flutters.

With my face aflame, I bite my lip and scrunch my eyes closed, muttering, "I'm so sorry." I peek one eye open at him. "I'm staring at you like you're a plate of fresh baked cookies, *again*. That's rude of me," I murmur, embarrassed.

Kyran gives me a crooked grin. "It's alright, I don't mind. If anything, I actually appreciate your honesty. I've, ah, found myself doing the same, you just haven't caught me yet," he admits, rubbing his neck with a light laugh.

We gaze at each other for a breath, then both of us laugh as the awkwardness fades into comfort.

Straightening, I propose, "Okay, how about this, if either of us does or says something that makes the other uncomfortable, it's up to you or me to explicitly voice that concern. Otherwise, we both have the opportunity to…*express* ourselves with each other, freely. Deal?" I raise my eyebrows at him, holding out my hand with a mischievous smile.

"Deal." He laughs, clasping my hand. His brow lowers a bit, and he quietly asks, "Is there *anything* you don't want me to do that might really upset you? I don't want to accidentally cause you distress, Selene." He reaches out and gently brushes his hand over my knee.

I frown at how his question triggers a few rough memories to briefly surface. I swiftly dismiss each one, not wanting to dwell on them at this moment. Slowly shaking my head, I look up into his eyes, knowing my answer.

"No, Kyran, I don't believe you would intentionally do anything that would upset me. I *trust* that you wouldn't. The only thing I can think of that might make me distressed would be if you were to, um, *touch me* in my sleep, or forcefully control me…physically," I say quietly, looking down and picking at the hem of my t-shirt with shame.

When Kyran doesn't respond, I glance up at him timidly. He's clenching his jaw, a stricken expression shadowing his face when he drags his gaze down to mine.

"*Selene,*" he whispers heavily, "I would *never* touch you sexually without your permission. Even now, after our agreement with one another. That is something that should be honest and real, not played on like a game or bending the rules. Whatever has happened to you, I am here for you *whenever* you need to talk, or even to just let it out, in any way you need to." He pauses to take a breath, his voice rough with his emotion.

Pain shines in his warm eyes. "Though I do not know your specific details, I do understand what it's like to be...*manipulated* in that way. I'd never—you are becoming so precious to me, I couldn't—"

Tears slip from my eyes at his words. With my heart leaping from my chest, I throw myself forward and wrap my arms around his neck, crashing my lips against his.

Kyran's warm hands splay on my back and he sighs against my mouth. His arms slide around me, holding me close. Electricity tingles beneath every part of my skin that touches his, and my blood sings with the warmth that blooms deep within my body. He feels *right*. He feels like *home*.

A few blissful moments pass before I pull back, my breathing a bit ragged, and he gently cups my face. He grins crookedly and I huff a laugh, grinning back. Leaning forward, Kyran briefly presses his forehead to mine before lightly kissing the place between my brows.

"So, what questions did you want to ask me?" he murmurs, the smile never fading from his handsome face as he strokes my cheek with his thumb.

Reaching up, I take his hand in mine and blink a few times, needing to focus my thoughts.

Remembering some details from earlier, I decide to ask, "You told me about mates earlier and it made me curious, what are the other aspects to werewolves? How do alphas differ from the regular wolves? And what exactly are the hybrids you mentioned? Oh, when my mother was explaining things, I heard you mention the white wolf, why was that specific? I know now that is *my wolf*, Luna. What does—oh, oops, I'm sorry." I press my hand to my mouth, feeling embarrassed for rambling incessantly.

Kyran's eyes crinkle from his wide smile and he chuckles. "It's alright, I followed what you're saying. I understand how overwhelming this all must be to learn." He sighs. "To start, werewolves' fur coats are colored the same as their natural hair in human form. Their eyes match as well, and mates are never of the same coloring, though I don't really know why. Alpha wolves always have black fur, and no other wolves will be. Besides black, regular werewolf fur ranges in all colors you'd see naturally in hair, and in all different shades as well. Some even have a mixture of tones, though no patterns. The older a wolf gets, the grayer their hair and fur becomes, quite similar to normal humans as they age." An easy smile spreads on his handsome face as he absently fiddles with my fingers.

"There are not any white wolves, however. There never has been, except for in the legend. He clears his throat, reciting in a dramatic voice, *'A mysterious, all-powerful ruling wolf once roamed the earth, her magic capable of healing the damned and strengthening those around her.'*"

I laugh, gesturing for him to continue.

"I've only met two wolves—a mated pair of elders in my pack—that claim to have seen this great white wolf, once upon a time. The story of your wolf stretched back over a millennium, and most wolves only believe it to be just that, a tale. I wonder if Luna would recognize them, Eirene and Chrestotes, if you met them again," Kyran muses aloud, tracing the lines on my palm.

A slight pressure pushes in my mind before Luna's voice murmurs, *Yes, I do know them. We helped them communicate while they were held imprisoned away from each other.*

Kyran smiles broadly at me, raising his eyebrows. "Well, I'm sure each of them would be *very* grateful to speak with you. If you would like, I can have them meet with you when you're ready," he offers kindly.

I smile back at him, nodding my head a little and wait for him to continue explaining the werewolf culture to me.

Kyran is quiet with his thoughts for a few moments before he clears his throat again. "In regards to alpha wolves, we hold power over wolves who swear allegiance or loyalty to us, forming our packs. Some have been known to abuse that power, behaving in a similar manner to that of a human dictator. Alpha wolves are either born through a bloodline, or assume the position by killing an alpha and taking his place. If an alpha willingly steps down, his eldest son becomes the new alpha through transference of power, or he can be challenged by his son in a fight for position. Any male can challenge an alpha, though the fight will go until one of them yields or dies.

"If a new male becomes alpha, his hair and fur color will magically alter to black, marking his status. Generally, many wolves do not respect an alpha through transference because they feel he did not *earn* the position. Likewise, some view outright murdering for it to be a despicable grab for power, unless it was death from an agreed upon challenge.

"As for our power, we can force any wolf in our pack to submit to our will, whether they want to or not. This is what I meant by the abuse of power. I personally only use this when *absolutely* necessary, *never* just because something isn't going my way or someone refuses my command. I don't believe in taking someone's free will just to suit my whims." His voice goes flat as he picks at the grass with a tight expression. "I actually had to do this recently, with someone who'd betrayed us."

I'm at a loss for what to say as I absorb everything Kyran tells me. When he looks at me once more, I meet his gaze with a soft smile, nodding encouragingly. After a few quiet moments, he takes a deep breath and continues describing his culture.

"When it comes to other wolves, either from another pack or a rogue, they naturally feel the instinct to submit when around an alpha. Most of the time, they keep a distance if he isn't their leader, to discourage the threat of a challenge. This happens when a male wolf won't submit or look away from an alpha in either wolf or human form. Most often the fight is brutal but quick, usually ending in the death of the challenger. If it's a female, it most likely means she wants to get laid, and she will," he says jokingly with a dry laugh. "Unless he's mated, then may she rest easy, because a pissed-off female mate is not fun to be around, *ever.*" He dramatically widens his eyes and I laugh, playfully pushing his shoulder.

Scrunching my brow, I curiously ask, "How did you become Alpha?" I draw circles on his palm with my fingertip, enjoying listening to his husky voice as he teaches me about the fascinating supernatural world.

The humor fades from Kyran's face and he pulls his hand from mine. Rubbing his mouth, he glances away. "I killed my father," he says quietly, not looking at me.

Stifling my shock, I sense there's more to it than that, so I gently ask, "Why, what was the reason?"

Watching his jaw clench, I can tell this isn't an easy thing for him to discuss. "You don't have to—"

"He was bitten by vampires, trying to protect my mother when she was abducted by them," he explains with a rough voice. "My older brother Einarr was supposed to be Alpha. Not me. But he died that day protecting our mother, along with our sister Kara, Trey and

Kira's triplet. I got there too late. I chased after the vampires that took my mother and tore apart any of the ones I could reach until they seemed to just…vanish." Kyran sighs roughly, fingers picking at the grass.

"My father's distress and rage at my mother's disappearance made him dangerous. He became berserk from his bite, slaughtering innocent wolves in our pack. As he lost control over his wolf, people feared for their lives, living in turmoil with him as Alpha that way. I had to…*handle* my father in order to protect everyone else from the same fate." His voice trails off as he stares away into his memories.

Feeling his pain, I grasp his hand tightly, remaining silent. No words could help soothe that kind of wound. After a moment, Kyran clears his throat, looking at me once more.

"Hybrid wolves are the product of a male werewolf impregnating a witch," he states with a change of subject, back to explaining the werewolf culture.

I give him a small smile and squeeze his hand reassuringly.

"They are werewolves who wield varying levels of magic, dependent on the power their mother harnesses. There aren't many hybrids, mostly because witches generally choose to remain impartial to other supernaturals and their affairs. If a witch decides to bear a hybrid child, it would be wise to assume she has reasoning to do so, who-knows-what for. You can always tell a hybrid wolf by her eyes. They will have some form of purple shading, similar to how a witch's eyes appear." He speaks indifferently, neither in favor nor opposed to them.

A memory flashes of my night at his bar. "That redhead, at your bar. The waitress. She had indigo colored eyes. Is she a hybrid wolf?" I ask curiously.

He nods silently, his mouth pulling into a flat line. Picking up on his distaste, I raise my eyebrow in question. Kyran sighs, leaning back on the hand I'm not holding.

"That was Vala, who you…*met*. She is—ah, *was*—my lead hybrid warrior. There are a total of eight hybrids in my pack, and each are trained in combat to use their witch magic both defensively and offensively. Eir is the only exception, she will not fight because she does not believe her powers are to be used to bring harm upon others. I am unsure if she even *is* a witch, though." He trails off for a moment before lightly shaking his head.

"Anyway, Vala is a powerful hybrid. She claims her mother raised her with ancient magic rituals and practice. She specializes in both psychic and illusion magic, she can make you believe anything she wishes. Vala can create an extremely realistic mirage, leaving her victim unaware unless they try to touch it. Pair *that* with physical combat training and she is nearly unstoppable to fight against." Kyran looks at me with a slight grimace.

"What's that face for?" I ask hesitantly, *hoping like hell* they aren't currently romantically involved.

My chest constricts at the thought as a foreign, prickly heat of jealousy courses through me.

"She happens to be my ex-girlfriend, and I have reason to believe she was involved with what happened to you at my bar Saturday night. I don't know *why* that happened, or her reason for involvement, but she has been...dealt with. I don't intend on speaking with her again until I learn more about that night, if I can." His face is hard as he stares out across the field.

My mouth twists a little as I think about this new information. "How long ago did you break up?" I ask with genuine curiosity, my chest relaxing with relief.

With a sigh, Kyran looks to the sky, mumbling, "You're really making me lay it all out there, huh?"

His sarcastic tone pulls a smirk to my lips. Composing myself, I quickly assure him, "If you don't want to talk about it, I completely understand." I smile gently and twine my fingers with his.

Meeting my gaze, he lifts the corner of his mouth. "It's alright. I'm past it now, even though it did affect me for quite some time." He pauses, taking a breath to collect his thoughts. "Years before becoming Alpha, when I was still young, I met Vala in a...shady part of the city. I wasn't home often, and thinking back on it, my relationship with her could have been avoided had my mother been aware of it. She knew me too well, my mother, she would've known something was wrong." He sighs heavily, briefly closing his eyes.

"Anyway, Vala was the first female to actively pursue interest in me. A few had tried to before, but I was not the most approachable guy back then. We had a noncommittal hookup one night after she incessantly followed me for days, showing up in places I wouldn't have expected to find a woman. After that night, I thought she was my mate. I was infatuated with her, couldn't get her off my mind, and she became an obsession for a while. We would constantly have terrible fights over things I can't recall now, but they felt like the biggest issues, at the time. Our relationship wasn't healthy and I knew it, but I didn't care much to make a change because I believed I'd found my soulmate. My life was very volatile with her and I wondered for a while, if this was really what mate bonds were like, why would people fantasize about them like they were a dream come true?" Kyran's voice drifts away as he absently rubs his chest with his free hand.

Giving the hand I hold a little squeeze in encouragement, he meets my gaze once more and finishes explaining.

"It wasn't until my mark appeared that I discovered her illusion. Vala had been magically manipulating my emotional reality into believing she was my true mate. So, upon learning *that,* I had to process that my *real* mate had just died. My pain was so immense that the despair was too much for me to handle. I wanted to kill her at that moment. My hatred became so intense that I feared I actually *would,* so I left, disappearing from everyone for years. No matter how much my father commanded, I wouldn't return. Not until the night my mother was taken." He lets out a deep breath, running his hand over his face.

A small exhale leaves my parted lips and I grip his hand in both of mine. "That is just awful, Kyran. Truly awful. How—*why the fuck* is she still around today?" I ask harshly, a rare anger flaring inside me at the thought of him being around someone who has caused him so much pain.

He lets out a humorless laugh and his mouth twists to the side. "Once I became Alpha, I knew our pack needed her power and I chose to set aside my personal bullshit to protect them as best I could. Given the fact that I was pretty awful at being an Alpha for a while, it was the best place I could think of to start, with the intention to be a good one. I had requested her allegiance in exchange for my forgiveness for her despicable actions, and she eagerly accepted.

"Over time, Vala worked her way higher in the pack, proving her place through her capabilities. I had made her swear a binding vow to never use her abilities against anyone in my pack. She has, in the past, made attempts at regaining my affection, but after learning the truth of what she'd done to me, I have never looked at her as more than a member of my pack. I'll admit, I still harbor regret of ever meeting her. But I have to say, life has a very peculiar way of working itself out," he murmurs and smiles crookedly at me, lightly tugging on my hand.

Leaning over, I let go of his hand and wrap my arms around his middle, squeezing him tightly. Kyran curls an arm around my shoulders, running his hand along my side.

"I am sorry for the pain you've endured because of my mark," I whisper against his chest, "as well as everything else brought upon you by others." My lip quivers with sudden emotion and his arm tightens around me comfortingly.

"It is nothing you need to apologize for, sweetheart. I am just grateful to be sitting here today, with you," he murmurs into my hair, lightly squeezing my shoulder, and I close my eyes with a smile.

We sit in comfortable silence together for a while, with me listening to his steady heartbeat while he glides his hand through my hair. Glancing up, I abruptly realize how long we must have been gone for. Faint specks of stars peek through the clouds as dusk slowly dims the sky and I let out a soft sigh. Kyran follows my gaze and rubs his hand down my arm before withdrawing, making me yearn for his touch as his warmth fades away.

"Let's get you home," he murmurs. "I'm more than content to sleep in the woods, but I doubt you are."

I scrunch my nose in distaste and he smirks, leaning forward to kiss the top of my head.

"Thank you, Kyran. Not just for taking me on a run, but for being open and trusting me with the vulnerable parts of yourself," I say quietly, resting my hand against his chest, over his heart.

"*Mmm.*" His chest rumbles. "I don't think I could keep anything from you that you ask of me, sweetheart," he murmurs, pressing his forehead to mine before swiftly shifting to his wolf.

He licks the side of my face and gives me a toothy, open-mouthed grin.

"*Argh!*" I laugh, playfully pushing him away and scoop up my sweatshirt as I stand. Pulling it over my head, I can't help but breathe in his rich, earthy scent and I smile at the ground. Kyran nudges my belly with his snout and crouches low, waiting. I climb onto his back just behind his shoulders and wrap my arms around his neck, hugging him tightly. As he stands, he lifts his head toward the sky then takes off at an easy lope across the field.

"How do you know where to go?" I ask in wonder, the wind lightly blowing my hair around my face.

*The stars. I know where your cottage is beneath the sky. We're not too far, maybe only a few minutes away.* His husky voice caresses my mind and I shiver, most certainly *not* from the wind.

I let my thoughts drift as he expertly carries me through the dark woods, feeling completely safe from danger with him. I brush my fingers against my mouth, recalling the warm softness of his lips against mine and smile wide. It seems crazy, the intensity I feel toward him with only knowing him for such a short time, but it doesn't *feel* crazy. It feels *right,* like pressing the final puzzle piece into its place, or turning a key in its lock.

A gentle humming resonates from within me, lightly vibrating my body, and I find that my hands are glowing when I push up against Kyran's back.

Euphoric laughter bubbles and pours out of me as I sit upright, adjusting to the movements while Kyran runs. Feeling completely free, I grip his sides with my legs and throw my arms out wide, more laughter escaping me. Tipping my head back and yelling recklessly at the sky, Kyran joins me, his deep howl resonating all around us as we race through the trees. My voice screeches into a shriek when Kyran's back disappears from beneath me and I hurl through open air, my limbs flailing frantically.

Strong, warm arms wrap around my waist, catching me before I hit the ground. My breath leaves me in a *whoosh* as he swings around, my legs flying out in front of me. Giggling wildly, I grab onto his arms, tipping my head back against his chest until he stops spinning and plops us down beside a tree, placing me gently on the ground between his legs. The stubble of his chin scratches my neck before he rests it on my shoulder, squeezing me tightly around my middle.

"I am really grateful to have found you, Selene," he murmurs in my ear, burying his face at the crook of my neck. "I wasn't even looking." His whispered words tickle against my skin.

A warm smile spreads across my face and I chew my lip nervously, thinking about a question I feel I already know the answer to. Pressing my lips together, I take a slow breath and prompt in a whisper, "Ky?"

I bite my lip again in the short silence.

*"Hmm?"* He rumbles quietly, his breath caressing my neck.

"How is the mate bond formed, when the woman chooses to accept the man?" I murmur the question, lightly gliding my fingertips across his thick forearms.

He flexes his arms around me. "If she doesn't say the words of rejection—"

"What's that? Oh, I'm sorry," I mutter, grimacing at my interruption.

Kyran breathes a laugh against my neck. "It's alright, don't apologize. The female has the choice to reject the male by saying, *'I reject this bond,'* or *'I reject you,'* but she'll use his name. It's the opposite for acceptance. If she accepts, the pair then lay with each other, hence the name of 'mating bond'. Much like the old human marriage tradition of consummation, werewolves become truly bound to one another through body, mind, and soul in that moment. The stories I've heard tell of an experience unlike anything else, some of pure euphoria and some of extreme emotion. It's a beautiful thing, really." His voice drifts off and he presses a light kiss to my shoulder.

Pushing myself upright, Kyran releases his hold around me and I turn to face him. My cheeks flush when I meet his gaze and he gives me a lopsided smile, making me grin widely. Another question rises and I narrow my eyes, wondering how this works.

Pursing my lips, I ask, "How long does the pair have before a choice must be made? Is it instantly upon meeting, or can they continue on living without the decision being made?"

Kyran tips his head back against the tree and takes my hand, absently playing with my fingers. "Most are usually decided very shortly after meeting, though I do know of some pairs that had gone weeks without a choice being made. I do not know the reasons why, but I do know that they all had a hard time focusing on anything else other than getting back to one another. It was as if the bond magic became magnetized, pulling the pairs together regardless of how far apart they were. I, uh, kind of experienced it myself this past week," he admits, lightly rubbing his free hand across his bare chest.

"What do you mean?" I ask curiously, trying to keep my gaze on his eyes.

He lifts his hand and runs it through his hair, slightly grimacing. "Please don't take this the wrong way, but every night I would find myself here, in these woods. I didn't understand what it was at first, but I was being drawn to you, to be close to you. Valdr would run here unknowingly. He said it felt like a pull from within that got stronger if he went in any other direction. That blackthorn over there is where I'd wake each morning at sunrise." He gestures past me and releases my fingers.

Rising to my feet, I take a few steps away from him, observing the large shrub he indicated. I notice how the earth beneath it is packed down and cleared, showing its disturbance compared to the messy forest floor around it. Glancing upward, I push some branches out of the way. I'm at the edge of the woods with my favorite willow not far beyond, my bedroom visible from where I stand. Recalling how Kyran said he'd find himself here at sunrise, my lips part as I realize that's when I would wake on my balcony each morning as well.

Looking over my shoulder, I turn to tell Kyran this realization, but I squeak in surprise when I find him standing behind me. "You're *so quiet!*" I huff with a laugh, playfully swatting him on the chest.

"I'm sorry, I wasn't trying to sneak up on you." He takes a step backward and runs his hand through his hair. "I know how this looks, but please trust that I never watched you. I left quickly each time I woke, I only ever saw you standing on your balcony. I wouldn't—"

"Ky, it's okay, it's alright. I believe you," I reassure him quickly. "I was going to tell you that I've been waking at dawn every day, finding myself on my balcony as if I was sleepwalking. I would have a reoccurring dream, which actually happened to play out in real life yesterday. I think...I also feel the pull, deep in my chest. It eases whenever I'm near you, and my head doesn't hurt. I think that's Luna, pushing at her barriers and responding to the bond magic. It all makes sense now," I whisper, staring blankly out into the dark woods.

Kyran hesitantly takes a step forward, drawing my attention back to him. I'm abruptly reminded of his nakedness and my eyes involuntarily roam his body. My body flushes warmly when my gaze drifts below his tapered hips, and I swiftly recall how we were sitting moments ago. It doesn't feel off-putting to me, though. *I am comfortable with him,* I realize with a smile as I continue to appreciate his powerful physique. His body is thick with well-defined muscles, his bronze skin taut over the chiseled dips and full, rounded edges, and I find myself longing to caress every inch of him. When my gaze flits over his face, his amber eyes flash brightly and I press my hand to my mouth.

"I'm sorry!" I quickly apologize, glancing away from him with a furious blush.

He laughs and I peek back at him, seeing the amused ease on his face. "Have me as much as you'd like, sweetheart. I have nothing to hide from you. I'm all yours," he rumbles softly, spreading his arms wide and giving me a heated smile.

I bite my lip as I step towards him and reach my hand out, slowly tracing the network of small scars visible through the tattoos on his broad chest. Electricity buzzes beneath my skin as I glide my fingers over his body. I follow the thick lines that run up his shoulder and along the side of his throat, watching Kyran's face as my fingers rest at the nape of his neck. He closes his eyes and reaches up to press his palm to my fingers, but he does not remove my hand from his brutal scars.

"What happened, Kyran? If werewolves have healing capabilities, how come you have these scars, all of them?" I ask him softly, my brow creasing with concern and sorrow. "These two feel very deep, what would cause something like this?"

He takes a slow breath and opens his eyes to respond. "I—" he huffs out a sigh, "I got these from—"

Kyran's entire body goes rigid, his face twisting into a mean snarl. A menacing growl rips from his chest and I drop my hand immediately, afraid that I've upset him. He clenches his jaw, and his arms and chest thicken as he flexes in anger.

"Kyran, I-I'm sorry, I didn't mean to...I won't ask again," I say meekly, worried I brought memories back he'd rather not share.

*"Hekate!"* He bellows and I jump from the sudden noise.

With a gust of wind, my mother appears beside us, her violet eyes whipping between him and I. Misunderstanding seeps into anger on her face and her gaze pierces into Kyran.

"No, Mother, it's nothing like—"

"Hekate, I need you to send me home," Kyran interrupts me hastily, rage making his voice hard and cold.

I look at him pleadingly, feeling so sorry for causing this. It hurts to know that he carries the pain of his past with him. I know all too well how that can affect life, and I do not want that for him.

A painful throb pulses through my head and I wince, a whimper escaping me as I press my hand to my temple. Kyran looks at me sharply and gently cups my face in his warm hands. My pain immediately dissipates at his touch.

Luna's urgent voice bursts in my mind.

*Go! I wish I could help you. Please stay safe,* she breathes hurriedly.

My brow pinches in confusion, but before I can speak, Kyran leans forward and kisses my forehead softly. He presses his head to mine, looking into my eyes.

"I am not upset with you. I will explain another time, but I *have* to go. My pack is under attack." He speaks gently, but his voice is tense.

As he pulls away, I lean up and kiss him lightly, whispering, "Please be careful. Let me know you're okay."

He silently nods and turns to Hekate. She raises her hand, asking, "Anyplace specifically?"

Kyran's eyes are unfocused for a moment before a grimace pulls his mouth downward. His gaze snaps to my mother's. "Eastern fields, near the woods."

She nods once and Kyran swiftly shifts. His enormous wolf bares his teeth and looks extremely intimidating. I don't feel any fear, though, just concern and some awe at his powerful presence. My mother waves her hand and Kyran vanishes.

"Be wise, *Custos*," she whispers, her voice quietly echoing behind him.

Concerned for what he will be going up against, I ask, "What does he mean by his pack being under attack?"

My mother turns to me, her mouth drawn into a tight line. I rarely see her angry, so I know this must be really serious, and I clasp my hands together anxiously.

"Vampires. They have his sister," she answers me gravely.

# CHAPTER FIFTEEN

## BRUTALITY

### KYRAN

My paws hit the ground running, pounding into the earth toward the chaos in the woods. The pungent metallic tang of blood assaults me, the grassy field coated in it from both vampires and wolves. I force myself not to look closely at the lifeless bodies littering the ground, keeping my attention on the trees as I break through the forest edge. Tearing into an oncoming vampire's neck with my jaws, I rip his head off and keep running without missing a step.

*Where is she?* I demand, mindlinking all of my warriors around me.

*The big pine tree, to the south,* a voice yells back amidst the cacophony of screaming, snarls, barks, and hissing.

I pivot to my right and quickly come upon a swarming mass of fighting bodies. Blood splatters the air. Limbs fly through branches, either attached to bodies or severed from them. A sharp whine peals from a warrior. I howl deeply and the wolves immediately separate themselves from the teeming swarm. They swiftly circle the large tree, corralling the vampires inside the swirling ring of blurred wolves.

A cold body slams into my side, arms scrambling to grasp my torso. Sharply whipping around, I fling the vampire off me and harshly stomp on his chest, savoring the way the bones crunch beneath me. He hisses in pain, baring his fangs at me.

I snarl back viciously. His eyes bulge in fear before I snap my jaws over his face, tearing the flesh from his skull and crush the thick bone with another harsh bite.

Leaping off the corpse, I throw myself into the seething mass of vampires and all the circling wolves dive in at once. We work as a unit, quick and efficient. I latch onto an arm and tear it off, sending the vampire down with the force of my bite, and a wolf appears to finish him off as I spring onto another one. Spitting another head out, I glance around, finding some warriors in their human form trying to climb the base of the pine tree while vampires rip them away in defense. Snapping my attention upward, I search through the branches and notice a pair of long, slender legs dangling from up high.

*Kira! Kira, can you hear me?* I mindlink her directly and the legs flail vigorously.

*Kyran! I can't—*

Her scream pierces the air and I snarl, bounding toward the base of the pine tree. I clamp my jaws around a cold leg, repeatedly slamming the vampire against the wide trunk. Tossing my head, I throw the limp body aside and pounce on the back of another one, crushing his skull between my jaws. I lope away from the tree and turn to sprint toward it, shifting midair as I leap and quickly pull myself up onto a branch.

A cold hand latches onto my ankle. I kick out hard, hearing the satisfying *crunch* of bones breaking as the vampire falls back to the ground. Pushing off the branch, I jump to grasp another, making quick work climbing up the tree. When I get a few limbs away from my sister, four vampires drop around me, hissing and scrambling forward.

One lands on my branch and I wait for him to lunge. Grabbing his wrists, I whip his body sideways and use him to knock another out of the tree, the echo of snapping branches following him down. I release my hold and the vampire screeches as he is flung out into open air.

A burning scratch tears down my back and I yell out in rage, breaking off a thick branch before I turn. Swinging it like a baseball bat, I crack the vampire across his head and kick him in the chest, sending his limp body crashing down through the branches. Glaring sideways at the last vampire, he bares his fangs at me and hisses, but he hesitantly takes a step backward. His red eyes dart around and when they land on me again, I hurl the broken branch at him like a spear, piercing his heart.

I climb higher as the last body falls away and pull myself onto a wide limb, finding Kira thrashing against a large vampire. He has her arms pinned behind her and holds her neck in a chokehold, her legs kicking the air uselessly. She isn't afraid, though. She's pissed as hell and tries relentlessly to land a blow on him, but he's too tall. When her eyes meet mine, her body goes still and the vampire holding her growls at me in warning. As I consider a way to get her out of here safely, a mocking laugh makes me bristle.

"Fancy meeting you here, *dog*. Do you come here often? The food is subpar at best, I'm afraid," Caedes cold voice calls out from the next tree over.

A limp body crashes through the branches below him as he appears, blood spilling over his chin and neck. Rage boils my blood at the sight of him here, on my lands, attacking my people. I quickly search my sister's body, and seeing her torn, bloodstained clothes, my body tenses with fury. I am relieved to only find a few rapidly fading cuts and bruises, thankfully not seeing any bite marks.

Meeting her gaze, I mindlink her quickly before Caedes can notice. *When I take my third step, I want you to bite his arm hard, okay? When he releases you, swing down to the branch below, and press yourself against the trunk.*

*Got it,* she responds immediately, keeping her body still.

I take a step forward and the vampire holding my sister tightens his hold on her. I pretend not to pay him attention, speaking to Caedes instead. "You realize you've lost most of your subjects, right? Was it worth it, bringing them here to slaughter? Maybe they misbehaved and you wanted to punish them, teach your people a lesson?" I taunt him dryly.

"*Tch*. I got what I wanted, I don't care who gets killed in the process," he scoffs and grins wickedly, nodding toward my sister.

I step forward again, laughing humorously. "You don't have anything, Caedes."

"Oh, I have more than you know, *dog*." His cold voice cuts me and I take my third step with a snarl.

Kira bites down, tearing flesh from the vampire holding her. While he bellows in pain, she drops her body, quickly sliding off the branch. I lunge forward, grabbing his bloody arm and jerk him toward me. Gripping the back of his neck, I slam him against the tree. He harshly kicks backward.

I narrowly avoid his foot and try to throw him off the branch, but he lands a blow to my stomach, knocking me off balance. I block the second and third punch, swiftly jabbing out and cracking his jaw, grinning as blood flies from his mouth. I quickly follow with a kick to his gut and grab the back of his head, slamming his face into my knee. His body slumps forward before he lashes out, his fangs going for my leg, but I kick hard against the side of his face. I crouch and grab ahold of his head, twisting my hands sharply.

The echo of his neck *snapping* reverberates off the quiet treetops before I unceremoniously dump his corpse over the edge of the limb.

Whipping around, I stalk toward the end of the branch as far as I can go and glare at Caedes. His eyes are wary and he takes a small step backward, briefly glancing down. The bastard grins at me before he darts away over the branches. My instinct screams to chase him, but I force myself to remain still, trying to regain control of my breathing as my mind flashes back to my mother. Seeing my sister held captive reminds me too easily of the day I lost half of my family, how Kira looks *just* like our mother, and how I was almost too late *again*.

I grip the sides of my head, a roar of rage escaping me. The branch beneath my feet shudders and my eyes snap open, finding my sister walking carefully toward me.

"Kyran, I'm okay. I didn't get bit, I'm healed now. I'm fine," she reassures me, her hand held out.

I drop my hand into hers and step forward, pulling her into a tight embrace. Taking a deep breath, I look into her bright green eyes. "What the fuck happened? How did you end up here?"

Before she can respond, a loud commotion rises from below, and my sister urgently pulls my hand as she descends the tree. We make quick work dropping from the branches. As my feet land on the ground beside hers, a warrior runs up to us, his chest heaving.

"Treyvar, by the lodge," he says breathlessly. *"Traitor,"* he gasps, placing his hands on his knees.

Kira bursts into her small honeyed wolf and takes off toward home, a few wolves quickly following her.

I clap my hand to my warrior's shoulder and raise my voice above the others, yelling out, "Hybrids, gather the vampires and burn the bodies. Take your time with our fallen and bring them home when you can, I'll have a pyre prepared. Warriors, with me!"

I shift and sprint westward, the ground rumbling behind me as dozens of wolves run. The air fills with growls and low howls in the tense moments it takes to catch up with my sister. She falls in behind me with the rest of the wolves melding into one group. A few minutes pass until I see a cluster of wolves out near the prison cells, and I push my legs faster, my anger fueling me.

The crowd parts at my arrival, revealing my brother on top of someone, pounding his fists into their face mercilessly.

I pause for a moment, realizing I've never really seen him be violent, not truly. The only time he's ever lashed out aggressively was when our family was torn in half by the loss of our mother and siblings. Even then, Trey just broke a bunch of things and screamed at people. He didn't brutalize them or take his pain out on anyone.

*He's the opposite of our father. Unlike me.*

Shaking my head, I stalk over to him and listen to the way he spits his words out while he beats the man beneath him.

Trey's voice is thick with anger as he yells close to the guy's smashed-in face, hands gripping his neck forcefully. "You fucking piece of shit! *I knew it!* After everything we've done for you, *given* to you, this is how you repay us?"

*Treyvar, what is going on? Explain to me,* I mindlink since I don't think he realizes that I'm standing beside him.

Whipping his head around, my brother's bloody face falls and he slumps backward onto his heels before slowly rising to his feet. He's breathing heavily. They must have had an intense fight for him to be bleeding and weary.

Trey shoves his hand into his pocket before angrily tossing something to the ground in front of me. Peering down, I scratch my paw across the grass and find an old key, immediately recognizing it as one of the oubliette keys. Snarling, I glare at my brother and wait for his explanation, though I have an idea of what has happened now.

"Vala is gone. A group of vamps and a witch suddenly showed up, mere moments before the warriors mindlinked me about a swarm attacking in the east. I think that attack was a diversion. Caedes appeared by the lodge as I was running to the cells and tore Kira from the house. The bastard disappeared before I had a chance to do anything about it. By the time I got to Vala, she was being carried away unconscious. The group vanished with her and the witch.

"That's when I saw *him* trying to sneak away through the trees. I intercepted him before he threw that key into the woods. He released Vala. He's been the one, *this entire time,* letting the vampires onto our lands! *Fucking traitor!*" Trey seethes and kicks the laughing man in the side, earning a groaning snarl in return.

I push past my brother and with one sniff, I know who has betrayed me, my family, my entire pack. I should have done something before, should have pushed him when my brother warned me. Stepping on top of his body with my full weight, I stand on the man I had felt was one of my closest friends. Who I trusted to hold the security and safety of my pack. Snarling, I gnash my teeth above his mangled face and his entire body twitches in response.

*Sigurd,* I mindlink not just to him, but to everyone surrounding us as well, *heal yourself and speak to me, to the pack. You have this one chance to clarify your actions.*

Disagreements rise from the group, shouts ringing out to kill him or torture him for his betrayal. I want to fulfill these demands myself, but I know I must give him this opportunity to show that I won't act rashly in retaliation. I don't move as I watch the wounds mend on his face and he tries to take a deep breath. Grimacing, his face slick from fresh blood, Sigurd turns his head and spits to the ground before glaring up at me. I lower my head and bare my teeth, silently waiting for him to speak.

"I had to. I had to do what he demanded of me. He has my mate," Sigurd mumbles, not meeting my gaze.

*Why not come to me immediately? Because of you, he had my sister, she could have died! We lost lives, unnecessarily! You—*

*You don't have a mate!* Valdr seethes at him and a collective gasp rolls around us.

Taking control, Valdr stomps down on Sigurd's chest and his ribs crack loudly, an agonized groan tearing from his mouth. Growling viciously, he quickly reaches up and grasps my throat, shoving upward. Slipping out from beneath me, Sigurd throws a knee into my side with a fast punch to my throat before he shifts into his wolf, leaping a few feet away.

I lunge at him as he turns to face me and we collide in a snarling tangle of gnashing teeth, tearing claws, and dripping blood. I sink my jaws into his shoulder and rip downward, gouging a large chunk of flesh off his body. He whines loudly, but moves to bite my throat and I duck my head, his jaws snapping the air above me. Twisting, I firmly latch onto the base of his throat, but not hard enough to puncture deeply.

Sigurd goes still, his chest rumbling with a long growl.

*Shift!* I use my alpha command and his body immediately blurs. I shift back as well and throw him to the ground hard, his head bouncing with the impact.

"I *trusted* you. For over a century, I trusted the safety of my pack with you in charge," I grit out between clenched teeth.

He laughs humorlessly and sneers at me. "Your father was a better Alpha than you, and he was a shitty man. At least he had the balls to execute those who betrayed him. You just exile people, too weak to do what you should. Why do you think we sided with the vampires against you? Your brother was supposed to be Alpha, not you, but you weren't there that day, and *he* died instead of *you*. Our intentions were to wipe your bloodline out and we'd create an unbeatable pack, combining wolves and vampires together. Nobody would've stood a chance against us with Einarr and Caedes in charge, especially if we'd captured the white wolf. Her power is untouchable, and with her in our control, we would be *invincible*." Sigurd spits again, smiling haughtily.

My body shakes with rage at the mention of Selene, but I restrain myself from showing how his words affect me. It's obvious the vampires still don't know who she is or where to find her, since they tried taking Kira earlier.

Focusing only on one thing he'd said, I glare down at the traitorous bastard and demand, "Who is *we*? Who else has been involved with the vampires from this pack?"

He just laughs in response, so I snag his wounded arm and whip him across the grass, his body slamming into a nearby tree. Blood seeps from his torn shoulder and he slowly heals his wound as I stalk toward him. With a yell, he dives for my legs and I jump over him, planting a foot on the ground, kicking into his side.

Grabbing my ankle, Sigurd rolls and tries to drag me to the ground, but I move with his force, landing on my knees beside him. I strike him hard in the side of his head with my elbow and push to my feet as he rolls onto his back, baring his teeth at me.

"Fight me honestly, if you think I'm *not enough* to be Alpha. Challenge me for my position if I'm *so weak*." I growl at him, clenching my fists at my sides.

He heals for a moment and rises to face me, raising his chin. "I, Sigurd Svik, challenge you, Kyran Gennaíos, for your position and power as Alpha of this pack." He spits at my feet.

*"Challenge accepted,"* I grit between my teeth, chest rumbling loudly.

I know Sigurd. I know how he thinks, how he fights. I rely on my instinct and experience, allowing him to make the first move. He crouches into a fighting stance and sidesteps around me, my eyes carefully following his movements. Keeping my back away from him, I slowly turn in place and notice the way his eyes shift focus from my face to different parts of my body, assessing where to strike first. I never remove my eyes from his, catching how his gaze lingered briefly on my left knee before flicking his eyes up to mine.

I narrow my gaze at him an instant before he strikes with his leg, and I step back, dodging his kick. Sweeping my foot outward, I pull him off balance, throwing a quick succession of punches to his throat and gut before stepping back out of his reach. He growls lowly and feints to his right while jabbing his fist toward my face. I throw my arm up to block him and wrap my hand around his wrist, pulling him hard toward me. I slam my fist into his face twice before he stumbles a bit, and I use this moment to lash my arm out, snapping a thick branch off of a nearby tree.

Discarding the broken limb, I step back a few paces, positioning myself across from the sharp protrusion, baiting Sigurd in front of me.

He stalks toward me angrily, throwing his weight behind a punch as I dodge him and turn to grip the back of his neck. He grasps my arm and twists around, the force of it turning me away from him. I wait for a breath, feeling for the moment he puts pressure on my arm behind me. Quickly reaching behind me with my free hand, I grip onto his wrists and throw myself forward with a yell, dragging him over me and slamming him against the ground.

The muscles around my shoulder tear from the strain. I heal as fast as I can.

Growling through the pain, I bend down, wrapping my hands around his throat in an iron vice.

Rising to my full height, I lift Sigurd off the ground and his feet kick me futilely. Without hesitation, I surge forward, impaling him on the sharp, broken branch. Sigurd roars as I shove him back, the jagged wood emerging just below his sternum with a gush of dark blood. Squeezing his throat tightly, I watch with sick satisfaction as his face begins to discolor.

His eyes widen in fear, mouth gaping silently like a fish out of water.

*"Tell me who else from this pack is involved with you,"* I command savagely, pushing my hands harder, glaring at him mere inches away.

Names whisper through his mindlink and I tally a dozen of my warriors. Relaying their names to the pack through a command, the traitorous men and women begin to emerge. Some are shoved from the crowd and some fight loudly against the alpha command, but they all unwillingly drag themselves forward.

Releasing Sigurd just as he is about to lose consciousness, I let his body drop onto the broken branch and he howls with pain and rage.

"Hold him," I demand as I turn away, and Trey and Jeger rush over, pinning Sigurd to the tree.

Facing the line of traitors, I glare into each of their eyes with contempt, slowly pacing back and forth. "Whoever has betrayed me willingly, *step forward*," I command, clenching my jaw.

Watching as eight out of the twelve betraying warriors grudgingly move out of line, I circle behind the group and cross in front of the remaining four. They each look afraid, whereas the people in front of them looked angry. Now that I have discerned who has had direct involvement conspiring against me, I know death is not a justifiable punishment for these people.

"Although you did not *outright* defy me, you have held the awareness and knowledge of this betrayal." I speak gravely to them all, holding their gazes individually. "You've chosen to withhold this information from your Alpha and are therefore deemed traitorous wolves. *I exile you from my pack, branding you as untrustworthy, and sentence you to a rogue life, never to be part of a true pack again,*" I seethe, baring my teeth and a thunderous growl rips through my chest.

I press my palm to each of their foreheads, my alpha magic severing our ties, marking their souls. The loss of each pack bond stings as I go. When I remove my hand from the last in line, I step away from them, nodding once.

A few people come forward and grab hold of each traitor, removing them to escort them off our lands. Two of the four are females, and their shrieking sobs echo as they are dragged away. I feel pity for them, but not guilt. Not when they deserve exile.

"*Tch.* Weak, like I said." Sigurd's voice drifts over me as he mumbles beneath his breath.

Ignoring him, I face the wide gathering of my pack members and address them loudly. "Who here has been directly affected by the vampire attacks? Either your mate or a family member has been stolen from you, or you've suffered loss through berserker disease as a result of our attacks. Please, come forward."

My heart clenches at the large amount of people moving toward me, how so many people have endured loss in my charge because of *Sigurd*. Sweeping my gaze across the group, the pain I find in their eyes echoes through my bonds with them.

"I offer each of you the opportunity to seek vengeance against those who've brought you unforgivable pain and suffering this past century. I only ask that their torture be fatal. Their death is the price they must pay for being part of something so harrowing for our kind. Their evil has no place on this earth, and they should feel the pain they've brought upon us before departing this realm." I glare at the closest traitor, receiving a snarl in response.

Turning toward the line of traitors, I command, *"You will remain still where you stand."*

Nodding at the growling pack beside me, I turn my back on the eight traitorous warriors. Stalking toward Sigurd, I grin viciously when the gruesome cacophony behind me rises. His eyes widen, staring over my shoulder. Blood seeps from his chest and mouth since he cannot heal himself while impaled, and he spits at my feet before meeting my gaze.

My grin morphs into a snarl and I snap my fist out, his cheek *crunching* on impact. My brother and Jeger release his arms when I grab his shoulders, forcefully tearing him off of the tree. Before Sigurd has a chance to heal, I slam him to the ground by his throat and shove my hand into the gaping hole in his chest. Clawing upward as Sigurd screams in agony, I grip my fingers around his heart.

The rapid beating intensifies when he glares into my eyes.

*"If I am weak, then what does that make you?"* I hiss viciously.

His glare melts into terror, fingers scrambling to find purchase against my unyielding grip. Holding his wild gaze, I release a roar of rage and clench my fist, crushing his heart before tearing it free from his body. I stare into his vacant, horrified face with sick satisfaction.

My chest heaves with the turmoil roiling inside, and I slowly open my hand. A wet thud hits the ground as I turn away and shift. Howling long and low, I throw my head back, and many of my pack join me as songs of anger, pain, and sorrow fill the air. Rage thrashes within me relentlessly.

I catch Jeger's gaze, mindlinking him directly. *Give me the location of the nest you found Vala at.*

I recognize the address he tells me, and knowing where I need to go, I bound away from my pack into the woods. Jeger and Trey shift, quickly loping after me and I let them follow. I might need their backup if the place is heavily occupied.

As I run, I think of Selene and wonder how she would react to this side of me. It has been a long while since the last time I lost my control, but part of me *thrives* in brutality, as if a switch flips off. I don't feel anything other than rage. I become unhinged. I am a monster.

Tugging on the faint bond connected to her, I hope she can understand that it means I am sorry.

Sorry for who I am, for what I'm about to do.

*Please forgive me, sweetheart,* I whisper to her before closing off my mind completely.

# CHAPTER SIXTEEN

## BONDS

### SELENE

My mother and I sit on our porch sipping herbal tea, and I consider something I want to ask her. The thought has bothered me since we came inside after she sent Kyran home, but I needed a moment to rehash things in my mind before speaking with her. I pull my feet underneath me and turn sideways on the bench swing, my mother mirroring me.

"Why don't you help them, against the vampires, if you created the werewolves?" I ask her quietly, raising my brow. "I'm still not entirely certain on the details of everything, but I can assume that the power of a *goddess* surpasses all others, correct?"

"You're not wrong." She chuckles briefly before sighing, "I can't. My involvement in the affairs between races would be perceived as a direct attack on Nyx, and *trust me,* nobody wants a war between goddesses. *Especially* her and myself." She runs a hand down her face and scrunches her nose.

"She might not be able to, but I can." Asteria's sharp voice startles me as she appears in front of us.

"Asteria—"

"No, Mother. This is getting out of hand. Caedes has recruited *witches* to do his dirty work for him. Through scrying, I've uncovered the identity of who he's been working with. I'm fucking pissed to learn it has been *Hazel*. I am unsure if Melody is involved, but it'd be wise to suspect her as well. That *bitch* was the one who poisoned you at the club and hindered my magic. I believe she knows *who* you are. The only way she would have been able to discover your identity is through your blood, which is why that bastard ex of yours ripped your hair out. I fear it is because you've lived with us that raised suspicion, and Caedes cannot attack you while you are here." The anger in her voice cuts through the night air and she crosses her arms, pacing back and forth.

"Earlier this evening, the attack Kyran's pack suffered was intended to find *you* there, not his sister. The hybrid wolf Vala, she created an intelligent glamour for their females to use. It alters their physical appearance, and the blonde women are disguised in plain sight. There was a traitor communicating with Caedes from within Kyran's pack, divulging sensitive information, and I'm assuming his sister wasn't wearing her glamour. The vampires believed her to have been you. I was shown a man speaking over the phone about *you* being with Kyran, and his sister was mistakenly taken from their home by Caedes himself." Ria drops her arms, scowling.

She turns to our mother. "I tried to follow Caedes through the astral plane, but after he ran from the fight, his signature vanished from earth. I think he has another realm to hide in, with the aid of the witches' magic. He took Vala as well, though I am unsure if she is willingly involved with him or not. Regardless, we're facing a *much* larger issue than we originally thought." She wraps her arms around her middle and plops down into a chair with a huff of frustration.

My lips part as I connect the dots, fully understanding how vulnerable I am now. I look at my sister's frustrated face, then glance over at our mother. Tension lines her eyes and mouth. I need to awaken Luna, and *soon*. Thinking, an idea forms and I rise to my feet, catching their attention.

"We should try to unlock my memories through Luna, now that she is present in my mind. I can pull her forward and maybe you both could channel her directly? I'm willing to do what is necessary to awaken her. I need to *try*. I can't let Caedes succeed. At the very least, getting my memories back could help me to mentally prepare myself with how to navigate things going forward." I speak firmly, fighting against the anxiousness pooling in my belly.

Ria nods, glancing at our mother, and I turn to see her also nod in agreement. A smile pulls my cheeks up just as a tight *pang* yanks at my chest. I press my hand over my heart, concerned, and take a deep breath.

"We will need some time to prepare for a sleep-dive, how about tomorrow evening? Selene—" My mother's quiet voice changes from light to worried as she hurriedly stands beside me. "Are you alright?"

"I...yeah, I'm alright. I think I feel Kyran? Although, it doesn't feel *good*," I mumble, rubbing my chest.

"Do you feel pain?" she asks me, grasping my shoulders.

"No, no. Not pain. It feels...like I'm very angry, deep inside, with sorrow mixed in. I also feel...despair." I pull my brows together and look into my mother's deep violet eyes.

*It's so heavy and suffocating,* I wonder sadly, making soothing circles with my palm.

"Your bond with Kyran can share feelings as well as thoughts to one another, though the feelings are felt involuntarily, whereas thoughts are intentionally sent. They call that the mindlink, but only mates can sense what the other is currently feeling," My mother explains, her brow pinched with worry. "Emotions, as well as physical sensations, may be communicated through your bond with him as a way to speak without words. It can become overwhelming to the recipient if pushed to the extreme, however. There is a way to disconnect the transmission, though it leaves both mates with an emptiness that can only be reversed once physically reunited. I have only known of this to happen in the circumstance of torture or imprisonment, in the hopes of saving their mate from suffering with them." Her voice drifts away, and she watches me warily.

I blink my eyes slowly, astounded by the complexity of this new information. Just as I open my mouth to ask a hundred questions, Kyran's voice faintly whispers through my mind.

*Please forgive me.*

A sharp pain radiates through my head. Wincing a little, I recognize the sensation as Luna's presence and I take a slow breath, trying not to fight it. As I relax, the pain thankfully lessens to a dull pressure.

*We'll get you out soon, starting tomorrow.* I try to direct the thought toward Luna, and I receive a pulse in my head in response.

I smile at our improvement and Asteria rises to her feet, spreading her arms out to me. I meet her in a warm embrace, both of us squeezing tightly. She pulls back and smiles widely.

"Get some rest, you're gonna need it for tomorrow. I have a good feeling about this time." She winks at me before disappearing, a light gust of wind rustling my hair.

I blink owlishly and my mother glides away, glancing back at me. "Would you like more tea?" she asks quietly, holding the door open.

Shaking my head, I absently reply, "No, thank you. I'll just sit here for a while. I'd like to think things over, now that I have some more information."

She nods and closes the door gently behind her, only to reappear in front of me with a thick, fuzzy blanket. I jump at her sudden presence, unsure if I'll ever really get used to the ability she and my sister have. We both chuckle and I wrap the blanket around myself.

"I will send the boys over to you, to keep you company," she murmurs before vanishing with a puff of wind.

Heavy thudding echoes around the house before a sharp *bark* announces Phylax and Machitis' arrival. They both bound up the steps, bodies shoving the bench swing in their battle for attention. Laughing, I bend over to scruff their fur affectionately and get them settled before I sit down, pushing the swing lazily with my feet.

I spend the night listening to the crickets and tree frogs, wondering where Kyran might be, and what had happened with his pack this evening. I think about what it means to have a mate bond, how Luna not being physically present affects it, and how it might feel when she is awakened.

Yawning, I lie on my back, gazing at the stars. Glancing at the moon, a slight pressure pulses in my head and I smile at the thought of Luna, wondering what she looks like. My mind drifts to Kyran again, hoping he is okay and wanting to know what he meant by asking for my forgiveness.

The darkness I'd felt earlier weighs on me, and tears well in my eyes as I recall the anguish he suffers inside, recognizing it for what festers within me as well.

*He has only been kind and gentle with me, never once has he made me feel uncomfortable or afraid. So what could he possibly ask my forgiveness for?* I wonder solemnly.

The twinkling of the night sky and the sway of the bench lull me as I think about Kyran. Closing my eyes, I remember our day together and smile warmly through my unshed tears, wishing for another day like that again soon.

A menacing growl sends my eyes flying open as my dogs launch to their feet. Another deep rumbling rolls out from beside me and I bolt upright, placing my hands on each of their shoulders. My heart races, a million scenarios flashing in my mind as I search the dark woods across the lawn. The hackles raise on both dogs' backs as their growling intensifies, and my breath comes in shallow puffs.

If I gave them the command, they would take off after whatever it is that has alerted them without hesitation, but I don't want to send them into the unknown, or leave myself here alone and vulnerable.

Rising slowly to my feet, I glance down to follow their line of sight. Peering into the tree line, a shadow separates from the woods. My mouth goes dry as I imagine vampires running toward me and I nearly scream before the low moon illuminates two amber eyes.

A pent up breath *whooshes* out of my chest and I place a hand to my galloping heart in relief. I try to walk toward the stairs, but both of my dogs press themselves against my legs, preventing me from moving forward. Gently brushing my hands across their heads in reassurance, their growling fades away.

"It's alright boys," I murmur as I pet them and they relax beside me.

Giving them both a final pat, I step off the porch and notice the light of dawn creeping through the sky. Glancing at the large wolf, I smile as I cross the dewy grass toward him. I turn around to hastily run back and grab the blanket. Hurrying to Kyran, I hold out the blanket and wait for him to return to his human form.

He shifts his weight from one paw to the other, but he remains as his wolf, his glowing amber eyes intently holding my gaze.

I lift my arm and step toward him, running my fingers through the fur at his neck. Gasping, I immediately snatch my hand back when I feel slick, sticky wetness and stare down in horror at my bloody fingers.

*It is not my blood,* Valdr's gravelly voice murmurs in my mind.

"What happened? Are you alright?" I ask quickly, dropping the blanket to the ground.

*I am unharmed,* is all he replies, still staring intently at me.

Raising both hands, I gently stroke his face and he closes his eyes for a moment. When he opens them again, he licks my bloody hand, meeting my gaze once more.

*I must tell you something, Selene. Kyran has…receded. After the attack, he sought revenge against Caedes and we disrupted his influence by eliminating many of his powerful fighters. Kyran has blocked his mind and will not speak with me. I am unsure if he can even hear me or see what I see. I still feel him, but it's as if he is far away and not here with me,* Valdr explains in a tight voice, his eyes shining with concern.

His discomfort is evident in the way he shifts his weight as he speaks, and I stroke his cheek comfortingly. "Why would he do this? Valdr, what has happened? Is his sister alright?" I ask quickly, my chest constricting.

*Kira is unharmed. We were betrayed by someone we kept close, and by others we were unaware of in our pack. I don't feel emotions the same as Kyran does. Things are much more plain for me. I view things as action and reaction without the trivial burden of emotional connection or reasoning behind it. Kyran's past weighs heavily on him, and he has been balancing on a precipice for a long while. Tonight has pushed him, mentally, back into a place he has fought hard to escape from.*

He growls lowly, nudging his nose into my hand.

My eyes fill with tears at his words, feeling empathetic as I can relate my own inner battle with what he describes. Sniffling, I lean forward and lightly kiss his cold, wet nose. Valdr licks my cheek in response. I wipe my face with my forearm, not wanting to get anymore blood on me, and take a step back.

"Would you like to stay here, with me?" I ask Valdr hopefully, thinking of Kyran and wishing he was here.

His voice comfortingly rumbles in my mind. *Yes. I came to you with the hope that you'd be able to bring him back. I also don't want to leave you alone with the way things are.*

I give him a small smile and gesture for him to follow me. I turn around, making my way to the other side of the cottage and reach across the front porch, grabbing my tote bin with the grooming supplies. Stepping back, I grin at Valdr as his eyes flick to the bin and back to me a couple times.

*What is that?* he asks warily.

I place the tote bin on the ground and walk over to the hose reel, clicking the head to the shower position and turn the spigot open. Glancing over at Valdr, I laugh as his ears flatten in adamant refusal.

*No, no. Absolutely not.* He growls lightly and I laugh again.

"It's just water and some soap, it won't kill you. You're filthy. I promise to be gentle." I step in front of him, raising an eyebrow.

Valdr snorts out a sharp breath and glares at the hose before relenting, *Fine, but be quick.* I grin as he rolls his eyes.

Chuckling, I squeeze the handle and wet his neck, moving around him to rinse the bloody grime from his fur. Standing in front of him, I can't help the guffaw that escapes me when I notice the blatant antipathy emitting from Valdr. His ears are pinned back with squinty eyes, and his nose is scrunched in pure disdain at being sprayed by a hose.

"I need to wet your face," I try to say seriously, biting back another laugh.

He just stares at me for a silent moment, and slowly closes his eyes without changing his expression. I giggle in amusement and was his face quickly, booping his nose with a sudsy finger. Laughing at his gentle growl, I rinse his face clean and squeeze the shampoo bottle down his spine, making him shiver a little. I chuckle as I dig my hands into his fur, scratching my fingers through his thick coat. Valdr rumbles softly as I work and his body relaxes while I scrub him clean. A few spots have him shifting around and it's fun finding the areas he enjoys most when his rumbling intensifies.

After a thorough rinse, he vigorously shakes his body, completely soaking me in the process. I glare at him mockingly and laugh when he lowers his bottom jaw in amusement.

With a devilish idea, I grin and let him know I'll be right back. Quickly putting away the hose and tote bin, I cross the driveway toward a small storage shed and pull out the Shop-Vac I use when I need to dry the dogs. Lugging it back over to Valdr, he immediately growls at it, baring his teeth. I can't help the giggles that bubble out of me as I plug it in and brandish the long nozzle like a weapon.

*Absolutely not going to happen,* he refuses, taking a step backward and shaking his head.

"It is, if you want to stay with me. I will not have a sodden wolf traipsing around my house." I struggle to speak firmly, and I bite my cheek to stop myself from laughing.

Growling deeply, Valdr plops his rear on the ground and I drag the Shop-Vac over, hitting the switch with the nozzle. It whirs loudly, but I can easily hear Valdr's rumbling protest over the noise and I grin wickedly as I sweep the nozzle around his body.

*This is beyond demeaning,* he grumbles in annoyance, stomping a paw to the ground with a huff.

I laugh deeply, enjoying this time with him, appreciating him for allowing me to do it. It takes a while for his coat to fully dry, but when I finish and turn the blower off, I snort in amusement when Valdr shakes his fur. He looks like a puffed out, angry ball of fluff. I swiftly yank my phone out of my pocket and snap a photo of him, trying to keep the camera steady through my laughter. He bounds over to me, lifting his front paw and pushes me to the ground. He licks my face relentlessly until I beg him to stop.

I shove him off me, completely covered in slobber.

*"Argh,* Valdr!" I pretend to be disgusted, swiping my face with my sleeve, but end up laughing some more at the gleam in his eyes.

I push to my feet and wrap my arms around his neck, hugging him tightly. "Come on, let's go inside. I need a shower," I mumble as I release him, heading toward the front door.

Neither my mother nor Ria were in the house when we came inside and I led Valdr to my bedroom, telling him to get comfortable wherever he'd like while I took a shower. When I emerged from my bathroom, I found him sprawled on my bed, taking up almost the entire space while he napped. I quietly went down to the kitchen to eat a quick breakfast, and upon my return, he lazily lifted his head to greet me before dozing back off to sleep.

I lie on my side, curled up against his warm fur, listening to his deep, even breathing. Gently brushing my hand down his soft coat, I think of Kyran and feel sorrow at the thought of him suffering in pain alone.

*I hope you're alright in there. I'm here for you,* I tell him in my mind, squeezing my eyes shut against a wave of sadness.

*Shh,* Luna's soft voice whispers, and I'm gladly reminded how I can hear her while touching Kyran or Valdr. *Don't wake him, he needs rest.*

Concentrating on just her presence, I ask, *Can you feel him? Kyran, I mean. Can you sense him right now?*

*Yes, I can. Though he is distant, I can feel him.* She sounds hopeful and I smile at her words.

*Could you help me find his connection?* I ask her, keeping my eyes closed and holding still.

My chest slowly blooms with warmth, and at the center a soft pressure tingles. Focusing on it, I imagine a golden light forming a string and I pull on it gently, thinking of my concern and care for Kyran.

*I'm right here with you, you're not alone. You don't have to face this by yourself,* I whisper, hoping he can hear me.

I stay here for a few breaths before I slowly release my hold on the connection, nearly missing the faint tension that returns to me. I hold firmly onto our bond and remain there, focused only on keeping my energy entwined with it. I continue to think about my care and empathy for Kyran as I pour these feelings through our bond.

I realize I must've drifted to sleep at some point when Valdr stretches beside me and I open my eyes, noticing the dimness of my room. Yawning, I stretch with a groan and grab my phone, checking the time. My stomach gurgles and I sit up, reaching a hand over to ruffle Valdr's ear. He cracks his eye open and lolls his tongue out as he yawns, putting his sharp teeth on full display.

"Are you hungry? I'm going to make myself some dinner, what would you like? I can check for some meat in the freezer, though I don't really know how appealing that is," I mumble, scrunching my nose at him.

*No, thank you. I'll go hunt in the woods while you eat. It won't take long,* he responds as he slides off my bed, rising languidly.

"Don't make a mess," I say sternly, smirking when he looks over at me.

Valdr rolls his eyes up toward the ceiling and I laugh, climbing out of bed and crossing to my door. I shuffle down the stairs, finding Ria and my mother ladling stew into their bowls. Asteria barks a laugh when she sees Valdr following behind me, but my mother places her bowl down and hastily comes over to us.

"Is everything alright? Why are you in wolf form?" She looks from me to Valdr, her brow pinching with a concerned frown.

Before I say anything, I notice how she intently looks at him and realize he must be speaking with her privately. She closes her eyes and nods her head once. Glancing at me, she gives me a gentle smile, placing her hand on my upper arm.

"He will return when he is ready, dear. Have patience with him. I trust you will come to understand his reason," my mother says softly before returning to the kitchen.

I place my hand on Valdr's shoulder and rub my fingers into his fur while we walk toward the front door. Pulling it open, I turn to him and give him a small smile, focusing on our bond.

*Come back to me soon,* I whisper in my mind as he steps onto the porch.

He turns around and presses his head to mine for a moment before silently bounding away into the darkness. I leave the door open and head into the kitchen for dinner, the three of us keeping quiet and allowing the deafening silence of our thoughts to take hold while we eat.

## KYRAN

Burning rage sears my mind, its flames consuming me in this dark hell I'll never escape. Years of brutality that I've both inflicted and endured has laid brick upon brick over my soul, leaving me with this stifling, exhausting weight to silently carry as it slowly suffocates me. It's as if I have been drowning in the blood that pours from invisible wounds within my own mind, screaming endlessly with nobody to hear for two hundred years.

At one point, I had fallen into a numb existence, far beyond the reaches of pain, despair, turmoil, anger, fear. A point of emptiness inside, a hollow man with nothing worth living for. A point of cold death walking the earth. I was made for destruction, and I had destroyed myself.

I learned how to behave in ways the people around me expected, never truly showing the disguise that was my mask, hiding the nothingness within. For years I lived in that farce.

Until I met her.

She ignited my chilling darkness with her light, warming me back to life with her laughter and giving me something to *live* for. Her soul is so pure. It cannot be tainted by me, by my personal demons that I cannot defeat. Her presence is closing the gaping hole inside me that I've been floating in eternally, sending me back into the boiling pit I evaporated from. She has become an oasis in the barren desert of my existence. A safe haven I fear I will burn to ashes if I stay too long.

Keeping her safe is of utmost importance, and to do that, I must face myself and allay the anguish that has festered inside of me. The problem is, *I have absolutely no idea how to accomplish this.* So I remain here, burning in this inferno as the fire roars on.

Amidst my chaos, a slight pull tingles deep within me, and Selene's melodic voice drifts through my mind.

*I'm right here with you, you're not alone. You don't have to face this by yourself.*

Her presence is a shower of rain, soothing and snuffing out the flames that surround me. If I were awake, I could cry from the relief she brings me. Too soon, the rain dissipates and the fire pushes back, its heat blistering as it rises. Cowardly, I scramble to grasp our bond in hopes that her energy will return and keep the flames away.

I am abruptly enveloped in soothing comfort, floating in a pool of moonlight. Breathing deeply, I bask in the weightlessness of her light curling around me, savoring the serenity of her energy. I drift peacefully, and eventually focus my mind toward finding the roots to my turmoil without suffering through the agony that it has become.

The ocean of tranquility that Selene bestowed upon me gradually fades and I find myself facing a row of shadowy doorways. Hesitantly, I step forward and peer into the arch directly in front of me. Immediately consumed with physical agony, my body burns all over, recognizing the torture I'd suffered as a child that my father had called *training*. His voice grates my ears as he demeans me and I throw myself backward, landing hard on my ass.

My chest heaves and I grab my head, the loathsome fire springing to life in small bursts around me. Squeezing my eyes shut, I desperately gain control of my breathing, only opening my eyes once the heat disappears. I drop my hands into my lap as I stare at the arched doorway and glance around, shaking my head at the other four.

*I don't know. I don't think I can do this. Not alone. I need help. I need Selene.*

I desperately wish she was here with me.

The tightness in my chest vanishes at the thought of her and I rise to my feet, tethering this place in my mind as I reach for Valdr's connection. Everything around me whirls quickly, coming to a dizzying stop as I focus on Valdr, seeing and hearing through his senses. I recognize the living room in Hekate's cottage as Valdr lies next to the warm fireplace, watching Selene and her family in the kitchen. Seeing her makes my heartbeat quicken and I feel Valdr's attention when he notices my presence.

*Welcome back,* he says dryly, but I sense the apprehension behind his words.

*Don't welcome me yet,* I mumble. *I need to speak with Selene, please,* I add quietly.

Valdr silently rises to his feet and pads over to Selene, nudging her lightly with his nose. As she turns to him, the affection in her eyes makes my heart swell, and I realize they must have bonded while I was…away. She reaches out, gently rubbing his face with a smile and Valdr licks her palm, making her laugh.

Taking a step back, Valdr announces, *Kyran is here.*

Selene's hand flies to her mouth, and Hekate murmurs to Asteria before they vanish, giving us privacy. I appreciate their courtesy and shift into my human form, shamefully unable to meet Selene's gaze.

I run my hand through my hair and rub the back of my neck awkwardly, unsure of what to say.

She jumps to her feet and drags her chair over. Climbing onto it, Selene throws her arms around my neck without a word. My arms loosely wrap around her at first, but when she squeezes me, I hold her firmly, burying my face into her hair, deeply breathing in her sweet scent.

*"Kyran,"* she whispers, slightly pulling back and holds my face in her soft hands. "Are you okay?"

"Yeah," I huff automatically, glancing at her. "Actually, *n-no.* I'm not," I admit tightly, gazing into her bright crystalline eyes.

Tears spring forth and she hugs me again before stepping off the chair. "Come," she murmurs, grabbing my hand and pulling me toward the stairs.

We ascend to her bedroom and she lets go of my hand as she crosses the room toward her closet, mumbling something about needing more clothes. As I reach for a blue throw blanket to wrap around my waist, Asteria manifests holding some sweatpants and a t-shirt. She tosses them to me and I immediately recognize my scent on them. Opening my mouth to question her about it, she just winks at me and vanishes with a brush of wind.

Selene snorts as I stare at the empty place her sister just occupied, wondering how she got my clothes. Slightly shaking my head, I get dressed quickly and glance over at Selene. She pulls the puffy comforter off her bed, nodding toward the balcony. I open the doors for her and we settle ourselves on the deck, sitting on her blanket facing each other.

Reaching out, Selene takes my hand and squeezes it tightly, her face pinched with concern. "You can tell me as much or as little as you need to. Whatever it is that pulled you away must be hard. *I am here for you, okay?"* She says seriously, holding my gaze intently.

Nodding, I look down at our entwined hands as I rub my thumb over her fingers, thinking about what to say. Taking a breath, I meet her gaze again and let out a sigh.

"There is a lot to me that you are unaware of. I have a...dark past." I glance away for a moment before continuing. "With everything that has been going on lately...things have resurfaced within me. Things that I have tried very hard to move past, unsuccessfully," I admit quietly.

She nods in understanding but remains silent, giving me the space to speak freely. I turn her hand over and absently play with her fingers as I consider my words.

My chest tightens with unfamiliar anxiety. "I've experienced and done *terrible* things that have haunted me my entire life. Now that I have met you, I fear—" I growl, frustrated with how difficult it is to say this.

"I fear that being fucked up will either bring you harm, trouble you, or send you away." I grit my teeth at the admission, glancing away from her.

Selene withdraws her hand. Mine clenches into a fist in her absence. To my surprise, she kneels in front of me, pulling me into a firm hug. She slides her hand up behind my head, holding me tightly for a moment before sitting back on her heels. Taking both my hands in hers, she kisses my fingers and holds my gaze.

"Kyran, listen to me." She shakes her head, murmuring, "Your past traumas do *not* define you, it is how you *choose* to act upon it that does. You sitting here and openly sharing this with me shows your strength and *choice* to heal. Your past-self is not your present-self, though you must not suppress the parts of you that have suffered. There are many facets to you, and collectively, each individual piece of you forms the Kyran that I know now." Her voice is hard with her conviction and my heart thumps at her words.

I shake my head stubbornly, my throat tight with apprehension. "You don't know what I've done. You don't deserve to be with someone like me...I am not worthy of *you*," I rasp with pain in my heart.

"This entire time that I have known you, Kyran, you have *only* been kind, gentle, and respectful towards me. I cannot throw that away based solely on your past. That would be cruel," she responds seriously, squeezing my hands.

Staring into her eyes, I feel her truth as she speaks and I nod once, taking an uneven breath.

"Selene, I-I need your help. I think I have to relive the worst memories I've buried deep within my subconscious. I tried to do it on my own, but I know that I cannot do it safely. When I blocked Valdr out, I was...not doing well. You gave me reprieve through our bond and I was able to find where I'd shoved these memories. I…need you with me, in order to face this shit and move on from it, once and for all." I shakily let out a pent up breath as I search her gaze, my heart beating erratically.

"It is not easy to ask for help, and I am grateful for you coming to me," she whispers, her eyes never leaving mine.

I swallow thickly, knowing there's no turning back. "If you do this, you will learn everything there is about me as I bare my shadowed soul, and I will not blame you if you choose to deny me afterward. I just need to *try*. I want to be a better man. I cannot continue living with this…suffocating darkness inside me. *I don't want to be like this anymore.*" My voice cracks and I bow my head, ashamed.

Her hand grasps my forearm as she murmurs, "I want to help you. I know all too well how it feels to be alone, drowning inside. I will do my best to assist you in your healing, though it is up to you to break free from your bonds. I can only show you the key, okay?" She gives my arm another squeeze.

Lifting my head, I give her a small smile which she instantly returns. Pulling lightly on her hand, I wrap my arms around Selene and kiss the top of her head before turning her around. I scoot back against the wall and drag her against my chest, caging her in with my arms. Tilting my head back, I gaze up at the stars, breathing slowly.

Finding Selene has awoken a desire to live again. After drifting through life expecting to die alone, her presence has given me something precious to cherish.

*Hope.*

Being bonded to her makes me want to be a better man not just for myself, but for her, because she *deserves* that. This bond has given me the hope that there is more to this life than suffering and misery. I know facing myself is what I must do to be ready for Selene and our potential life together, and I will do *anything* to ensure our bond solidifies between us.

"Thank you," I whisper to Selene, to the sky—to anyone willing to listen—immensely grateful just to have her here with me.

# CHAPTER SEVENTEEN

## HEALING

### KYRAN

We spend the rest of the evening quietly sitting on the balcony, gazing at the night sky. A few hours ago, Selene fell asleep against my chest. I'd pulled the blanket around us to keep her warm and have been holding her while I think about what I must do in order to properly be with her.

Looking up, I judge the time to be close to midnight based on the position of the moon and gently gather Selene in my arms, careful not to disturb her slumber.

I rise slowly to my feet and carry her into her room, reaching out to quietly close the doors behind us with a soft *click*. I lay her gently in her bed, arranging her comforter around her like a nest, and I can't help myself from brushing her silvery hair away from her beautiful face. She looks so peaceful and calm, two things I have never felt, except in her presence. I lightly trace my thumb over her cheek before pulling my hand back with a sigh.

Turning to take my place on the floor by the balcony doors, a softness glides over my hand.

I glance at Selene's sleeping face. I peer down at her outstretched arm, her fingers resting on my knuckles and flick my eyes back to hers, finding her squinting at me.

"Come here," she murmurs sleepily, rolling onto her side and lifting her blankets.

I lie down and take the blanket from her as she wiggles her way beneath my arm, curling into my chest. Wrapping my arms around her, I pull her in tightly and press a kiss to her head, feeling more comfortable than ever before. I listen to her breathing as it quickly evens out, her sleep returning to her so effortlessly, and I smile at the thought of her feeling just as comfortable as I do.

Closing my eyes, I release the trepidation about what Selene will choose to do once she discovers my harsh truths. I only focus on enjoying the time I have spent with her as I drift off into a restful sleep.

A low rumbling rolls through my chest as silk caresses my back and I flex my shoulders at the sensation. Feathered hands glide up my neck, kneading the tension away, making me sigh with pleasure. Gentle fingers run through my hair, and the electric tingles they emit shoot down my body with a sultry heat. I stifle a groan, lifting my head from the pillows. Selene's bright smile greets me as she giggles, running her hands through my hair again and I close my eyes, enjoying the feeling of her touching me.

"Good morning, Ky," she whispers, her voice soft.

"Good morning, sweetheart," I whisper back, rolling onto my side and brushing my knuckles against her jaw.

Her smile widens as she props up on her elbow, sliding her free hand into mine. "So, I've been thinking," she murmurs, drawing circles on my palm, "what if my mother or Asteria could assist us with your healing, somehow? We were going to attempt to unlock my memories before you had come back, and I wanted to ask you first before bringing it up to them, to see if it would be something you'd be open to?" she asks quietly, giving me a small smile.

I raise my eyebrows at her thoughtfulness and lightly nod in agreement. "Yeah, I think that is a great idea, Selene. Thank you." I smile and she beams at me happily.

"I'm not really sure *what* they can do for it, but I would be willing to bet they've got something we could give a try," she says hopefully, giving my hand a squeeze.

A quick rap on her door announces Asteria before she pushes her way into the room and tosses a glass bottle at me. I barely manage to catch it, mere inches away from hitting Selene on the head. I snap my gaze up, a light growl escaping me as I glare at Asteria.

The witch-goddess grins. "Meet me downstairs in a few minutes. Drink up, both of you. You're gonna need it!" she chirps before pushing the door closed and poofing away.

I look sideways at Selene as she sits up and she meets my gaze, letting out a laugh. I chuckle with her, shaking my head. "That woman is something else," I tease, smirking.

"I am well aware," Selene drawls with another laugh.

Thinking out loud, I murmur, "If I'm not mistaken, I believe Asteria is a prophet. She has the ability for precognition." When she gives me a blank stare, I clarify, "She can see the future."

Selene's mouth puckers while she slowly nods, probably realizing instances that make more sense to her now after hearing me say this. It strikes me how she's lived so much of her life unaware, yet she has accepted it all with such grace. I can't say that I would handle it very well if our roles were reversed, that's for sure.

I sigh, glancing at the bottle Asteria left us with. "I guess we're doing this now." *I don't know if I can face her after this.*

"Excuse me for a moment," Selene murmurs with a sigh as she pats my knee, pushing to her feet.

She stretches her arms over her head before disappearing into her bathroom. I turn the glass bottle over in my hands, observing the metallic copper liquid swirling inside. *Well, what have I got to lose?* Shrugging, I uncork the bottle and swig it down, leaving a little less than half for Selene. The potion is sweet and sour, but not entirely bad, and it seeps warmly into my stomach as if I just downed a handle of liquor.

*Only our fucking mate bond! We could've figured this out ourselves, just…I don't know, tell her the shitty things we've done? That won't be too bad, not like what you're about—*

*Enough!* I cut off Valdr's oddly anxious voice. *We must do this, it's the only way.*

Selene walks over to me, changed into a flowy white t-shirt and black leggings with her hair piled in a bun, and holds out her hand for the bottle. I stare at her, awed by her simplicity being as attractive as the night she came into Howler's. *She's so beautiful.*

She sniffs the bottle before carefully taking a sip, and I laugh when she scrunches her nose at it. She glares at me and squeezes her eyes shut, tipping her head back to drink it down. The way she makes a twisted face is adorable and I laugh again, feeling slightly lightheaded. Selene rests her hand to her belly, no doubt feeling the pooling warmth by now, and glances at me with a slow grin spreading on her face. I rise to my feet, smiling like an idiot, holding my hand out for her.

We clumsily make our way downstairs, laughing at each other the whole time until we see Asteria and Hekate waiting for us in the living room. Asteria grins at us and gestures toward the floor by the fireplace. A few cushions and blankets have been laid out with candles and random bowls spread around. Hekate steps forward, clasping her hands with a worried expression on her face.

"How do you feel?" she asks, looking from Selene to me.

*"Hammered."* Selene drags out the word and starts laughing, swaying unsteadily.

I can't help but laugh too, I feel fucking fantastic. Asteria laughs with us and shakes her head as she moves to the other side of the room. I lightly tug on Selene's hand and we topple to the floor, flopping onto our backs.

"The potion I gave you is intended to ease your mental barriers," Asteria explains quickly. "I'll be able to work easier this way with the both of you. I will be sending you into the dream realm, and you should have full control over your conscious-self while there. Your physical body will remain unharmed. Though what you experience may *feel* real, remember that what you see and feel is only in your mind. Everything is just figments of your memories and nothing more. Understand?" she asks intently and I try hard to focus on what she has said, nodding once in acknowledgment.

She waves her hand around, getting Selene's attention. "You might be able to unlock your memories through the sleep-dive as well, if you choose to focus on your subconscious while in the dream realm. Mother will provide me with extra power to sustain you both for as long as possible. I am unsure *how long* I will be able to maintain the transportation spell, though, so try to be as efficient as possible."

Asteria turns to me again. "If—for whatever reason—you need to be extracted, focus on Valdr's bond and I will cease the spell. His soul will remain here with your physical body, to act as a gateway for communication if needed. Most importantly, do not let go of Selene, *no matter what.* If she becomes lost in the dream realm, she may never wake again. I have no tether to her except for you, Kyran," she states gravely.

I swallow thickly at the seriousness of Asteria's voice and nod, clarity briefly allowing me to fully grasp her words. Glancing over at Selene, her eyes blink owlishly at the information before she looks at me with worry. I give her hand a squeeze in reassurance. She lets go for a moment, snaking her arm beneath mine and tightly clasps my hand again.

"Are you both ready?" Asteria asks, raising her glowing hands.

We nod silently, and her eyes flood black, only the glowing white irises visible as she begins chanting. Around me, the room melts away like candle wax, and I feel nothing except for Selene's firm grip in mine. Darkness overcomes me with a sensation like diving into water and I am abruptly floating over my body ethereally, looking down at our sleeping forms on the floor. Hekate glances up at us and gives me a small, sad smile.

"This is quite similar to astral projection. You can move freely as if you would normally, though add flying to the mix with some psychic teleportation, and you can go literally anywhere. Envision in your mind's eye where you want to go and you will be there. Good luck, Kyran," she murmurs, waving her hand and everything completely disappears.

The silent, utter blackness is extremely disconcerting. Selene grips my hand and I immediately squeeze back reassuringly. Searching within my mind, I find the mental tether on my repressed memories and the row of five doorways manifests before us with a curl of smoke. Curiously, I envision a bright night sky above us with a soft, grassy field beneath our feet, and everything springs to life around us, drawing a startled gasp from Selene.

"*Whoa,* this is so amazing! Can I try?" she asks eagerly, pulling me around to face her.

I grin at the awe on her face and nod. "Just imagine anything you want and put it somewhere," I inform her, aware of how lucid dreaming works.

She squeezes her eyes shut for a moment and smiles as hundreds of floating white candles appear in the air, along with wildflowers in the field and leafy vines along the stone arched doorways. The warm light of the candles sets the wildflowers aglow like fireflies and gives the whole area a calming, serene feeling. I grin at her when she opens her eyes and lets out an excited squeal at the view she created. Her joy fades when she looks at me again, her brow pulling down in concern.

"Are you sure you're ready for this?" she asks me softly.

Glancing at the arches, my chest tightens and I turn back to her, replying honestly, "I don't know. I...feel a bit anxious."

"Maybe talking about them first will help you?" she asks quietly, rubbing her thumb over my knuckles.

*It's not me I'm anxious about,* I want to tell her.

I ponder her idea for a moment, thinking it might make it easier if she knew what each one was before going in.

Nodding, I murmur, "Yeah, I think so."

I arrange the archways into a wide circle around us and turn to face one of them, the one I had tried to enter before. Sighing, I explain tightly, "This is my first experience of what my father had called *training.* I didn't realize that it was actually torture until I was older, though. His methods would change as time went on, getting stronger and harsher as I grew. This was only two years after I first shifted. He said that he *'could sense the power in me,'* and told me how he wanted to use my potential to his benefit. This moment here, I think, is the start of everything else. I want to get through this one first in hopes that the others won't be as strong afterward." My voice drifts off as I stare at the foggy air swirling around inside the doorway.

Selene takes a slow breath, processing what I've told her. She steps in front of me, blocking my view of the arch. "I want you to focus on what you wish to tell that little boy inside there, inside your mind, and hold on to those words. When you push through the torment you'll uncover, remember that you have already survived this, that what happened to you was *not* your fault in any way, and allow yourself to *feel* it all. Let the energy run its course and fade away, spent and disbursed, rather than living inside you, festering in a wound desperate to heal. However it comes out of you, let it out *fully,* and let it *go*." She speaks gently, but she has a hard look in her eyes that tells me she's gone through something like this with herself.

My throat constricts and I pull her tightly into a hug, clenching my jaw against the emotions her words have brought out. Selene leans up and kisses me softly before stepping aside. I take a measured breath and am about to cross through the arch when she clasps my hand firmly in both of hers.

"No matter what, hold onto my hand, and feel that you are *not alone* in this, Kyran. When it overwhelms you, feel my hand in yours and know I am here with you, okay?" She lifts my hand and kisses my fingers.

Nodding silently, I gaze into her bright eyes and brace myself before I step through the doorway.

*Agony sears my skin, my back tearing open from the lash my father whips at me. A scream claws at my throat and I sag forward, staring into my reflection in a puddle of my own blood. My boyish face grimaces back at me, collar clanking against the chain tethering me to the wall. Torn fingernails scream beneath me, scraped raw from scrabbling against the concrete floor as I try to avoid my father's whip, the chain keeping me just within his reach.*

*"Face me like a man, you fucking coward!" he screams from the side of the cage, raising the whip above his head.*

*My body trembles, ready to shift and fight my attacker when another burning strike hits my back. I roar out in anger and burst into my wolf, lunging at my father with snapping jaws. My neck snaps backward, legs flying out in front of me, reaching the end of my chain just inches away from him. Before I can fully rise to my feet, a hard kick to my face sends me sprawling.*

*My father squats down in front of my face. "You're weak and pathetic." He spits at me. "I should just leave you here to rot, you piece of shit."*

*He reaches out, unbuckling my collar and throws it at me when he stands to leave. Shakily, I push off the floor as the cage door clangs shut behind him and shift back to my human form.*

*"Heal yourself and wash up before coming to dinner," is all he says without a backward glance.*

# LUNAR SHADOWS: AWAKEN

*I let out a harrowing bellow of rage until my lungs lose air and fall to the bloodstained floor, curling into myself to sob in the pain he's left me with.*

I separate from my inner child and stand beside him as pure fury rages around me, fire igniting and burning everything around us to ashes. I scream and scream until my chest is raw, feeling through the immense anger and resentment I've lived with for so long.

Desire courses through me to follow my father and torture him the way he did to me, to tear his skin from his flesh and rip his nails out one by one. Smash his teeth in until he chokes on them, break every bone in his body without letting him heal. I lose myself in the fury, feeling vengeful for his maltreatment, grieving the life I could have lived.

My hand tingles warmly and I remember Selene, of how she told me to think of the little boy and what I wanted to say to him.

I grip Selene's hand and feel her presence with me, taking deep breaths to calm myself. Focusing hard, I crouch and gently lay my hand on my inner child's head. I pour healing magic through his body and watch as the torn skin mends, the bruises fade, and the blood dripping from his nose ceases. I pull the boy into my lap, cradling him.

"Your strength is greater than you know. What you have been through does not define who you are. How others treat you is a reflection of themselves, not you. You are loved and cared for, you have great potential to be a powerful man with the ability to love and care for others in return. You *deserve* love, you always have. You did not deserve this unjust torture. *I love you,* and I thank you for not giving up, for keeping your strength, for allowing me to be where I am today." My voice cracks as a tear streams over my cheek, and I let it fall away.

Rising slowly, I carry him out of the doorway and place him on his feet beside me. He looks up at me with hard, amber eyes and glances at Selene. A wide grin slowly spreads across his boyish face. He laughs joyously, beaming at me with pure happiness and turns to run away, fading into the ether with his laughter trailing behind him.

Another hot tear escapes as an immense weight lifts from my chest, feeling like I can *finally* breathe.

The doorway slowly turns to dust and blows away on an invisible wind. I let out a huff of a laugh in disbelief. Selene wipes her cheeks and pulls my arm around her, squeezing my middle with all her strength.

"You should be very proud of yourself, Kyran. What you have just accomplished is not a simple thing to do," she mumbles against my chest. "You're absolutely adorable as a child, by the way."

I laugh as I wipe the tear away and look down into her eyes. "Thank you for your strength, Selene. I don't think I'd be able to do this without you," I admit quietly. "I know I would've gotten lost in the rage and pain of that memory if you weren't with me."

She smiles warmly and stretches up for a kiss, which I return deeply. After a moment, I pull back and take a slow breath. Walking over to the next arch, I sense what lies beyond it. Frowning, I bring forth the memory to share with Selene and it flashes across the archway in snippets like a TV screen.

"This happened shortly after my father's torture started—maybe a year or so had passed—time was hard to keep track of back then." I sigh, running a hand over my face. "I had a best friend. His name was Sisu, and I looked up to him like an older brother. He could do anything and never be affected by it. He feared no one and nothing, he was definitely a risk taker. One night, vampires attacked our pack and took his mother from their home. Sisu was only a child, but he fought with everything he had and even killed a few of them before he had been bitten. He was the first child in our pack to go berserk and it impacted everyone immensely. He was well-known and loved dearly by all. When Sisu began to lose control, my father had ordered his death, with *me* as the executioner," I explain tightly, clenching my jaw as I recall how that felt.

Selene gasps, her hand flying to her mouth with tears pooling in her eyes. She shakes her head in disbelief. "How could he? That...that is just *cruel*," she whispers harshly.

"He called it *resilience*." I scoff at the memory of him and his sneering smirk when he demanded it of me. "I refused him, in front of our pack. My father used his Alpha will on me and *commanded* that I kill Sisu, then and there. It was awful," I say lowly, dropping my head.

Selene gently rubs my arm. "When you go in there, remember to allow yourself to feel everything fully, and to let it go. It is very important that the energy dissipates outside of you."

I nod, giving her a sad smile before stepping through the archway, immediately staring into the red eyes of my angry, distraught friend.

*My entire body tenses as my muscles flex, refusing to obey the command set upon me. My legs painfully drag me forward against my will. I stare into Sisu's eyes and he snarls at me, his lean body quivering as he fights the urge to shift. The crowd surrounding us murmurs both in encouragement and dissent, the majority of the voices opposing my father's demand. I resist with everything I have when I come to stop before Sisu, holding his gaze for as long as possible.*

*"I don't want to do this, Sisu," I plead, shaking my head fervently as I clench every part of my body to remain still.*

*"Kyran, please, I don't want to hurt you! I don't want to hurt anyone, I can't fight it any longer." His voice is ragged as he paces back and forth. "Just do it. Do it!"*

*"Si—"*

*"Kill him!" my father demands harshly.*

*I bare my teeth at my father with hatred and lunge at Sisu, striking him in his face as he jumps at me, shifting mid-stride. I throw my body to the side and wrap my arms around his neck, trying to choke him, but he claws at my leg and pushes free. Sisu's brown wolf snaps his jaws at me, barely missing my face. I throw my fist into his throat and kick his ribs as hard as I can. Mid-shift, Sisu sinks his razor sharp fangs into the side of my neck and I scream in pain, tearing my body away as his teeth drag down to my shoulder, taking strips of my flesh with him.*

*Valdr assumes control, shifting fast. He lunges at Sisu, clamping his jaws around his throat. Without hesitation, he rips downward, blood flooding over his face and onto the ground. Sisu staggers for a moment before dropping dead, his body hitting the ground with a sickening thud.*

*Silence radiates as I shift and collapse to my knees. People immediately surround us in a cacophony of exclamations.*

*I can't hear what everyone is saying as I stare at my best friend, lying dead in the dirt because of me.*

*My first kill that wasn't a hunt.*

*Blood seeps from my wounded neck, but I make no move to heal it. I grow numb, remaining there in the bloodstained dirt long after everyone has gone home.*

*My father never spoke a word to me about it afterward. I focused only on the rage and hatred toward him, vowing to kill him one day for making me do this.*

Taking a deep breath, I lean forward, pressing my hand to Sisu's body and bow my head. I let the grief of his death flow over me.

The heavy waves threaten to drown as I mourn his loss and I struggle to breathe through it. My chest feels as if it will cave in, my limbs trembling slightly. I instinctively tighten my fingers around Selene's. She immediately grips onto my hand, her warmth and comfort surrounding me, and it releases the pressure built up inside. I don't fight against the tears that fall, allowing them to pour from me freely as I remember my friend.

I still wish that things could have been different, but I finally accept things for how they are.

Once I expel the grief I've carried my entire life, my body feels lighter and...*peace* settles within me. Now, the thought of Sisu feels like melancholic longing, rather than the sharp stab of a knife it once did, and I'm okay with that. I'll always miss him and wish for him to still be here with me, but I don't have to carry the negative memories like a punishment anymore.

Rising to my feet, I wipe my face as I step through the arch and look into Selene's concerned eyes. She silently pulls me into a hug, holding me for a while until I lean back, letting out a deep sigh. She threads her fingers through mine and nods to the side, taking a step away from me. I glance at the plush swinging bench she conjured and give her a smile as we sit down together.

I clear my throat, trying to dislodge the thick lump that has taken residence since we first began. "You had asked me about my scar," I say quietly, pulling the collar of my t-shirt down to show her. "It was from this night, from Sisu. I chose not to heal it because I wanted a reminder for what I had done to him. As if I could ever forget." I scoff, glancing up at the candles floating around us.

"Kyran, look at me," Selene says seriously, and I turn my head to face her. "Sisu's death is not your fault. You are not to blame, your father is. Though it was your body that ended his life, your father used you like a tool to do his work for him. You were only a child. That should not have been forced upon you." She speaks firmly, her gaze intense.

I nod slowly as her words wash over me. "You're right. I know this now, seeing it again for what it truly was. I've always held guilt over his death, feeling like a monster for murdering my best friend. I have come to realize that my father is to blame for the fucked up mess that I became, not me. It wasn't until a few decades ago did I come to understand that I could *choose* to be better, that I didn't have to be the monster he created. I think...I can finally forgive myself for this," I say quietly and smile wondrously at my words.

The doorway disintegrates and blows away, showing me that I have truly let go. Selene squeezes my hand, smiling warmly at me. I take a deep breath, feeling better for not harboring the heaviness any longer. Pushing the swing with my foot, we sit in silence for a little while.

Knowing I don't have the luxury of taking my time, I pull another arch in front of us. This memory will hurt differently than the others, but it is equally as painful to feel. A realization creeps over me as I recall this moment in time, and I have confidence I will surpass it more swiftly than the last two.

Gesturing toward the smokey archway, the scene silently plays in fast-forward. "This was the moment my mother was abducted. I arrived home *just barely* too late to make any difference, and I have carried the guilt of it since, always thinking I should've done something to save her. I just realized now, though, that there was nothing I could have done to change it, based on how things were going in my life at the time." Leaning forward, I rest my elbows on my knees as I explain my past.

"I had separated from my pack for a while before she was taken. I was living in darkness for a long time after discovering my mate had died without meeting her, and dealing with the fallout from Vala, as you now know," I murmur, glancing at Selene. She gives me a sympathetic nod and I continue. "I had been heavily involved in the Underground, which is basically a supernatural fighting ring, except where only one being leaves alive. It is a violent, nasty place to be, and only the vilest of beings participate, the prize being a large sum of money from a betting pool."

I sigh heavily, running a hand through my hair. "I had originally been there because of my father. He wanted to display the power his pack held, intending to intimidate the other packs and rogue wolves with my abilities. The Underground had become a sort of twisted addiction for me. The self-inflicted pain and torment of the fighting was like fuel to my fire, allowing my rage to unleash monstrously." I take a breath, gritting my teeth with the memories.

Selene strokes her fingers down my arm, resting her hand atop mine.

"I had been there, that night, when I heard my father's pleading mindlink to get home, begging me to help fend off the vampires. Believe it or not, there is a portal to the Underground in the center of town. Every pack has one near the vicinity of their territory for easy access. Sometimes Alphas will recruit wolves or other beings from the Underground to work for them in various ways. You know that old, dilapidated diner that sits in the middle of the shopping district? Yeah, that's the portal. It has never been a real diner." I laugh humorlessly at the thought.

"No way," Selene mutters with wide eyes. "Um, if you don't mind me asking, when was the last time you fought there?"

"Over a hundred years ago, and I don't have *any* intention of ever going back there," I say flatly with a shake of my head.

Sighing, I push to my feet and Selene gets up as well, giving me an encouraging smile. We cross over to the arch and I step right through, expecting the despair that washes over me.

*I'm sprinting across our field, trampling hundreds of dead bodies, my eyes locked on my mother's flying blonde hair as she is hauled over the shoulder of a large vampire. My father is swarmed by vampires. Einarr and Kara fight viciously to chase after our mother. I whine when I see my younger sister fall, pounding my paws harder into the earth to reach them. Einarr catches the vampire who killed our sister, tearing him in half, and rushes toward the group of vampires running away with our mother.*

*My brother's sharp howl of pain radiates into the night as he falls, but I cannot bring myself to look away from my mother's limp, dangling body as they disappear into the woods.*

*I follow the scent trail for miles until it simply vanishes, as if they left earth entirely. I circled the woods for hours, searching for any kind of clue as to which direction they could have gone. My father's distant howl pulls me back toward home and when I arrive, I stop short at the sight of my dead siblings. If only I could've—*

I shake my head and pull out of the memory, reversing it to the beginning and watch it like a movie. No, there is nothing I could have done differently, I did what I was able to do. Although I am unsure about my brother, I know Kara died honorably defending our family, and her death was something she would've been proud of. I cannot blame myself for her loss, or my brother's.

Thinking about my mother as I watch her capture, the heavy grief of her loss washes over me and bow my head. Whatever it was that she had endured, I hope her death was a reprieve for her. I trust she knew that I would've done everything and anything to prevent this from happening if I could have, and that's what matters most. I even sought out and killed those who were responsible that day.

All except for Caedes now.

Opening my eyes, the scene slowly fades away as I accept the past for what it is. I cannot blame myself for things that were entirely out of my control.

Life just fucking sucks like that sometimes.

I step out of the archway holding the memory of killing my father as it blows away behind me. His death at my hands formed a festering illness inside me because most of my issues had been essentially tied up with him. Killing him had been a mercy since he was berserk, but it was also a curse upon me.

I used it as my way of punishing him for every pain he caused me, for every bad experience and resulting fallout. I acted out of anger and spite, not through mercy for his life. Harboring that ill will toward my father pushed all of this *shit* deep down inside me, instead of it being released upon his death. I don't think I could ever truly forgive him for what he had done to me throughout my life, but in a twisted way, I understand where he was coming from in choosing to do so.

With that understanding came the ability to let go of the burden I've carried for so long, of the immense pain I never let myself validate or feel through.

Selene's gentle touch pulls me out of my thoughts and I sigh tiredly, feeling extremely worn out. I glance at the last remaining archway and smile, knowing I don't have to enter it for me to move past it for good. She looks up at me patiently, and I gaze down at her, brushing my fingers over her cheek.

"This was the moment I got my mark, when I learned the truth of losing my real mate and of Vala's deception. It was an extremely distressing moment full of despair, remorse, grief, and anger. This was essentially the breaking point for me, the final straw that really sent me over the edge. I didn't see a point to my life anymore, not after everything I'd already gone through. Everything I had endured before could have been worth it, holding onto the chance that I'd meet my mate and be loved by her.

"When that got ripped away from me, I felt that my life no longer held any meaning. I had no purpose. I wanted to die after this happened. I think that was a huge reason why I went to the Underground, I had hoped someone would be able to accomplish what I couldn't bring myself to do." My voice drifts away as the despair I'd lived with for so long rises to the surface for the last time. I swallow thickly, taking a calming breath and letting it go.

I squeeze Selene's fingers as I look into her bright eyes. "I don't feel that way anymore. I don't have to go in there because that pain no longer exists within me. I'm standing here with *you* literally holding my hand through what I thought would never happen. My healing. I feel lighter than I ever have. I feel free now, Selene, thanks to *you*. If not for you, I would still be going around that endless cycle, over and over until I died, and I can finally say that cycle has been broken. *You* have given me my life back, and it has meaning. I have people I care for who care for me, I have my family and my pack. I cannot express how grateful I am to have found you, and I am wholly yours, if you'll have me," I murmur, my heart beating heavily in my chest.

"Now you know my dark truths. You have witnessed the ugliest parts of me, of what I've done, and I will not deny that I chose wrongly when I had the choice to do good in my life. I chose to remain the same, even though I could've changed for the better. So here I stand now, accepting who I am, and I bare my raw self to you, if you'll have me. Even if you won't, I honestly understand. I will always be grateful for the time I've had with you, and for the immeasurable help you have given me to forgive myself. To truly *heal*." A tear slips free and runs over my smile as I hold her beautiful face.

"*Thank you, Selene,*" I whisper on a breath, shaking my head. "You do not have to answer right now. I want you to take as much time as you need. Just know that I will always be here for you, no matter wh—"

Diamonds fly from her eyes as she leaps, crashing into me. She wraps herself around my body, kissing me deeply. I hold her tight, the kiss more passionate and intense than any I've had before. Her fingers grip the hair at the back of my head as her soft lips glide over mine and it feels like I'm flying. Selene's touch is like electricity, shooting tingles through every inch of me. She gasps against my mouth and I open my eyes.

We're completely surrounded by thousands of glittering stars.

I glance down, seeing the floating candles hovering below us, and realize we *are* flying. I laugh deeply with joy and bury my face into her neck, kissing her soft skin. She shivers against me with a sigh. Keeping an arm locked around her waist, I caress her back and run my hand through her hair as I slowly kiss along her jaw, working my way to her mouth once more. We remain here for a while, floating in the night sky, holding each other tightly.

Selene leans back, her mouth swollen and flush, the rosy color matching her cheeks when she meets my gaze. I grin widely and kiss her nose, pulling her legs from around me and hold her closely to my chest. She bites her lip and smiles back at me, resting her head on my shoulder as I descend to the ground.

My legs are shaky beneath me—an entirely strange sensation—and I finally understand the old saying of 'weak at the knees'. With a shake of my head, I huff a laugh at the thought. Sitting on the bench swing, I rest Selene in my lap and gently sway, feeling completely at peace for the first time in my life.

After a few quiet moments, I reach out and touch Valdr's bond.

He immediately asks, *Is everything alright, do you need to come back?*

*I'm fine actually, more than alright. How much longer do we have in here? I want to try to get Selene's memories unlocked before Asteria has no energy left.*

I wait for a few heartbeats, assuming Valdr is speaking with either Asteria or Hekate, and I smile at Selene's curious expression. I wonder if I make a face while talking with Valdr and am about to ask her when he responds.

*She is doing okay, though you have about a third of the time that you've used, if that helps. I will come back to warn you before she pulls you out,* he informs me and his presence fades away.

"Hey, I just reached out to Valdr, we don't have much time. Do you still want to try to find your memories of your life before your stasis?" I ask quietly, and she nods enthusiastically.

"Yes! Let's go," she chirps, pushing out of my lap and grabbing my hand as she stands. "Wait, how do I find that?" She abruptly turns around.

I laugh at her scrunched face. "Think of inside your mind, the spot where you can recall people, places, or events, and envision something that can depict that energy. For your case, you might be able to feel the blocked area of your memory. If you focus on *that,* maybe your subconscious can manifest it for us to explore," I prompt, watching her face as she closes her eyes.

She squeezes my hand as her eyebrows bunch together, a frown pulling her mouth down. Our field vanishes, replaced by a vast forest. Enormous trees stand around us blocking out the sky, and loud wind and crashing water echoes nearby. Curious, I glance at Selene and she just shrugs, looking around at the woods surrounding us.

I'm drawn to the trees and reach my hand out to brush the trunk nearest me. The bark glows at my touch. A golden sheen appears, showing me a younger Asteria running around with their dogs at the cottage, and I can hear Selene's laughter as she sprays them with a hose. I smile and withdraw my hand, turning to Selene.

"These trees are your active memories. This is a beautiful way to picture your long-term memory," I murmur, looking around us again.

I notice how the trees vary greatly in type and wonder how that correlates with her memories, thinking about how each type could be parts of her life representing different people and things within them. Selene tugs on my hand and I follow her, walking closer to the sound of crashing water I heard when we arrived. Within moments, we break out of the forest and Selene gasps.

I can't believe what I see.

A high cliff stretches before us with a rocky face, and at the edge sits a large silver cage with a bright golden cord threading around the bars, disappearing like a rope into the ether above. Pacing around in circles within the cage is Luna, her pure white fur coat beaming like moonlight. She is *absolutely magnificent.* Our eyes meet and she goes stark still for a breath before thrashing against the bars. The entire cage rattles, but it remains intact.

*I cannot wait for Valdr to meet her, he is going to lose his mind,* I wonder with awe. She is breathtaking and I grin widely at the sight of her, turning to share the excitement with Selene.

Her face is not turned up toward her wolf, however. Her eyes are wide with fear as she stares below us, her breaths coming fast. I rest my hand against her back and quickly follow her line of sight. A vast, dark ocean churns, and giant waves crash angrily against the shore, white froth spraying from the force of impact. On the horizon, I notice a tiny island with something shining on it like a beacon.

Fear, anger, and anguish permeates the air around me as I focus on the raging sea.

"Selene, what's wrong? Look at me. *Selene*," I say sharply, stepping in front of her when she doesn't move or respond.

She blinks and her eyes flick to mine, filled with tears. Harsh wind whips her hair around as she shakes her head, biting her lip with tears dripping down her cheeks. I cup her face gently and look into her eyes, fear rising into panic behind them.

"I think this ocean is from...*Bolvi*," she whispers with a sob, pressing the back of her hand to her mouth.

I take her hands in mine, raising my voice over the lashing wind. "We can try to go to Luna if you'd prefer, but there is something out there in that water. It seems important to be surrounded by this ocean. I am here with you no matter what, Selene, in any way you need me to be, okay? You *do not* have to go in there. We can talk about this if you want to, or we can leave to come back another time when you are prepared. Whatever you choose, know I will be by your side. Always." My deep voice booms with the crashing waves.

She meekly nods and steps aside, raising her hands to her face for a moment to collect herself. Concerned, I run a hand over my mouth, watching as she turns to look out at the stormy waters with so much pain on her face.

"I...I don't think I'm ready. Not yet. I've been silently fighting this...this *agony* for a while, trying to just *move on* with my life and leave this shit behind," Selene whispers raggedly, shaking her head as she takes a step backward. "I can't face this yet, it will drown me." Her voice is thin, void of the strength she had with me in the starry field.

She looks at me over her shoulder with deep despair in her eyes, reaching her hand for mine.

I immediately step toward her.

The moment I raise my arm to take her hand, a monstrous wave rises up, ripping me off of my feet and swallowing Selene as it pulls her into the ocean.

"*Selene!*" I bellow out to the sudden blackness.

Her terrified screams pierce my heart before the violent water silences her. Without hesitation, I scramble forward, diving over the edge.

# Chapter Eighteen

## STRENGTH

### SELENE

Icy fear drowns me. Tumbling through the darkness of the churning waters, my arms and legs flail helplessly as I sink deeper into the abyss. I was about to take Kyran's hand and walk away from the turmoil that I wasn't ready to face. Though I have spent a long time sorting through all the shit Bolvi did to me physically and mentally, there was a lot of energy I had yet to fully release from within me.

Traumatic energy that threatened to consume me if I paid it too much attention.

Bubbles fly from my mouth when I scream in terror. Frigid water pours into my lungs, suffocating and weighing me down. I kick harshly, desperate to find the surface, but I cannot tell which way is up or down. Panic seizes me, fearing I will not survive this, and I thrash wildly to try and get *anywhere* but here.

Blazing heat envelops my arms, holding them still against my sides and I whip my head around, finding Kyran's glowing amber eyes boring into mine. He looks terrified and drags me against his warm chest for a moment then pulls back, mouthing silent words at me.

I can't hear him over the pounding in my ears and I shake my head vigorously as we float beneath the raging water. He clasps my hands tightly before opening his mouth and taking an exaggerated breath, widening his eyes at me in a silent plea to understand. I belatedly realize that he is *breathing underwater.*

I squeeze my eyes shut and *believe* that I can also breathe. I take a tiny inhale through my nose as a test. A bizarre sensation fills me as the cool water flows around my skin, but my chest is light with air. My eyes fly open and stare wildly at Kyran, taking a deep breath myself. A shrill laugh spurts from me, a few bubbles floating upward.

Dizzy, I try to wrap my head around everything that just happened and uncontrollable sobs escape me in another torrent of bubbles.

Kyran pulls me toward him again and holds me in his strong arms, running a hand over my hair. *"Shh,* it's okay. I've got you, sweetheart, you're okay," he whispers, comforting me.

I take a moment to collect myself and consider what makes up this ocean. I realize that all my trauma has built up into a single, overwhelming sea of energy, each drop of water from the awful experiences I went through with Bolvi. Many of them were based on fear, and I have shied away from fully facing it because any time I tried, the beginnings of a panic attack would rise to the surface. Instead of processing things, I'd push it down, down, down, shoving it deep within me.

I look up at Kyran with a frown, clutching him tighter. "I'm afraid," I admit with a shaky voice. "I don't think I can get rid of this, it's too much. I just want it to go away. I don't want his energy inside me. I can't go through that again, it will ruin me." My voice breaks from the emotions roiling within me and I can't stop myself from crying.

"I know, I don't want you to have to face this if you aren't ready to. It's okay to be afraid, Selene. I may not know the details of everything you have faced, but you did not deserve *any* of it. I can tell Valdr to have Asteria pull us out, okay?" His voice is gentle, but there's a tightness to it that shows in his eyes as well.

I want to agree and leave here immediately, and I almost open my mouth to say so, but I abruptly understand that is what I have always been doing, running away. If I turn my back on myself again, this won't go away and it will only grow worse with time, making the next time I face it that much more difficult to deal with. Steeling myself, I shake my head and Kyran's brow scrunches downward.

"I can't run away, not anymore," I say firmly, my voice gaining strength as I speak. "I don't know how, but I need to release this once and for all. I don't want this *mess* affecting me any longer."

Glancing away with a blush, I murmur, "I also don't want it getting in the way of bonding with you."

A warm smile pulls at the corner of his mouth and he leans down to kiss my forehead. "I'm here for you however you need me to be," he mumbles against my skin.

"Thank you. I-I don't know where to start." I sigh deeply, regulating my breathing.

I focus only on us for the moment.

Kyran pulls back a little and slides his hands down my arms. The muscle at his jaw tics. "What would you say was the worst part about being with him?" he asks quietly, his voice rough.

Averting my gaze, I chew on my lip as I think about that, having tons of issues to choose from. With a nod, I know where I need to start. "Control. Or the lack of it, I should say. I always felt like I had absolutely no control around him. He would do whatever he wanted with me—*or to me*—whenever he wanted to. If I ever denied him or disagreed, I would've been hit or shoved down in retaliation, forced to fear speaking against him. I had the choice of either suffering physical abuse, or going along with what he wanted to save my body from the pain. I know now that I was only trading physical pain for mental abuse when I had to succumb to doing things I did not want to do," I grit out between my teeth in anger.

My breath comes faster as ire rises with the resurfacing memories. "He was a predator, seeking out weakness to prey upon. That asshole manipulated me into believing I would never be loved by anyone else, convincing me that nobody would want to be with someone as pathetic as me. It's all *so fucked up!* I truly hate him, I despise the thought of ever having been involved with a piece of *shit* like that," I seethe, my trepidation melting away into frustration and shame.

Kyran remains silent, and I fight against the tears threatening to fall. I slide my gaze toward him, finding him staring out into the abyss with a cold, stony expression.

His body is rigid, almost statuesque as he hisses through clenched teeth, *"If I ever see that fucking bastard again, I will rip his beating heart from his chest, and savor watching the worthless life bleed from his eyes."*

His dark words stir something buried deep within me. I drop my head, angrily scrubbing my face with the memories swirling around me. A gap through my fingers reveals a dark shadow circling below us and I tear my hands from my face in shock, my heart leaping into my throat.

Gasping, I grip onto Kyran's shirt in fear and stammer, *"K-ky, Kyran!"*

I point a trembling finger at the looming shadow. He grasps my hands and glances downward, swearing at the sight of the shark rising closer. Pressing his fingers to my chin, he pulls my face toward him and looks me hard in the eyes.

"Selene, you called him a predator. That shark is the manifestation of Bolvi, and you've got to kill it to set it free from your soul. I could do it for you, but I want *you* to save yourself, to show you how much strength you hold within. You are capable of more than you know. I have faith in you that you will succeed. I will be here with you the whole time, okay? I won't let him hurt you ever again." Kyran's voice is hard with conviction.

A tear slips down my cheek.

I nod, breathing shakily, and turn away from Kyran, scrambling to figure out how to approach this. The shark grows bigger the closer it gets and I swallow thickly, my nerves jittering. Its large gray tail lazily flips back and forth as it circles us. With haste, I envision a long blade attached to a lengthy handle, manifesting it into my hands. I roll it between my palms nervously and Kyran lets out a low whistle of approval. I turn over my shoulder to grin at him, and he smiles back encouragingly before I glance down again, startled to find the shark swimming alarmingly close beneath me.

Slowly floating backward, Kyran follows me and I warily lift my weapon in defense. The two of us stay side by side as the shark bends around, its flat black eye facing us. Before I have time to react, it jolts forward on a burst of speed.

I hastily lash out the blade with a scream, catching it in the gills as it passes by me. The huge shark thrashes to the side and darts at me again, this time closing its massive jaws around the handle and snapping it in half. I shriek, totally freaked out, and fail at conjuring a second weapon as the beast prepares to strike at me again. All I can see is the deep, gaping pit of its mouth. A mouth ringed by dozens of jagged points coming straight at me.

I try to swim away and squeeze my eyes shut in fear.

A loud *clang* echoes through the dark water.

Startled, my eyes fly open, relief flooding me at the sight of the metal cage surrounding me. Searching wildly for Kyran, I find him floating above with a long metal harpoon held loosely in his hand. He winks at me before focusing on the shark again.

It circles back toward us, gaining speed, and with a surge of anger and fear, I snag the harpoon from Kyran. Drawing my arm back, I aim the weapon and wave my free hand to dissolve the cage. Waiting for the right moment, my heart pounds heavily, constricting my chest with fear as the shark opens its wide jaws. Kyran grabs my hand tightly just as I scream and launch the harpoon upward into the shark's mouth with all my strength.

Inky blood spills around us, clouding the water as the shark thrashes with the harpoon lodged inside its head. The beast slowly sinks into the abyss beneath us. I can't help the cries that leave me, the fear and anger seeping out of me, falling behind the dying monster into the depths below.

My entire body shakes and I meet Kyran's gaze, letting out a laugh of disbelief. A second laugh follows and then another, each one becoming more jubilant as they escape me.

Kyran smiles widely, holding out his arms. I fly into him and he holds me tight, swinging us around.

"You did it, Selene! How do you feel, now that it is done?" he asks proudly, pressing his cheek to the top of my head.

"Terrified. But, also more free. I don't want to experience that again, but I have to admit, it was quite a rush." I laugh again, pulling myself up to peck him on the cheek with a kiss.

He laughs with me and I push off his shoulders, swimming toward the surface. My head breaks through with a splash and I spin in a circle, noticing that the waters have calmed a bit, though large waves still rear up around me. Kyran appears a few paces away, looking around as well before meeting my gaze.

"What has been left within you, Selene?" he asks quietly, nodding toward the heavy, crashing waves.

I suck in my lip and take a deep breath before answering.

"Intimacy," I whisper, reaching for his hand. "He ruined it for me. I don't know what it feels like to be touched by a man and enjoy it. I always dreaded him putting his hands on me, forcing me to comply when I would tell him no. It always resulted in him *hurting me*, outside and in. He would…hold me down, yell at me to shut up or hit me until I did. I couldn't sleep peacefully without the fear of being disturbed. I ended up keeping myself awake, always expecting the worst. It got so bad that I wanted to die, Kyran," I admit with a sob, squeezing his hand tightly.

"*No,*" he rasps, his face stricken as he pulls me into a warm embrace.

The opened floodgates of my memories overwhelm me, and I reveal details I haven't been able to speak aloud. "He-he would only leave b-bruises where my clothes would cover, so nobody would see them," I cry out between gasps, my emotions threatening to consume me. "He would get me drunk and ridicule me for not handling my alcohol, then take advantage of me in a vulnerable state. He kept revolting photos of me as blackmail, threatening to display them to the world if I ever left. The worst of it all is he killed the hope inside of me that one day I would know what *real love* felt like. His *love* was all that I knew, and it has marred me ever since." I end on a ragged whisper, feeling a little sick, and my lip quivers as I desperately try to hold back my tears.

Kyran remains silent, and after a few moments I pull back to look at him. His handsome face is contorted with rage, but he holds me gingerly in his arms. He moves slowly before gazing intently into my eyes.

"That's why you had me make you that drink, isn't it? And the way you reacted to me running into you at the park…*Fuck!*" He growls the swear with heated anger, releasing his hold on me and roughly drags a hand down his face.

Kyran meets my gaze again and gently cups my face in his warm hands. "I am *so sorry* that you had to experience that horrible shit, Selene. How could someone *do that*—" He clenches his jaw and shuts his eyes, his nostrils flaring with ire, hands trembling against my skin.

When he opens his eyes once more, unshed tears glisten in them and he roughly whispers, "Selene, the pain you have endured, the pain you *still carry*, it…it affects me deeply, and I promise you that I *will never—*"

A looming shadow tears my eyes from Kyran's, and I glance past his shoulder at the gigantic wave rising behind him.

*"Ky—"*

It swallows my shout when it crashes down, devouring us in the tumultuous current and countlessly flipping me head over heels. I'm torn from Kyran's grasp, flailing around blindly for him.

The light snuffs out beneath the cold water, leaving me in pitch blackness and my chest clenches with fear. A pressure blooms against my back and I relax, relieved that Kyran found me so quickly amidst the chaos.

Icy fingers grip the back of my neck as more roughly grope my body. Horrified, I let out a shrill scream when I realize it is *definitely not Kyran touching me*. Hands squeeze too hard, bruising my throat, arms, legs.

I desperately claw at them as panic seizes me.

I'm blind in the darkness, sobbing helplessly while my clothes are torn off. My skin crawls from the painful, unwanted touches. A cold, slimy lick trails up my neck and I shudder in disgust, wildly slapping my skin at the sensation. I can't focus on how to make it stop, I can't think of anything except my fear and repulsion.

My shrieks and cries echo in the cold emptiness.

A stinging hand slaps across my face, hitting me hard enough to steal my breath. Prickly hands grate against my belly, roughly dragging downward and I cry out desperately for it to stop.

The sickening touches suddenly vanish from my skin, replaced by a blooming heat, soft and gentle across my hips. I search the darkness in front of me, unable to focus on anything solid and I flail away, scared without my vision.

Squeezing my eyes shut, I envision the floating candles again.

When my heartbeat slows to a safer pace, I peek through my lashes at the candles illuminating the deep waters with an ethereal glow. Opening my eyes wider, Kyran floats below me, gripping his head with a pained expression on his face. At the sight of him, my body relaxes for a moment, feeling much safer now that I can see, knowing he is with me.

Another pair of gross, cold hands wrap around my torso and dig their fingers into my ribs. I let out a dreadful whimper, scratching at them futilely. My pleading eyes flash to Kyran's and he swims toward me, glaring in horror at my bruised body.

His gaze meets mine with a desperate questioning expression.

My eyes flicker between his, and I silently nod in agreement.

Kyran immediately reaches out with both hands and lays his on top of the phantom ones, his warmth melting the icy touch away as he presses his palms to my sides. With a feather-light brush of his fingers, he glides them over my skin and I relax in his comforting touch.

Slimy fingers slide over my breasts and I grimace at the sensation before they pinch my nipples *hard*. I cry out in pain, my hands flying uselessly to my chest in defense.

Kyran frowns and meets my gaze. "Tell me to stop and I will, okay? If at any moment you feel uncomfortable, let me know right away." His voice is rough and tight with anger.

I sob helplessly as the vile memories assault me.

*"Okay,"* I whisper with a nod, and pull my hands away against the instincts raging inside of me.

He holds my gaze as he glides his hands up my body, his eyes searching my face as he gently cups my breasts in his warm palms, the pads of his thumbs lightly grazing over my nipples. I close my eyes as little sparks radiate from his touch, and my mouth lifts into a small smile.

*I am safe with him.*

Sharp nails dig into my back, scratching down my spine and squeeze my ass so hard I yelp, arching away from the vile touch. A tear spills from Kyran's eye as he glides his warm palms around my ribs and reaches up, resting his fingertips behind my shoulders. He massages me gently, and I sigh when he slowly traces his fingers over my spine. Electricity tingles behind his touch. He splays his hands around my ass, caressing me in soothing circles.

Looking into his amber eyes shining like firelight, I let out another sigh, running my hands up his strong arms. I accidentally dig my fingernails into his shoulders when an icy grip stabs my inner thighs, forcing my legs apart.

I glance down with a sob and Kyran growls fiercely, his hand flying between my legs to protect me. He holds still, carefully keeping his hand in place as he lifts my chin to look into my eyes.

"Are you alright?" he murmurs, rubbing his thumb across my cheek to wipe away my tears. His face is hard with tension as he seems to struggle with keeping his emotions under control.

I wait a moment, anticipating more violation, but it thankfully doesn't return. My heartbeat settles from the perilous rhythm it was pounding, and I take a moment to catch my breath. Slowly, I nod my head in response, and Kyran glides his other hand across my cheek, cupping my face in his heated palms.

Relaxing against him, I slide my arms around his neck as more tears fall, dripping over his hands. Lifting myself, I wrap my legs around his waist and press my forehead to his. He effortlessly embraces me in his strong arms, holding me close, keeping me safe.

"I am, with you," I whisper, nodding again with a sniffle.

He gives me a warm smile before kissing me deeply, his hand caressing my face and I glide my fingers up his neck, burying them into his thick hair. Heat blooms in my chest, the warmth spreading throughout my body as I sigh against his lips.

After a few heavy breaths, I pull back and smile at him, tracing his eyebrow with my finger. He grins at me crookedly and I am struck by his rough handsomeness up close. Kyran kisses my eyes still wet with tears, rubs his nose to mine and looks upward. Smirking at me, we hurtle toward the surface.

I cling to his neck at the sudden movement as we quickly shoot out of the water. Droplets fly everywhere, glistening like diamonds. All around us the ocean is calm and beautiful, the sky a bright blue with puffy white clouds floating by. From up here, I see the island Kyran had mentioned before I got swept away and I point to it, guiding his sight.

We slowly float over to the small piece of land in silence. Lowering toward the beach, Kyran gently sets my feet in the sand and takes my hands in his.

"*I am so sorry* you had to go through that Selene, both now and in the past," he says with a thick voice, rubbing his thumbs over my knuckles. "It sickens me to know you've experienced such awful treatment, especially from someone I was once responsible for. You did amazing, and as you said to me, you should be proud of yourself for your courage and strength to go through it again."

I swallow back the tears that I can hardly keep at bay. "Thank you, Kyran. I would have drowned in this without you here, and I know that I will still have things to overcome from it, but the darkness isn't as consuming. I feel lighter, more free now that I have faced what I've suppressed for so long. I wasn't ready to go through that and I didn't want to, but with your help *I did*, and that is something I won't forget. We make a kick-ass team," I mumble with a smirk, easing the heavy mood.

He laughs lightly, though his eyes hold a hardness within them.

"I am always here whenever you need me. For *anything*," he murmurs, his voice growing serious once more as he reaches up to gently cup my face. "Always remember that, sweetheart."

I step forward and wrap my arms around his middle, squeezing tightly. Kyran strokes my hair, resting his chin on my head and holds me close. We stay like this for a little while, gently swaying with the light breeze.

After some time, I lean away, taking a deep breath. Though I told him the truth, I wasn't completely honest with him about how I'm feeling, and frankly I'm not in the best place of mind to face it at this moment. I let my breath out slowly, glancing away from him. A flash of shame runs through me, and I clench my jaw before giving him a small smile.

"Ready to go find that shiny thing you saw?" I ask quietly, taking his hand in mine as exhaustion threatens to claim me.

"I am when you are," he murmurs with a tight smile. "Actually, hold on a moment."

Kyran gently pulls my hand, lifting my arm up high. He grasps my fingers and spins me around, silky material fluttering over my body. Glancing down when he brings me to a stop, I smile at the pretty pastel blue dress he manifested for me.

"Huh. I would've expected a t-shirt and jeans," I jest, scrunching my nose at him playfully.

He laughs and takes my hand again, turning us toward the trees.

It doesn't take us very long to get through the forest and I enjoy the peaceful walk with Kyran. The calm quiet is a reprieve from the exhaustive turmoil of today. We come across a gorgeous grassy opening with a small waterfall and sparkling pool, bright flowers blooming throughout the greenery.

Sitting in a patch of sunlight is an illuminated, shiny silver chest. I hurry toward it, knowing *this* must have been what Kyran had noticed. Hesitantly placing my hand on the cool metal, I gasp at the jolt of energy that painlessly radiates along my arm. I slam my palms against the lid, pushing forcefully to no avail.

A frustrated groan escapes me and I drop my hands, walking around the chest to observe it.

The metal is ornate with intricate filigree, large rivets line the edges over the smooth face panels, and I cannot find a lock or keyhole anywhere. Confused, I glance up at Kyran, and he looks puzzled as well. He crouches, curiously running his fingers over the chest.

I stop beside him, murmuring, "These are my memories, I can feel it. I have no idea how to open it, though. I think there is some sort of spell or enchantment—*Asteria!*" I slap my hand on the chest. "I bet she could open it, maybe it's locked with her magic somehow? And she couldn't reach it before because it got buried deep into my subconscious. Now that I know where it is, maybe I can direct her to it and I'll get my memories back." My words rush out hopefully and I wring my hands together.

"That would be wonderful." Kyran grins, rising to his feet. "Would you like me to let Valdr know we've found it and have Asteria pull us out? Though, we should probably rest before attempting to unlock that," he mutters, quickly glancing at the chest and narrowing his eyes before meeting my gaze, a look of concern etched onto his face.

I almost nod in agreement, but a thought darts across my mind and I step around the chest. "Wait, what about Luna?" I ask tightly, remembering her cage.

His brow pinches and he nods, murmuring, "Let's go to her, quickly, before we run out of time."

Kyran holds out his hand and I lace my fingers in his, focusing on the cliff I saw her on. I imagine we're standing next to Luna's cage and in a flash, the windy cliff top appears around us.

The sight of my wolf makes me press my hand to my mouth in astonishment. She is absolutely *stunning* with her bright white fur, her crystal blue eyes shining like starlight, and the poise she carries herself with. I dash over to her cage and shove my arms through, immediately overcome with a sense of deep longing at seeing her.

She eagerly presses her head into my hands.

"*Luna,* I am so glad to see you! I don't remember being with you, but I can *feel* you and I know I miss you. You are gorgeous! Wait until Valdr gets his eyes on you, *woo.*" I whistle jokingly, and a laugh bubbles up from my chest as tears spring in my eyes.

Kyran chuckles beside me and he rests his hand on my back. "I said the same thing when I first saw her. Luna," he greets her, bowing his head deeply, "I am honored to meet you, and I look forward to running with you beneath the moon." He grins mischievously as he straightens.

She leans forward, pushing her snout through the bars, and Kyran brushes his hands over her face. She gives him a lick then lightly nips at his fingers, a feathery growl leaving her chest. I laugh at the same time as Kyran, and he ruffles the fur on her head.

"Yeah, he's gonna roll over when he meets you," he jokes, his eyes crinkling happily.

*I'm pleased to see you here.* Her melodic voice floats around Kyran and me like a ringing crystal bell. *Can you get me out? I've tried endlessly, but it doesn't budge. I'm trapped here. I want to run.*

Kyran shakes his head and I reply, "No, I don't know how yet. But I am going to try. I will talk with Ria and Mother about this as soon as I can. I hope you aren't in here much longer." I sigh, grasping the bars.

Looking at the cage, I take a few steps back and follow the seamless metal bars around in a circle, finding a large padlock on the other side. I grasp it, wondering where the key is to unlock it. I blink, belatedly recognizing the gleaming silver metal.

"The chest!" I exclaim and they both turn to face me. "There is a padlock here made of the same metal as my memory chest. If I can open that, I'd bet the key to opening *this* is inside of it, somehow. Luna, I don't think I can get you out until my memories are restored, but I believe Ria can do that part for us," I tell her with hope brightly coloring my voice.

"We've gotta go, I need to let her know about this," I say to Kyran, holding out my hand for him.

When he slides his fingers through mine, I reach up and grasp the golden thread woven around the cage.

*Selene, are you alright?* Valdr's rough voice immediately rumbles through my mind.

*Yes, I'm okay. We need to leave. I know where my memories are, but I cannot access them, and I believe Luna cannot be freed until they are returned to me,* I quickly inform him.

*I will let them know,* he responds tightly, his anxiousness evident through our bond.

I place my hand against a bar, murmuring, "Luna, I will be back as quick as I can, okay? You'll be free soon."

She just huffs a breath in response and dramatically lies down with a flop. Kyran laughs and I roll my eyes at her attitude, though I can't hide the smirk that tugs at my lips.

Dizziness washes over me and I tighten my hold on Kyran as everything fades to black around us, just like it was when we first started this journey.

I yearn to finally feel whole again, but I'm anxious to get started, because the darkest part of me is clawing its way to the surface, and it's difficult to hold back the anguish threatening to consume me.

# CHAPTER NINETEEN

## UPLIFTED

### SELENE

When my eyes fly open, taking in the dim room, a heaviness settles over me, spinning my head violently. My gaze briefly meets Ria's and I roll onto my hands and knees, retching painfully. Squeezing my eyes closed, I clamp my jaw shut before I vomit, breathing deeply through my nose. It takes a few moments for the room to stop whirling before I sit back on my heels, pressing a hand to my belly.

Kyran crouches in front of me and rests his warm palm on my forehead. The disorientated sick feeling immediately dissipates. I smile my thanks at him and he smirks, winking at me in response. My belly flops, opposite to how I felt moments ago.

Pushing to my feet warily, my mother steps over and rests her hands on my shoulders, her deep violet eyes pinched with concern.

"How did it go?" she speaks softly with a tight, apprehensive expression. "Valdr mentioned you found your memories."

Exhausted, I run my hand over my face. "I found them, yes, but I cannot access them." I drop my hand and let out a heavy sigh.

Glancing at Asteria, I find her sitting slumped against the wall and she gives me a wan smile. I cross the room and slide my back down the wall to sit beside her, resting my head on her shoulder.

"I believe that you have to unlock the memories for me. I think I felt a spell or enchantment on the chest when I tried to open it." I yawn widely, rubbing my eye. "We found Luna as well, but she's trapped in a cage, and the lock looks like the same metal as the chest. I'm guessing she can't be freed until my memories are," I mumble sleepily.

"*Mmm,* that makes sense. I'll have to think about how to best approach it, but right now I need sleep," she replies tiredly, yawning as well. "Oh, maybe Mother can put us into a temporary stasis for a day, and I can travel the dream realm with you back to where you found your memories!" My sister's voice pitches higher as she widens her eyes, leaning forward.

I place my hand on her shoulder, shaking my head. "You need to rest, I think we all do. We can discuss this tomorrow, but for now, go sleep in your bed," I murmur, gently patting my hand in comfort.

Nodding absently in agreement, she vanishes and a curl of wind ruffles my hair with her departure. I chuckle as I slowly push to my feet again. Kyran finishes his hushed conversation with my mother and comes over, embracing me in a warm hug. He kisses the top of my head and straightens, taking my hand in his.

"I've got some matters to attend to back home, but I can stay here with you for a little while longer," he murmurs, pulling his eyebrows together as he examines me.

With a tight smile, I quietly reply, "That would be nice, but I think we could both use some time alone to process everything we've just gone through."

He nods in agreement and lifts my hand to his mouth, pressing a light kiss to my knuckles. I suck in my lip at the tingles that race up my arm and he smiles warmly at me, reaching out to brush his thumb across my cheek.

"You know how to reach me if anything happens. Remember that I will *always* be here for you, sweetheart." He releases my hand, stepping toward the door.

Swallowing thickly against the lump forming in my throat, I follow him onto the porch. Kyran undresses, handing his clothes to me with a crooked smile, and shifts into his massive midnight wolf. He bounds down the steps and silently disappears into the dark woods like a shadow, and for the first time, I long to run with him.

*I can't wait to chase them through the trees,* a soft voice sighs in my mind.

With surprise, I say excitedly, *Luna! I can hear you!*

*Really? You can?* she responds in disbelief.

*Yes! This is amazing,* I chirp, turning around and darting toward the kitchen.

Pouring tea, my mother turns to me with a grin, clearly having heard our exchange. I wrap my arms around her in my excitement and she laughs, setting her cup down before embracing me tightly.

"This is great news! We are much closer to your awakening than before. I want to hear about your journey, but you must rest as well. Your body needs to recoup the energy you spent. Now, *shoo,*" she murmurs with a wide smile, waving her hand at me.

Before my lips part to reply, a gust of wind turns me upside down, and I abruptly find myself standing beside my bed. I press my hands to the side of my head, blinking rapidly, and huff a laugh as I walk dizzily toward my bathroom.

Turning the shower on, I toss my clothes in the hamper and brush my hair absently, staring blankly as my mind replays everything that had happened. Stepping into the steam, I wash slowly, letting the water run over me for a long while until I am wrinkled and drowsy, feeling uncomfortably numb.

Wrapping my fluffy black robe around me, I smile at the irony of it and pad across the floor to my bed. Crawling under the blanket, I notice Kyran's warm, earthy scent. I breathe deeply and close my teary eyes, letting sleep quickly pull me under before the unwanted darkness does.

# KYRAN

As I leave Selene, I mindlink Trey to let him know I am on my way home. He sounds relieved to hear from me and offers to make breakfast so we can catch up. My stomach gnaws at me angrily and

I'm grateful for my brother's attentiveness. I didn't want to leave her, but I would feel rude eating Selene's family out of house and home.

There *is* a pack meeting I need to have, though. Sigurd's betrayal has left me without a head warrior. The Convocation is coming up fast as well. I groan at the reminder.

*Fuck, I forgot all about it with everything that has been going on, and there is a lot of preparation that needs to be done.*

Weaving around trees, I recall my experiences in the dream realm, glad that the heaviness has lifted from both my mind and body. Though there are memories and residual energy left I need to work through, I feel like a new man today. With this in mind, I vow to help those who are fighting the invisible battles within themselves by sharing my experiences openly, rather than stuffing them down in shame and pretending I'm fine. I have gained the insight that many who seem okay on the outside could be screaming internally with no one to hear, and I want my pack to know that I am here to listen to them about anything, no matter what.

My legs grow weak as the light of dawn creeps through the trees. When I break through the forest, I greet the warrior who is patrolling and make my way toward home. Crossing through the villages, I slow to a trot amidst people milling about, opening their shops and waving at me as I pass by. Some faces are somber, no doubt from residual feelings of the recent attack, combined with Sigurd and the warrior's betrayals.

I come upon Stjarna's crystal shop and pause my steps, noticing how her ever-glowing windows are dark. Feeling for her connection, I curiously find it to be distant. Wondering where she is, I make a mental note to ask Trey about it, and continue up the street toward my home. I could reach out and ask her, but with respect, I give her space and ponder the reasons for her distance as I make my way up the long drive.

Shifting at the top of the steps, I glance at the unfamiliar beat up truck parked in front of my garage. Realizing this must be what Trey mindlinked me about as soon as I was out of the sleep-dive, I push open the door, wondering who could be visiting. I am greeted by the savory aroma of breakfast and my brother's bright laughter. Closing the door softly behind me, I snag the sweatpants hanging on a hook in the entryway and quickly pull them on before padding around the corner.

A large, lumbering man sits hunched at the island, his faded green flannel sleeves rolled to the elbow on thick, scarred arms. My footsteps cause Trey to turn over his shoulder from his place at the oven, and he gives me a wide grin. The mop of black curls that raises in response to my brother reveals the man's identity immediately. I grin widely as well.

A loud bark of a laugh bursts from me at the unexpected surprise, and Alpha Felagi drops his phone onto the counter at the sudden noise.

He's on his feet in an instant, his burly frame belying the speed and grace with which he moves. His joyous, booming laugh rattles the pots and pans. Felagi stands a few inches taller than me, and easily weighs close to a hundred pounds more than I do, judging by the paunchy stomach pushing at the buttons on his flannel. He pulls me in close, his wide palm slapping against the bare skin of my back before he claps my shoulders, giving me a slight shake. I can't help but laugh at his rough way of greeting, remembering the way he'd throw me around as a pup during our visits.

"Kyran! How the hell are ya'?" His deep voice is full of warmth and his sage green eyes crinkle as he looks me over. "Yer lookin' a bit rough, eh? The hell have ya' been doin'?"

"I'm looking better than you, fat man," I jest, slapping my hand to his belly.

I yank his overgrown, peppered beard.

He growls before swinging his thick arms toward me. I duck beneath them agilely, laughing in earnest. It's been a while since we've had a chance to meet up, and I am glad for the surprise. Felagi was a long-time friend of my father's, and he has been a part of my life for as far as I can remember. He catches me off guard and slams his elbow into my gut, making me grunt out another laugh.

Felagi wrings his arm around my neck, messing my hair playfully. "Good to see ya' haven't changed, boy." He lightly shoves me away, his smile fading into a line. "I'm sorry to hear 'bout yer head warrior, among everythin' else ya' got goin' on lately," he mutters, shaking his head solemnly.

"It's a shame, really. It's why I'm here early, ahead of the Convocation. I want to help with preparations and lend ya' some of my mated pack members for extra security measures. Treyvar called me the other day 'bout it all, and I said I'd be there in a jiff, no questions asked." He grunts in a serious tone, and nods his head once, clapping his hand on my shoulder.

I mimic the gesture and glance at my brother, silently thanking him for his effort. "I appreciate the support, but I don't think the vampires would be so bold to attack us. Not with all the alphas present during the convocation, let alone the number of extra wolves that will be staying here for the week," I reply assuredly, thinking out loud as I take the seat beside Felagi.

Noticing the way his stool creaks when he sits down, I smirk at the childish idea forming in my mind.

He sighs deeply. "Ya' can never be too cautious, 'specially with how things've been goin' lately. I swear, I'm gettin' calls weekly 'bout women goin' missin' from all the packs. Some of 'em are even bein' taken from their own damn beds at night. One of my wolves claimed to have seen that fucker Caedes roamin' too close to our territory the other week, an' I had all the light-haired women gathered up an' taken to our cells in my best attempt at keepin' 'em protected. Fer fucks sake!" Felagi's voice raises gruffly, his clenched hands thumping against the counter with his frustration.

I rest my hand on his shoulder, just as irritated as him. This shit has gone on far too long. Remembering our phone call a little while back, I give him a slight push to get his attention. Turning over my shoulder, I call out to my brother, "Hey, Trey, could you run up to my room and grab my phone for me real quick?"

I just realized that Selene needs a glamour bracelet. *Fuck, how could I not have given her one yet?* I grimace at the thought as Felagi turns in his seat to face me, his stool groaning in protest.

"Felagi, remember the call I made about the abductions, how I learned that younger blonde women were being targeted?" I prompt, and he nods with concern.

"Well, my lead hybrid gathered some women together and created a bracelet that puts a glamour over the wearer. It alters their physical traits, varying their skin tone and darkening their hair to help better disguise them. They can hide in plain sight. It is quite ingenious, if you ask me," I say offhandedly as I focus on my sister's bond.

*Kira, could you meet me in the kitchen as soon as possible with all the remaining bracelets, please?* I quickly mindlink her.

Felagi stares blankly at me.

*On it!* her bright voice chirps in my mind, and I raise an eyebrow at my old friend.

Felagi absently wipes his mouth with his hand as he ponders the information, and slowly nods his head. "That's…incredible. Ya' seen this work?" He glances at me skeptically.

I raise both my brows as I nod in affirmation. "Yeah, Kira is on her way here with the rest of the available bracelets. I want to show you how it works and give them to any pack members you have coming ahead of the convocation." I give him a small smile, a bit distracted by my thoughts of Selene.

He whistles as he crosses his arms, thanking me for my generosity. Trey reappears and hands me my phone before returning to the stove to finish his cooking. I murmur my thanks to him as I check the screen, finding no calls or texts, and open up Selene's messages. I grin at the photo she sent me a few days ago before sending her a quick text asking how she is doing, letting her know that I have something for her, and to let me know when she is ready for me to drop by to talk about the sleep-dive.

I slide my phone into my pocket just as Trey sets down a few platters full of breakfast food and takes the other stool beside me.

"You should eat, you really do look like shit," he says lightly, but concern shines in the tight set of his eyes.

"I'm alright. Much better than I look," I mumble and reach for a plate, piling it high with pancakes, eggs, sausage, and bacon. Felagi stands to take the farther plate piled with jellied toast and biscuits. His stool complains once more as he sits back down, scarfing his food without flatware like a starved animal. Trey leans past me to watch him with a fake horrified expression on his face.

I smirk, enjoying the comfort of having them around, regardless of the bone-deep exhaustion blanketing me. Felagi turns to us with jelly smeared over his mustache and a half-eaten biscuit in one hand. I can't help the chuckle that escapes.

"What? Yer' a right arse half the time, add in ya' lookin' like that," he waves his biscuit at me, "an' good luck findin' yerself a mate!" He slaps his free hand on the counter with a deep, grating laugh.

Trey snorts a laugh at our old friend's antics.

I grin and sharply kick my foot out, snapping the weak, protesting leg off his stool. Felagi crashes through the crumbling pile of wood, the plate of baked goods he held clattering to the floor beside him. A piece of jelly toast splats onto his face, muffling his cry of surprise.

My brother and I laugh hard enough that our eyes water, and Felagi's glare quickly evaporates as his booming laugh joins ours. He wipes a hand over his face and smears the jelly onto his shirt with another grating laugh. Bending over, I extend my hand to him and pull him to his feet with a childish grin. He clasps the back of my neck and gives me a light shove before dragging the last remaining stool over.

We finish our breakfast lightheartedly, sharing lots of laughter and catching up with each other's lives over the past year.

Our conversation trailed late into the morning. Felagi was extremely impressed when Kira arrived with the bracelets. She demonstrated how it works and Felagi insisted on trying it on himself, much to all of our amusement. He had asked more questions about the people involved with the bracelet's creation, and I begrudgingly explained Vala and her betrayal. This led into the events with Sigurd, and Felagi had many colorful words to express on that matter. We talked about the vampire attacks some more, and he had just excused himself to make a phone call after I discussed pertinent details about Caedes with him.

I'm rolling the braided strands of the bracelet between my fingers when Trey drops onto the couch beside me. Sliding it into my pocket, I turn to face my brother. He smiles easily at me, but I can tell there's something weighing on his mind by the set of his shoulders and the tightness in his eyes.

"What, Trey?" I ask gruffly and sigh, rubbing a hand over my face. "I'm sorry. I'm beyond exhausted after what I went through yesterday.

Well, the past few days, actually, now that I think of it." I sigh again, dropping my hand with a slight groan.

He silently nods before narrowing his eyes. "I was going to ask you about that," he says lowly, glancing away.

He clearly wants to say more but isn't sure how, and I wonder if I should just lay it all out there or not. My brother nods toward the hall and we make our way out back into our mother's garden. Neither of us speaks until we reach her favorite bench, carefully sitting down. Treyvar looks at me with concern and for the first time today, I notice the dark circles that line his eyes.

"What happened, Kyran? The last time I heard from you—before this morning—was when we separated after eradicating Caedes' vamp nest the other night. I know it was a lot to take on, especially after Sigurd and all the shit involved with him, but for you to look like this? You haven't been in *this* condition since..." His voice trails off as he quickly glances away, twisting his lips to the side.

"Since the Underground, I know. I know what you mean. And to answer your next question, no, I did not go there. I don't ever want to be there—*be a part of that*—again," I growl, my hand clenching automatically at the memory of the brutal fights that make up a large portion of my past life. Relaxing my hand with a measured breath, I run it through my hair and meet my brother's gaze once more.

"What happened?" He repeats his question, this time more solidly.

"Honestly, Trey, I have been silently living in agony since I came of age. I never wanted to show it and did all I could, every single day, to keep that part of me hidden from everyone. Our father—" I correct my words at the sharp look Trey gives me from the mention of him. "He was...very hard on me, and it took a toll, slowly hollowing me out until I did not recognize myself. I was made of rage, hatred, and pain. A cold nothingness that numbed me entirely. This is something I've dealt with silently, and it has taken me until only a few years ago just to *be able* to begin to overcome, let alone even *try*."

I sigh heavily, rubbing a hand over my face. "I just went through it all again, earlier this morning. It was done with the purpose of letting it all go, though. That's why I look so worn out."

Treyvar stares at me for a few heartbeats. He lets out a weighted breath before quietly commenting, "You haven't spoken of him in a very long time."

"Since I killed him, you mean," I say flatly, leaning back on the bench and sliding my hand into my pocket.

I grasp the bracelet for Selene in the silence that stretches between us, wondering if she has woken yet and how she is doing. Trey sits back as well, clasping his hands in his lap.

*I hope she's alright,* I worry.

*Kyran,* Valdr's voice cuts through my thoughts.

Before I can respond, my brother blurts, "I don't blame you, or hold resentment over what happened. Neither does Kira. I hope you know that, Kyran. Honestly. It really hurts to hear you've been in such *pain* most of your life. I don't know the exact details of what he put you through, but I understand enough, and it's fucking bullshit that you had to go through that, *and* to do it alone…I'm sorry. I am really sorry. If I had known—"

"Nothing would have been different," I cut him off. "Shit happens, and life moves on. You just gotta learn how to deal with it. I couldn't learn—I *refused* to—and suffered the consequences of it. It wasn't really until Selene came into my life that I fully acknowledged to myself that I can either choose to take the burdens of my past with me, or lay them to rest and move on. It was because of *her* that I was finally able to let it all go," I admit quietly, rolling the bracelet between my fingers as I stare blankly at the ground.

I glance at my brother and his brows silently raise while he processes everything I just said. I'm surprised to find that I don't feel awkward about being open with him like this. A ghost of a smile pulls at my mouth.

He asks me questions about the sleep-dive and our father, remarks on my ability to maintain my position as alpha and hold it respectably with everything I've endured. I thank him for his understanding and brush off his praise, the only thing that actually makes me uncomfortable in all of this. I chose not to discuss Selene's experiences because I felt that they were not mine to share, and the thought of her makes me pull out my phone once our conversation comes to a lull.

Checking the screen, I find a text from Kira about the pack meeting, along with a notification on my calendar for a scheduled delivery later this afternoon.

I'm a little bummed to not have heard from Selene yet. Sighing, I put my phone away and rise to my feet. Trey stands, briefly rubbing at his arm before huffing out a breath.

"I know we don't do this, but...I love you." He rushes out the words and claps a quick, one-armed hug around my shoulders.

I chuckle and snag his arm as he pulls away, tugging him back toward me and hold him tight for a moment. Patting his back, I release him with a light toned, "I love you too, *baby boy*," and laugh at the appalled look he gives me.

Growing up, I used to tease Trey about the way our mother would talk to him in a singsong voice, and it feels good to be so lighthearted with him once more. He gives me a small shove and I shove back harder, making him stumble a bit. Just as he is about to push it further, Kira's bright voice rings out from the doorway.

"If you two are finished being cute, we have a few cranky elders waiting in the Great Hall for us." She laughs with a warm smile, shaking her head.

Trey dramatically clears his throat. "We were just discussing sports," he says seriously and ducks as I push at the back of his head.

His eyes crinkle with his laugh, and I grin at him as the three of us make our way to the meeting.

After the arduous task of staying conscious during the dry pack meeting, I mindlinked Jeger, informing him of his new role as head warrior. He thanked me for the honor and swore to never let me down, to which I let him know it was never a concern of mine. I delegated the task of delivery acceptance to Trey, and asked Kira to make arrangements for housing the wolves from the other five packs during the Convocation.

I decided mid-afternoon that a nap was better than passing out in public and slept until dusk.

Sitting at my desk, I spin my phone around in circles as I consider sending Selene another text. I'm becoming concerned that I have not heard from her today. It has been thirteen hours since I left her place, she must be awake by now.

Tapping my screen, I open her messages and begin typing, only to see that my last two texts from this morning have been read. My brow creases as I wonder why she didn't respond, and I erase what I had been saying. Re-typing, I tell her that I hope she is alright, and if she needs anything to please let me know. I hesitate a moment before pressing send, having an insecure thought that she might feel I'm being incessant. Sighing, I drop my phone onto the desk and sit back in my chair, lacing my fingers behind my head.

*Kyran,* Valdr's urgent voice jolts me from my thoughts and I sit upright at his sudden presence.

*Wha—*

The landline blares loudly, cutting me off. That phone is only used between alphas and I snag it off the receiver immediately, clearing my throat before I answer.

"Alpha Castian," I greet plainly, noting the caller ID, "is everything alright?"

"Alpha Kyran, yes, things are fine. Well, as good as they can be, all things considered." His tired voice crackles over the line and I find myself nodding my head. "I'm calling to ask you if it would be possible for my pack to arrive a few days early for the Convocation? My mate is pregnant, and I'd like to give her extra time for travel. I want to get her situated before the celebration begins."

My eyebrows raise and I quickly reply, "Yes, of course, that will not be an issue. Congratulations, by the way! That's big news." I smile genuinely.

For the past few hundred years, it is not often that females have successful pregnancies, so I understand his concern in regards to his mate.

"I am more than happy to accommodate Mira as much as she needs. When should I be expecting you?" I ask, sliding a paper over with notes for the coming week scratched on it and pick up a pen.

"In two days' time. We are already on our way, though we're moving slowly. I cannot thank you enough." His voice is relieved and he audibly sighs.

We make small talk for a couple minutes, and I bid him safe travels before placing the phone back on the receiver. Castian and I have been amicable since he became alpha of the South Eastern Region pack one hundred and fifty years ago, after his father had died unexpectedly. He is a good man, even-tempered and neutral when it comes to the egos the other alphas tend to carry.

I find myself actually looking forward to meeting with him and his mate this year. Now that I have Selene with me, their sickly-sweet affections for one another won't make me want to drown myself in liquor like all the other Convocations I've had to endure. I decide that other than Felagi, they will be some of the first people I introduce her to once the celebrations begin.

The bonding of an alpha female is a huge cause for revelry within each pack. My excitement grows at the thought of announcing it this year, especially in my own territory.

*I'll have to order a special cake, just for her,* I think happily, jotting down the idea on my overfilled paper.

*Kyran!* Valdr's sharp voice sends a pang through my head and I wince, dropping my pen.

*Valdr, what the fuck?* I berate him, but he quickly cuts me off.

*It's Selene.* His rough voice cuts through me like a hot knife. *Something is wrong, I've felt Luna's distress since this morning. Although I cannot communicate directly with her, I know they aren't well.*

*Shit!* I'm on my feet and out the door before my thought has finished. *Why didn't you fucking say anything sooner?* I lash out as rising fear pushes my anger aside, my heart racing.

*I tried. Twice,* he responds curtly.

*Fuck!* I burst out the back door and immediately shift, knowing that running would be twice as fast as driving. *Fuck fuck fuck!* My mind reels with possible scenarios, and I push my legs to their limit.

*Trey! I need to get to Selene, something has come up. Take over for the night, I'll get back to you when I can,* I hastily mindlink my brother, my words rushing out of my mind.

Unease weighs heavily in my chest, and I sprint through the forest faster than I've ever run with my heart clenched in a vice the entire way.

# CHAPTER TWENTY

## SPIRALING

### SELENE

*I'm falling, hurtling toward a gaping pit of blackness as my breath rips from my chest in a silent, never-ending scream. Bleak emptiness swallows me whole. Spiders claw up my spine, their razor-tipped legs scrabbling against my skin in places I can't reach. Ice courses through my veins, weighing me down, down, down into the abyss where my worst fears starve. I can't breathe. I can't find my way back. I will die here, alone and forgotten. Perhaps I already have…*

"*Selene,*" a distant voice calls to me, faded and wispy like smoke in the wind. "*Selene, please be okay.*" The faint noise grows closer.

A sharp sting bites my cheek and my black world erupts with blinding light, forcing my eyes to squeeze shut painfully against the stark contrast. Incessant blaring—no, *screaming*—pierces my ears and I raise my hands to block it out, except, *I can't move my arms. Why can't I move? I'm trapped! I need to escape!*

Panicking, I freak out at the sensation, my heart beating in erratic bursts as I wildly thrash in my bindings. The wailing echoes unending around me.

"*Selene!*" Asteria's shrill voice cuts through the chaos, and I blindly search for her through my flooded, blurry eyes.

Recognition dawns on me as I take in my bedroom around me, and I understand with horror that it is *me* who is the source of the manic screaming.

Asteria—no, *Bolvi*—straddles my legs and has my arms pinned to the bed beside me, my body writhing relentlessly out of my control. My skin glows brightly, illuminating the fear in Asteria's wide, violet eyes as she mouths words I cannot hear.

Her face melts into *his* with that awful sneer and flat, hollow gaze. Instinct takes over and I let out a strangled cry, heaving my hips upward and I wrench my arms free of his grasp. Releasing a fearful scream, I shove him away from me as hard as I can. A burst of light rips from me at the contact, sending him tumbling across my room. He crashes through the closet doors in a heap.

I scramble off the bed and crumple to the floor, crawling away to press my back against the wall. My chest heaves with hyperventilation as I clutch the sides of my head, sobbing uncontrollably. I squeeze my elbows around my knees, rocking back and forth as I stare across my room at the darkness in my closet.

Light wind ruffles the sheets hanging off of my bed, my mother appearing before me. Her pretty face is stricken as she crouches and reaches a hand toward my head. I absently notice the sparkle of a tear on her sharp cheekbone before everything goes black.

"*Selene.*" My mother's soft voice catches my attention, drifting toward me from everywhere and nowhere at once.

Part of me doesn't want to acknowledge it, to ignore her. I've been floating for what seems like an eternity, and I have no intentions of ever leaving. Pure comfort surrounds me, luxurious, golden silky rays of sunlight bathing me in a pool of warm bliss. I sigh contentedly, utterly relaxed.

"*Selene, I'm bringing you back to us now.*" Her voice is hesitant, something I've never heard before.

My heavenly waters dissipate and I groan in protest, feeling lethargic. My weight settles beneath me once more, and someone holds my hand lightly in theirs. I give the hand a small squeeze as my senses come back to me.

Crickets chirp in the distance and the rich aroma of petrichor comforts me. A soft, warm blanket covers my legs, and I clench it in my fist before cracking my eyes open.

"There you are, dear." My mother sighs with relief, her face coming into focus. "How do you feel?" she asks tentatively, her black brows knitting with worry.

I run a mental check over myself. "I feel mostly…numb," I respond, my tone flat.

She nods her head in understanding and leans away. My gaze becomes unfocused on the spot she just occupied before drifting toward the open balcony doors. The faded light of the sky is either early dawn or dusk. I can't tell, and I don't really care.

I force my eyes to find my mother's once more, realizing that I have no idea how long I've been unconscious for. "What's going on?" I quietly ask in a monotone voice.

Her mouth pulls into a tight line, eyes narrowing slightly before she responds. After letting out a small sigh, she takes my hand in hers once more and softly answers, "You were having an episode of extreme hysteria, which I believe was triggered from what I can only assume to be night terrors. I'm unaware of what went on during your sleep-dive with Kyran, but from my point of view, it was most certainly not good. I was forced to magically…*tranquilize* you, in order to gain control of your mind. I can keep you here, like this, if you wish. Or, I can taper it off, and let you get a hold of yourself slowly."

I think I understand what she is saying, but it is difficult to process thoughts at the moment. I don't entirely like the sensation of this nothingness, though. I must make a face because my mother looks at me intently.

"I don't know," I murmur, and her brow pinches with concern. "What I mean is, I can't really form coherent thoughts enough to remember *what* was going on. I don't want to stay numb like this, though. Please take it away," I mumble, holding her gaze as best I can.

She nods and pats my hand. "Okay, I will. I'll be back in about an hour and see how you're doing with it, alright?"

"No." I shake my head, pushing myself up and turn to face her. "I don't want it at all. Take it away. Now." I speak firmly this time.

Staring at me for a moment with a narrowed gaze, she nods once and raises her hand. Gently pressing her fingers to my forehead, she murmurs something incoherent and the fogginess evaporates from my mind.

Everything comes crashing down on me like a frigid tidal wave.

I close my eyes at the sudden onslaught of emotions and memories, sucking in a breath and holding it tightly as I wait it out. Once I recall the moment my mother arrived, I exhale slowly, relaxing my grip on the blanket and open my eyes.

I glance at her and offer a wan smile as I rub my temple at the sharp headache blooming. Without prompt, I explain the nightmares of despair and anxiety, how I woke to my own screaming and confused Asteria for my abusive ex-boyfriend. I immediately ask if she is alright, feeling concerned and guilty that I hurt her. My mother assures me that she is fine, just resting for the moment since she exhausted herself earlier this morning.

We discuss some of my experiences in the sleep-dive, and I decide not to go into much detail about it with her, only admitting that I was not intending to face my suppressed trauma when it consumed me. My mother nods in understanding, and though her eyes are tight with concern, she doesn't push the matter further.

"If it's alright with you, I think I'd like to be alone for a little while," I say quietly, pulling the blanket up around my shoulders.

"Of course, dear. If there is *anything* you need, I am here for you." Her voice is stern and she offers me a small smile.

"Thanks," I mumble, glancing away and she vanishes into thin air.

I can't help but replay my panic attack once more, feeling both shame and anger about it. My mind flashes through the sleep-dive, recalling the things I saw with Kyran and I close my eyes against it. Tears trickle down my cheeks and I let them flow freely, trying to not hold anything inside.

He wasn't wrong when he told me there was a lot to him that I was unaware of. Pulling the blanket up over my head, I lay on my side and curl into a ball.

*With the weight of all of his own problems, it isn't fair for him to carry all of my shit as well. I'm too…broken, too damaged,* I admit to myself dejectedly.

A small sob escapes me as the emotions I've ignored for too long creep out of their hiding places. Everything feels overwhelming.

It is all just too much, and the only thing I am able to do is succumb to the flood with the hope I'll come out of it alive.

I lay there for a while, endlessly crying as my mind unravels the awful experiences, and the emotions tacked to each one runs me over again and again. I feel beaten, inside and out, utterly battered and broken.

My shoulder protests from being squished beneath me for so long, but I can't find the energy to move. The thick stuffiness to my nose makes it difficult to breathe, and my lips have grown chapped from the countless heavy gasps.

*I wish I could help you through this,* Luna's clear voice slides quietly through my mind. A gentle pressure blooms in my chest at her words, bringing me a foreign sense of comfort. *It would be easier if you had your memories returned, to give you a better sense of severity to compare to.*

Hot anger flashes through me at that comment, and I am about to lash out at her when she interrupts my train of thought.

*This is in no way meant to invalidate what you are feeling or what you have been through. What I am trying to tell you, Selene, is if you were to remember your past—our past—you would have a plethora of experiences to compare the intensity of what your mind is desperately trying to process at the moment. For you, this situation is the worst thing you have ever been through. However, with your full conscious memories, I can assure you we have been through many harsh, negative experiences. What feels like a tidal wave that you are endlessly drowning in could feel like a rainstorm instead. Do you understand what I am trying to tell you?* Her voice is gentle yet firm inside my mind and I sense her true intentions, though I don't know if I can acknowledge it at the moment.

I squeeze my eyes shut, feeling as if I'm teetering on the edge of another breakdown, and take a deep breath through my mouth since my damned nose isn't functioning properly anymore.

Focusing on the fact that *I don't even know who I really am* makes me slightly nauseous. Not to mention that the man I'm falling in love with is a *fucking werewolf,* which I apparently am as well. Without any recollection of all the shit involved with *that,* it all has me feeling more than slightly crazy. A manic laugh bubbles out of me and I can't control it.

Everything that has taken place these past couple of weeks is pure insanity, and I've just been living in fantasy land or something, because *this can't be happening.*

*It certainly has happened, and you need to pull your shit together.* Luna's voice is harsh now, slicing through the wild thoughts racing in my mind.

My crazed laughter is cut off by a strangled cry as I realize I'm suffering a mental breakdown and have zero control over it, which only makes all of this ten times worse. My skin feels like there are millions of tiny ice snakes writhing beneath the surface.

I'm also emitting an eerie glow into the room like a freaky lamp.

I am beyond distressed at this point, fearing what this means.

*"What is happening to me?!"* I cry out as I fling the blankets off of my bed, gawking at my luminescent skin.

*Shit—Selene, be careful!* Luna demands, her voice laced with worry. *Argh! Hekate!* She calls loudly and I wince at the sudden volume.

My mother manifests across my room and her hand flies to her mouth at the sight of me. I stumble out of my bed and take a few steps away from her, holding my arms around my middle as I shake my head. I have no idea what is going on with me, but I feel like it could be dangerous if Luna is worried, and *especially* if my mother is as well.

I just want to get away, to run away from everything and everyone right now. I swipe at the never-ending tears pouring from my eyes as I take another step toward the only exit closest to me. My balcony. Maybe the evening air will help me find some reprieve from the onslaught of tumultuous emotions wreaking havoc in my mind.

"Selene," my mother whispers softly, holding up her hands as if trying not to startle a wild animal.

I shake my head, continuing backwards and refuse to meet her gaze. I just can't, I need to get away before something bad happens. My feet step into a pool of moonlight that peeks over the trees. I am instantly shrouded in cool mist and swirling wisps of inky blackness, my stomach bottoming out sickeningly as my body whirls around.

Wind brushes over exposed skin. My bare feet connect with soft grass before I finish inhaling for the scream clawing its way free from my chest. I lose my balance, falling to my hands and knees with a small shriek, overwhelmed with confusion and fear.

# LUNAR SHADOWS: AWAKEN

*"What the fuck was that?"* I cry out loud as I turn over to sit on the ground. Outside. In the middle of the woods.

*Shadow-walking,* Luna sighs, her voice tired and quiet.

*"Huh?"* I respond dumbly, glancing around and feeling more than a bit lost, both mentally and physically.

*Shadow-walking. Think of it as teleportation, in a sense. It is an ability we wield with our magic, among a few others…we'll discuss this later. Right now, what is important is that we get back to safety. It is dangerous to be out here alone.* I sense her trepidation growing as she speaks.

Swallowing thickly, I shut everything away as best I can. I look around and try to figure out where the hell I ended up, without focusing on the *how.* All I can see is an enormous clearing ringed by a thick forest in the distance. Lifting a hand to wipe the tears from my eyes, my fingers brush over tall stems, and I glance down at the ground. In the dim light, I find that I am surrounded by wildflowers and my brow pinches with familiarity. As I rub a soft petal between my still-glowing fingers, it takes a few moments for it to register that this must be the clearing Kyran had brought me to.

The memory of riding on the back of his wolf as we raced through the woods causes warmth to pool in my chest, and a tiny hint of a smile ghosts my lips. The darkness of the sleep-dive wipes away any sense of comfort, leaving me again in cold despair.

I have absolutely no idea how to get home. Feeling helpless, I flop onto my back and spread my arms wide, staring absently at the budding stars far above me. My hands glide back and forth over the tops of the wildflowers, their velvety texture oddly soothing me into a false calmness.

I spend a few moments like this, actively thinking of nothing in a desperate attempt to stave off the inescapable mental anguish. The sharp *snap* of branches breaking sends my heart into my throat and I shove to my feet, hastily turning around in search of the source. The darkening sky makes it difficult to distinguish the trees from one another. Fear grips my spine with an iron fist as a large shadow bursts from the forest.

Stumbling away from the dark mass rapidly approaching, I don't register Luna's voice through my pathetic cries of fear until she is nearly screaming at me.

*Selene! It's alright, stop running! He's here, you called for him and he found us.* Her voice quiets into a softer tone when my feet clumsily come to a stop.

I turn to look over my shoulder and find Valdr standing a few paces away from me, his body heaving with the effort to breathe from running. Stepping toward him, I slowly raise my shaky hand and he closes the distance between us immediately, pushing his head into my illuminated palm.

Tight with apprehension, a mix of Valdr's and Kyran's voices fill my mind. *Selene, what happened? Are you alright?*

I am abruptly reminded of the shit storm that today has been. Snatching my hand away with the fear I could harm them, I hold it to my chest as fresh tears spring forth and I shake my head in a silent response.

Valdr swings his head around, searching for any threats. His bright eyes meet my gaze again before asking in that eerie dual voice, *Why are you out here? Are you hurt? Did someone take you?* Their last words are spoken roughly with a low growl.

Again I shake my head, tears dripping down my face.

"Take me home, please," I whisper, refusing to speak about my psychotic episode and the subsequent loss of control over powers *I didn't even know existed.*

I can't meet his gaze, shifting my weight uncomfortably as I try to hold back my crying. Valdr blurs and Kyran appears, his face stricken as he takes a step toward me with his hand outstretched. I vehemently shake my head this time as I step away, wrapping my arms around my middle.

"Selene, what is going on? What happened?" Kyran sounds alarmed.

I turn, watching his hand clench into a fist as it drops to his side. My eyes twitch up toward his distressed face and the hysteria threatens to overcome me again, so I squeeze my eyes shut, taking shaky breaths as slowly as I can. I stare at the ground beneath my bare feet, sensing Kyran take a tentative step toward me.

"Don't," I rasp, my fingers digging into my upper arms. "Please," I add quietly, feeling awful for a thousand reasons.

"Sel—"

Hot anger irrationally courses through me and I wrench my hands downward, balling them into fists as I grate out, "I can't look at you right now, not after everything that's happened."

"What?" he breathes, his voice quietly incredulous, and my heart cracks at the sound.

"Kyran, just…*please take me home,*" I whisper raggedly, my chest threatening to cave in on me.

He growls lowly and I glance his way, though my eyes don't travel farther than his broad chest. His muscles flex with tension as he tries to regulate his breathing, and I notice how eerily still he's become. I cannot bring myself to look into his eyes, not right now. I know that I would completely fall apart if I do. Kyran lifts his hands to his face for a moment before slinging them around the back of his neck, taking a heavy breath.

He begs, his voice thick and rough. "Selene, I need to know wh—"

*"Just take me home, dammit!"* I shriek and icy pressure flashes through every cell in my body, the silkiness of it coursing down my arms and bursts free in writhing tendrils of obsidian smoke.

All of my distress, anguish, confusion, and pain collide into this one sensation streaming through my body, and it *freaks me the fuck out.* I cry out in horror, shaking my hands to dissipate the shadows wrapping around me and it swirls away on a soft breeze.

Dragging my terrified gaze to Kyran's, he pushes to his feet, staring at me with his mouth parted. Pain flashes in his bright amber eyes. Guilt and shame drags my gaze to the ground.

I swallow thickly, my throat hoarse as I whisper, "I-I'm so sorry. I didn't mean—I c-can't be here. I need to speak with my mother."

Kyran doesn't move for a few moments until he grunts with frustration and shifts into his wolf form. Valdr instantly moves forward, but I automatically step aside with the fear of causing him harm. He abruptly stops at my avoidance.

Valdr silently lowers himself to the ground beside me and I hesitate for a moment, staring down at my glowing hands. With a deep breath, I close my eyes and focus on *not* doing anything as I shakily reach out to grab hold of his fur, swinging my leg over his back.

He waits for me to get situated before rising to his feet and immediately turns us around, silently loping toward the dark woods.

After a short while, I lower myself and press my cheek against the back of his neck, feeling as if a train ran me over. My pathetic attempt at walling off the turmoil crumbles, my tears silently spilling down my face, into his soft fur. I don't bother to wipe them away as we ghost through the trees.

None of us say a word the entire way home.

# KYRAN

A million tiny, angry wasps buzz around my mind, stinging me and sending thoughts down dark paths. When I left Selene earlier this morning, she seemed normal, besides looking as exhausted as I had felt. Seeing her now, with her bloodshot eyes wild and frantic, her skin void of color, and that power...

*What the fuck is going on? Why wouldn't she look at me? Can she not stand to see me after learning of my past? I said I'd understand, but fuck, this hurts. Really bad. Why is she out here, so far from home? How did she get here? She looks as if she's in pain, but I couldn't see any injuries on her. Argh!* I fight against the growl that threatens to tear free with my roiling thoughts.

I hardly pay attention to where Valdr is going, letting him take over because I can't separate myself enough at the moment to give her the space she is clearly asking from me.

*If someone hurt her, I'll fucking kill them,* I seethe, my anger simmering.

I'm frustrated at not understanding what exactly has happened to her, and with not knowing how to help her. Whether she wants me to or not, I will do anything for her until she tells me to leave. It would rip my fucking heart out, but I will obey her wishes, whatever they may be. Even if it kills me to do so.

I want to reach out to her, to comfort her in any way she needs. The desire to care for her consumes me, fanning the flames of my irritation at this situation and spiking my anger once more.

*Did she get her memories back while I was gone? Does she see me differently now? Those shadows, is that her power? They looked...tangible. Like she could command them as beings if she wanted. But she was scared, terrified, as if she didn't know she could do that. Fuck, why won't she talk to me? What changed?* My mind reels with a looming panic, my heart beating wildly.

*I need you to get a grip on yourself. We're here.* Valdr's rough voice startles me from my thoughts. *She needs us. I don't know with what exactly, but I can feel Luna's attempts at reaching me, as if Selene is blocking her out right now.*

*Shit, why would she do that?* I wonder fearfully, both to him and myself. All Selene wanted was to be able to find a connection to her wolf, to hear from her. *Why would she shut her out...Fuck.*

At that thought, I am reminded of myself just days ago, how awful I felt about myself, unwilling to face her in that way.

*No. No no no. I don't want her to feel alone in this, whatever it is she's going through,* I worry and my heart gives a slight pang at the thought of Selene suffering, especially feeling as if she doesn't have support.

As we break out of the forest, Hekate and Asteria rise to their feet on the porch. Valdr comes to a stop at the foot of the steps and Selene slowly slides off his back, taking a couple small steps to the side. She positions herself away from both the stairs and Valdr. Hekate moves toward the steps and Selene raises her hands with alarm. She quickly drops her arms to her sides an instant later, pressing them tightly with a grimace.

"No, please, don't come near me. I feel dangerous, out of control. I don't know what's going on with me, and I honestly don't think I can handle anything anymore." Her usually soft voice is broken and haggard, as if her throat is raw from screaming. It sets my teeth on edge.

I force Valdr to shift and glance at Hekate with worry, her face mirroring how I feel. Asteria wordlessly removes her cloak and holds it out for me to take, but I ignore her, turning toward the beautiful, distraught woman beside me. She wraps her arms around her middle and shakes her head at me, not meeting my gaze again.

My brow furrows as irritation flares, and I can't help demanding, "Why won't you look at me? Why won't you talk to me, tell me what's going on?"

Selene remains silent, her throat bobbing with a heavy swallow as she glances at Hekate. I clench my fists and jaw tightly for a moment, taking a measured breath before releasing the tension coiling within me. She's scaring me now. Something is really, really wrong, and I don't know what to do.

"Selene, *please*. I just want to help you. Tell me what to do, I'll do anything. It hurts to see you like this. I don't want you to suffer, I don't want you to be in pain," I plead, straining not to close the distance between us and take her into my arms.

"I can't be around you right now," she whispers roughly, gripping her arms around herself tighter.

Her words are like a punch to the gut and I just shake my head in disbelief, never taking my eyes off her face. She's frowning, her bottom lip is chewed raw and tears glisten in her eyes. I can't understand where this is coming from, not at all.

My limbs grow heavy as I watch the turmoil in her eyes, looking everywhere except at me.

"Why?" I say on a breath, needing to hear her tell me.

*Is it because now the truth to me is out there? I know I can't stand to look at myself half of the time. Why would she love me, if I hate who I am? I was a fool to believe that would ever change. What's happened cannot be taken back, and I live with it every day. I just thought...with her...I'd have a reason to be better. To want to be better. For her, and for me. For us.*

My heart fractures in the gaping silence between us.

She finally turns to face me, raising her bright blue eyes to mine, and the agony I find in them steals the breath from my lungs. My breaking heart races as she takes a shaky breath and I clench my fists tighter, letting my nails dig into my palms. Her eyes close for a moment, and when they open again, there's a bleakness in them that terrifies me.

"I need you to go," she says lowly, her lip quivering before a tear drips from her eye.

*"Selene,"* I rasp as my heart all but freezes at her words, thumping sluggishly in my tight chest.

My breath painfully whooshes out from my lungs. I instinctively lift a hand toward her, desperately wanting her to take it and let me hold her. Her eyebrows bunch upward as she steps away from me with her palms raised.

I plead with her again, my pain nearly overwhelming at the thought of her pushing me away. *"Please—"*

*"Leave!"* she cries harshly, and an icy dark blast of magic bursts from her hands.

The inky smoke slams into my chest and sends me hurtling off my feet across the grassy yard, slamming my back into a wide tree. A deep grunt escapes me as my head cracks against the bark. Selene screams my name with terror and pain, and I wrench my gaze toward the cottage. I watch morosely as Hekate places her hand to Selene's forehead, cradling her neck as she goes unconscious. They vanish and Asteria disappears as well, leaving me dazed at the edge of their woods.

A gust of wind warns me of Hekate's arrival and she is instantly in my face, her deep violet eyes boring into mine. Under normal circumstances I'd shove her away, but with what just happened, I can't bring myself to do anything at all other than breathe shards of glass. Her cold fingers prod at the skin around my eyes for a moment before she nods once and rises to her feet, holding her hand out for me to take.

I just stare at it before rolling my head to the side, my mind focused on Selene and *how could this be happening*.

Hekate's slim hand smacks my cheek. I glare up at her with a growl rumbling from my chest. She just sticks her hand out again and I bat it aside, shoving to my feet. I turn away from her, aimlessly walking deeper into the woods.

She protests, calling me back to her.

I ignore the words, not giving two fucks about anything other than Selene at the moment. Part of me wants to tear the trees out of these woods in a rampage, and another part of me just wants to crawl into a hole.

*My mate is distressed, clearly in pain, and there's nothing I can do to help her. She doesn't want my help. Doesn't want…me.*

I let the dejected thoughts roll over me as I blindly push through the branches. Valdr's unease sinks heavily in my chest, and I absently rub a hand over my bare skin in response.

Hekate's voice calls out to me again, but I just continue stalking away.

"Kyran, I said *stop*," her voice rings out sharply, and every muscle in my body turns to stone.

My eyes remain open, but I have absolutely zero control over my body as Hekate manifests before me, her sharp face pinched with irritation. Her long black hair billows around her, giving away her emotional state as she points a black razor-tipped finger at me, harshly speaking through clenched teeth.

"It is not my place to discuss matters with you, and I will leave the details up to Selene to decide if and what she wants to share. However, I feel it is necessary for you to understand that she has suffered a great amount of distress. Her mind has essentially broken under the weight of everything she's been carrying. This probably would have never happened to her if our issue with the magic barrier between her and Luna didn't exist. I believe it has put an extreme strain on her mind in general, and whatever had happened during the sleep-dive became too much for her to bear.

"So please understand, Kyran, that what she just did to you was entirely out of her control. Her lunar abilities are breaking through, which means she is extremely close to having access to her wolf bond. This *should* be a good thing, though with her hysteric state, she is far too dangerous to be out of control. I do not wish to speak for her, but I feel that she certainly did not intend to cause you any harm. Have patience, *Custos*, and see things from a greater perspective if you can. This is all I will say on the matter, the rest is up to the two of you." Her voice grows quiet as she steps away from me, gently pressing a cool palm to my face before vanishing into the night.

Hekate's power releases me and I stumble forward a step, reaching a hand out to lean against a tree as I process what she'd said. Logically, everything makes sense, and I *do* understand what she told me.

But all my mind can focus on is the fact that my soulmate does not want me with her.

I turn my back and slide down the base of the tree, closing my eyes at the bite of the bark and drop my head into my hands.

*Valdr, I need you to take over for a while.* I send my thought out quietly, hoping he understands what I mean.

Shifting silently, I let him have control so I can take some time to try and wrap my head around everything that just happened. I don't want to lose the hope that grew since the moment I met Selene. I try to see this from a bigger perspective like Hekate advised and mull over the reasons as to why Selene had such a drastic shift. I know her being forced to face her trauma the way she did was not easy on her—hell, it was difficult even for me to get through—so I can only guess at the severity of her emotions because of that.

What scares me is how she continued on afterward, even up to when I left in the morning, how none of her anguish showed on her face. Sorrow surges at the thought of her living her life well-versed in masking her pain, living in silent agony unknown to the world around her. How such a gentle, caring, and beautiful woman could be torn to shreds on the inside, enough to be able to destroy her mind this way...it is too much for me to accept.

I don't think she's aware of the strength she wields to be able to live life in this way. I find myself admiring her within this...*mess.*

Because what a mess this has all become.

She told me she couldn't be around me right now, and also said before that she couldn't look at me. I'm not sure exactly *why,* and I'm terrified to find out, especially after hearing her words about everything that has happened.

I can't imagine my life without her in it, not after really getting to know her. I'd rather die than not have Selene in my life. I want her—I *need* her. She has shown me that there's more *to me* than what has *happened* to me, and I need to have her realize that for herself as well.

That is, if what she's learned about me isn't the reason for her distance. Because if it *is,* then I don't think I can withstand the agony of her walking away.

# CHAPTER TWENTY-ONE

## FORTITUDE

### SELENE

I wake groggily to canned laughter coming from the television, and crack open my swollen eyes to find Asteria sitting on the floor below me. She's watching some corny sitcom while painting her nails, her usual weekly habit, and I roll onto my back with a groan.

My limbs feel like they have been stretched in all directions, and my face aches, inflamed from the never-ending crying. I assess my body functions for a moment and I have full control over my movements, except my mind is shrouded in a warm blanket, numbing my overall psyche.

I am a bubble, floaty in the sense of being lightheaded, but without the dizziness. It takes a year to blink.

Ria glances at me over her shoulder, giving me a sympathetic look. She pushes to her feet and lifts my legs to sit with me. I drag myself up against the arm rest and pull a throw blanket around my shoulders, not really thinking about anything in particular.

Ria pats my leg and gets my attention, her manicured brow pinching with concern.

"Hey, how are you feeling?" she gently asks, her sharp voice uncharacteristically soft.

I have to consciously focus on my emotions, finding that I don't have them floating around freely like I usually do. It takes some effort to pull them forward to assess how things are within me. I can feel the distraught emotions if I look closely, but they don't have much of an affect on me at the moment, so I answer her truthfully.

"I feel okay. Kind of…high? Haha, I don't know. I'm a bit numb, but also kinda floaty?" I blink lazily at her and she nods with a small smile.

"Yeah, that would be from Mother's spell. She placed a sedative enchantment around your mind after rendering you unconscious. She and I both agreed it was probably the best course of action, with all things considered. Your powers are manifesting, and without your knowledge of how to wield them, shit can turn *real bad*, if you get what I mean." Ria widens her lavender eyes dramatically, giving me a smirk. "You're badass, by the way, and this is coming from *me*," she adds with a hair flip and I giggle childishly.

My mother pushes through the porch door clutching a basket in her hands, and the bright sunlight pouring into the dark cottage with her arrival stings a little. I squint my eyes from the harsh change and she quickly closes the door, placing her herb basket on the counter. Her skirts float around in waves, their swaying mesmerizing me for a moment.

I don't hear what she has said to me.

My mother's face is concerned and I have to blink a few times to focus on her directly, clearing my throat a little before I speak.

"I'm sorry, I didn't hear you. Things are…a little hazy." My voice is languid, and I smile loosely up at her.

She glances at Ria who laughs and shakes her head with a shrug. "Could be worse," she says offhandedly, her smile fading away.

"I think I overdid it with the incantation," my mother mutters, crouching before me, and gently presses her fingers to my temples.

She closes her violet eyes and murmurs something incoherently, her voice shifting into a lower cadence as she speaks. Something cool slithers through my head at her words, the way water feels running over your hand, and the haziness to my mind dissipates, leaving only the veiled, muted emotions and partial numbness behind.

Sighing, I blink a couple of times, regaining my clarity. I give her an appreciative smile as she leans back.

"Thank you. That is much better. Not to say it wasn't good before, it was *great,* but I don't want to cover all my shit up without addressing it at its core," I say quietly, glancing away from them both.

"You should have the ability to access what ails you at your discretion. My intention with the enchantment is to give you a means to handle yourself on your own, without feeling too much of everything all at once. When you are ready, I will remove the spell from your mind and you will return to your natural state. Until then, take as much time with it as you see fit, dear. We all want you to feel well soon." My mother gives me a reassuring smile and I nod in gratitude.

Glancing toward the window and the bright blue sky, I try to recall the last thing I remember happening. I wince as I see myself exploding with dark shadow magic and throwing it at Kyran in my desperation to get him away from me, ultimately doing the *one thing* I was trying so hard to avoid.

I turn to my mother, asking quickly, "Is he okay? Did I hurt him? I didn't mean to, I don't know what overcame me. None of this has been making much sense." My voice is frail and sore, and I raise a hand to rub my throat.

Asteria vanishes for a moment and reappears with a glass of water, silently holding it out for me. I take it gratefully and gulp half of it down while my mother takes a seat in the armchair beside the couch. I finish the glass with a sigh, realizing how thirsty I am and that I haven't had anything to eat in almost...*two days?*

"What time is it? How long have I been out?" I ask them both, setting the empty glass on the end table.

I watch with fascination as Ria swirls her fingers around and liquid splashes behind me. I turn to find my glass refilled with water and gape at Asteria with an astonished smile.

"That is seriously so awesome," I say under my breath, taking the glass in my hand once more.

"He is alright, for the most part," my mother answers my earlier question with a reserved tone. "It is eleven forty-seven in the morning. You were asleep for more than a day."

I peer at her over the glass as I swallow down a few more gulps of cold water and my eyebrows furrow. "What do you mean by *for the most part?'* Is he hurt?" I ask immediately, a stone of worry dropping into my stomach.

"Kyran is unharmed physically, due to his healing ability. However, I am not one to speak for how someone is on the inside." My mother holds her hand out and a steaming cup of tea appears in her palm. "I am certain he is…having some difficulty, though," she murmurs and takes a sip of her tea, her violet eyes watching me over the rim.

Asteria shifts on the couch, pulling her legs up and faces me. She sighs heavily and I notice the darkness beneath her tired eyes. Her hand gently pats my leg still perched in her lap, and she gives me a small smile. "I'm sure he's okay. Just go talk with him once you've regained some of your strength."

I shake my head, glancing down and knitting my fingers together. "No," I whisper, "I don't think I can face him right now."

Neither of them say anything in response and I chew my lip as I think about my behavior toward him last night. I feel ashamed for him to have seen me in that way, and for using my power against him. I groan internally at the memories of yesterday playing in my mind.

*I'm a fucking mess.*

*You got that right,* Luna's exasperated voice weaves through my head and I snort a laugh.

My sister looks at me weirdly and I ignore her, raising my hand to scrub my face. *Ugh, I need a shower. A long, hot, thorough cleanse.* Dropping my hand with a sigh, I place my glass down and slowly get to my feet. My sore body protests against the movement as I stretch my arms over my head.

"I have a lot to think about, and I'm going to start in my shower. Then in my tub. I'll check back in once I've become a swelled up raisin," I say blandly, waving a hand at nothing and heading for the stairs.

As I take the first step, I pause for a moment, turning back toward my family and give them a small smile. "Thank you, both, for everything. I appreciate your help and patience through all of this—"

The television emits a harsh, incessant droning noise. We all flinch from the loud interruption. *'Breaking news'* flashes across the screen, and video footage shows a reporter running through smoky chaos in a city.

Her voice is frantic over the din of screaming people and blaring car horns.

"...*We have yet to identify the cause of the explosion, or how many buildings have been affected. Police are on their way to evacuate and restrict the immediate area. Several EMS teams are assisting injured people as they emerge from the rubble...*"

Her voice cuts off over the boisterous background and she coughs heavily into her arm, the air on the screen hazy and dark from the fallen buildings.

The banner streaming across the bottom of the screen shows '*Times Square, NYC in uproar after sudden explosion detonates, collapsing several buildings...*' I lose focus on the words as more images and videos appear showing people bloodied and panicked, cars crushed on top of one another and hanging from torn out sections of broken buildings. Huge pavement chunks are strewn all over the place. It's an awful sight and just as I am looking away, the camera pans over to a cleared out area.

A woman rises from the destroyed ground. Her clothing looks odd, almost like she is wrapped in a bedsheet, though it's hard to distinguish with the dirt, blood, and the shakiness of the video.

My mother gasps loudly, her hand flinging to her chest before she vanishes with a heavy gust of wind. I push my hair out of my eyes and look at Asteria with confusion, her face mirroring mine.

"What the hell was that about?" I ask, resting my hand on the banister.

She just shakes her head, glancing back at the screen as the video cuts out to black and flashes to another perspective, which also cuts out as well. All the subsequent shots are now blacked out and the news reporters' voices grow frantic.

Ria turns back to me with a worried expression. "I don't know, but I have a feeling she knows who *that* was." She waves her hand toward the television. "Go upstairs try to relax. I'll stay here and wait for her return. Just shout if you need me for anything, okay?" Her voice is back to that unfamiliar softness and I just nod in response.

Thinking about the awful situation in New York, I hope the affected people can pull through the ensuing turmoil, and feel guiltily grateful that I don't know anybody there.

Opening my door, I find my room tidied and send silent thanks to my sister as I shuffle to my bed, sitting on the edge for a moment. I grab my cell phone off the nightstand and open my texts, tapping on my messages with Kyran. I notice there is a new message beneath the few texts that I didn't respond to yesterday. I quickly put my phone back down, dropping my head into my hands with a groan, unable to bring myself to read what he has said.

I push to my feet with a huff, not having the energy to sift through my volatile thoughts. Taking advantage of the magical sedative, I let the numbness block everything out as I walk into my bathroom. I am fully aware that I am being ignorant, but introspection can start in an hour or so, after I'm clean and with a full belly.

I sigh contentedly, wrapped head to toe in a matching set of a white fluffy towel, robe, and slippers. It's amazing what some soaps, oils, and hot water can do for the soul. My stomach gurgles and I consider making my way down to the kitchen like this when a *clink* echoes across my room. I glance toward my vanity, finding a dinner plate filled with my favorite foods, and a glass of what I can only assume is Merlot. Smiling, I pick up the wine glass, take a long sip and sigh in satisfaction.

"I'm gonna need a lot more of this if I'm supposed to make it through today in one piece," I jest out loud, holding the glass aloft.

Ria's laughter echoes up the stairs.

A wine bottle appears beside the plate a moment later with a *thunk*.

Smirking, I pick up the plate and step onto my balcony, settling in the spot Kyran and I had sat together a couple of nights ago. My joy fades away as I think about him and what has happened. I shake my head lightly, knowing that I can't deal with that at this moment and shut it out for the time being. Sitting back against the wall, I gaze over the yard as I eat, letting my mind drift naturally.

Thoughts of Luna surface, and I am glad she's a part of my life. I feel fuller having her here. It wasn't something I noticed before I was aware that all this shit existed, but since learning about magic, my mother and sister, Kyran and me—and *everything* involved with us—I felt like a part of me was missing. As if I wasn't whole. I understand why I still feel that way, not fully *myself* without my memories, even though Luna can speak with me now. I hope once we figure everything out and release her, I'll feel...complete.

My thoughts drift in the direction of the mate bond and I push it away, picking up my wine glass and finishing it.

Reaching for the empty plate, it disappears when my fingers graze the edge. As I rise to my feet, I chuckle my thanks to my sister again, assuming she can hear me somehow. Stepping over to the worn railing, I lean on my elbows, dangling the glass between my fingers as I watch the clouds float lazily overhead.

I sigh heavily, not knowing where to even begin within myself as I contemplate which thoughts to sort out first. After a few more moments of watching the sky, I close my eyes and sift my way back through all the shit to the beginning of the sleep-dive. Memories and images of Kyran flash through my mind, of him going through his own troubles and I let it fade away. My chest tightens at the thought of him right now. I can't face him in reality, and apparently I can't face him in my memories, either.

I push forward through my recollection. The terrifying sensation of being swept underwater overcomes me and I gasp out loud, quickly backing out of the memories. Sharp, shattering glass startles my eyes open and I realize that my hands are empty.

"Selene? Are you alright?" Asteria's voice calls out, alarmed.

"Y-yeah, sorry, I wasn't paying attention," I yell back, scrunching my nose with embarrassment.

"It's okay," she responds reassuringly, her voice less tight now that she knows I'm alright. "Hey, watch this!"

I'm about to ask what when glittering shards of glass float upward over the railing, shimmering like stars in the sunlight. I watch with wide eyes as they swirl around one another and coalesce into the wine glass once more. Hesitantly, I reach out to grasp it, a laugh bubbling from my chest in astonishment. Quickly leaning over the banister, I meet Ria's wide grin with one of my own and hold the glass up.

"That was *awesome*," I gush, honestly impressed.

"*Tch*, that was nothing." She scoffs, shaking her head with a laugh. "Wait until you remember all the crazy shit we used to do with my magic."

"I can't wait," I say earnestly, smiling down at her.

My towel slides off my head and I straighten, draping it over the railing. Crossing my room to snag the bottle of wine, I take it downstairs and meet with Ria in the kitchen. I set the bottle on the counter, taking a sip from my refilled glass as she turns around and hands me a spoon.

Raising an eyebrow at her in silent question, she just smirks and holds out her hands, palms facing upward. With a *snap*, two pints of ice cream manifest and she holds one out to me. I gleefully take it and hurry over to the couch, the wine quickly forgotten.

My sister joins me and turns on the TV, choosing an episode of *Sabrina the Teenage Witch*. I narrow my gaze at her with a grin as we settle in together, quietly enjoying our sweet treats.

Bright golden light rouses me, and I squint against the morning sun beaming through my windows. I yank the covers over my head with a groan, rolling over in bed. Asteria and I stayed up late talking, courtesy of the wine bottle that never ran dry. At first, our conversation was mostly about little things, but it grew heavier as the night went on. She'd asked me how I was doing, and I was tempted to lie and say I was doing fine, but I figured that would completely defeat the purpose of trying to heal. I quietly admitted that I was struggling to face anything at all.

She was very kind and understanding, listening to the things I chose to talk about and we had a few moments of shared tears. I decided to let her know the full story of Bolvi, and she was visibly holding back her fury while I spoke. Ria had vowed that if she ever saw him again, she would rip his heart out, and I laughed until I realized she was serious. I told her that Kyran had said the exact same thing, but it probably wouldn't be necessary since he's most likely dead or damn close to it from the berserker disease. To be honest, I hadn't even thought about seeing him again after the incident at Kyran's bar. I guess I just figured with Kyran around, he'd never show himself again, and I pushed him from my thoughts since that night.

We talked about my sleep-dive experience and I explained how I didn't intend on facing my suppressed trauma when it ended up swallowing me whole. Ria gave me insight on how the astral plane works, with energies and the powers woven through them, how memories hold energy and mine must have been quite strong to take me over in that way. We talked about the chest again, and that maybe soon we could try getting it open.

Recalling what Luna was trying to tell me amidst the chaos of my hysteria, I found myself agreeing with her that having my memories back would definitely help me in wading through everything weighing on my mind.

I sigh, pushing my covers aside with a flop of my arm and roll onto my back. I have to admit, the light, fuzzy feeling blanketing my mind has helped me tremendously, and I want to properly thank my mother for placing the enchantment over me. She never returned last night, at least not while I was awake, and I want to see if she is home now. I shove my legs over the edge and sit up, stretching my arms high.

I do feel better after my night with my sister. Saying and expressing things out loud released some of it from within me.

*Maybe the whole energy thing works on this plane as well. Maybe some of the negative energy transferred from my mind to dissipate into the ether as I spoke the thoughts aloud.*

I wonder at this train of thought while I get dressed, and head downstairs for breakfast. I intend on making the most of today and let go of the weight I've been carrying for too long. With this in mind, I consider what I should focus on working through first when I enter the kitchen.

I smile, glad to find my mother sitting at the island. As I'm about to ask her what had caused her to leave so abruptly, Asteria pushes through the porch door.

"Hey," she says with a hesitant smile. "Um, Kyran's outside, if you'd like to talk with him," she adds quietly, pulling her brows in.

I chew on my lip, wrapping my arms around my middle, and lightly shake my head. "I don't think I'm ready to see him yet," I admit, shame coloring my cheeks warmly.

She nods in understanding and disappears for a few moments. I awkwardly stand in the kitchen with a lost appetite.

Ria reappears with a sad look on her face before she composes herself and takes a seat beside mother. My chest aches in protest of my held breath and I release a sigh with a *huff*, shuffling over to the couch to sink into the corner section. I must have zoned out for a little while because a nudge to my knee catches my attention. My mother is sitting next to me, holding out a banana walnut muffin.

Accepting the treat with a small smile, I meet her gaze and ask her about yesterday. "What made you leave so quickly? Is everything alright?" I pinch my eyebrows together, hoping that nothing else is adding to her stress right now.

Her violet eyes meet mine, cheeks puffing out before she releases her breath on a heavy sigh. She gently shakes her head. "No, I am afraid things are not alright. In fact, things may just get much, much worse in the world if we are not careful…" She trails off, staring into nothing.

I quickly glance over at Ria. She turns over her shoulder in her stool, a bite of food held aloft halfway to her mouth. Her face pinches with concern, and I look back at my mother as she sets her mouth in a grim line.

"What do you mean by that?" I ask cautiously, unsure where this could be going.

She pats her hand on my knee, giving me a tight smile before admitting, "I left yesterday after that newscast broke out, because that woman shown in the wreckage, the one rising to her feet in the center of the chaos? That was…" She clears her throat. "That was Lilith. She is my sister." Her words detonate like bombs.

Asteria spits her tea onto the island at the admission and a shrill, *"What?!"* peals from her.

She manifests directly in front of us, her wind buffeting me against the couch. I blink owlishly at both her sudden appearance and my mother's revelation, and I can only watch the scene unfold before me.

"You have *a sister?* I have *an aunt?"* Ria's voice is still shrill, and I nod along in agreement at her bewilderment. *"Lilith?"* Her voice is high with disbelief as she runs a hand through her silky auburn hair, gripping her scalp tightly.

My mother nods and slumps back against the couch. "Yes. Though, she is not what mortals have portrayed her to be." She sighs with a wave of her hand.

Asteria just gapes at her, and a thought crosses my mind. "Why did you leave so abruptly, though?" I ask, trying to wrap my head around all of this.

My mother takes a deep breath before mumbling, "I haven't seen her for a few millennia." Her eyebrows raise as she sits deep in thought.

A squeak escapes Asteria at this new insight and I flick my eyes to hers, watching as her mouth fails to form words. I empathize with her in discovering something about her life that she had been unaware of for, well, *ever.*

"Why?" I ask simply out of pure curiosity, glancing back at our mother.

"The sake of humanity was under threat and she was involved. I had no choice other than to open a rift and send them into the future—" She pinches the bridge of her nose and inhales sharply, cutting herself off. "You know what, it's a long story, one I'll explain at a later time because frankly, I don't have the energy to deal with this right now. What is important, however, is that I know what spell to use to unlock your memories."

Ria's eyes nearly bug out of her skull. "*What?* How? Did you meet with her? Did she tell you? Why would she know that? Is she a witch, too? But how, if you're sisters…you're like, *the* witch, though. Do you share power? Are you both split from—"

"*Asteria,* enough." My mother raises a hand with a dry laugh.

Ria looks like her head is going to implode.

I just blink at them, only mildly affected with the benefit of my enchantment.

"*First of all,* I am not a witch, I am the *goddess of witchcraft,*" my mother breathes irritably.

"*Tch,* semantics," Asteria says flippantly, waving her hand.

My mother stares flatly at her before curtly responding, "No, *dear daughter,* there is a distinct difference, one you are very well aware of."

Again, Ria waves her hand dismissively. "Demons-shmemons, whatever, you know what I mean. If Lilith is your sister, what does *that mean*, exactly?"

*Wait, what?*

"Demons?" I query, raising a finger, though neither of them seem to notice.

*Once you hold your memories, this will all make sense,* Luna's voice drifts through my mind. *None of this is new information, besides Lilith being Hekate's sister. I'm equally shocked as Asteria.*

I just nod along, absorbing everything as best I can. My mother rubs her forehead and closes her eyes for a moment, as if this discussion causes her physical discomfort.

"*It means* that Lilith is the creator of demons. Her power is paralleled with mine, though her focus lies in the realm of the...underworld. Look, a long, *long* time ago, someone pissed her off, *royally,* and in her wrath, the demon race was born. She intended to use the demons to seek revenge on them, but things got out of control when she got caught up in a battle with—never mind. Like I said, I will explain her story another time." She sighs exasperatedly, and I can't help but just stare blankly at her.

Words are registering on the same level as reading off a diner menu.

Taking a heavy breath, she opens her eyes and explains, "What is important here is that I had to send her into the future, and I had to enchant her memories away someplace safe as a means to bide time to figure out what the hell to do with the dilemma we were faced with." My mother lets out another tired sigh. "Yes, to answer one of your questions, I did meet with her and in doing so, I realized that the issue *we* are dealing with here can be solved by something I forgot I had done only once before." Her voice grows quiet as she gazes at the both of us.

Asteria's hands slap against her thighs, her breath whooshing from her chest in disbelief.

I glance at the two of them for a moment before rising to my feet and announce flatly, "Well, let me know whenever you're ready to free my memories, because I want to get it over with sooner rather than later, and preferably with this enchantment still in use." I gesture between them with my uneaten muffin. "Especially with the way the both of you look right now." I raise my eyebrows with a slight shake of my head. "I'll be outside in the gardens for a while."

I spend the rest of the day wandering the gardens alone, and give myself space to let my feelings run their course. I take the necessary time needed with each thought and emotion, to allow them time to pass without pushing any part of it away. Utterly exhausted, I rest on the edge of the large fountain, stroking my hand though Machitís' fur as he sits with his massive head perched in my lap.

My body is worn, as if I'd run a marathon today, and I realize how draining it is to endure emotional pain.

I've waded through a decent amount of emotional baggage, I'd like to think, and now I allow myself some peaceful quiet away from the memories and the feelings that come with them. Deciding I want to do something for my mother as a show of gratitude and care, I contemplate which flowers to pick for a bouquet.

Rising to my feet, I pat Machitís' head once more and tell him to go find his brother, watching with a smile as he bounds away into the darkening forest. Meandering through the gardens, I select a variety of flowers and enjoy breathing in their scents as I go.

*I want to apologize for my behavior, before,* I direct my thoughts toward Luna, sensing that she has given me some distance for my privacy.

*There is absolutely nothing for you to apologize for, Selene.* Her crystal voice rings sharply in my mind and I smile faintly at her intensity. *What happened to you was truly awful, and with your discovery of your entire life being a lie on top of what you'd already been carrying, it is no wonder for you to have reacted the way you did. Do not feel ashamed for feeling too much.*

*I understand, though I do feel embarrassed by it all. Especially with my behavior toward Kyran.* I admit, my voice sounding small. *I was in a panic. My mind felt out of control, and this is not including my supposed powers coming to life without my knowledge of them. I just did not want to harm anyone, most of all him.*

I feel a comforting pressure from Luna, almost like a hug, and she quietly responds, *I know. I see things from my side differently than you can, and I know you would never intentionally cause him harm.*

*Exactly.* I'm relieved she understands. *This is why I can't be around him right now, not while I'm like this. I feel...broken. And I don't want my suffering to cause him pain, because I know he cares, and I know my hurting would in turn hurt him just by existing. I won't allow that to be, so I can't be with him right now. I hope he will understand where I am coming from with this.*

I let out a sigh as I pick the last flower, a small clutch of sweet jasmine, and add it to the white bouquet I've gathered.

As I step across the path toward the cottage, a soft whine catches my ear on a brush of wind and I turn over my shoulder.

The dim light of dusk makes it hard to see farther than the garden. I don't notice anything out of the ordinary until a dark movement catches my eye near my favorite willow.

I almost brush it off as one of the dogs and am turning back toward the house when the glint of amber flashes briefly in the setting sunlight.

*"Kyran,"* I breathe, my chest tightening painfully at the sight of him.

He takes a few steps forward in his wolf form, fully emerging from the shadows of the woods and stops beside the willow. He truly is beautiful. I'm overcome with the strong urge to run to him, to wrap my arms around his neck and never let go.

But I know that would not be fair to either of us, to hold onto him in order to stand on my feet. It would be a disservice to us both if I don't sort out my issues first, especially when he has finally freed himself from the binds he'd been trapped in for so long.

I stare at him for a few shallow breaths, my heart pounding with the effort to stop my legs from moving forward. I tear my eyes from his, begrudgingly walking up the path toward the cottage.

His low keening howl washes over me, making my chest ache painfully with every step I take. Tears spill over as I open the door, not daring to look back. Because if I do, I wouldn't just fall apart.

I'd shatter into thousands of pieces.

# CHAPTER TWENTY-TWO

## WOE

### KYRAN

Two days have passed since Selene pushed me away. I haven't been able to bring myself to leave her woods, my worry for her outweighing my responsibilities at home with my pack and the Convocation preparations. Valdr had mindlinked Treyvar only to tell him we would not be home that first night, to which my brother accepted without question. It wasn't until late last night that he had reached out to me to see if there was anything I needed help with. I thanked him for his concern, but only asked if he could manage things without me for a little while longer. He assured me that things were going along fine, and told me to take whatever time I needed.

Yesterday afternoon, I watched Selene have a meal on her balcony. She seemed lost in thought, almost dazed as she looked out over their property. I haven't been stalking her, I've respected her choice to have personal space and distance, though it is tearing me up inside. My only reason for remaining out here is to ensure her safety. I don't entirely know what has happened, or why she was out in the forest on her own, but I can't leave without being sure no harm will come to her.

Jeger reported to me the night before that small nests of vampires have been appearing in the surrounding towns and cities, although they haven't seemed to cause any issues.

Yet.

No news of Caedes has surfaced since his attack on my sister. The last I've heard of him was from Felagi letting me know he was sighted in the North East. I have no idea what the hell he is up to, but Jeger informing me about new nests is a major concern.

This knowledge is what made me show myself to Asteria earlier this morning. I felt she and Hekate should be made aware of a prevalent threat to Selene. Asteria had thanked me and asked if I would like to speak with Selene, which I immediately agreed to, only if she would ask her first out of respect for her privacy.

Asteria let me know that Selene was not ready to meet with me at the time and she gave me a sympathetic smile, asking me to have patience. She assured me that though Selene is struggling, she is doing as well as she can, and that they are taking care of her. I thanked her for letting me know, feeling awkward at being so vulnerable in front of another powerful being. I dejectedly returned to my place beneath the blackthorn with the hope I had been clinging to slowly dying within me.

The day passes sluggishly as my mind wanders, thoughts threatening to shroud me in darkness as time goes on. I try not to succumb to self-loathing and focus on Selene's needs. She's been through a lot of shit and her space is necessary in order for her to begin to heal. Fuck, it took me *way too long* to figure that out with my own life, and I refuse to be a reason it continues on with her.

Little shadowy snakes of doubt slither through my mind, though, embedding themselves deep with tiny, icy fangs.

*What if it isn't just her pain causing her distance? What if it is me, if I'm not who she thought I was when we first met? She knows now the shit I've done, things I've chosen to do. Hell, things I never told anyone about before. What if it is the reason she can't face me now?*

My chest aches at these thoughts as I pace around the woods, the setting sun casting long shadows between the trees. Valdr has grown as restless as I have been, the both of us anxious at the prospect of losing our connection with our soulmate. Our mind swarms with incoherent fearful thoughts, creating a wild tangle of undulating emotions.

Distant rustling catches my attention and I peer through the tree line. Selene picks flowers in the garden behind her home, her dogs bounding into the woods across the field. My heart beats achingly at the sight of her and Valdr suddenly takes control, stepping out from the shadows of the trees with a pained whine.

Her bright eyes flit around in search of the noise and my chest tightens when she doesn't seem to notice me. Just as she is turning to leave, our gazes happen to meet. Hope blooms from her sharp intake of breath at the sight of me.

I step forward out of the shadows, stopping beside the old willow tree outside of her balcony, the place where I first revealed myself to Selene. The anguish in her eyes sends a stab of pain to my heart as we silently watch each other.

My leg twitches to run toward her. It takes everything I have to remain where I stand, fighting against Valdr's desire to disregard my demand of respecting her boundaries and do as he pleases.

A heavy, sinking weight fills the pit of my stomach when she doesn't move or speak, despair clawing its way through my skin to burrow into my lungs and steal my breath. Her gaze leaves mine when she turns her back and walks away from me. The hollowness that seeps from her absence swallows me whole. Immense sorrow overcomes me and a deep, morose howl rips from my chest when she opens the door, walking through it without a backward glance. Any hope I had left died at the resounding *click* of the door, closing resolutely on what would forever be the best thing to have ever happened to me.

My body reacts and I'm running, my bleeding heart stinging with every stride. Skidding to a stop where Selene stood only moments ago, I breathe deeply, scenting fresh jasmine.

*Of course she was picking jasmine.*

The aroma makes me weak and my legs give out on me as I shift, desolation bringing me to my knees. My palms crash into the gravel and I bow my head.

Hot tears stream down my face.

I grate my fingers into the rough ground, seeking *anything* to lessen the burning agony igniting deep within me. An anguished groan escapes me and I clench my jaw against it, my breath hardly leaving my constricted chest.

It takes me a few moments to get a hold of myself, though Valdr's unbridled distress makes it immensely difficult. I slowly push to my feet. With a long look at the light in Selene's windows, I roughly swipe a dirty hand across my face in agitation and turn away, shifting back into wolf form. I resolve myself to accept that I am no longer needed here. Hekate is aware of the vampire threat and she is more than capable of handling things on her own. My heavy paws crush the ground beneath me as my insides turn to stone.

I am forced to switch off my emotions, fearing they will consume me again, afraid of tumbling into the fathomless pit I only *just* crawled out of. By the time I make it across the patrol boundary, both my mind and heart are encased behind a thick wall of ice.

My movements are automatic, thoughts only focused on the task at present. I don't bother to acknowledge the warrior who greets me, or any of the pack members milling around the village as I trudge up the roads to my home. I hardly even notice anyone anyway, my attention only on the steps that I am taking, carrying me further away from Selene.

The entry door shuts with more force than I intended as I stalk across the house, the joyous conversation in the lounge above quieting at the sound. I take the stairs two at a time, barely giving the group of people a glance as I round the corner to take the short flight up to my rooms.

"Oi, Kyran!" Felagi's raucous voice booms. "Now it's a party, haha!"

I ignore him and the laughter that follows, not able to join in the lighthearted fun they're having. The clack of pool balls and upbeat music just grates against my ears, and I grit my teeth as I wrap my hand around the door handle.

The stairs behind me creak and I wrench my head over my shoulder, glaring at the intruder before I realize it's my brother. Briefly closing my eyes, I sigh through my nose and drop my hand, crossing my arms over my chest as I wait for him.

"Hey," he greets in a light voice. His smile drops immediately when he looks at me. "You okay? What happened?"

My only response is a glare and he nervously runs his hand through his hair. Trey's face pinches a little before he drops his arm and leans against the wall. He shoves his hands into his pockets. I cock an eyebrow at him, silently asking what it is he needs to tell me.

"Right," he sighs, accepting my silence. "Well, Felagi's pack arrived earlier today, as you can tell." He gestures down the stairs at the noise below. "Everyone is situated for the most part. Kira made sure no one but Felagi was to stay here in our home. Many people brought their own tents and whatnot. Anyway, Alpha Castian has just arrived with his mate and their pack. They're making their way through the villages at the moment," he quietly informs me.

I nod in acknowledgment, waiting a beat to see if there's anything else he wants to add before pushing my door open and stepping through.

Turning over my shoulder, I catch his eye as he is about to head back downstairs and mutter, "Greet them for me and make sure their room is accommodating for Mira's pregnancy. Let them know that if she needs anything to ask me directly, or to get someone who will find me for them."

His green eyes widen at my words and he smiles brightly. "No shit, she's pregnant? That's great news! I'm happy to greet them and I'll let Kira know they've arrived." He turns to step down the stairs and pauses, glancing back at me.

"Oh, Alpha Marx called a little while ago, he and Alpha Luric are traveling together, and they'll be here within the next couple of days. I haven't heard from Daine, but I'm sure he'll show up at the last minute with all the pomp and circumstance, as usual." Trey rolls his eyes dramatically.

I just nod again as I turn, forcefully closing the door behind me.

In my bathroom, I crank the shower as hot as it will go. Bracing my hands on either side of the sink, I glare at my dirty reflection in the fogging mirror.

The darkness in my mind swirls the longer I stare, and my fingers grip the edges of the sink basin like a vice.

*I'm here if you need anything,* Trey's voice quietly floats through my mind.

His words trigger something within me, cracking the ice inside.

I bare my teeth at myself as I rip the sink off and smash it down onto the countertop with a harsh snarl. Porcelain shards fly everywhere.

I lose control, yelling my frustration as I tear the cabinet free from the wall and hurl it across my bathroom.

Wooden splinters explode against the wall and broken chunks of tile litter the floor. Water sprays me in the face from a severed pipe and I crush it in my grip, deeply slashing my palm against the metal.

Hot anger courses through me and I smash my fist into the mirror, shattering the rage-filled reflection. Bloody glass rains down around me, cutting my forearm along the way.

None of the physical pain registers. I couldn't care less about it anyway.

In my agitation, I swipe my bloodied hands over my face and grip my hair tightly, trying to rein in the simmering rage. I know I'll regret the damage I've caused here, and I feel shame at losing control, but *fuck, this really hurts.*

I catch a glimpse of myself in the good mirror, fog obscuring most everything except my blood-covered eyes. I turn my back on the despicable reflection and stalk over to the shower, the blood on my hands smearing the glass door as I step under the scalding water.

With ragged breath, I close my eyes and press my hands to the wall as I bow my head. I remain like this for a long while, focusing on locking down my pain until I have a safer place to let it out. Valdr is restless, his agitation palpable, and I struggle to breathe through the tightness in my chest.

Washing myself mechanically, I emerge from the shower once it runs ice-cold, not giving the destroyed bathroom a second glance. I get dressed for the night, forced to play the part of host and meet with the other packs.

Besides silently living in my own personal hell, the night had gone well and I let everyone know that the Convocation is set to formally begin in three days' time. After my announcement, I quietly excused myself from the socialization and tucked myself away in my room, hardly managing to get any sleep.

I kept waking up and checking my phone, even though I know it had never gone off. She hasn't responded to any of the texts, and I haven't sent anything more since she walked away from me.

I irrationally want to crush my phone, so I drop it on the bed as I get up. The aroma of breakfast being prepared drifts into my room and my stomach tightens needily at the scents, though the pain of my hunger doesn't register. Everything is numb within me, unless I acknowledge what lurks just beneath the thin veil I carefully shrouded myself with.

I kick away some of the debris in my bathroom, ignoring it as I leave my room and head down the stairs.

In the lounge, I find Mira holding her large belly, bracing herself against the back of the sofa and I hurry over to her. "Are you alright? Where's Castian?" I ask in a rush, placing my hand on her shoulder in concern.

She lets out a sigh and smiles up at me, brushing her copper hair away from her freckled face. "Yeah, I'm alright, just winded. This little pup likes to kick the crap out of my lungs," she murmurs with a chuckle, rubbing her belly as she straightens. "Castian is in the kitchen. He wakes really early, likes to get his personal stuff out of the way so he can tend to my needs when I get up for the day. He's just the sweetest." Her pale face blushes as she speaks about her mate.

A sharp pang of envy spears through me.

I give her what I hope is a smile and offer her my hand as she waddles her way toward the stairs. She accepts the support and we slowly make our way down the steps. I release her hand when both of her feet are on the floor. A chair scuffs loudly and Castian appears, stuffing half a bagel in his mouth to take both of her hands in his, leading her toward the dining table.

"You should've called for me!" he chastises lightly, ushering her along to take a seat.

Mira swats him away before she carefully sits down. "I'm pregnant, not disabled," she mumbles under her breath.

I huff a dry laugh as I fill a plate before taking my seat at the head of the long table. Kira, Trey, Felagi, Castian, and Mira all pause and glance at me, no doubt wondering what the chaos was from the night before. I just grunt and stuff a forkful of eggs into my mouth, dropping my eyes to my plate. They all resume conversation unaffected and I am grateful for the given privacy.

I doubt I'd be able to explain it calmly anyway.

I eat my breakfast in silence, mostly keeping to myself as I fill a couple more plates and finish them at the island. I quietly thank my brother for the food as he makes his way outside and I head into my office, forcefully closing the door behind me.

My ass barely grazes the chair when Castian bellows my name in fear, and I'm bolting out the door in less than a second. I find him holding up Mira, sobbing and clutching her belly as a large patch of blood blooms over her pale pink dress.

*"Fuck,"* I breathe, grabbing the towel off the oven handlebar and toss it at Castian.

He quickly presses it to Mira, his fearful gaze meeting mine.

*Eir!* I hastily mindlink her, panic lacing my voice. *I need you in my kitchen, now!*

I wipe my hand across my mouth, unsure what I can do for them. A small popping noise announces Eir's arrival beside me. Her back is to Mira and her golden eyes shine brightly, pinched tight with concern. She holds a worn leather strip in her slim hands and raises it to tie her silky copper hair back.

"Kyran, what's wrong?" she asks quickly, and I grab her shoulders, spinning her around.

"Oh! Oh, *oh no,*" she breathes, rushing over to Mira and immediately begins barking orders. "Kyran, get me fresh clothes and a clean, soft blanket. You," she points a finger at Castian, "lay her down and find a large bowl."

I do as I am bid, bounding up the stairs toward the linen closet in the lounge that Kira keeps stocked. I take out the entire stack of sheets and blankets, hurrying down the hall to my brother's room to grab a shirt and sweatpants from his closet, figuring the clothes are for Mira and baggy would be best in this situation.

I leap down the stairs to find Eir cradling Mira's belly with golden light emitting from her hands and a look of determination on her face. Castian is openly crying as he sits behind his mate, supporting her head and shoulders with his body.

My heart lurches for him and I carefully set the pile down on the floor a little ways away from them. Knowing Eir would tell me what she needs, I remain silent, staying in case I could be of help somehow.

She assures Mira that her baby is okay and asks when she is due to give birth, which turns out should be anytime this week or the next. Eir tells her that she is going to guide the baby out with her magic, and will try to help ease the sudden pain as best she can. Mira agrees and begins to lift her skirts.

I quickly turn away and go out to the garden, quietly closing the door behind me to give them some privacy.

I don't know exactly where Eir came from, only that she's been living on these lands for as long as I can remember. She had been a close friend to my mother and aided with delivering all six of her children in this house. I never asked my parents where they met her, only knowing that she's been the head healer in our pack for centuries.

Once, when I was a pup, I boldly asked her if she was a witch. I knew she wasn't entirely a wolf because when she shifts, her scent differs from the hybrids. Since I had never met a witch at that time in my life, I didn't know what one smelled like, so I couldn't use it as a comparison.

Her response was, *'Don't ever insult me like that again,'* and to this day, I have yet to understand what exactly Eir is.

*Maybe it's time I ask her again, though this time with some respect,* I muse as I wander aimlessly.

My thoughts drift around Castian, hoping that everything will work out well with their baby. As I blindly walk through the streets. images of Selene holding a little blonde-haired bundle flash in my mind's eye. I shake my head fervently at the sudden thought, the unexpected sight causing my steps to falter. A longing pain drags over my heart and I forcefully shove it down, swallowing thickly as I round a corner in the main square of the village.

I pass through the busy common areas, noticing how well things have come together for the Convocation. A trace of guilt runs through me for not being a part of the preparations. I make my way up toward the Great Hall, finding that it is fully decorated and set up for the commencement ceremony. The wide fields behind it are dotted with large piles of wood for bonfires, and various stations are prepped for food and drinks. The surrounding forest, lampposts, and roofs are strung with lights, as well as crafts and artwork from the people in my pack.

Making a mental note to thank my brother and sister for their efforts, I realize there isn't much for me to do, other than to make it through the next few days until the full moon is upon us and the celebration begins. Not really sure what to do with myself, I head back to my home to maybe catch up on some logistics and check in with Jeger, see how everything is going on his end of things.

The thought of doing such mundane tasks in the midst of the shit-storm looming over me seems so trivial. Forced with no other option than to keep moving forward, I mentally fortify my ice wall so I can better focus on the responsibilities required of me.

# CHAPTER TWENTY-THREE

## AWAKEN

### SELENE

I spent the last two days doing much of the same thing, focusing my energy on sitting with my emotions as I recall memory by memory, allowing everything to run its course and let it go. The work is slow-going and painful, but the intensity lessens as the days go on. Most of today, I sunbathed in the garden after I tentatively prodded a particularly sensitive memory of Bolvi. It took a long while to work through it.

My soul lightens with every small step I make in healing. My body is exhausted as much as my mind, and sleep has not come easily since the night I left Kyran standing in the yard. I've wanted to reach out to him a few times, but had to tell myself it will only complicate things at the moment.

I need to get through this shit on my own first.

My mother let me know that today we would get my memories back. I'm equally excited and apprehensive about it, though I'm not entirely sure which way I'm leaning toward more at the moment.

Pushing the porch door open, I sniffle thickly through my inflamed nose and wipe my face with the hem of my t-shirt. Ria turns from the oven, holding a tray of chocolate chip cookies. She gives me a small smile and grabs a platter, transferring the cookies onto it at the island. I take a seat on the other side, snagging a warm one from the tray. Taking a bite, I savor the buttery feel of the fresh baked cookie for a moment before scrunching my nose and glaring at it disappointingly.

"What? If there's something wrong with it, it's your fault." Ria waves the spatula at me with a raised eyebrow. "I made these from your dough stash in the freezer," she informs me dryly.

I snort a laugh and point at my red, puffy face. "Is there anything you can do for this? I can't taste a damn thing," I mumble, emphasizing my words with a thick sniffle.

She laughs, stepping around the island and wipes her hands on her thighs. Lifting two fingers, she murmurs, *"Recupero,"* and traces her fingers over my eyebrows, down my nose and across my cheekbones.

The pressure in my face immediately dissipates and I can breathe regularly again.

"Damn, where was this when I was a teenager?" I joke with a small grin. "Thank you."

All the heavy crying lately has made my sinuses inflamed and my eyes feel like I rubbed shards of glass in them. Asteria's magic just wipes it away as if it never was a problem to begin with. She laughs again, giving me a warm smile and goes back to filling the plate.

I take another bite of the cookie and this time, I groan in satisfaction at the delicious taste. Hopping off my stool, I snag two more and make my way to the couch, anxious for our mother to arrive. My sister joins me and I silently consider what having my memories back will be like.

"Hey, Ria?" I ask quietly, and she hums around a mouthful of cookie, raising her brow.

After swallowing a bite, Asteria clears her throat and turns toward me on the couch, asking, "Yeah?"

She twitches her brow, looking at me expectantly when I don't immediately reply.

"Am I...different?" I gesture vaguely at myself, waving my hand around my head. "How I am, how I behave, I mean. Am I different now compared to the person you knew before we had to go into stasis?"

The question drifts through the room, and my heartbeat quickens with anxiety at her unspoken answer.

Her eyebrows pinch and her mouth twists to the side before she shakes her head. "No, not really. If anything, you're just more reserved overall. You're still kind, compassionate, and have always had a gentle soul. Though, I will admit, Luna's sassiness definitely bled into your personality at times. You had an edge to you, like, even though you didn't *want* to harm anyone, you'd be *ruthless* in the name of justice or morality. I think that comes with Luna's soul, though, and yours has not changed. This current part of you is simply the foundation block of the part of you I knew back then. I'm confident that when you hold your memories once more, the life you've lived here will bring a more well-rounded self forward when combined with your past self." Ria smiles warmly at me with love in her eyes.

I smile back, nodding as I finish the last cookie, absorbing her words.

Our mother arrives with a burst of wind, flickering the candle flames around the living room. Her straight, cropped hair flutters over her shoulders. She smooths her slim hands over her plum velvet dress, a movement I've grown to understand to be a nervous habit since she is always impeccably well-kept. Her violet eyes have a slight shimmer to them as she holds my gaze, her mouth drawn tight.

"If you are ready, I have everything prepared," she quietly informs us, glancing from me to Asteria.

I nod once. "I am. As much as I can be, I guess. Although, there is something I would like to see, before my memories are restored. Kind of like a fun new experience, to give me a little bit of a fresh memory to tie with an old one, perhaps?" I roll my lips between my teeth, suppressing a grin.

She narrows her eyes at me, shifting her weight and crossing her arms. "What...are you asking?"

"Would you show me your triple form? I know from the lore and mythology that the...*humans* have is that you are depicted with an appearance as a three-headed goddess, one face each for the maiden, mother, and crone." I raise my eyebrows expectantly, clasping my hands in my lap.

"Is this really necessary?" she intones dryly, pinching her nose with closed eyes.

"*Ugh,* she used to do this to me as a child to get me in line when I wouldn't *obey.*" Ria pushes off the couch and flaps her hand at our mother, making her way back into the kitchen.

I laugh at them both and nod eagerly, gesturing for her to proceed. My mother drops her hand and sighs dramatically before stepping around the armchair.

"*Fine,* if it makes you feel better. But we must begin our work immediately afterward, I need the light of the rising full moon to strengthen the magic within you," she mutters and looks at me pointedly, a small crack of a smile pulling at her mouth.

I nod once in agreement, and she shakes her hands at her sides. Lifting her arms, she sweeps them in a wide arc, pressing her palms together at her chest. Her violet eyes flash, glowing brightly. With a mischievous smile, she claps her hands then spreads her arms wide.

The air around her shimmers for a moment as two shoulders and arms appear on either side of her outstretched ones, and two slender necks raise identical heads in opposite directions. I can't help the gasp that escapes me as my eyes flit over her. Their movements are individual, like three people sharing one main body. She lowers her arms and raises an eyebrow at me, her mouth lifted in an amused smirk.

"*Whoa,*" I breathe, pushing to my feet. "Can you see all around you?" I ask, fascinated.

"*Yes,*" all three mouths respond simultaneously, three identical voices with different tones joining harmoniously.

I step around her to look at each face and all six eyes track my movements, her heads swiveling as I walk. It's *totally* freaky and cool at the same time. The head on her right side is youthful, pretty in the way that nature is, and she gives me a pleasant smile. This face is the same as the mother I've always known, just younger, more childlike in its features. Her middle head is the original and I smile at her as I pass by, peering around her left shoulder at the third head. Wrinkled violet eyes greet me warmly, and her soft jowls wiggles a bit as she inclines her head in greeting.

I turn and stand in front of my mother with a wide smile, delighted at the magical wonder of her.

She raises all six arms a little as if she's stretching, and her voices murmur, *"It's been some time since I've held this form."*

Her three expressions are reminiscent. She sways a little for a few moments before whirling her hands and returns to her original form, smoothing her now waist length, wavy black hair over her shoulder. I can't resist the desire to hug her and wrap my arms around her slim waist, feeling lighter than I have been since the sleep-dive. I whisper my thanks, and she gently pats my head before I pull away with a sigh.

"Alright, tell me what I need to do. I'm ready," I say sternly, feeling sure for once. "Should we remove my mental shroud? Luna said that she believes having my memories back will help me to be able to process things within myself, and I agree with her. It feels right. I just want to feel *whole* again." My voice grows quiet with weighted emotions.

My mother nods in agreement and holds out her hand for me. I place mine in hers without hesitation. The sensation of a rocking boat washes over me and I find myself in a dark room, lit only by four fat candles placed on the floor at each center point of the walls. When my senses fully return, I notice that we're not in a *room,* but a cavern of stone with a missing ceiling open to the twilight sky. Soft, mossy vines climb the walls and encircle the craggy edges, giving the area a deep earthy aroma.

A gentle breeze tickles the back of my neck as Asteria manifests holding some crystals and what looks like a glass vial of ink in her hands. She gives the vial to our mother and summons an intricate athame into her empty hand. I step aside as she passes wordlessly, placing the various crystals on the ground before turning to face me with a small smile.

"I need your blood. It has to be given freely," she states simply and I give her an incredulous look. "Not much, just enough to coat the crystals." She rolls her eyes, handing me the ornate thin blade.

I loosely grasp the carved black handle, eyeing it warily as if it'll embed itself in me on its own and glance back at Ria. "Does it matter where the blood comes from?" I ask, unsure how to go about this.

She just shakes her head and summons another athame, the carvings and shape similar to the one I hold. She swiftly slices her palm on the blade and hovers her dripping hand over the crystals. I wince at the thought of cutting my palm.

Without much thought, I move to stand beside her and quickly drag my blade across the back of my forearm. A sharp hiss escapes me at the hot flash of pain and I angle my arm downward, letting my blood drip over the clustered crystals.

The moment the first drop splatters, silvery light blooms from the center of the cluster and radiates outward, growing larger as more of my blood coats the crystals. Asteria brushes her fingers over my wound while murmuring something under her breath. My skin tingles as it seamlessly knits itself back together.

I stare confoundedly at my arm, smooth and clean as if the gash never happened.

*I guess I could've done my palm,* I think dryly as I watch Ria wave her hand over the glowing crystals.

The cluster levitates a few feet off the ground before separating into small pieces, each one floating away to form a wide circle. The ring settles onto the smooth rock floor with a series of soft *clinks*. At the sound of my name, I turn over my shoulder to find my mother beckoning me to come to her. I stand before her and she raises her inky fingers to my face, swiping them intricately across my forehead and over my temples before tapping my nose with a smirk. I chuckle as I turn back to the illuminated circle, finding Asteria with pretty runes adorning her face as well. She glances up toward the full moon cresting over the edge of the cavern.

"It's time," she quietly announces.

Ria turns toward the crystal circle and holds her hand out to me. I swallow thickly before I grasp it. We carefully step over the glowing crystals and turn in the middle to face our mother. She raises her palms as she closes her eyes, tipping her head back. A cool breeze swirls around her and caresses me gently. Ria tugs my hand as she crouches and I follow, the both of us laying side by side.

I stare nervously into the indigo sky as my mother's voice calls out to me.

"Selene, I won't remove your enchantment until you are in the stasis, though when you awaken, I will not replace it unless you ask me to. With Asteria's magic, this will feel much the same as the sleep-dive, though you both will have better control over what goes on. It will feel more like reality, just with a few extra perks. I wish you the best of luck, and I will be here when you come back." Her voice fades away for a moment before returning lower, chanting in a language I don't understand.

The crystals surrounding us brighten, emitting glittery ribbons of translucent light that float above us lazily, swirling around one another. Each stream forms a pool that stretches wider as my mother's chanting grows louder. The shimmering pool descends slowly, laying over my skin like a cool blanket of misty starlight. Tingles erupt all over my body at the contact.

My mind grows hazy, the sensation similar to the moments right before sleep claims its stake, how the heavy drowsiness is too strong to resist, and my vision quickly fades to nothing.

My conscious is aware that I am not asleep, yet I can't access any of my senses. The feeling is extremely disconcerting, and I would *definitely* start panicking if my mind wasn't still enshrouded with the sedative spell. With no touch, sight, sound, or smell, how the hell could someone *not* panic?

*Is this what a coma feels like?*

My thoughts echo around me into nothingness.

A blurry, dim light appears in the distance. Latching onto the one thing I can see, my mind intently focuses on the glow, immediately surrounded by a hazy silver light.

Misty wisps lazily float by.

A bright white flash darts through the haze.

Another disappears as quickly as it arrived, moving out of view.

Another, and another.

White light blindingly flickers all around and Luna stands before me, her icy gaze aglow from within. If I had breath, it'd be stolen from my lungs at the sight of her.

*She is magnificent.*

Though she doesn't stand as tall as Valdr, her presence definitely demands just as much—if not more—respect and attention than he does. She has a powerful aura about her, with eyes that pierce through to my soul.

*Took you long enough.* Her crystal voice sings around us and her eyes squint a little, as if she's smiling.

*Luna!* I cry, my consciousness pushing toward her.

With our connection, my body manifests and I wrap my arms around her fluffy neck. I hold onto her for a few heartbeats, but she dissipates into mist beneath my arms. My hands flail out, catching myself at the last moment. I push to my feet, spinning around in the foggy nothingness, searching for her to no avail.

"*Luna!*" My cry echoes around everything and nothing. "*Luna, where are you?*"

"*Selene?*" Asteria's distant voice calls back to me.

"*Ria! Over here! Follow my voice. I'm not going to move until you find me because this is weird as hell and I don't want to get lost forever inside my own mind, not when I haven't even finished sorting it out myself and I have so many things I still need to do, I can't get stuck here in this freaky-as-fuck smoke. What the hell even is this? Is this my brain? No wonder I fucking lost my shit—*"

A hand grabs my arm, cutting off my wild rambling and Asteria appears, pulling me in tightly for a hug. I hold her just as strong for a moment before leaning back to take a deep breath. At her touch, the misty haze slowly slides away, revealing the giant trees of the forest Kyran and I had seen.

We're standing in the manifestation of my memory. I recall him making a comment about this being a beautiful way to see my long-term memory, and I reach out to the closest tree, placing my palm against the bark. It glows brightly at my touch. The tree becomes a translucent video, playing a memory of Asteria starting a food fight in our mother's kitchen when we were little. She throws crumbled cupcakes at me, and I fling spoonfuls of icing over the island back at her.

I smile widely at the memory and remove my hand, my gaze drifting through the forest and the vast variety of trees it holds. I assume that each type of tree is categorized with specific sets of memories, and my mind itches to explore.

Just as I take a step away, Ria takes hold of my elbow and pulls her gaze from the forest to meet mine. "Where is that memory chest you were telling me about?" she asks, brushing her knuckles against the food fight memory tree.

In the distance, the crash of ocean waves looms ominously and trees sway with the winds they create, making me grimace. I *really* don't want to go back in there if I don't have to, so I close my eyes and focus on the island Kyran and I had found.

Imagining the little beach with the jungle and private waterfall pool, I pour my energy into the image and wrap my hand around Ria's wrist. In a heartbeat, the ground softens beneath my feet. I open my eyes, standing on the small white beach overlooking a stormy, turbulent sea.

"Whoa," Ria whispers, sweeping her gaze across the dark frothy waves.

"Yeah." I sigh, watching it with her. "That forest was my long-term memories, and Kyran guessed correctly that *this* is my unresolved trauma and negative energies." I gesture at the roiling waters with a frown. "We got caught in it unexpectedly when we were here. It was awful," I whisper, lowering my eyes to the sand.

The ocean isn't quite as violent as it was the first time, but it is far from a calm, tranquil lake, that's for sure. Though the waves don't tower as highly, they are still ominous and intimidating. I turn my back on them, taking a couple of slow, measured breaths. After a few moments, the loud crashing noises lessen, and I reach behind me to take Ria's hand as I step toward the jungle.

She pulls herself around with me, silently following along the path until we reach the sparkling pool with the gleaming metal chest. Asteria gently tugs my arm, and I turn to face her. With a pained look on her face, she wraps her arms around me tightly, rocking us back and forth a couple times before she lets go. I give her a slanted half-smile and shrug, turning back toward the chest.

I frown at how nothing has changed since I last saw it.

Ria turns to say something, but before she speaks, a heavy sensation drops through my mind as if I'd been swimming for a while and finally stood on solid ground. I blink a couple times and shake my head, pressing a hand to my temple. Glancing at Ria, I wonder if she felt it too. When she only watches me curiously, I realize the sedation spell must have been lifted off of me.

Anxiety crawls over my skin, sending little prickly spiders skittering in every direction, overcome with a sense of dread at being trapped in my tumultuous subconscious mind.

Asteria must notice a look on my face or sense the change in me because she grabs my hand tightly, looking me hard in the eyes.

"Selene, I won't let anything happen to you, I promise. *This,*" she points a manicured finger at the chest, "is our goal here. Not *that.*" She waves at the whooshing of the ocean behind me.

I nod woodenly, trying to control my trepidation and breathe it out slowly. "Okay, just do it. I don't want to be in here any longer than necessary." I shake out my hands and turn to face the chest once more.

Asteria gives me a long look, then nods once in agreement and faces the chest. While we were waiting for our mother to return from preparing for the stasis, she told me how this spell requires precision and a lot of energy to execute properly. I take a step away to give her some space and glance around the clearing, trying to distract myself from the crashing waves on the other side of the forest.

Ria chants a spell and firmly presses her palms against the metal chest, her fingers splayed wide as she imbues her magic. She pulls her hands away and straightens, her brow furrowing in confusion when nothing happens. I watch as she repeats the process, again getting the same results. Ria presses her fingers to her mouth, staring at the chest with narrowed eyes.

Leaves rustle nearby.

Glancing behind Ria, some of the large ferns sway back and forth rhythmically, the odd movement catching my attention. Ria chants again louder this time, forcefully projecting her voice and slamming her hands against the chest.

Dark water laps over the jungle floor, creeping closer and closer toward us with every ebb and flow, the whooshing sound of the ocean growing with it.

"Um, Ria…" I murmur, anxiety making my voice thin as my wide-eyed gaze remains fixed on the rising waters.

"Hold on, Selene, I can't understand why the spell isn't working," she mutters, stepping around the chest to look at it from another angle. "I'm reciting it just as she told me to, exact incantations and everything."

I swallow thickly, raising my trembling hand to point at the encroaching ocean, now spilling into the pool at the base of the waterfall. The jungle plants are quickly consumed by its murky depths.

*"Asteria, I don't think we have any time left,"* I croak with fear.

My tight, shaky tone must finally catch her attention, because she glances at me worriedly and follows my line of sight.

"*Shit!*" she yells with rising tension. "*Shit shit shit!*"

A horrified squeak escapes me, paralyzed with fright.

Ria whirls around and slashes a hand in an arc, shouting, "*Expello!*"

The water pushes back a small distance before surging forward, greedy waves crashing over my feet and sending me careening forward. I let out a yelp of surprise and reach for Asteria, our fingers just missing each other as I hit the ground and tumble into the cold, frothy sea water.

My hands scramble blindly for purchase and I grasp onto something solid and smooth. The metal chest radiates silver light at my touch and Asteria's stricken face glows in the reflection, her eyes widening with realization.

"You have to touch the chest while I'm doing the incantation!" she yells over the deafening noise of the ocean crashing eerily close.

I open my mouth to agree when a large wave pummels me, filling my throat with icy water and tearing me away from the chest. My body flips end over end until I slam into a tree and sharp pain radiates along my spine.

*Fuck, she was right to tell me it would feel like reality.* I groan, trying not to lose control and freak the fuck out.

A memory of Kyran eases my distress, how he taught me that I should treat this place like a dream and envision what I want into existence.

With him I mind, I tell myself, *Relax, you can breathe.*

Wincing against the iciness in my chest, I am relieved to only feel air when I inhale. Opening my eyes, I am surrounded by inky blackness and can't tell which way is the surface. I visualize Ria and the chest with a bubble of air surrounding her, keeping her safe from the water.

Praying that it works, I push off the tree with my feet and swim in the direction I'm only completely guessing is where Asteria—hopefully—remains with the chest.

A flash of green whizzes past me, followed quickly by two more, and I cautiously trail after them. Another slashes through the frigid abyss like an angry serpent. Vines dash in and out of the water. My head breaks the surface to find Asteria wielding the earthen whips, lashing them toward the rising water and breaking its surface with her magic. I swim as fast as I can toward her, snagging the end of one vine and giving it a tug to get her attention.

*"Shit, Selene! Are you okay? Hold on tight!"* she yells frantically, tossing the other vine and making a yanking motion with her hand.

I'm forcefully dragged toward her, the vine efficiently towing me through the thrashing water. She latches onto my shoulders, hauling me onto the grass beside her feet. I scramble on my hands and knees to get away from the vengeful, icy sea, beyond grateful that my envisionment actually worked.

Chest heaving, I turn to look back at Ria. She motions her arms in great sweeping patterns, her body swaying rhythmically as she chants a spell. The water surrounding us swirls into a hollow ring at her command, forming into an undulating, ominous wall.

*"Asteria! I'm going to try to freeze the water so you can do your spell! It's the only chance we have!"* I cry out over the din of the violent ocean.

It has swallowed up the little island entirely, leaving only this tiny patch of land with us and the chest left to consume.

The ring she created has crested into a churning sphere with us trapped inside the dome. Shadowy figures taunt me from the other side of the water wall, and I tear my gaze away to look into Ria's bright eyes. Her brow pinches with concern but she nods, understanding we don't have another choice.

I glance up at the racing waters and envision a thick wall of ice. My mind pulls any association I have with cold, solidity, walls, *anything* that can help me barricade us from the ocean of agony that seeks to devour me. I imagine forming a glass bubble, projecting all my previous thoughts into it as hard as I can, and the rushing noise ceases around us, the only sound the echo of crackling ice as it forms.

The frozen dome is rippled with ribbons of waves, glistening from the light that emits from me like millions of stars crushed to dust and sprinkled into my skin. Asteria gapes at the ice wall and drops her hands to her sides, giving me an incredulous look.

The ice creaks overhead.

She snaps her gaze toward the chest and we rush to it together. I slap my palms against the cold metal at the same time she does. An ominous *crack* sounds above us, a fissure fracturing the ice sends shards raining down. The jagged pieces cut harshly into my cheeks and arms, and I hiss against the pain as another resounding *snap* sends larger pieces flying.

*"Asteria!"* I scream in terror and she squeezes her eyes shut against the sight.

She bellows the incantation one last time, a vein in her neck straining with the effort as the glowing chest begins to vibrate. A tear streams down her cheek and more chunks of ice come crashing around us. Water trickles over me in icy rivulets. As the last word of the spell escapes Ria on a sob, the chest explodes open, knocking us both onto our asses.

Glittering silver light pours endlessly from the burst top, nearly blinding me. The swirling beam fountains up and outward, the misty streams intertwined with inky black shadows. They billow throughout the light as they coalesce into one thick, iridescent ribbon dancing on the wind.

I gasp as the magic rushes me, crashing into my chest and igniting me with blinding white light. My body is electrified, every cell swelling with immense power as my mind flows with images, sounds, places, people, beings, tastes, smells—*with everything.*

Memories fly by me like the blurred window of a car on a highway, too fast to identify any one thing, but enough of an idea to know what I'm looking at. I can't breathe, my chest constricting as it feels like my mind and body is being separated into thousands of pieces only to be sanded, polished, and put back together again.

Euphoric—*possibly slightly manic*—laughter erupts from me as the last of the powerful light absorbs into my body. Opening my eyes, I'm startled to see that I am floating high above the dark ocean now.

My joy is immediately snuffed out when I realize the little island and Asteria are nowhere in sight. I whirl around frantically, only finding the vast waters stretching into the distance.

A sharp whistle catches my attention and I snap my gaze up to find Ria floating on her back above me. She has her arms slung behind her head as she leisurely kicks her feet over a puffy cloud hammock.

She grins widely at me over the edge.

I laugh carelessly in my immediate relief, throwing my arms out wide and spinning in circles amidst the stars that manifest around us.

I catch her hands as I whirl past and take her along with me in my flight of glee. I am finally, *finally* back to my whole self again. My gaze meets her bright lavender eyes and I picture the cage Luna has been trapped in, pushing my energy toward it. Soft grass tickles the bottom of my feet a breath later.

Ria's squeal of happiness pierces my ears and she strangles me half to death in her excitement. I can't help but just laugh and hold on tightly.

*"Holy fuck,* that was intense!" She barks a laugh, gripping my shoulders and giving me a slight shake. "I don't know what I would've done if the spell didn't work, but *damn that was a rush!"* She grins and lets me go.

"Yeah, well, I'm really glad it did. I feel *amazing,"* I breathe, the wide smile never leaving my face.

A *chuff* catches our attention. Luna stands at the edge of her golden cage, one ear flattening while a paw stamps the ground in annoyance. Ria snorts before breaking out into a giggle fit and I join her, our adrenaline making us a bit giddy. Clearing my throat, I step forward and press my palm against the lock of Luna's cage.

A flash of light stretches out in a band around the bars and the cage disintegrates, leaving only my wolf and the iridescent golden bond behind.

Luna dramatically shakes her fur coat and haughtily saunters over to me, making me chuckle. I throw my arms around her neck and cry into her soft fur. So much time has passed with us being separated, and now that I finally understand what it is like to have her as a part of me, I *never* want us to be apart again.

A gentle rumble comfortingly rolls from her chest and I know she feels the same way. *Prissy attitude be damned.* I laugh through my tears, sensing her inner eye roll. Taking a few moments to collect myself, I release her and wipe my cheeks dry.

"Hey, Luna, it's good to see you," Ria murmurs and smiles warmly, rubbing her fluffy head.

*Mmm,* Luna hums as a reply and primly sits on the grass.

I grin widely at my wolf, feeling free and whole as I shout an excited cheer to nothing, the sound a yelp of joy. Her eyes narrow before she throws her head back and howls, making Asteria laugh joyously and dance in a circle.

After a miniature celebration, Ria chats with Luna about nonsensical things and I turn toward the dark ocean, happy to let them catch up knowing we have *all* the time in the world for us to talk.

Now that I have my memories back, I have full understanding of the position and *power* that Luna and I hold. Not only are we the most powerful werewolf to exist, we are the fucking *queen*, and *dear, sweet Caedes* will suffer my wrath.

He has caused unforgivable amounts of turmoil and death within *my* race, and I fully intend to make Caedes beg for his life before delivering him to the underworld myself.

The three of us take our time in conversation and relaxing, conjuring ridiculous things to laugh about and enjoy while being in this astral plane. With the knowledge of how the stasis magic works, we know we can stay as long as we want. The runes on our skin are powered by our own magic and the spell is enhanced with moonlight. Hekate is mostly there just in case something goes wrong or to adjust things accordingly.

I think about how my recent memories in life contradict what I now know to be the *real* truth. Asteria implanted a false past in my mind that made me think I had been adopted as a teenager, and it altered how my time was perceived to pass by for only a few years, rather than more than a hundred. I do not hold any grudges against her for it, knowing why I had agreed to be placed into stasis. It was to save the werewolf race from potentially being wiped out, and I'd make the same choice again without hesitation.

I consider my relationship with Hekate, and how for the past fifteen years with her—though *technically it was over a century and a half*—she was solely in the role of my mother and nothing else. What perplexes me now is if I should continue to call her Mother or like I always had, simply addressing her by her name.

*Though she did have a part in my creation, technically the moon goddess Selene and the great wolf Fenrir are my…parents? Ugh, no.* I shake my head at the thought and let it go, deciding I'll bring it up to her once we are back in the earth realm.

Sighing, I sit up from my soft bed of grass, looking out over the cliff at the churning ocean water. The waves aren't undulating highly anymore, the water appearing like any normal sea. The size of it, though, is what concerns me.

Rising to my feet, I step toward the ledge and raise my arms out before me. Wind blows my hair around wildly as it picks up with my intentions. The vast ocean water swirls into a funnel, and I conjure a large glass bottle between my outstretched hands. Envisioning the sea water streaming into the bottle, a long ribbon of the icy dark liquid rises from the center of the whirlpool and stretches toward me. The ocean rapidly shrinks as the water flows into the glass until there isn't a drop left below.

Squinting my eyes at the trapped torrent of water, I place a wooden pirate ship inside with a realistic thunderstorm added for effect, and cork the bottle closed.

Turning around, I heft the large bottle with a grin and Asteria laughs with her eyebrows raised, commenting on the ingenuity of my mind. I smile at the bottle, the once all-consuming power of it becoming something I can pick up off the shelf and interact with if I choose, or just watch from a distance if that's all I can do.

The harsh experiences my 'human' life gave me have become comparably minor when faced with the hundreds of years I've lived previously. This does not negate the impact it had on me, however. The bottle of tempestuous water I hold in my hands is proof of that, and I *will* have to break it open at some point to release it from me for good. At least for now it is easily manageable, and that is all I could ask for.

I push the bottle up into the air and watch it float toward the forest of giant trees before turning to face Asteria and Luna.

"Ready to get back? There's a lot to be done," I say with a smirk, reaching out to take my sister's hand and rest my fingers on Luna's head.

"I am if you are," Ria responds with a grin, and I nod my agreement.

She lifts her free hand to swirl it through the air around us, whispering, "*Tempus est ut evigilet.*"

My body tingles before my vision slips away.

Cool air fills my lungs and my eyes flutter open at the sensation. I sit up groggily, rubbing my face with a groan. Asteria stretches her arms overhead and she sits up beside me, looking as disheveled as I feel. I grin at her, giving her a quick hug before rising to my feet. The crystal circle surrounding us has gone dormant, returning back to its original state.

A short distance away, Hekate stands with her arms clasped behind her back as she stares up at the full moon high overhead. Her head turns toward us as we step over the circle and Ria collects the crystals with a sweep of her arm.

Hekate's hands flutter in the air around me, her words coming out in a rush. "Selene, how did it go? How do you feel? Are you alright, were you harmed?"

I laugh, pulling her in for a hug. "Hekate, I'm fine. I'm really well, actually. It wasn't easy, but we were successful." I lean back and give her a wide smile which she returns in earnest.

"That is *wonderful* news!" she breathes and quickly hugs me again before pushing my shoulders back, her thin eyebrows pinched with concern. "What of Luna? Is she finally here with us again?"

*Yes, Mother, I'm home,* Luna's light voice sarcastically chimes, and we all laugh out loud from it.

Hekate's eyes crinkle with happiness. "Luna, old friend, I am overjoyed for you to finally awaken. Let us replenish our energies, and then we must see you run free." She looks deeply into my eyes with a teary gaze.

*I would like nothing more than to oblige, however there is something Selene must do first before I will shift,* Luna declares, her tone quieting.

Hekate and Ria both glance at me curiously. My smile falters as apprehension tightens my chest and I nod slowly, knowing what Luna means.

"Yes, she's right, though I am *starving* right now. If we're done here, let's have dinner together before I must go." I look between the two of them and they nod carefully. "Great, see you there!" I chirp, relishing the caress of my *long* unused power.

Giving them a wink, I shroud myself in darkness, shadow-walking home.

# CHAPTER TWENTY-FOUR

## CRESCENDO

### SELENE

I manifest in my room and immediately take a much needed, long, hot shower. Wrapped in a fluffy black bathrobe, I cross my room to the door and pause for a moment. After *everything* that has taken place, I want to collapse into my bed right now and bury myself in the blankets. But Luna was right, there is something I have to do.

My gut clenches at the thought.

Making my way down the stairs, the hearty aroma of dinner makes my mouth water and I pad into the kitchen to find Hekate and Ria arguing over which herbs to use in the potatoes. I smile warmly at them, feeling a thousand times better now that I've gotten my whole self back. Plopping into a stool at the island, I snag a warm roll and tear off a bite, commenting offhandedly, "You know, you could just separate it into two bowls and season them *both* how you'd prefer. I'll take my share from Hekate's, though." I smirk and Ria throws a dish towel at me.

"Fine, whatever, just finish the damn potatoes," she grumbles, pushing the boiling pot across the stove and leans against the counter with crossed arms.

Our gazes meet and we both crack a smile. Hekate just shakes her head, waving her hand over the pot and the water evaporates from it, leaving perfectly mashed potatoes inside. She gestures toward her herb shelves and dried seasonings float into the pot as butter and cream fly out of the fridge, dropping in. Asteria lifts a large ceramic bowl and snaps her fingers, placing the full dish on the island beside a roasted chicken and platter of vegetables.

We eat dinner together with the full moon peeking through our windows and talk about what happened within the stasis. I smile to myself, glad that nothing feels at odds within me, and I can *finally* begin to relax.

The three of us sit together chatting for a while as the moon creeps high over the trees. While Hekate and Asteria catch up with Luna, my mind wanders toward Kyran and how I need to meet with him. My nerves tense as the night goes on, and I excuse myself to my room to sort through my thoughts.

Sitting at the edge of my bed, I finally pick up my phone and open my texts, tapping on my messages with Kyran. Guilt washes over me when I notice the messages he sent a few days ago, texts I never responded to, asking me if I was okay and to let him know if I needed anything. His messages progressed with concern before the last one only said that he is sorry for what I'm going through, and that he will always be here for me. A tear drips down my nose and plops onto the screen, my apprehension making my chest tight.

*I hope he understands.*

I consider how exactly to go about what I need to say to him. Steeling myself before my anxiety gets the better of me, I wipe my phone clean and tap out my message, quickly hitting send in case I chicken out.

> **Kyran, I'm sorry for being so distant, things have been difficult for me this past week…I know you must be busy with the Convocation tonight, but if you have a free moment, I need to talk with you. You don't have to get me,**

# LUNAR SHADOWS: AWAKEN

> **I can travel on my own. Just let me
> know when you have some free time**

I stare at the screen for a few moments, debating if I should say anything else. Deciding to just wait for his reply, I slowly place my phone on the nightstand. Flopping onto my back with a sigh, I stare at the ceiling fan as it spins lazily above me.

My phone vibrates twice and I fling myself over to grab it.

> **I have to perform
> the commencement
> ceremony in half an hour**

*Right, of course. It's been a while since I've been to a Convocation.* I sigh, nervous about being unsure how to say what I need to.

> **You can arrive at any time though
> Just let me know.**

His second text was sent immediately after the first and I chew on my lip as my nerves tense, knowing that I'll be seeing him soon.

> **Okay I'll let you
> know when I'm there**

I drop my phone onto the bed when he doesn't respond and push to my feet, pulling the towel off my head while I walk into my bathroom to get ready for the night. I methodically dry my hair and curl it at the ends, leaving it down to flow over my shoulders and around my waist. Frowning at the dark circles under my eyes, I turn to call out to my sister and smile, seeing her standing in the doorway to my bathroom with a mischievous grin.

She whispers something incoherent and taps her fingers to my cheekbones before flicking my nose with a wink. Without a word, she vanishes.

I laugh at her antics and glance at my reflection, finding my skin clear and bright.

Any trace of exhaustion has been completely wiped away.

I may be an all-powerful werewolf queen, but my magic lies in defense and movement rather than elemental and glamorous like that of Asteria's. The thought of my powers has me narrowing my eyes, and I glance across the room, focusing on my makeup bag sitting on a shelf. With a slight push of intention, the bag levitates and flies into the bathroom, coming to a gentle stop on the white countertop.

Grinning into the mirror, I swipe makeup over my eyes, thinking about how *dull* life has been without my abilities. It has definitely been humbling, I'll admit that. I choose a soft, dusty pink color for my lips and leave the bathroom, heading to my closet. I want to look commanding yet sexy and flip through my clothes, my mouth turning down at the side because nothing seems...*right*. My clothes are more on the plain side, leaning toward comfort over style, and I'm pulling out a simple black dress when a breeze brushes my hair from behind.

Smiling before I even turn around, I place the dress back on the rail and glance over my shoulder, grinning at the white outfit laid out for me. Leaping toward my bed, I hold up the hanger and hum my approval at the shimmery white silk of the clothing, my fingers brushing the fabric, admiring the choice Ria sent me. Peering down, I don't see any shoes and open my mouth to ask for some when a pair of silver strappy heels *whump* onto the bed, and I laugh out loud.

"Thanks, Ria! I owe you one," I call out to the house, a wide smile spreading on my face.

*"I'll take repayment in the form of a week's worth of red velvet and cream cheese cupcakes. You know what? Make it two!"* Her tinkling laugh dances through the halls and I laugh as well, nodding my head.

"You got it," I chuckle, carrying my new outfit over to my closet.

I slip into the fluid fabric, pulling the crop top over my arms, tying the wide band behind me, and lacing the high-waisted skirt tightly over my hips. Looking into the floor length mirror, I run my hands over the flowy skirt in awe. It has a high slit on one side that cuts diagonally across my knees, the white silk draping elegantly as it floats around me.

My top has a sweetheart neckline and is a smooth, fitted panel over my torso, stopping just below my rib cage. It leaves a couple of inches of bare skin above the skirt. I adjust the thin, sheer capped sleeves, sliding them off my shoulders and push my hair behind me.

Twirling over to my vanity, I choose simple jewelry and turn toward my bed. Perching on the edge, I slide my feet into the heels and grasp the wispy long straps, crisscrossing them up my shins and tying them with neat bows at the back. The leather along my feet is speckled in little gemstones that reflect light like stars as I step carefully over to my mirror. Distant howls echo through my open balcony doors, marking the beginning of the Convocation, and I smile at the sound as I look myself over.

*This is sure to make quite an impression,* I muse as I twist to look at my back, adjusting the low v-cut of the tied bow holding my top together, and turn to face myself one last time. My stomach dips with apprehension and I press my hands to my middle as I inhale deeply, letting my breath out slowly.

My fingers tremble slightly and I drop my hands, shaking them out. I cross my room and grab my phone, realizing I have nowhere to put it. I look up at my ceiling with a groan and a soft chuckle startles me from the doorway.

"Here," Asteria says lightly, holding out a small white purse lined with little crystals.

"Thank you, Ria, really. This is so beautiful." I gesture my hand over my outfit as I take the purse from her, tucking my phone inside.

I give her a warm smile which she returns before she moves her hands in a 'turn around' motion. Silently obeying her, I sling the long, thin strap over my shoulder as I turn my back to her.

"Final touches," she says quietly, and a gentle breeze ruffles over my hair. "There, perfect. You needed to wear something equally as impressive as yourself, and I just *knew* you wouldn't own anything remotely close to what tonight—*and tomorrow*—calls for."

She crosses in front of me with a sly smirk and I can't help the laugh that escapes me.

Ria takes my hand and pulls me in front of the mirror, my hair dramatically styled with larger curls throughout, and..."Is that glitter?" I ask incredulously, shaking my head to see if anything falls out.

Ria laughs and shrugs, mumbling, "Sure, let's call it *glitter.*" She grins wickedly and I take a couple steps closer to the mirror.

Leaning over to get a better look at the shimmering in my hair, I notice something off about it and stand stark still, even holding my breath to be sure I don't move.

The tiny flecks in my hair twinkle on their own, like stars.

I gasp at the sight of actual *starlight* embedded in the strands of my hair and whirl around, gaping at my sister.

"Asteria, how the *hell* did you do this?" I ask in amazement, a light laugh escaping me.

She just shrugs again. *"Eh,* I had a lot of free time on my hands while you were in stasis, and I made a friend with a fun elf nearby. She showed me some cool tricks. Okay, bye! Have a good night! Or, a good *week,* I should say." Ria snickers, waggling her eyebrows at me and I swipe at her, my cheeks flushing.

She vanishes before my fingers can grasp her hair.

"Ria! An *elf?* Where the *fuck* did you find an elf around here?!" I yell out to her, knowing damn well she can hear me.

Her laughter floats around me and her disembodied voice swirls around my room. *"Oh, you'll find out soon enough. Now, go!"*

Her words echo with mischief before the ether swallows me whole.

My agitation is easily outweighed by my amusement and I laugh as I'm deposited on the wide stone steps in front of Kyran's home. Brushing back my windswept hair, I hiss through my teeth at the sky. *"You're incorrigible, you know that?"*

Asteria's laughter is chased away by the wind. My grin fades and I nervously roll my lips between my teeth as the weight of this moment settles over me, pooling deep in my stomach. I take my phone out of my purse and send a text to Kyran, letting him know I'm here.

A cacophony of cheers, yips, and howls echo throughout the vast forests surrounding his home, the thrum of music beating rhythmically into the night sky. Nostalgia relaxes me a fraction, listening to the celebratory noise. I smile as I imagine how Kyran must have looked at the head of the ceremony, raising the spirits of the thousands of unmated wolves around him with the hopes of finding their soulmates this week.

I glance at the full moon high overhead and close my eyes, taking a deep, calming breath as I wait for him.

# KYRAN

The past few days have been fucking tough. Trying to manage my duties while my mind gets buried deeper in suffocating darkness as each hour passes has been nearly impossible.

After Selene never responded to any of my messages, and then her walking away from me, I lost all hope of ever having the chance to be with her.

*Fuck the mate bond. I would've been completely content with just having her with me.*

A low rumble rattles my chest from Valdr's displeasing growl at my thoughts. I ignore him, pushing wearily out of bed to take a shower.

The commencement ceremony begins at midnight when the full moon is at its peak in the sky. I spent most of the daylight hours ensuring everyone had what they needed for the week-long celebration, begrudgingly walking through the bustling villages as thousands of high-spirited wolves roamed eagerly, mingling in the hopes that they would find their soulmates.

The whole purpose of the Convocation is centered around just that, unmated wolves bonding with their fated soulmate, as well as for the alphas to convene and make amends between packs. I could not find it within myself to take part in any of the celebrations these past few days, merely just playing my role as hosting alpha to the five other packs on my territory.

Castian and Mira welcomed a healthy baby girl a few days ago. I met with them once Eir informed me that everything went well, but I refused to hold her when Mira offered, mostly out of fear that my carefully erected wall of ice would crumble once I looked into the face of the infant werewolf. They named her Eudora in honor of the gift of life the moon goddess blessed them with.

Yesterday morning, alphas Marx and Luric of the Southwest and Midwest regions arrived with their packs. Unlike Marx and Daine, Luric is a reserved man with a stoic demeanor. I've never heard of any ugliness spoken about him in the three hundred years he's been an alpha.

He took his position shortly before my father's demise and they had a positive standing with one another, a relationship that has continued with me to this day. We aren't necessarily friends, but we don't hate each other, so at least there's no animosity between our packs.

Marx, on the other hand, is violent by nature and has tendencies to act without thinking in tense situations. He's been the alpha of the Southwest region for over five hundred and fifty years, brutally laying waste to anyone who has the balls to challenge him for his position.

My father wanted to take him out for political reasons. He had a friend in Marx's pack whose son *'would've made a good ally'*. He pitted me against Marx once, sent me out to provoke him into a fight with the intent to kill him. My father demanded I portray it as the young wolf's doing to get him into power.

It was a fairly even match between Marx and I, though his cockiness led to a few small mistakes that allowed me to eventually get my teeth around his neck. I would have followed through with his death without a second thought if that kid hadn't begged me on his knees to let him live. Marx is only alive today because that wolf adamantly refused to take the place as alpha when he did not earn it himself, even though he was too afraid to challenge Marx on his own.

Seeing Marx yesterday was *fun*, his pissy glares at me throughout the afternoon hardly registering as I blatantly ignored his presence. He is damn well aware I could have claimed his place a long time ago, and I am fucking certain the result would be no different now.

A couple hours ago around dusk, Daine arrived with the least amount of unmated wolves out of all the packs. It's no wonder since all they do is fuck and fight, and fight while fucking. His pack in the Pacific region is nearly lawless. They terrorize humans for sport and infiltrate other packs around the country in their own search for mate bonds, resulting in many conflicts that strain the balance of power between packs.

Due to their reckless lifestyles, a lot of his wolves end up dead before they reach three hundred years of age, often getting involved with vampires and becoming overwhelmed with berserkers.

Having a lack of support from the other packs definitely doesn't help.

I've known Daine since we were pups. Our fathers were friends in the early days of their lives until my father had to kill his mother from the disease. Daine was only a hundred years old at the time, and he lost his mother a little bit before I did. He turned hateful toward our family afterwards, and even killed his father while he slept out of spite for being weak, for letting his mother get bitten instead of himself.

Daine has been an arrogant asshole for as long as I've known him. I intentionally greeted his arrival late to show my lack of respect for him as a man. I made him wait for me in the village square for an hour until my only acknowledgment of his presence was to walk past him in wolf form and piss on the ground at his feet.

Valdr commended my greeting, though he said I should've pissed *on* his feet instead.

Daine couldn't retaliate against me since being the hosting alpha for the Convocation, an act of violence against me would equal a declaration of war during this week. Tensions are already running high because of it.

*I hope it rises higher and he tries something. I need an excuse to let my frustration out, preferably with my fists and his face. Someone needs to feel the way I have these past few days, might as well be him.*

I sigh heavily, hanging my head until the water runs cold.

I'm swiping a towel over my body when my phone vibrates on the lone remaining bathroom countertop. With a sigh, I step over the debris still laying around the cracked tile floor. I haven't bothered to clean up the mess I made a few nights ago, figuring if I was to lose control again, it might as well be in here since shit has already gone to hell in this room.

The only new addition to the destruction was my shower door last night. I couldn't contain my thoughts from overwhelming me and in my frustration, I smashed the door to pieces in an attempt to get the fucking awful feelings outside of my head.

I honestly *cannot* prevent myself from seeking release from the mental agony that the thought of losing Selene brings.

Shame tries creeping up to the forefront of my mind about my lack of physical control, but I stuff it down deep. As I reach the counter and pick up my vibrating phone, I find a text from Selene.

My heart constricts and I lean my weight against the sink, staring at the screen before hesitantly tapping on her message.

> **Kyran, I'm sorry for being so distant,**
> **things have been difficult for me this**
> **past week...I know you must be busy**
> **with the Convocation tonight, but if**
> **you have a free moment, I need to**
> **talk with you. You don't have to get**
> **me, I can travel on my own. Just let**
> **me know when you have some free time**

My stomach drops as I read her text a second time, my heart kicking into a shallow racing beat when I realize what this means. I try tapping out a few different responses and erase them all, at a loss for what to say. Shuffling into my bedroom, I sit on the edge of my bed and rest my elbows on my knees as I stare morosely at the screen. Realizing I have to say *something,* I tap out a short reply and hit send before I erase it.

> **I have to perform**
> **the commencement**
> **ceremony in half an hour**

My brow scrunches as a pang runs through me when I tap out another reply, backspacing on the last few words before sending it.

> **You can arrive at any time though**
> **Just let me know.**

I want to tell her that I'll find her, I always will, but I don't want to sound pathetic so I leave it at that. I toss my phone onto the bed and it vibrates as it flies toward the mattress.

My hand snaps out to catch it before it lands.

> **Okay I'll let you**
> **know when I'm there**

My phone slips away as I drop my head into my hands, trepidation washing over me. The yawning pit in my gut fills with cement, and my heart feels like it might splinter into pieces. Valdr grows restless, undoubtedly feeling as uneasy as I do.

*I don't think I can do this.*

I shake my head, gripping my hair tightly. Swallowing thickly against the tears that threaten to fall, I take deep, shaky breaths to try and slow my thunderous pulse.

*Kyran?* Kira's voice quietly floats through my mind.

*What,* I mindlink back flatly, not bothering to mask my dejection.

*The ceremony is supposed to begin in five minutes, where are you?* Her voice is pinched with concern and I ignore it.

*Shit.* I sigh heavily. *I'll be there in a minute.*

Not realizing how much time just passed, I drag my hands down my face with a low growl and shove to my feet, stalking toward my closet. I hurriedly pull on a pair of jeans and a dark leather belt, grab a black dress shirt, rolling my sleeves to the elbows and buttoning it three-quarters closed before I haphazardly shove it into my pants. Stepping into a pair of dark leather boots, I snag the towel off my bed and quickly swipe it over my hair as I wrench my door open, taking the stairs three at a time.

Darting through my empty house, I push through the front door and jog toward the Great Hall just in time to see Kira stepping through the side entrance. Her smooth, rusty colored dress looks good with her darker glamoured complexion, and I would've complimented her on it had she not scowled at me like a hag.

*"Where the fuck were you? We have less than a minute!"* she hisses under her breath, her fingers like iron daggers on my biceps when she loops her hand beneath my arm.

My sister clucks her tongue as we walk through the door. *"You look like a fucking mess, Kyran,"* she mutters, flicking her eyes up to mine irritably.

I just grunt in response, not caring about anything at the moment. My only focus is keeping a grip on my sanity, just so I can get through this fucking bullshit and leave to have some time alone before I willingly pulverize my heart to smithereens.

I step robotically across the floor and plaster a mild expression on my face, mentally preparing to put on a show. My teeth are clenched so firmly, I'm sure one is bound to crack.

As we approach the dais, I let Kira step up first to stand with Treyvar before I take my place at the front.

Raising my gaze, I blindly look over the sea of people sweeping through the Great Hall and spilling out the enormous double doors opened to the fields beyond. Massive bonfire piles lie in wait to be consumed with flames, just like my soul tonight. Tearing my gaze away from the fields, I pretend to make eye contact with the people closest to me in the crowd as I begin the fake as fuck speech.

"Tonight commences the twenty-fifth Convocation that I have hosted as the Alpha of the Rocky Mountain Region pack," I announce in faux excitement. Cheers erupt throughout the crowd and I force a grin in response before I continue.

"I am honored once more to ask our moon goddess to bless us with the gift of our soulmates." I fight back a grimace and lift my arms wide, tipping my head back as I raise my voice. "May our cups never run dry as we fill this week with bonds, joy, endless feasts, and celebration!"

A raucous cheering erupts and I drop my gaze back to the riled up crowd to finish my bullshit performance. "Set aside the invisible barriers and give way to divine fate, let her light guide you, may you find your mate!"

I throw my head back and howl wildly, streams of my pain and torment filling my voice as everyone screams and follows along with their own echoing cries. Lowering my head, I don't bother to watch as the crowd buzzes with excitement. People hastily move outside in their enthusiasm to begin celebrating, and I turn to step off the dais.

My intentions are to go back to my room, but Kira snatches my arm and drags me around the building toward the fields flooded with wolves. I don't want to hurt her feelings, so I swallow down my misery and trudge along next to her chipper steps.

The night air glows as the bonfires ignite, sending embers swirling up to dance with the stars, and the hundreds of streaming lights flicker when music blares to life around us. People pass by endlessly, often gliding their hands out to graze others as they go in an attempt to feel a connection. I instinctively flinch away anytime a body steps too close to me, grateful for my size as an alpha to stand above most everyone here. My position gives me a sort of bubble that most people respect.

Kira brings us to a stop near a bonfire and Trey turns around holding a few beer bottles, handing one to the both of us with a wide grin. *"This year is my year, I'm sure. I can feel it!"* he announces loudly over the din.

Kira gives me a sidelong look as she takes a swig of beer and rolls her eyes. He says this *every* Convocation. I pop off the cap and drink absently, my eyes unfocused on the large dancing flames in front of me.

Daine's and Marx's voices call out nearby, and I slide my gaze toward them, not wanting them anywhere near my sister. I can't stand the cocky looks on both of their faces.

They're surrounded by a drove of women who croon and pet them, writhing around to the music while the alphas behave like they're the goddess's gift to earth. Daine's shit-brown gaze meets mine over the fire and I glare at him unblinkingly, not holding back any of my disdain for him. He holds my gaze for a few moments until a woman steps in front of me, blocking my view of him. She says something I don't care to hear. I look over her shoulder at Daine and find that he's turned away, pretending to pay attention to someone else.

I huff a dry laugh with a shake of my head.

*Coward.*

The female that I forgot was standing in front of me asks in a whiny voice, "So, what do you think? *Wanna give it a try?*"

I silently turn away without even looking at her.

*I don't fucking want to be here.*

I grumble as I stare down at my full beer bottle. Kira leans around me to speak with someone and I peer over my shoulder. My gaze catches a pair of young females' eyes, and they yelp as they turn tail, darting away into the crowd.

I swipe a hand over my face, losing patience.

Kira gives me a sympathetic look before she turns back to talk with her friends. I'm about to tell her I'm leaving when a clammy hand grips my forearm. I whip my head around to find the female from before who apparently can't take no for an answer.

A deep snarl rips from my throat at the contact and Valdr hovers near the surface, making me snap my teeth in her direction. Pissed that she disrespected me by touching me without permission, I forcefully wrench my arm away from her, sending her careening back a couple steps. Her pinched face fills with terror, and she stumbles back a few more steps before running away, passing the other alphas.

Daine glances over, following her trail. His eyes meet mine again, narrowing with a smirk and he lifts his beer bottle toward me.

"What's the matter, Kyran?" he tauntingly calls out, "ya' get rejected by your mate?" His obnoxious laugh carries over the celebrations and Marx joins him, clinking their bottles together.

I react without thought, hurling my full bottle straight into his dickhead face. It smashes into pieces, soaking him with beer. He roars with rage and Marx's gaze latches onto mine.

I bare my teeth at him in challenge.

*Fucking try me, I dare you,* I mindlink him directly.

I sense his tension as clearly as I can see it straining over his body.

People cry out in cheers at the sound of the breaking glass, the violence nothing out of the ordinary on a night like tonight. With the high energy of the Convocation, people get testy competing to find their mates—especially the males—and fights break out often throughout the week. It's almost expected.

I continue to stare Marx down, my heated glare unwavering. The look on my face must display how vicious I feel because the fucker drops his gaze and turns to his group as if nothing happened.

*Coward,* I mentally call out to him.

His shoulders tense, but he doesn't turn back around.

I could've said these words out loud, called him out for everyone to hear, but I couldn't give less a fuck what other people thought. Both he and I know who he really is, someone who preys on the weak to make himself more powerful. A reason why I will never respect a leader like him, or his ass-hat of a friend.

Daine is still seething, undoubtedly wanting to start a scene. I just narrow my eyes and cross my arms, silently daring him to do something about it. With the way I feel right now, I'd *gladly* go to war with his pack if it meant wiping out the filth that disgraces our race.

Valdr growls in approval when Daine averts his gaze, clenching his jaw and throwing his bottle into the fire.

I turn around to find Kira staring openmouthed at me, gesturing wordlessly in a *'what the fuck'* manner. I just shrug a shoulder at her. Trey bursts out laughing, clutching his belly with one hand and our sister throws her hands up with a growl.

My mouth tugs at the corner just as my pocket buzzes.

I nearly fumble my phone in my haste to pull it out, reading a text from Selene saying she's outside my house, and I take off without a word, stuffing it back in my jeans as I run.

It's difficult to maneuver through the throng of wolves, wincing as I accidentally knock over a few people as I go. Once I push free of the crowd, I break into a sprint. I have no idea what I'll say to her when I see her, but all my thoughts are consumed by the urge to beg her to stay.

I prepare for the worst and tell myself that no matter what, I'll always be here for her, to be someone to care for her unconditionally, and to always have her back because it's what she deserves. I vow to accept whatever it is she says without lashing out, knowing that she's coming from a place to better herself and not to hurt me intentionally.

When she goes to leave, I'll place my heart with her because I know it belongs nowhere else.

Crossing the field in seconds, I dart through the trees of the forest near the Great Hall and come up to the back of my house. My boots slide along the grass as I round the corner and stop dead in my tracks. Selene stands there, gazing up at the sky in a silky white dress that flows around her like water. She looks like pure moonlight poured from the heavens.

Her stunning eyes meet mine, piercing straight through my ice wall and directly into my soul.

*She is breathtakingly beautiful.*

I choke up, my chest constricting in a vice at the sight of her.

Selene gives me a soft smile as she turns, knitting her fingers in front of her and chews on her bottom lip. I want to reach out and smooth my thumb over it, to wrap her in my arms and never let go.

Instead I just stand there, helplessly waiting to watch my life disappear.

## SELENE

I grow anxious while waiting for Kyran. He read my text but didn't respond, and I assume he must be caught up in managing the Convocation. My thoughts tumble over themselves as my nerves get the better of me, and I watch the stars as I resolve myself. After everything that has happened, after learning Kyran's truth, I know what I must do now. I feel apprehensive and contemplate how I want to go about this with him, the words never quite forming clearly in my mind.

Kyran appears around the corner of his house, coming to a racing stop an arm's reach beside me. I pull away from the sky to look into his eyes. Wringing my hands, I give him a small smile and worriedly chew on my lip. His handsome face is lowered, watching me with his bright amber gaze.

There's tension in his eyes.

I take a small step toward him, nervously tucking my hair behind my ear, unsure how steady my voice will be.

"Hey," I say quietly.

"Hey, sweetheart," he whispers roughly and my stomach flops a little.

Composing myself, I stand straighter and pull my shoulders back before asking, "Would you mind going for a walk?"

He nods his head, then immediately shakes it and winces, scrunching one side of his face. His scar jumps with the movement. I want to reach out and brush it with my fingers, to comfort him. He runs a hand through his already messy hair, then slides it down his face with a sigh.

"Come this way," he says quietly, gesturing back the way he came, his eyes cast toward the ground.

We walk silently through the garden, following a dirt path that leads into the woods. We quietly wander along, passing by a few random strangers who are giddy as they run, disappearing like wisps into the night.

I smile in their wake as they go.

Out in the distance beyond the trees, large bonfires illuminate fields packed with people as they talk, laugh, and dance the night away.

Glancing sidelong at Kyran, I notice his tightly clamped jaw and stiff gait, wondering what could have happened for him to be so tense.

I softly clear my throat. "I got my memories back," I say lightly with a small smile, and his head whips around to look at me with surprise.

We come to a stop in a small clearing, the noise of the celebrations a faint hum in the distance. I wait for him to say something.

When he doesn't, I murmur, "I've reunited with Luna as well."

He releases a held breath and smiles warmly at me. "I am truly happy for you, Selene. This is great to hear. I hope you weren't hurt in the process. How did it go?" His voice grows sharper as he speaks, and the tension in my chest eases in his presence.

"Well," I sigh, "it started out alright. Asteria was with me, of course. It got a bit...*stressful,* I'll admit, but we managed to make it work." I give him a slanted smile, scrunching my nose.

His brows pull up at that, and a faint smile tugs his lips before fading just as quickly as it appeared. He glances at the ground for a moment, shuffling his foot over the dirt.

"How did it feel, finally letting Luna run free for the first time again?" he quietly asks, glancing up at me with a slight gleam in his eye.

"I, ah, haven't shifted yet. We returned only a couple of hours ago. I wanted to wait until after—to come and speak with you first." I clear my suddenly thick throat and exhale heavily.

"I...don't know where to start. I never thought I would be doing this," I mumble, my nerves getting to me.

Kyran backs up a step while still staring at the ground, and I take a deep breath in an attempt to slow my racing heart.

It doesn't work at all.

My throat dries uncomfortably when I try to speak, arms tingling with apprehension. Swallowing thickly, I try once more to breathe before getting his attention.

"Kyran?" I say softly, waiting for his eyes to meet mine again. Biting my lip, I stammer, "K-Kyran, I—"

*Shit, I didn't think I would be this nervous.*

I let out another heavy breath before trying again. "I...reject..."

My heart beats so hard I'm afraid it will burst.

*Breathe, deep and slow. You can do this,* I reassure myself as my stomach pitches sickeningly, and I hold my breath for a moment so I can do this properly.

# CHAPTER TWENTY-FIVE

## SHATTER

### KYRAN

**D**espair claws at my throat, strangling me while the vice around my heart refuses to yield. I fear I might pass out. *No. No. No no no. This…this can't be real. She…why? I…I can't lose her. I can't.*

Thoughts race desperately as my mind spirals.

Devastation gouges out a gaping pit in my stomach as I frantically search her face. She closes her eyes, inhaling slowly. I stagger back a step, my body betraying me as I involuntarily reach out toward her and I wrench my hand to my side.

My fist clenches into stone. A sharp, stinging heat trickles down my palm and through my knuckles. The pain focuses me for a moment and I grit my teeth, steeling myself to endure the absolute worst agony I could ever imagine.

Losing Selene is the *one thing* that would break me; I knew that from the moment we first touched. She is an angel I never deserved. I would cherish her always, and will forever be there for her in any way she needs, even if it kills me.

Severely gritting my teeth, one cracks sharply under the pressure. I lose control.

Hot tears spill from my eyes and I don't bother to fight it, letting them flow freely as I burn alive in silence. At first, I couldn't believe she would be my soul mate. It seemed impossible for my darkness to be bonded with her light.

I did hold on to a small seedling of hope, though. It planted itself deep within me, nurtured by every smile, every laugh, every touch of her soft, gentle skin. Kissing her had bloomed that seedling into a bright, stunning flower when she didn't shove me away.

*I love her,* with my entire soul, with every fiber of my being. I love her unconditionally. I always will.

Swallowing thickly, I don my mask. It is a well-versed skill that I mastered promptly in life, one of which I never thought I'd use with her. Arduously straining my face, I put up a facade of calmness, though the roiling storm wreaks havoc just beneath its surface.

She releases her held breath.

I can't breathe.

Her beautiful eyes glisten as they open and when her gaze meets mine, a searing pain of finality stabs through my heart.

I collapse to my knees as the wave of despair crashes, crumbling my fortitude in one fell swoop. My hands claw into the ground, and I cannot hold back the small sob ripping from my chest.

Without strength to keep myself together, I shatter into millions of irreparable pieces at her feet.

# CHAPTER TWENTY-SIX

## LOVE

### SELENE

My heart is a hummingbird ready to burst from its cage and fly free. I let go of the tension seizing my chest and my breath flows out slowly, taking all of the anxious nerves with it. Resolved, I gaze at the worn ground for a fleeting beat of my spasmodic heart.

Flicking my eyes to Kyran's, I'm startled to find them brighter than ever before.

Pools of molten amber burn like sunlight, halting my racing thoughts, my breath, *my everything*, holding me captive in this single moment in time. Just as my lips part, Kyran collapses to the ground.

I inhale sharply with alarm, pressing my fingers to my mouth. "Ky? Are you alri—"

*"Selene,"* he rasps, haggard and muffled.

I can't see his face as he's bowed into the ground, but his voice freezes me solid. He sounds agonized, my name a knife slicing through him and cleaving straight into my heart.

*Kyran, no. No no no. I've caused him immense pain.*

Tears well in my eyes and blur the sight of him hunched broken on the ground.

"Kyran," I croak through a sob as I reach a hand toward him.

He lifts his head heavily, tears falling like rain. His beautiful face twists in anguish, and ever so gently he takes my outstretched hand in his. With the faintest pressure, Kyran draws me closer and I stagger forward, my legs about to buckle with grief. He reaches up with his other hand while rising to his knees, releasing me only to wrap his arms around my waist and legs. I twine my fingers through his hair as he presses his head against my belly, holding me tightly.

Tremors vibrate from him, muscles rippling throughout his body. *He's fighting himself from shifting,* I realize morosely and I curl myself over him, wrapping my arms around his head and shoulders.

"Kyran," I whisper in his ear, turning away for a moment to sniffle and wipe a tear.

"I will let go, I promise." His voice is thick and coarse. "This is the hardest thing I've ever had to do. I don't…*I can't lose you,*" he whispers hoarsely on a breath, squeezing me harder.

His words detonate inside me and my gut roils with sudden nausea. I didn't get to say what I intended the right way.

*I've hurt him, so deeply.*

My legs give out on me.

I am grateful for Kyran's strength when I barely drop an inch and my hands scrabble over his head, blindly searching through my tears for his face.

The rough prickle of his jaw grazes my palms and I latch on, blinking fiercely to clear my sight. My sorrowful gaze meets his broken one. I stroke my thumbs lightly over his burning eyes, wiping away fresh tears, and I push forward with my feet, forcing Kyran to sit on the ground. Without letting go of each other, I lower myself onto his lap and wrap my legs around his waist.

His brow pinches but his intense gaze never leaves mine, silent confusion replacing his distress, and I give him a watery smile. Swallowing thickly, I breathe slow and deep as my racing heart threatens to completely suffocate me.

"Kyran, I am *so sorry.*" I give a slight shake of my head and bite my lip. "I was beyond nervous coming here, and I needed to calm myself to speak properly with you, to be able to tell you how I feel. I can *feel* how much I've hurt you. *It's not what you think,*" I murmur soothingly, rubbing small circles at the nape of his neck with my fingertips.

His eyes flicker between mine, still as a statue beneath me.

"You don't understand, Ky, what I was trying to say. Though your reaction more than shows just how much you truly feel for me, I knew a while ago. Little by little I could feel it. I didn't want to believe it at first because trust isn't something I can give easily, but with you, I could give you all of me without fear. I found myself relaxing in your presence. You bring me peace like I could never have imagined, and with you *I am safe,* in all ways possible. That alone, I…I never thought I'd find," I whisper as I slide my hands up to cup his face.

I hold his teary, bewildered gaze. "You don't walk before me, paving my path. You don't walk behind me, following my lead. You don't hold me down from below or pull me up for support. You stand beside me, an ever-present strength to catch me when I fall, to take my hand when I need courage, to hold me when I need solace, and most importantly to just *let me be me,* as I am. You've become my best friend, Kyran, and I truly cannot imagine living the rest of my life without you beside me." My voice catches as wild emotions threaten to overwhelm me.

Swallowing again, I take a measured breath and smile warmly. One of his hands releases my waist and his heated palm smooths my hair away from my face, his thumb trailing delicately over my brow and down my wet cheek. He returns my smile gingerly, his brow still locked in a deep furrow as he listens to me speak.

With another breath, I continue my quiet declaration. "Kyran Gennaíos, *I reject anyone who is not you.* I could not ask for a better man to be my soulmate, and I will be forever grateful for him to be you. I trust you with not only my heart, but also my soul. I promise that I will hold yours with the utmost care, protection, and devotion. I am eager for our life together, excited for the journeys we will experience, and dream of the family we will one day share." I sniffle and grin at the flash in his wet eyes.

"I know you and I both have things that need work, but with each other's help, we can heal, grow, and flourish. *Together,*" I murmur, gripping his face tighter as fresh tears pour from both of our eyes.

"I accept you, Kyran, now and forever. I accept you as my mate. *I love you, Ky, always.* Don't ever forget that," I whisper, leaning forward to press my forehead to his, the tips of our noses brushing lightly.

We stay immobile for a few heartbeats, the weight of my words settling between us. Kyran's hands mimic mine, caressing my face with feather soft gentleness, and he pulls himself back to gaze deeply into my eyes. His warm breath puffs around me from a hollow laugh of disbelief, his eyes closing and opening gradually, as if he can't quite process what I have said.

Blinking once, twice, his eyebrows pull in and up. A toothy grin grows on another breathy laugh. I can't help but chuckle, my tears still falling away, and I nod in encouragement.

Leaning forward, I gently kiss his forehead. Kyran wraps me in his arms once more and launches to his feet, my legs still tightly wound around him. His laughter bubbles out, flying through the night air as we spin wildly, and his palpable joy fills me with glee. I join him, throwing my head back and release my elation, feeling entirely free.

He winds us to a stop with a heaving chest, and I lift my head to be met with the brightest smile I have ever seen. Holding me with one arm, he brushes his hand through my hair and clasps my neck tenderly. I trail my fingers along the top of his spine, a warm smile melting on my face as I raise my eyes to his.

*"Selene,"* he breathes, affectionately resting his forehead on mine once more. "I…you…that—" His breath whooshes out of him.

I press my fingers to his lips. *"Shh,* I know. I know," I whisper, slightly shaking my head. "I truly did not mean for you to think I was denying you, Ky. I am so, *so sorry."*

He shakes his head, our noses rubbing gently. "I don't want you to apologize. It's just that," he sighs heavily, "the thought of you leaving nearly severed me. I thought I'd let you go, too, though that almost killed me to even consider it," he murmurs, closing his eyes.

"I will *never* leave you, Kyran. Not willingly, at least. I'd rather die than be apart from you in that way. You don't have to fear that," I assure him, caressing his cheekbone lightly.

"I am yours, Selene, entirely yours. I've known this for a while, wanted to tell you a few times, but I…I guess I was afraid of scaring you away," he says softly.

His hand slides up into my hair, holding me tightly against him. "You chose me. You actually *chose me,"* he whispers, his voice distant, as if not entirely intending to speak aloud.

I scoff lightly. "Of cour—"

*"Ég elska þig, engillinn minn. Ég hef alltaf gert. Ég mun alltaf, sama hvað."* His husky voice sends a shiver down my spine, raising the hairs along my arms.

"Whatever you just said sounded really sexy," I whisper on a laugh, heat flashing over my cheeks.

Kyran's breath rushes out and he quickly repeats, *"I love you, my angel. I always have. I always will, no matter what."* He swallows thickly as a stray tear drips from his eye.

"I—*mmph.*" I sigh as his lips consume mine.

Lightning races through every nerve in my body as if my skin will catch fire. Gasping at the sensation, I break our kiss and he mirrors me, clearly feeling the way I do. I drag my hands to the back of his head, gripping my fingers into his hair, eliciting a soft groan from his sinful mouth. His hands match mine, though one is in my hair and the other slides down my waist, cupping my ass with a pleasurable squeeze. I meet his heated gaze and he cocks a brow at me, making me breathe a laugh before I crash my mouth to his once more.

Kyran kisses me deeply without hesitation and effortlessly carries me through the trees. The sharp sting of bark bites delightfully into my back. A soft cry escapes me and he smiles against my mouth, a low rumble echoing from his chest. Nipping at his bottom lip, I pull it into my mouth, slowly gliding my tongue across until he groans deeper and it's my turn to grin.

Widening his stance, he slides me down the tree until my thighs meet his and he presses himself flush with my body. I release a heavy breath against his shoulder and lick the base of his throat.

Kyran tilts his head back, his rumbling louder now that I'm close to his chest.

*Fuck is it sexy.*

He pushes me into the tree and his hardness rubs me deliciously, dragging a moan from my throat. I dig my nails into his solid biceps before I tenderly bite the crook of his neck. He moans deeply and I lightly scratch down his arms, gliding my tongue along his throat.

"*Fuck, gemæcca,*" he groans, his voice heavy in my ear as his hand massages the side of my ass.

Kissing my way up his jaw, I purr in his ear, *"Mmm*, I like that, *'gemæcca'*. Say it again," I quietly demand, pinching his lobe between my teeth.

"Tell me what else you like, *gemæcca,"* he growls softly, and his dark chuckle resonates as he pushes against me sensually.

Tilting my head back, I stroke my fingers gently down his chest, gliding them beneath his half-buttoned shirt while his hands continue to knead my ass. I lick my lips slowly, his eyes tracking my tongue intensely and I purse my mouth in a coy smile.

Leaning forward, I ghost my lips over his, stopping once more at his ear to whisper, "I'd rather you find that out on your own." I teasingly lick the soft spot behind his jaw.

His growl is loud this time as he snakes a hand up behind my neck, gripping me tenderly and pulls my face close to his. The sinful smirk playing on his lips makes me bite mine and I grin at the game we've begun.

Kyran glides his hand around my throat and across my jaw, delicately grasping my chin. He kisses me softly. I melt around him, winding my arms around his neck, squeezing him tight against my body while he passionately deepens our kiss. Cool air caresses my back as he pulls us away from the tree and lowers to his knees, sitting back on his heels.

His kiss is consuming, coaxing the roaring flames beneath my skin to an inferno and I grow dizzy with the headiness it brings. Releasing my hold on him, I relax my legs and fold them beside his, straddling his lap. His tongue glides across mine and I moan into his mouth, slowly grinding myself against him. His hands grip my waist, pushing me down.

After a tantalizing few moments Kyran pulls back, panting with flushed cheeks and gently kisses my nose.

"How do you feel, Selene? The bond is driving our desires out of control at the moment. I want to be sure that you are comfortable with this," he says softly, his molten amber eyes searching mine.

"I completely understand if you'd want to wait. I am more than happy just to be able to hold you like this. I can't promise I won't stop kissing you, though. I can't believe you accepted me." He smiles with so much tenderness that it radiates within me.

His arms snake around my body, constricting my waist and shoulders affectionately as he envelopes me in a blissfully warm hug. I squeeze him just as hard and bury my face into his rounded shoulder, closing my eyes to bask in his comfort.

*Safe. He keeps me safe.*

The thought is answer enough and I nod silently against him, more than sure of what I want.

I want him, in every way, and I want him *now*.

"I am sure, Kyran," I murmur, pulling back to look him in the eyes. "I trust you, wholly, and I want to bond with you, mind, body, and soul. I want to show you how you make me feel, and…it pleases me to please you," I whisper with a flushed smile.

His eyes crinkle, chuckling lightly. "I feel the same way. Though to be honest, *I want to be the one doing the pleasing,*" he whispers softly, pressing a gentle kiss to my forehead. "At any moment, you tell me to stop and I will without hesitation, okay? No questions asked, no explanation needed. Please promise me that." His tone is serious and he cups my face with one hand, his bright eyes burning into mine.

Grateful tears spring forth anew as I breathe a laugh, nodding slightly. I am immensely appreciative of his care, of how thoughtful he is with me and how I feel. His attentiveness is something out of a storybook, something I've only read and dreamed about, and it is one of the things I love most about this man. My smile grows wide as I nod more assuredly.

"*I love you,*" I whisper, his gaze holding me captive.

"*I love you,*" he whispers back with a lopsided smile.

Pulling my bottom lip between my teeth, he licks his and I lean forward to kiss him. Raucous laughter bursts through the trees, startling us upright. Kyran glances over his shoulder, a dry laugh escaping him before he raises an eyebrow.

Leaning in conspiratorially, he flicks his gaze to mine with a smirk and murmurs, "What do you say we find somewhere more private?"

Squinting my eyes, I purse my lips and nod, our grins breaking out at the same time.

He slides his hands under my arms and lifts me gently, rising to his feet. Placing me on the ground, he offers me his hand and I take it with a smirk, his warmth flooding my arm immediately. Kyran laughs and pulls me through the trees, rushing past the small group of people stumbling away from the celebration. Giggles escape me like a teenager sneaking out late, giddiness filling my veins with bubbles as we run through the dark woods.

Firelight flickers throughout the forest, bonfires illuminating hundreds of unmated werewolves as they laugh and dance the night away.

In my carelessness, I catch my foot on something along the ground and stumble. Thankful for Kyran's firm grip, I laugh and swing upward with his arm. Turning away from me, he lets go of my hand and crouches low, waving me behind him impatiently.

"C'mon, get on." He nods his head at an angle.

I laugh incredulously. "You can't be serious!"

Shaking my head at his sidelong smirk, I climb onto his back, stringing my arms around his thick neck and lock my ankles over his waist. His warm palms stroke up and down the sides of my bare thighs, sending shivers skittering across my body. Hooking his elbows under my legs, he caresses the sensitive skin inside my knees and I squeeze his middle tightly in response. Kyran's deep chuckle echoes around us and I laugh with him, feeling almost drunk with joy.

He bounds forward, earning a squeak from me and I cling to him as he lithely weaves his way through the woods.

Confident of his hold on me, I slide my hands down the open collar of his shirt and graze my fingers across the large expanse of his hard chest. His skin is hot beneath my palms. I press my fingertips into the firm muscles, savoring the way they bunch at my touch. Vibration rolls from his chest when I drag my hands upward and across his collarbone, scraping my nails as I go.

I snuggle my face into his neck and kiss the place where it meets his shoulder, deciding to give a little nibble as well.

Kyran's growling deepens as his hands clench tighter around my knees, and his gait falters for a moment. Smiling, I tilt my head higher and lightly bite his neck a second time, turning his rumbling into a groan.

Grazing my nose along his jaw, I press my lips to his ear and murmur, "You're growling is sexy, it turns me on." I clack my teeth sharply with a sultry laugh.

His ribs expand as he takes a deep breath and sighs roughly, making me laugh again. Teasing Kyran is fun, especially when he's not in a position to do much about it, so I run my tongue around the shell of his ear and the sensitive skin just behind his jaw. My fingers trace patterns along the base of his throat as I drag my teeth over his neck. Just as I'm about to bite down once more, I'm torn away from his back.

A startled cry escapes me when I swing out into open air. My back hits something hard, wrists wrenched above my head. Pinning me one handed, Kyran hikes my ass up and flattens himself against me once more, pressing his forehead to mine with a thunderous growl. Lava flows in my veins, pooling low. I bite my lip harshly, acutely aware of everywhere our bodies touch. Using my feet, I pull him closer and lock my legs around his waist.

Kyran's eyes burn, his lush mouth parted and breathing heavily. I must have been too distracted to realize we were already at his home, I assume, but I honestly couldn't care less at this moment where we are when all I can focus on is the intense heat radiating between us. A small whimper slips from me as I ache deliciously. His pupils expand in response.

"I hope you enjoyed your play time, *gemæcca*, because now it's my turn." He growls lowly, pressing against me harder.

I breathe a moan, my eyes falling half-closed and bite my lip as I grin. He doesn't give me a chance to respond when his mouth crashes against mine, devouring me completely. He releases my wrists and smacks my ass, clamping onto it as he pulls me away from the wall. I rake my fingers through his hair, dragging another growl from him. Tumbling through a door, he spins us around and closes it by firmly pushing against me. I groan into his mouth, our consuming kiss becoming a frenzied clash of lips, teeth, and tongue.

Pushing against the door, I nudge him backward to get him moving again. He laughs against my lips and complies, carrying me through his home and up the stairs. I'm completely enthralled with him, his taste, his sunlit cedar scent, the feel of his skin as my hands roam freely.

I could stay lost in him forever.

Another door crashes open, and the pungent aroma of the plants and flowers in his room blanket me, causing me to pull my mouth away from his for a moment. I take in the spectacular sight of his atrium at night. The clear, starry sky through the glass is a beautiful backdrop and I breathe the scents deeply.

Kyran kicks his door shut and hurries us across the floor. His sultry mouth finds the crook of my neck and I groan loudly, tilting my head to give him better access. His hands knead my ass as he devours my throat and I grip the back of his head, pulling at his hair.

He growls softly against my skin before capturing my mouth once more and leans over, gently laying me on the bed. Rather than releasing my hold on him, I pull his body toward mine and he drops his arms on either side of my head.

His body is massive, filling my entire vision with just his upper half. A foreign sense of security washes over me and I smile up at him, meeting his heated gaze for a moment before I reach up to pull his face toward mine.

Licking my swollen lips, I murmur, "I don't want this night to ever end." I brush my fingers through his hair and kiss him softly.

"You don't gotta worry about that, sweetheart," he whispers, gazing into my eyes. "If I could, I'd stay right here forever."

Kissing me tenderly, he winds his fingers through mine, pinning my hands above my head. I lift my hips to push into his, seeking his hardness and I moan into his mouth at the sensation. Tugging my hands from his, I reach down and slide my fingers under the hem of his shirt, gliding them up his firm back, forcing him to arch into me. Kyran's lips part with a groan and I push my hands higher, skimming my palms over his taut muscles. His shirt bunches around his shoulders and he pulls away from me, leaning back on his knees. Without hesitation, he tears the shirt in two and tosses it aside in one fluid motion.

I hum my approval and immediately glide my hands down his bare chest, admiring his beautiful body. Every inch of him is thick, solid muscle, his palpable strength a sight to behold. I hardly notice the scars that pepper his skin beneath his wide array of intricate tattoos, my hands gleefully roaming as much of him as possible. Kyran watches me while I explore him, his muscles tensing with every touch I press to his skin.

The feel of him beneath my palms heightens my desire and I slide my hands up to his face, pulling him back down.

"You're so beautiful," I whisper, gazing into his warm eyes.

He shakes his head slightly. "How can I be, when I'm next to you?" he whispers back, brushing his lips across mine.

My heart swells and I yank his head down firmly, crushing his mouth to mine. Pulling his head aside, Kyran trails kisses along my jaw and down my neck, causing a line of fire to burn straight to my core. At the base of my throat, I hold him tightly against me, my breath growing heavy. He bites me lightly, mimicking me from earlier and I softly moan as tingles race over my body. His kisses travel across my collarbone and a small growl escapes him before his weight disappears.

He slides his hands beneath me, lifting me as he undoes the tie of my top, his fingers brushing over my skin like electricity. Kyran slowly drags the dainty sleeves off my arms before he discards my blouse, chest rumbling his approval. He gently lays me down, one of his calloused hands softly gliding down my sternum, trailing his fingers between my breasts.

When his fingers catch on the material of my white lacy bra, his gaze flicks to mine. Holding his stare, I raise my brow at him, earning a devious grin in return and my bra pulls against my back for a moment before it tears away.

"You're going to replace that," I breathe, a smirk tugging at my mouth.

Kyran chuckles lowly and I bite my lip, the cool air heightening the sensitivity of my bare flesh. Lowering himself slowly, his gaze catches mine as his tongue snakes out, circling my peaked nipple. My eyes flutter when his hot mouth closes over my breast and I roughly slide my fingers into his hair. He sways over to my other breast and repeats his tantalizing kiss, softly caressing my sides with his palms. Lifting his head, Kyran replaces his mouth with his hands, the heat of him fueling my desire and I place my hands over his, kneading his fingers with my own.

Wanting to take control, I push myself up and rise onto my knees. Kyran sighs as I lightly run my hands over his shoulders and down his chest, splaying them on the solid expanse of his abdomen. He leans back onto his hands and closes his eyes, savoring my touch.

I bend over to run my tongue along the center of his abs. His muscles flex beneath me and I grin, skating my fingertips downward as I go, watching the goosebumps mark the trail of my hands.

His breath grows heavy when I kiss along the line of his belt, my fingers trying to get it free of its buckle, and his rough hand glides over mine. He loosens it one-handed and I flick my eyes up to his for a moment as I unfasten his jeans.

Intentionally moving slow, I purse my lips at him, lowering his zipper one inch at a time. Kyran's hand twitches toward me and I bat it away with a smirk, enjoying the game of teasing him. Something about such a powerful man at my mercy is intoxicatingly attractive, and I hum my pleasure at the thought.

Reaching the bottom of the zipper, I hook my fingers around the hem of his jeans and tug them downward. Feeling bold, I snag his briefs on the way and shimmy his clothes down to his knees. I smile as his cock springs free and glance up, our heated gazes colliding.

Kyran sits back and removes his pants, stretching his long legs out on either side of me. He leans forward, kissing me softly. I bite his bottom lip and grasp him in my hand, smiling at the pulse of his pleasure at my touch. His rough hands gently cup my breasts and he rolls my nipples between his fingers, dragging a soft moan from me while I slowly stroke him.

Leaning down, I run my tongue along the silky warm length of him, circling his tip and lightly close my mouth around his cock. I take him as far as I can, his breath catching when I reach my limit. Kyran's throaty groan sends a shiver down my spine while I pleasure him.

His hands drift over me and find their way into my hair, fingers tightening in his grasp as he sucks in a breath. Grunting, he gently pulls me off of him with a sharp exhale. I smile coyly up at him. He grins devilishly down at me in return.

Faster than I can anticipate, his hands are under my arms and he tosses me onto my back, claiming my mouth with his. Kyran kisses me fervently, running his fingers down my sides and over my stomach, giving my hips a slight squeeze. I'm weightless for a moment as he flips me onto my stomach, his fingers quickly unlacing my skirt. His rough palms slide down my legs as he drags it off, the silky fabric caressing me.

Kyran smacks my ass with both hands, gripping my flesh with a low growl. I smile into the pillow, giving my hips a wiggle and his teeth graze my shoulder before he flips me over again, my laughter smothered by his needy mouth.

Pulling away, he kneels between my splayed legs and glides his hands from my shoulders over my breasts, along my abdomen and down my thighs, sending sparks in the wake of his touch. Tracing the edge of my lace panties, he slides his palm down my core, his gentle touch leaving me desperate for more.

One of his fingers glides beneath the fabric on the next pass of his hand and I moan, my hips squirming for pressure. A slight growl leaves Kyran's lips, the only warning I have before he tears my panties free and discards them to the floor. He slowly runs a finger through the wet heat between my legs and inhales sharply, his groan making me clench in anticipation.

*"Fuck, Selene,"* he murmurs, flicking his gaze to mine.

I lift my hips in response and he accepts the invite, dragging another finger along my center to rub tantalizing circles over my clit. Sparks ignite from his touch and I breathe a moan, reaching out to take him in my hand. He is slick with desire, and I stroke his cock firmly until he pulls away from me, leaning down to kiss the inside of my thighs. I thread my fingers into his hair as he glides his hot tongue along my core, his hands spreading my knees wide. I groan in pleasure and his responding growl vibrates deliciously.

Heat radiates from his intoxicating touch, spreading like waves over my body as I grind against his mouth while he devours me.

My breath grows ragged and I clench my fingers in his hair, every muscle in my body taut with pleasure.

Lightning strikes deep, fracturing along my spine and skittering down through my toes. I arch off the bed in ecstasy, his relentless mouth dragging my orgasm out longer than I ever thought possible. My hoarse voice echoes off the walls and I lose sight of the stars through the ceiling above me.

Kyran kisses my core once, twice, then pulls away, replacing his sinful mouth with his rough hand. The contrast jolts me and I groan deeply, writhing against his palm. He slowly slides two fingers inside and I clasp his neck, dragging him on top of me as he pushes them deep. His hand feels good, but I need *more*.

With a growl of my own, I pull him to the side, swinging my leg over him.

Planting my hand on his chest, I straddle him and press myself over the length of his hard shaft, grinding against him slowly. Leaning forward, I kiss him deeply, my hips rhythmically gliding back and forth. Kyran grazes his hands down my back and squeezes my ass, pressing me harder against him and groans into my mouth.

Pulling away, I whisper huskily in his ear, "Out there, you may be alpha and rule these lands. But in here, you are at *my* mercy. You obey *me* within these walls." I nip his jaw and raise my head to meet his intense gaze.

Kyran swallows thickly, licking his lips with a nod. "Of course, *my Queen,*" he murmurs in a rough voice, and tenderly cups my cheek. "I wouldn't have it any other way."

My heartbeat quickens and I smile lovingly at him, pressing my forehead to his. "Good. *Now fuck me,*" I demand softly on a breath.

His eyes widen for a fraction of a second before he flips us over, his hands cradling my head as his legs spread mine wide. His mouth captures mine the same moment he pushes his cock against my core and I sigh, relaxing completely in his embrace.

Kyran takes his time, edging slowly and giving me a moment to adjust when he fully settles inside me. I groan deeply, lifting my hips to meet his and grind against him greedily. Pressing our foreheads together, he gazes into my eyes as he pulls back and sinks himself firmly into me. Over and over, he moves at a languid, tantalizing pace.

My body rocks in time with his as we weave a beautiful song of love together.

I graze my nails along his sweat slicked back, clutching onto him tightly as my body winds tighter, creeping close to the edge of ecstasy once more. His hands grip the back of my neck and pull at my hair, kissing me passionately through my cries of pleasure. Pressure builds to a precipice deep within me and I dig my heels into his thighs, holding onto him with all that I have. Not once has he broken his sensual pace, his hips grinding me divinely and I wrap my arms around his shoulders in a vice.

"Kyran," I breathe on a moan, pulling him into me.

His eyes have never left mine, hypnotizing me as my body melds to his. His breath comes faster, growing heavier with each quickening thrust. I desperately groan his name again and he pushes deeper, forcing my eyes to roll back as sparks explode throughout my entire body. I dig my nails into his back with the intensity, eliciting a roar of pleasure from Kyran.

Breathy laughter escapes me as I transcend.

Electricity rockets through my nerves as molten lava flows through each vein, sending waves of pure ecstasy through every fiber of my being. White light illuminates behind my eyelids and Kyran's chest rumbles against mine. Our breaths heave in sync and I open my eyes, gazing into his smoldering ones.

Rubbing his nose with mine, he presses a gentle kiss to my lips and murmurs, "I love you, Selene, *so much.*"

I kiss him back softly, whispering, "I love you, Ky, *just as much.*"

Sighing with a contented smile, I release my hold on him and my limbs flop to the bed languidly. Kyran rolls sideways, slipping out of me and I immediately feel empty without him. Turning onto my side, I snuggle into his chest, admiring his warmth and he slides his arms around me.

Holding me tight, he presses a kiss to the top of my head before resting his cheek there and sighs deeply. I absently trace a small scar on his chest with my fingertip and notice blood under my fingernail. Pulling back, I look up at him with surprise and he glances down at me, furrowing his brow at my expression.

"Did I cut you?" I ask, alarmed, showing him my nails.

He laughs, his whole body shaking. My face flushes before I push myself upward and yank on his shoulder. I find little rivulets of blood dotted across his upper back and I glance at him once more, my eyebrows pinching together. I didn't mean to hurt him. I feel bad about it, and I intend to tell him this, but he cuts me off.

"Before you apologize, I'm fine. Fast healing, remember?" he says sarcastically with a nudge to my arm. "And anyway, *I liked it,*" he intones suggestively, lifting an eyebrow. "Though maybe next time you could do it harder, and drag them down some, *hmm?*"

My mouth pops open and pulls into a grin as I playfully push his shoulder. Kyran laughs again, his eyes crinkling as he wraps his strong arms around me once more and I kiss his cheek with a laugh. He turns his face and slides his mouth over mine, kissing me deeply. I twine my fingers into his hair, giving a sharp tug at the back of his head and he smiles against my mouth.

Hooking my leg over his waist, I forcefully pull his hips into mine and am delighted when his hardness rubs against my core. His calloused hand slides over my side and down my thigh, grasping my knee. Kyran hitches my leg higher before effortlessly pushing himself deep inside me.

I cry out with pleasure against his lips, pulling his hair tightly in my grasp again, and he growls his approval in return.

*Fuck, this is definitely going to be a long night,* I muse gleefully, my body tingling with warm bliss.

*You got that right, sweetheart,* his sensual voice drifts through my mind and we smile together.

I kiss him again, eager to learn his body and what pleases him most.

# CHAPTER TWENTY-SEVEN

## INTIMACY

### KYRAN

My fingers drift lazily, drawing patterns over Selene's soft skin while she lies asleep on top of me, her face buried into my neck. I absently stroke her hair as I stare up at the brightening skylight, watching as the stars slowly fade, breathing in her new musky jasmine scent. Before our bonding, she always smelled crisp like snowfall, sweet as a jasmine flower. Now, with my warm, earthy scent combined with hers, anyone will undeniably know she is my mate.

The smile that hasn't left my face since last night pulls a bit wider at the thought. I place a soft kiss to the top of her head.

*Nothing could beat this feeling of having the world in my arms,* I wonder as I wrap my arms around her, holding her snug against my body. She stirs a little, a soft sigh escaping her and she snuggles in closer to me, her short puffs of breath tickling my throat.

"Good morning," she whispers, gliding a hand along my shoulder and up my neck.

*"Mmm."* I groan as her fingers run through my hair, sending tingles over my body. "Good morning, sweetheart," I murmur, kissing her forehead.

I trail more gentle kisses over her temple and down her cheek, drawing a sweet laugh from Selene and I smile against her supple skin. She groans and stretches before rolling away, plopping onto her back beside me. I immediately miss the contact with her. Shifting over onto my shoulder, I prop my head in my hand as I reach out and brush her silky hair away from her icy blue eyes.

*You're so beautiful,* I tell her through our mindlink, and she grins widely at me.

*I love hearing you in my mind. It feels like a warm hug from the inside.* She giggles and her smile scrunches her nose a bit.

I cup her cheek for a moment before gliding my fingers over her jaw and trace the curves of her luscious body, savoring every inch of her with both my hand and eyes. The image of her lying bare in my bed, bathed in soft morning light, will forever live in the forefront of my mind. She sighs at my touch and closes her eyes, a peaceful smile lifting her sultry lips. Leaning over, I grasp her hip and pull her toward me before I claim her mouth with mine. She wraps her arms around my neck and buries her fingers into my hair *just right* at the base of my skull. A low rumble rolls from deep within my chest at her touch.

Selene smiles against my lips, lightly scraping her nails across my shoulders and I pull her lip into my mouth, dragging a soft moan from her. After a few long moments, she pulls back with a sigh and dramatically pouts her lips.

"I don't want to get up," she mumbles, looking at me through her lashes. "I just want to stay right here forever."

Selene tucks her head into my chest, wrapping her arm over my middle and drapes a leg over mine. I chuckle and glide my hand down her body from her head to her ass, giving it a squeeze.

"No one will be up for *hours*. We can lie here for as long as you want, sweetheart. I'm not going anywhere," I murmur into her hair.

She hums with pleasure, the sound making me pull her tighter to me before she lifts her head, narrowing her eyes at me. "What if I don't want to just *lie* here?" she whispers suggestively and smirks, biting her lower lip.

Grinning, I growl and roll on top of her, holding my weight off of her body as I rest my forehead against hers. My brow pinches and I inhale deeply, a heavy emotion washing over me as I gaze into her bright eyes. I feel *whole* now, complete, something that I have never felt in my entire life. Lowering onto my elbows, I cup her face in my hands, grazing my thumbs over her delicate cheekbones before kissing the tip of her nose. She glides her fingers along my arms, taking hold of my face as well, and I lean into her soft hands.

"I love you, Selene," I say quietly, turning to press a kiss into her palm. "You are the best thing to have ever happened to me, and I will always cherish you. I want to display my devotion and proudly present *my mate* to everyone, to proclaim in front of all the packs the arrival of our Queen. I want to have a bonding ceremony to honor you, to celebrate us, here, tonight. Will you do me the honor of accepting me again, publicly for all the wolves to see?" My voice is rough and thick with my emotion as I gaze into her beautiful eyes.

They sparkle with unshed tears as she bites her lip and eagerly nods. "Of course, Kyran, I would love to have a ceremony." She laughs, a tinkling chime of a bell ringing around me.

I grin and kiss her passionately, my thumbs brushing away her tears as they fall. Her hands slide down my neck and over my chest as I wrap my fingers around the back of her head to deepen our kiss. A weighted desire engulfs me, the headiness of it pulling a growl from my chest. I lean back for a moment to slide my hands over her waist and flip her onto her belly. Dragging my fingers down her back and around her round ass, I grip it tightly, leaning over her shoulder.

"As I said before, *we have hours,* sweetheart," I whisper in her ear, gliding a hand up her spine and reaching forward to gently grasp her chin. "How do you want to spend them?" I ask, my voice rough with a growl.

*"Mmm,"* she hums in response, her chest emitting a soft rumble of her own.

I can't help the groan that escapes me as I press myself against her. With my hand still lightly gripping her jaw, she turns her head to look over her shoulder at me, our eyes inches apart.

"I think I'd like to sort through the junk mail in my inbox," she murmurs huskily, smirking at me.

I carefully tighten my grip on her throat in response.

Her smirk widens as she narrows her sultry gaze and bites down on my index finger. Pulling it deeply into her mouth, she snakes her tongue around it and elicits a raspy groan from me. The sharp contrast of pain and pleasure sends me over the edge and I growl in her ear, dropping my weight over her soft body, slowly pushing myself between her thighs. Selene lifts her ass to meet my hips and I slide into her easily, both of us breathing a heated moan at the contact.

*You're right, sweetheart. I could stay here forever,* I murmur through our bond as I let go of my restraint entirely.

A soft, warm tingling pulls me from sleep, my eyes opening lazily to the golden glow of morning. Selene's hand glides languidly up and down my arm, her fingers leaving tiny electric sparks with each pass. Rolling my head to the side, I can't help the easy smile that spreads wide at the sight of her as she lies beside me, her bright eyes watching me with a hooded gaze. I brush the edge of her face with a knuckle, trailing it from her eyebrow to her jaw, lifting her chin for a gentle kiss.

*"Mmm,"* she hums, smiling against my lips. "Good morning. *Again,"* she adds with a soft chuckle.

I laugh and kiss her once more before reaching for her hand and raise it to my lips, pressing a soft kiss to her knuckles. "Good morning, beautiful. I hope you slept well," I murmur, my voice rough from sleep.

Her grin is bright enough to rival the stars and I automatically smile back with how infectious it is. She gives me a sly look and stretches lithely, sitting up with a yawn. I push up onto my elbows, watching her as she slides out of bed, the black sheets slipping away to reveal her gorgeous body. I'm mesmerized by the luscious sway of her hips as she takes a few steps. She turns over her shoulder with a knowing smirk and winks at me.

"I slept wonderfully, thank you." Selene smiles coyly, adding, "It was the best night's *sleep* I could hope for." She takes a few slow, exaggerated steps away.

A light growl escapes me and I throw myself over the bed. Laughter bubbles out of her as she takes off across the room, making me grin.

I easily catch her around the waist, her squeak of surprise trilling around us and I pull her close to my chest. Placing my lips to her temple, I kiss her a couple of times before dropping my mouth to her ear to murmur, "Keep it up, and I'll have you *sleeping* all day, sweetheart." I playfully nip at her earlobe.

Selene's tinkling laugh surrounds me as she turns in my arms, holding onto my neck and nimbly encloses my waist with her legs. My hands slide beneath her ass, holding her firmly while she kisses me. Her lips peck my face a few times before she rests her forehead to mine, rubbing our noses together with a contented sigh.

She chuckles, her crystal eyes full of light and murmurs, "We need a shower, and I'm hungry. Which, I could only assume, means you must be starving. There's also the matter of our *ceremony* to prepare for tonight." She grins widely, leaning back a little.

I nod in agreement, my heart feeling fuller and lighter than it's ever been in my entire life. My cheeks ache a little from how hard I've been smiling, and that thought has my smile growing even wider as I carry us toward the bathroom to shower.

As I step over the threshold onto the cold tile floor, my smile immediately falters at Selene's small gasp. I already know what caused it. Cringing with shame and embarrassment, I flick my eyes to hers and find her looking around the destroyed room with concern.

"I'd ask what happened, Kyran, but I'm sad to admit I could probably guess correctly," she says quietly and her gaze meets mine. "You truly believed I was leaving you, didn't you? I am *so sorry* for the pain I've caused you, Ky. I wasn't aware how things would be perceived from your side, or else I definitely would not have gone about things the way I had." She cups my face in her hands, tears welling up in her eyes.

Shaking my head, I place a hand over hers and assure her, "It is not your fault, sweetheart. Do not feel guilty for my inability to better manage my emotions. If anything, I should have confronted my fears instead of holding it in and letting *this* be the outcome." I nod vaguely at the room.

"It was a misunderstanding that hurt me—badly enough to lose my control—only because of how deeply I care for you, Selene. Though I need to work on my impulse control when it comes to anger like this, in a twisted way, it shows how greatly I feel inside. The thought of you leaving was almost too much for me to bear, and I couldn't bring myself to go against your need for space just to plead with you to stay. I haven't lost control of myself like this in a *long time*. It did not feel good, and I do not wish to have that happen again." I sigh, closing my eyes for a moment.

Her thumb strokes my cheek before her hand slides to my back, holding me tightly. I wrap my arms around her and bury my face into her neck as she runs a hand through my hair. Taking a slow, measured breath, I breathe in our new mingled scent and smile against her skin before pulling back.

Selene traces my eyebrow, trailing her finger down my neck and over my scar before her clear gaze meets mine once again.

"Well, let's try to be more open with communicating what's going on inside our minds. I can be a bit...stubborn when it comes to reaching out for help, and stars know that Luna isn't quite...*pleasant* when it comes to being tactful." Selene purses her lips, wincing a little.

*You got that right,* Luna's voice chimes with a hint of sass that makes us laugh, and Valdr stirs at the sound of her voice.

"I agree, and I promise to always let you in, even when I feel like protecting you from my shitty problems. To be honest, Valdr is really the better half of me. He keeps me in check, has a solid perspective on most situations...Well, except from you, I suppose, seeing how both he and I equally kind of panicked." I grimace as I look around and sheepishly admit, "Okay, we more than panicked. We freaked the fuck out."

*Kyran freaked out. I knew we were fine from the start,* Valdr's dry sarcasm slides through our minds, making Selene grin.

Her bright laugh pulls a smile to my face again and I kiss her cheek as I walk us over to the shower. Reaching out with one hand, I turn my body away to keep Selene from touching the jagged glass of what was once a door, and tug the lever to run the water. I grasp her waist and gently lower her to the floor in the shower.

As she turns, I can't resist the urge to grab hold of her ass with both hands and knead it firmly. She glances at me over her shoulder with a mischievous grin and wraps her hands around my wrists, dragging them across her body to pull me in close.

She slides my hands in opposite directions, moving one up to cup her full breast and the other down to glide between her thighs. I kiss her neck languidly, drawing out a heated sigh from her and with the enticing sound, the task of showering was quickly forgotten.

Selene stands by my bed with a small pout on her pretty face. The way her lips pucker make me smile as I pull a t-shirt over my wet hair. She's loosely holding a towel around her body in one hand and has the other on her hip. Crossing my room, I sit on the edge of the bed and take her hand, pulling her into my arms to give her a soft kiss.

"What's the matter?" I ask, lacing my fingers at the small of her back.

She sighs, dropping her hands onto my shoulders and sits sideways in my lap. "I have nothing to get ready for the day. I don't mind wearing my clothes from last night, I only had them on for maybe half an hour." She chuckles softly and scrunches her nose. "But I don't have anything for my hair or—"

Her voice is cut off by a small flash of light, a breeze tickling the back of my neck. I abruptly stand with her in my arms and whirl around to find a black canvas bag with a folded note sitting on my bed. My eyebrows pinch with a frown, and it only deepens at Selene's burst of laughter. I'm about to question her when she pushes out of my hold and steps over to the side of the bed.

"I've got to find a gift for her, with everything she's done for me," she murmurs, a warm smile pulling her lips wide as she reads the note.

"What? Who?" I ask stupidly, concerned with how something was able to be sent magically into this house.

When I first took position as alpha, I had the entire place heavily warded with the help of Eir and Vala. I wanted to be confident that my family was protected against unwelcome people or objects via teleportation while we slept, able to have our guards down in general within our own home.

"Ria, of course," Selene says on a chuckle as she shakes her head, unzipping the bag.

*"How?"* I ask incredulously as I watch her remove the contents of the small bag onto my bed.

Selene just shrugs as she takes out a smaller bag with flowers printed on it, a wooden hairbrush, a cylinder thing with a cord, and another wider, gun-shaped thing. She reaches in again and pauses, giving me a sly smirk as she plucks out a lacy sheer thong and drops it onto the bed. I raise an eyebrow at her with a smirk in return.

She laughs as she collects the items into her arms, carrying them into the bathroom. I follow her, leaning against the door frame to watch her as she gets ready.

I wait patiently while she brushes and dries her hair before asking her what she'd like for breakfast. While she does her makeup, we talk about what to do for the day, how I'd like for her to meet some people if she'd be up for it, and she eagerly agrees. Watching her is comfortable and has me thinking about what to get for my room to make it more inviting for her. An easy smile falls on my face as my mind wanders, thinking of options on renovating the bathroom, and what types of furniture to add to my room for her personal things to have places of their own.

Selene turns to me and scrunches her nose. She shakes her head before going back to the mirror, laughing softly.

"What?" I ask dumbly, realizing I must not have heard her and I stick my hands in my pockets from the mild embarrassment.

"I asked if you could get my clothes for me. What were you thinking about? You have a dreamy look on your face." She smirks, raising an eyebrow at me over her shoulder before leaning across the sink again.

"Making changes," I murmur with a grin and turn into my room.

On my bed, I find her white clothes freshly cleaned and pressed lying neatly across it. I glance at the note discarded beside the black bag and pick it up, reading Asteria's wispy handwriting.

*I'm beyond thrilled for tonight! You'll find everything you need in here. I told you that you'd need that dress for tonight, and you thought I was kidding. I love you, and we'll see you this evening. xoxo*

Just as I let the paper drift back to the bed, I notice black ink scratching across the bottom of the note, as if an invisible hand writes a message. Curious, I pick up the paper and read the new message I can only assume is from Asteria.

*Kyran, I have things for Selene to place in your home. Whenever you're ready, let me know, and it will be delivered at your discretion. Think of this as a sort of bonding celebration gift. Also, change out of your clothes. I've left you something much more appropriate in your closet. I will not have you wearing anything barbaric for your ceremony with Selene.*

I raise an eyebrow and glance down at my clothes. I'm wearing my usual jeans with a black tee and I huff a laugh, shaking my head. More words scrawl quickly across the paper and I continue reading.

*Also, I've spoken with Kira, and she's already getting preparations started, so you don't have to concern yourself on that matter. Enjoy the day, we look forward to meeting with you both later this evening.*

*P.S. she loves chocolate chip pancakes with strawberries and whipped cream, and this note will combust once this sentence is finished—*

I immediately toss the smoldering paper aside and watch perplexed as it dissolves into flames, the dusty ashes floating to my floor like snowfall. Running a hand through my hair, I look up into the skylight and shake my head with a small grin, knowing Asteria will get along quite well with my family. I have to admit that her power is impressive, regardless of how she managed to bypass the wards around my home.

Taking Selene's clothes into my arms, I turn to bring them to her and find her coming in through the archway. I hold them out with a lopsided smile, and she notices the condition of her clothes, then flicks her eyes to the pile of ash on the floor. She glances at me curiously.

"Your sister," I say dryly.

She laughs with a shake of her head, content with that answer.

I watch with a hooded gaze as she drops her towel, drifting my eyes over her addictive body. She smirks at me as she dons her shirt, leaving it dangling open as she steps into her silky skirt, sliding it slowly over her hips. Stepping behind Selene, I take the laces from her hands and tie them for her, grasping her hips and kissing her cheek. I reach up to tie her blouse as well, letting my hands linger over her bare waist for a moment. She takes them and pulls my arms around her middle.

Resting my chin on her shoulder, I breathe in our mingled scent and squeeze her tightly before turning her around. I wrap a curled lock of hair around my finger and smirk at the shimmer it holds, raising my brow in silent question.

"My sister," she replies flatly and we both bark a laugh.

I let go of her magical hair and take her hand in mine. "Come with me, I want to show you something," I murmur, suddenly feeling a bit nervous.

"I don't have my shoes on yet," she lightly protests, but follows me as I turn toward the bathroom.

"You don't need them, we're not leaving just yet." I smile hesitantly over my shoulder at the curious look she gives me.

I cross the bright atrium to step through a dark archway, leading Selene across the dusty floor to the far wall. Letting her hand go, I pull an old, creaking chain, the heavy drapes opening to reveal a floor to ceiling window that spans the length of the room. She gasps in surprise as the morning sun illuminates the small library.

The shelves are covered in a thin layer of dust and I wince at the sight, realizing how long it must have been since I've last come in here. *I should've cleaned before showing this to her.* I sigh and turn around, watching her gaze linger on the soaring shelves. Selene walks along one of the bookcases, gently running her fingers over the spines and knickknacks that have lived there longer than I have occupied these rooms.

Sliding my hands into my pockets, I wait as she wanders around with widened eyes, absorbing the energy this room holds. A few moments pass in silence until she walks over to me with a wistful smile on her face. I lift a corner of my mouth as I look around again.

"This is my personal library. It holds all my mother's favorite books, as well as my own. I will clean everything, and maybe bring in some plants to give life to the room again, but I want you to keep your favorites here, as well. That chair is the comfiest, and time can easily slip away from you in here." I nod to a well-worn, overstuffed armchair in the corner as I reminisce about falling asleep to stories my mother would read to me as a pup.

"This was our special room together, since none of my siblings cared much for reading. They'd all preferred sports or games as entertainment. My mother loved having one-on-one time here in the evenings, before my father began his…training," I say quietly as I pull my gaze back to Selene.

She gives me a warm smile and takes my hand again, rubbing her thumb across my knuckles comfortingly. "This is beautiful. I can feel the love in here, everything seems to have held onto both of your energies. I'd like to help you bring it back to life," she murmurs, resting her head against my shoulder and looks up at me with bright eyes.

I smile, dropping a kiss to the top of her head. My gaze catches on the boarded up archway half-hidden behind an old forest tapestry. Without a second thought, I let go of her hand as I cross the room. Stopping before the makeshift wall, I carefully remove the tapestry and place my palms against the rough wood, sliding my fingers into a gap between the planks. I bow my head for a moment.

This room has been closed off since the first day I slept here as alpha, the reminder of my mother too much for me to handle at the time. Now that I have Selene, I trust that I can walk through here with her at my side, and I want to make it hers. I tighten my grip on the old wood and yank it down, the nails clattering noisily to the floor as I place the plank at the base of the wall.

"Ky? What are you doing?" Selene's soft voice holds concern and her light footsteps approach.

I wordlessly pull each plank free and wave a hand at the archway as stale air thick with dust particles swirls from the movement. Kicking the nails to the side, I step through the archway, carefully making my way to the wall of windows. I pry one open to let in fresh air, the handle giving way with a small *pop* before the crank turns.

Selene calls my name from the entrance and I glance back at her, meeting her gaze with a small smile. I gesture for her to come in farther. Since the windows are covered in centuries worth of dust, just as the rest of the room is, I shuffle along the wall, rubbing my hands against the glass to let in some light.

Selene gazes around the room in amazement, and I tell her softly, "This room has been left untouched since before electricity was commonplace, and never received the renovations I had done to the home while modernizing things as time went on. There were days my mother would spend all of her time up here, especially while pregnant with the triplets, since leaving this floor was an arduous task on her body. I remember sitting beneath these windows to watch her work. She always created the most beautiful pieces."

I follow her gaze to the dozens of painted canvases dotting the large open room. Some were left half-finished on easels, and many lean against the mural covered walls. Everything in the natural world is depicted in her art. My mother adored the beauty of nature.

My eyes catch on an easel with a worn stool facing the canvas. There's a small table beside it holding old, cracked clay cups of paint with brushes sticking out of them, sadly waiting to never finish the faded woodland sunset.

Clearing my throat, I drop my gaze to the floor and murmur, "This is—*was*—my mother's art studio. I remember from some of our conversations that you enjoy creating art and wished you could paint more. I'd like for this room to be yours. I've never wanted to use it for myself, and it would've stayed boarded up till the day I died had I not met you. Before you refuse," I hold up my hand as she opens her mouth with a shake of her head, "just…think about it. You have total freedom here, with all of these rooms, to do what you please. What is mine is yours," I add quietly with a small smile.

Selene closes her mouth and her eyebrows pull inward. In the dim, dusty light, her eyes shine as brightly as the specks in her hair, and I reach out to brush some of it away from her face. "How long is it going to stay like this?" I wonder out loud, not that it bothers me, just mostly out of curiosity.

She just shrugs and mumbles, "I have no idea."

Selene glances around at the studio again. "Kyran, I don't think I can take this as mine," she whispers, shaking her head. "It's incredible, how it remains. Her *soul* lives on these canvases. I can't, it's not—"

"As I said, think about it." I interrupt her, lacing my fingers through hers. "I just wanted to show it to you, to let you know that this space is for you to have to yourself whenever you need it, for whatever you like." I guide her back toward the library. "I want these rooms to be yours as much as mine now that we're bonded."

Selene remains silent as we walk through the rooms and come to stop before my bed once more. Her full mouth twists to the side while she thinks, and I lightly push her down to sit at the edge of my bed.

Lowering to my knee, I lift her calf and grab one of her shoes, sliding it over her foot. I silently repeat the same for her other leg. She hums lightly, pleased, and my chest blooms with heat at the sound. She bends over to kiss my forehead and laces the thin straps up her slender legs.

Once finished, she rests her hands on the sides of my face and looks deeply into my eyes.

"Thank you," Selene whispers, "for everything. I love you." She kisses me softly and my chest rumbles at the contact.

"I love you," I whisper against her lips and we smile, pressing our foreheads together.

Her stomach gurgles loudly and I chuckle, rising to my feet. I hold out my hand for her. "Let's go make some breakfast. How does chocolate chip pancakes sound?" I offer with a smirk, and she bounces on her toes, lacing her fingers with mine as we cross the room.

"Oh, yes! Do you have strawberries?" she asks with a grin and I laugh, opening my door for her.

"I'm sure there's some in the fridge," I murmur with a wide smile.

Before Selene can take the first step down, I sweep my arms beneath her shoulders and legs, lifting her to my chest. Her startled squeak makes me laugh as I carry her down the stairs. I feel on top of the world after the night we'd spent together, and nothing could take away the warm, free weightlessness that has settled into my bones.

*My life finally has meaning, and I cannot wait to happily share the rest of it with this woman.* I smile at the thought, kissing the top of her head.

# CHAPTER TWENTY-EIGHT

## AMITY

## SELENE

Kyran graciously carries me downstairs and into the vacant kitchen, his home silent in the early morning hours. After gently placing me on a stool at the large island, he goes to work preparing breakfast. I offer to help, which he stubbornly refuses, insisting on doing everything himself. He even mockingly says that a *queen* should never worry herself with such menial tasks, and I promptly stick my finger in the pancake batter, smearing it over his face in response.

Sitting at the island, I smirk at the dried remnants of batter stuck in the stubble along his jaw. I stuff a fluffy bite of pancake smothered in chopped strawberries and whipped cream into my mouth. *"Mmph, thith ith delithith,"* I groan over my mouthful, rolling my eyes to the ceiling.

Kyran chokes on a laugh and swallows his bite, his warm eyes crinkling with amusement. "I'm glad you like it. Trey isn't the only one who knows how to cook. Where do you think he learned it from?" He raises an eyebrow, grinning widely.

"Definitely from Mom," his brother's voice drifts from down the hall a moment before he shuffles into the kitchen.

I smile around another bite and wave hello. He perks up at the sight of all the food Kyran made, scurrying over to fill a plate. Treyvar looks a bit disheveled this morning, as if he crawled into bed at some point during the night and didn't bother to change before coming downstairs. His sandy blonde hair sticks up at odd angles, and he has a red line creasing his cheek from an impression of his bedding. Kyran huffs a laugh at his brother and continues eating his third serving.

"Yeah, well, she taught me first," he taunts, waving his fork at Trey as he sits beside his brother. "You look like you had a good night?"

*"Tch,* not as good as you," he mutters under his breath, taking a long drink of water.

My cheeks flame with his implication and I roll my lips between my teeth. Kyran grasps my bare knee in his hand, rubbing his thumb soothingly over my skin. I can't help the smile that tugs its way free and I lean over to speak to Treyvar.

"We're fully bonded, I got my wolf back," I announce proudly, and his jaw parts in shock, a little rivulet of water leaking out at the corner.

A sharp squeal pierces the air and I'm almost out of my seat in alarm when Kyran's hand holds me in place. I quickly glance at him with concern, but he just rolls his eyes, nodding toward the grand staircase with an easy smile.

Turning in my seat at his gesture, I find a tall, pretty blonde woman hurrying into the kitchen, her bright green eyes squinting from her huge smile. I immediately recognize her to be Treyvar's twin sister, Kira. She rushes over and throws her arms around my neck, squeezing tightly as she rocks side to side with another shriek of excitement escaping her.

*"Ohmigosh,"* she breathes as she grasps my shoulders, pushing back to look into my eyes. "Oh, my—*fuck,* you're gorgeous! No wonder why Kyran's been such a mess." She grins widely as Kyran scoffs and Trey huffs a laugh.

Her energy is infectious and I laugh softly, giving a small wave. "Hi, I'm Selene. It's nice to finally meet you." I smile warmly, immediately taking a liking to Kyran's younger sister.

"When your sister sent me a message this morning, I just *could not believe what I was reading!* Then Eir manifested in my room, confirming everything, and I couldn't be more excited! I'm so, *so happy* for you both!" she gushes excitedly as she flits around the kitchen. "I've already got people working on it, so you don't have to worry about a thing. I've got it all taken care of. Oh! Speaking of which, I've gotta run to town for a few things. I'll be back in a couple of hours! Let me know if there's anything you both need!"

Kira plants a kiss on Kyran's cheek and disappears out the side door as quickly as she arrived.

I sit there baffled for a moment, blinking a few times before I slowly turn to look at Kyran, and he laughs at the expression on my face, wiping his cheek dramatically. Trey seems entirely unbothered by his sister as he chews on a piece of bacon, just shrugging his shoulder when our gazes meet. I shake my head with a slight laugh and pick up my fork, nudging Kyran's knee with mine.

"Looks like our only responsibility is to show up, I presume?" I tease and he smiles, nodding.

"Yeah, it seems that way. I think our sisters are going to divide and conquer this entire ceremony." His snort makes me laugh as I finish my breakfast.

"Ceremony?" Trey asks, leaning onto his elbows and raises an eyebrow at us both.

"Oi! We're havin' 'nother fuckin' ceremony?" a gruff voice bellows from the stairs, and I peer over my shoulder to see who it belongs to.

A large, heavyset man with unruly black hair and a matching beard tromps his way into the kitchen, stopping dead in his tracks at the sight of me. My spine automatically stiffens, his alpha presence stirring Luna's attention, and I slightly narrow my gaze. I don't recall ever meeting him in the past, nor do his features look familiar enough for me to place him from a long ago relative, either. Since I cannot properly greet him, I wait in silence for him to speak first.

"Selene, this is Alpha Felagi of the Northeast Region Pack, and my oldest friend," Kyran says lightly beside me. "Please excuse his lack of manners. He doesn't get out much," he quips, giving me a smirk and I stifle a chuckle.

Alpha Felagi glares narrowly at Kyran in response. He meets my gaze once more when Kyran continues our introduction. "Felagi, this is Selene, my mate."

His eyebrows pull in and upward at the revelation and he glances at Kyran in disbelief.

Kyran clears his throat, warning, "Be mindful of your respect. Not only is she my mate, she is *our Queen.*" His voice drops lower at the additional information.

Felagi whips his gaze back to mine with rounded eyes.

Trey spits out his drink and coughs harshly, his stool scraping across the floor as he shoves to his feet, gawking.

"*What?*" he rasps, swiping the back of his hand across his mouth before running it through his hair. "Did you just say what I *think* you said?" His green eyes are wild as they flash between Kyran and me.

I flick my gaze back to Alpha Felagi, watching the way his eyes dart from Kyran's and back to mine, narrowing a fraction as he *really* looks at me.

His head imperceptibly shakes, bushy eyebrows lowering when he whispers, "No, *no*. It can't be…can it?" He stares at me for a moment longer before looking at Kyran once more.

Kyran just nods once, his expression completely serious.

Treyvar still stands there with his hands gripping his hair.

I let out a small sigh.

The noise focuses Alpha Felagi's attention on me again and he immediately drops to his knee, bowing his head.

"Milady, m-my queen. My—your majesty," he stammers.

I wince, glaring at Kyran.

Treyvar bounces his eyes between me and Alpha Felagi before he drops to his knee as well. Groaning, I pinch the bridge of my nose with exasperation.

"Guys, please, it's not—" I sigh heavily. "It's not like that. *I'm* not like that. Please get off the floor," I mutter, their actions making me slightly uncomfortable.

*I am, and they better damn well know it.* Luna's haughty voice rings loudly, and the two men inhale sharply at the sound of her voice, lifting their heads to look at me and Kyran with disbelief.

I squeeze my eyes shut for a moment and let out a measured breath.

Leaning forward, I place both of my hands on their shoulders to get their attention before quietly saying, "Get off of the floor, please, this is not necessary." I look intently at each of them.

Treyvar glances out the corner of his eye at Alpha Felagi, waiting until he begins to rise. Once the both of them are on their feet, I push off my stool to stand with them and tilt my head back a bit to look up at the big guy's face.

"I do not see myself as being above others. I only hold my power to serve the werewolf race as a leader, through guidance and protection. And before you ask, please just call me Selene. My wolf is Luna, though she will most likely make you feel as if you need to treat her as royalty. Please don't, her ego is big enough as it is," I mutter, smirking when I feel her indignation roll through me.

Alpha Felagi cracks a grin at my words. He glances at Kyran and claps him on the shoulder, his tension slowly leaving his body. He announces in a rough voice, "I like her, boy. Ya' did good. Now, tell me, where the *fuck* did ya' find our *goddessdamned Queen?*"

His belly laugh bursts out of him, infecting all of us, and our chuckles ease the tense air.

"The grocery store, of all places. Can you even imagine that?" Trey's voice displays his incredulity as he takes his seat again, shaking his head. "The fucking *Queen of werewolves,* at the damned grocery store. How long have you been *here,* of all places on earth?" he asks, scrunching half of his face at me in disbelief and I let out another laugh.

"It's a long story." I wave my hand nonchalantly, but am surprised when they both shake their heads, insisting that I tell them everything.

Kyran suggests we take this conversation to the couches in the library, and the four of us sit together for a while as I tell them about my stasis and the reasons for being put in it. I explain my connection to Caedes and the vampires' actions, answer their endless questions about my creation, the Guardians, Luna, my powers, and basically anything they thought was made up stories about our heritage.

Through it all, Kyran sits beside me and basks in my words almost as much as they do, though he already knew most of it from speaking with Hekate and Asteria. His loving gaze hardly ever leaves me and I lean against him comfortably, relaxing into the openness of talking about these things while getting to know two of the closest people to him.

I agree when Felagi asks me if he could share the news with his pack. We inform him that we are holding a bonding ceremony tonight and would love to have anyone attend who desires to. He excuses himself after our long conversation and Trey rubs a hand over his face, claiming he needs to sort all of this out, leaving Kyran and me alone.

"I'm excited for tonight," he murmurs against my hair and I look up at him with a warm smile.

"Me too. I'm excited for *every* night from here on out," I say softly before I nip at his jaw.

He grins with a small growl and moves to seek revenge when a sharp knock comes from the front door. Kyran sighs before giving me a quick kiss and jogs across the floor, pulling the door open.

A muscular, shaggy haired man stands there with his arms crossed and he greets Kyran quickly before lowering his voice, speaking quietly in his ear. Kyran nods once and the man turns away, shifting into a wolf the color of tree bark before he bounds away.

Curious, I raise an eyebrow at Kyran as he walks back to me, his mouth pulled in a tight line. I push to my feet when he reaches the couch.

"That was Jeger, my new head warrior. He's also the best tracker in my pack. He caught trails of vampires outside of town, near pack borders. I want to follow them with him and see if anything comes of it." He narrows his eyes, and I can tell there's more he wants to say, but is deciding not to.

Filling in the blanks, I nod my head with understanding. "I know, you don't want me to be at risk by coming with you. It's alright, I don't mind staying here. I've got something I want to do anyway."

I give him a small grin, wrapping my arms around his waist. "Not that I can't hold my own or anything," I mumble sarcastically, laughing when he groans in protest.

"No, that's not, I didn't mean—*ugh,*" he sighs, exasperated. "I don't intend on being out long. I'll be back in an hour, maybe an hour and a half at most." He kisses my forehead. "I do look forward to testing out your capabilities, though. See if the legends hold true," he murmurs with a wolfish grin as he takes a step away.

"Yeah, I will *definitely* make you eat those words." I scrunch my nose at him. "I'll be up in *our* rooms, so whenever you're back, just let me know where you want to meet and I'll come to you." I smile warmly and he grins, nodding once.

"Sounds good." Kyran turns to open the door and glances at me over his shoulder, murmuring, "I love you, sweetheart. I'll be back soon."

*I love you too, Ky,* I mindlink him with a wink.

My smile stays rooted on my face as I explore the house, slowly making my way back up into the bedroom. Standing at the boarded up archway at the back of the room, I draw on my power, summoning my shadow magic.

I carefully twine it throughout the wooden planks nailed to the walls. With focused intent, the wood splinters and floats into a neat pile on the floor, the metal nails clinking as they fall. I push them aside as I step into the art studio.

Upon entering, I'm surprised to find that the studio is completely clean, no trace of the old dust, dirt, and cobwebs that covered every surface. The crystal-clear glass wall allows bright morning sunshine to fill the airy room, and soft wind drifts through the open pane, fluttering a note along the worn wooden floor. Picking up the paper, I read that Asteria had taken it upon herself to cleanse the space and replace art supplies, though she left the artwork alone for me to decide where to place them.

I hum to myself as I take my time with each finished piece, admiring the brush strokes and color placements of each one as I choose the best area of wall space to hang them. With my shadow magic, I gather the discarded nails from the boarded archways and fling them throughout the room into the spots designated for each canvas. Kyran's mother had a few unfinished pieces and I decide to leave them displayed on easels dotted throughout the space, giving the room a lived-in, warm atmosphere.

Perching on the well-worn wooden stool, I spend the rest of my morning painting in the peaceful quietness, enjoying the calm serenity that has blanketed me since jumping into Kyran's arms last night.

# LUNAR SHADOWS: AWAKEN

My hand floats a thin paintbrush over a canvas, gliding flowy streaks of cyan across tufts of white fur, and I lean back after the final stroke with a satisfactory smile. I admire the first piece of artwork that I have created in a long while, realizing that the last time I painted was before I'd met Bolvi. After he'd waltzed in and poisoned my life, I let go of anything that used to bring me joy. Everything that I did for myself seemed to only piss him off, and therefore make my life hell.

Now, though, I have *all* the freedom to do as I please, with all the support I could dream of from Kyran. It was because of this that I chose to paint my first piece as a gift to him, to show my appreciation for his care and his attentiveness towards me.

My smile grows warmer as I gaze at the bright amber glow of Valdr and Kyran's eye. The realistic detailed color is striking in contrast to the smoky midnight fur that surrounds it. Half of Valdr's lupine face takes up the left side of the canvas, and Luna's bright opposite matches him on the right. From her arctic gaze billows out a stunning stream of cyan smoke, drifting out across the misty gray forest background. Between the wolves is a smattering of tiny, golden sparkling stars depicting the cosmic connection we share.

Placing the paintbrush into a rinse cup, I rise off my stool and stretch my arms over my head. I cross the studio to the newly-stocked supply shelves and snag a fancy piece of paper, writing a note for Kyran. Pressing my lips to the parchment, I leave my mark at the bottom beside my name and grin, placing it on the stool with the fresh painting.

*I wonder where he will choose to hang this.* I smile at the image of our wolves together, excited for them to officially meet one another.

As if sensing my thoughts of him, Kyran's warm presence brushes through my mind.

*Hey sweetheart, I'm on my way back. Sorry it took longer than expected, I'll catch you up when I'm home. Meet me outside, in front of the house. There's a nice cafe I'd like to take you to, and hopefully introduce you to someone along the way.* His words float through me like honey and I savor his energy.

*You feel like sunlight, warm and cozy,* I murmur in my mind.

I feel his chuckled response rather than hear it as it languidly winds its way around me. *You feel like moonlight, cool and soothing.*

I smile, laughing softly as I stare at my painting, picking up the brush to fix a tiny smudge at Valdr's eye.

*If you could, please bring me some clothes to change into. I, uh, lost mine.* His voice is a bit thinner and I crease my brow in concern, hastily dropping the brush into the cup.

Bending over to quickly pull on my white clothes—I'd discarded them so I wouldn't ruin them with paint—I struggle to tie my shirt as I cross the bedroom toward his closet.

*Of course. Are you alright? Is Jeger?* I ask worriedly, knowing he must have needed to shift fast and shred his clothes if he's returning in wolf form.

As I'm reaching for one of his many black tees, my gaze snags on an entirely black formal suit, hung neatly with a pressed black dress shirt and silk tie to match. My eyebrows raise at the luxurious fabric as I run my fingers over the jacket, and a slow smile spreads on my face, imagining him wearing this tonight. I've only ever seen him in jeans and a t-shirt—not that I mind it at all—but something about him being primped and polished for me like this makes me feel...warm and fuzzy. Content. Important.

My smile grows into a grin and I bite my lip as sudden overwhelming emotions wash over me, knowing that tonight, not only will we be celebrating our bond in front of thousands of people, we'll also be declaring my presence to generations that believe my existence to only be a myth.

*I'm alright, nothing I didn't heal from. Jeger is unharmed, he was behind me when we were ambushed, and I took the brunt of the attack.* His nonchalant response pulls me back to the task at hand and his words jolt me into action.

With a shake of my head, I snag a shirt off a hanger and cross to his bureau to fish through his drawers, taking out jeans, briefs, and socks before dumping them on his bed to hurriedly pull on my heels. The thin straps frustrate me in my haste to wind them around my legs. I grunt irritably as I kick them off, snatching them from the floor, along with his clothes and my purse from the bed, and summon my shadow magic around me.

From one heartbeat to the next, I'm transported through the chilly dark mist onto the front steps of his home just as Valdr lopes along the grassy yard beside the long driveway.

My brows knit with worry at what he'd said. He trots up the steps and effortlessly shifts into his human form.

"*Ambush?*" I stress the question, taking a breath and demanding, "give me details, now. Please," I add with a scrunched nose as I realize how that sounded.

Thinking he'd only left to follow a scent trail, news of an ambush puts me on edge. Kyran senses my agitation and gently brushes his knuckles down my cheek.

"I'm alright, sweetheart. I didn't get bit and we took care of each vampire that we could find," he murmurs and gives me a half-smile. "It's nice to know how much you care, with your *queenly voice* and steely gaze." He laughs, giving me a teasing smirk.

My lips threaten to tug at the corners. I fight the urge to smile as I thrust his clothes toward him and grumble, "I'm serious. What would vampires be doing at the edge of your territory while the Convocation is active? And about you being bitten, now that Luna has awakened, your Guardian blood magic should've risen. You're immune to vampire venom, it's part of the Guardian's abilities. Speaking of," I purse my lips in thought, "which abilities do you possess? Have you felt anything take form within you?"

I watch with a hooded gaze as Kyran pulls the briefs and socks on before stepping into the jeans. His defined torso stretches as he tugs his shirt over his head, and I blink slowly as heat blooms inside my chest.

*Mmm, there's just something about a man wearing nothing but a pair of jeans.*

He pulls the hem of his shirt down, giving me a sly smirk. I twist my mouth to the side to stop myself from biting my lip, and his husky voice reaches my ears.

"*I can hear your thoughts, you know,*" he whispers conspiratorially. "Duly noted," he adds with a wink and I can't help the laugh that escapes me.

Kyran takes my hands in his and brings them to his mouth, kissing my knuckles. "I haven't felt anything, other than our bond fully forming. I feel the same in terms of power or strength. I guess I'm not really sure *what* I'd feel," he mutters and lets go of one hand, running his fingers through his hair with a sigh.

I lightly shake my head. "Actually, it's most likely because Luna hasn't shifted into her wolf form. Her magic hasn't fully materialized yet, and the Guardian magic is tied directly to *her*, so until then, I guess it'll remain dormant. Trust me, you'd know when you have it," I mumble, recalling a long-ago memory of the first Guardians' initial shift.

Kyran just nods as he steps past me and opens the front door, releasing my hand to grab a pair of boots. We quickly put on our shoes, and Kyran slides his hand under mine again. I smile at the gesture as we walk down the steps.

I glance up at him, curious about where we're headed. "Where is it you want to take me?"

He gives my hand a slight squeeze. "A cafe in the village. It's run by a mated pair of elders and they make the *best* coffee I've ever—" His voice cuts off, noticing the scrunched smile I give him.

Kyran frowns for a moment before letting out a flat sigh. "You don't drink coffee, do you?"

A laugh bubbles out of me at the dejected look on his face and I shake my head with a grin. "Nope. I'd still like to go, though," I offer, squeezing his hand in assurance. "Kind of funny, isn't it? How we've talked about *so much,* and have literally been inside each other's minds, but still have little things like this to learn? I'm curious about all of your little quirks," I muse, resting my head against his shoulder as we walk.

"Well, now that you have your full memory back, I'm sure we'll have countless nights of things to talk about, and I look forward to every single one of them," he murmurs, pressing a kiss to the top of my head.

I smile warmly from his affection.

The bustling streets pull into view as we reach the end of his winding driveway. Dozens of people mill about in high spirits carrying food and shopping bags, standing in clusters full of laughter, and the sights bring on a sense of unity and joy. More than a few people move out of Kyran's way as we pass, turning to stare at us with hushed tones, their whispers ecstatic at the sight of me.

I grin up at Kyran, and he glances at me with a similar expression. He whirls me around, clasping the back of my head as he sweeps me off my feet and brushes a kiss to my lips. Multiple gasps and cheers erupt throughout the village.

I can't help the joyful laugh that pulls free as he gently sets me on my feet. I'm sure by now everyone has heard of the ceremony taking place tonight, and his romantic display only confirms the rumors.

A young girl with a shy smile crosses our path, holding a white moonflower up toward me. I crouch down to her level, giving her a gentle smile as I look into her round, rich brown eyes. Lifting my palm, she gently places the large bloom in my grasp before pulling her hands to her chest. I pinch the small stem and tuck it behind my ear, earning a grin from the little girl and I thank her for her beautiful gift before rising to my feet.

She darts forward, wrapping her tiny arms around Kyran's leg and he chuckles, mussing her chestnut hair. The little girl squeaks and scurries away. I follow her path with my eyes to her mother who meets my gaze as her daughter takes her hand, giving me a warm smile and wave in greeting. I return the gesture, wiggling my fingers at the girl and take Kyran's hand once more.

We cross a couple more streets, moving closer to the center of the village based on the increasing volume of people. Kyran pauses at the sound of his name being called out.

"Kyran!" The worn voice echoes from an elderly woman frantically waving her hand over her head with a wide, toothy grin spread across her wrinkled face.

His eyes squint from the smile he gives her. I know instinctively this person is important to him and wonder who she is.

We quickly cross the busy street, coming to a stop before a little shop with a sign that reads *Window to the Soul*. I glance through the glass to find gleaming crystals of all sorts lining every possible inch of shelving and tables throughout the small space. I smile broadly at the sight, feeling drawn to go inside and hold the gemstones, clusters, and jewelry, to feel their energy and talk about where they were found.

Kyran chuckles and gently tugs my hand to get my attention. I smile at him sheepishly, and he gestures to the woman before us.

"Selene, this is Elder Stjarna. She is a dear friend of mine and a member of my council. Stjarna, this is Selene, my mate and—"

His words are cut off by a wild, barking laugh. Stjarna bustles over and throws her arms around me in a very motherly hug. Her grip is like iron, contrary to how old she appears, and I hug her back, grinning over her shoulder at Kyran. His eyes are bright with joy and my heart swells at the happiness that radiates from him.

Stjarna grasps my shoulders and pulls back to look me in the eyes, her bright emerald gaze sharp and assessing as she looks me over.

"I've heard all about tonight, and I am *over the moon* with joy. Now, tell me, do you have any jewelry for this evening?" She purses her lips as her gaze darts from my simple drop earrings to my bare neck, and then to the thin bangles at my wrists.

She tuts her disapproval with a frown. "Come, come. Inside."

Stjarna shoos her hands at me, and deciding I'm not fast enough, she turns me around and lightly pushes at me to walk into her shop. I glance over my shoulder to raise an eyebrow at Kyran, who just chuckles and shakes his head as he follows us inside.

Looking forward, I gasp as we enter the crystal shop and gaze around in awe at the thousands of shimmering stones. Stjarna scoots around me and passes through a beaded curtain before popping her head back out, waving us over.

I laugh, taking an immediate liking to the quirky old woman, and follow her into a dimly lit room adorned with large pieces of geodes and heavy clusters of crystals. She flutters around for a moment, collecting pieces of things as she goes and disappears behind a counter before carefully setting out a few options.

"As beautiful as you are, I cannot have our Alpha's mate attend her bonding ceremony...*unadorned*," she says lightly, glancing again at the modest jewelry I'm wearing. "Here, I've selected suitable pieces for you. Choose any you like, they are my gift to you." She smiles widely and lifts a few shiny gems for me to see.

"Stjarna, I thought you'd be thrilled to know something about Selene," Kyran says offhandedly as he steps up beside me.

"Ky..." I murmur under my breath in warning, having a strong feeling where he's going with this.

Her bright eyes widen a bit with interest as she flicks her gaze from his to mine. I wince a little, knowing what his next words are.

"I am sure you've heard the tales, and probably had known a few wolves who'd given their own accounts long ago about our Queen who'd once roamed our lands."

Stjarna nods, her brow furrowing.

"Well, she is with us once more, and I am honored to tell you that she is *my mate*." Kyran's voice is heavy with pride as his hand rests at the small of my back, and Luna brushes against our bond because of it.

Stjarna's eyes lock with mine and her jaw pops open, her gaze widening as his words settle around her.

After a still moment, she whispers, "Your eyes, *they're blue*. It's true. I never doubted your existence, and hoped to one day see this for myself to be true. Oh, Kyran," she sweeps her watery gaze to him, "congratulations, my boy! A mate! Our...*Drottning!*"

She gasps, dropping the gems in her hands as if they'd grown teeth and bitten her.

With a sharp shake of her head, she turns on her heel and flits about her shop once more, muttering incoherently. "No, no, this won't do. *Drottning!* In *my* shop!"

Stjarna disappears around a corner toward the back, more unintelligible words spilling from her lips as she goes.

I chuckle as I meet Kyran's gaze and squint at him, whispering, *"Really, did you have to say that?"*

He just laughs and shrugs, raising a brow.

I roll my eyes at him with a pursed smile.

Stjarna appears once more, carrying a few small ornate boxes and carefully sets them down on the countertop. She eases the lids open to display the breathtaking platinum set with large, pear shaped alexandrite stones. Their brilliant colors shift from a deep blue-green to a vibrant red-toned purple as she lifts the necklace and earrings up for me to see. My hand skims over my lips as I stare in awe at the jewelry, my eyes tracing the sparkling diamonds edging the large stones and clustered artfully at each tip. The gems appear to drip from the gleaming platinum.

When our gazes meet, I swallow past the dry lump in my throat, slightly shaking my head in disbelief.

"No, I-I can't accept *these*," I whisper, my eyes falling back to the magnificent pieces.

"They are absolutely stunning, but I can't take these from you. They are more than precious—these are beyond rare, especially at this size." I flick my gaze back to her sharp eyes.

Stjarna's thin mouth pulls into a wide, creased grin.

She shakes the fist holding the necklace at me and barks, *"Bah! I'm just an old crone and damn close to nearing the end of my time. These should belong to someone who appreciates them as much as I do, especially someone with a beauty to rival them, hmm?* I was gifted these a long, *long* time ago, and it only feels fitting now to pass the gift on to someone most deserving. Who better than my *Drottning,* no?" She raises her eyebrows into her silver hairline and beckons Kyran to move closer.

He steps around the side of the counter with an easy smile and lets Stjarna grasp his wrist, placing the necklace into his open palm. She closes his fingers over it and pats them before shooing him toward me, busying herself with removing the earrings from their box.

Turning toward me, Kyran's bright gaze meets mine, his warm hand grazing my neck as he sweeps my hair over my shoulder. A tingle runs down my spine at his touch, and I inhale sharply at the familiar *zing* of energy the necklace sends through me when it rests over my sternum.

My eyes flash to Stjarna who pretends to pay attention to the earrings, but I don't miss the knowing smirk at the corner of her mouth when her emerald eyes meet mine. She gives me a quick wink.

Kyran brushes my hair aside, pressing a kiss to my bare shoulder and I lean back into him automatically. I narrow my eyes at the old wolf. "How do you know Hekate?" I ask quietly, and her lips pull into a mischievous grin.

"Technically, all wolves know of Hekate," she mumbles, intentionally avoiding answering me properly.

"No, this necklace. It holds some of her power within the stone. Power that can only be given *freely,* and I know her well enough to trust that she does not *share* easily. So, tell me, how do you have in your possession an object—let alone what I can only assume to be *three*—infused with the goddess of witchcraft's power?" I ask tersely, eyeing the earrings she holds cupped in her palm.

Her green eyes twinkle as she smiles at me, nodding in silent approval.

"Yes, you are who these are destined for," she murmurs before clearing her throat. "You see, as a young pup, I had come to learn I held the ability of premonition. I could sense when something was about to go wrong—or right, though usually it tended to be in the negative—and as I grew into adulthood, this ability formed stronger, accompanied with obscure mental imagery. I had experienced a vision that *heavily* pushed me to seek Hekate, knowing that grave danger would befall the werewolf race if I didn't inform her that *something* was going to happen. I did not know the specific details, just the extreme importance that she must be made aware of it. After I found her and her daughter, she looked into my mind to view the vision I'd seen. Afterward, Hekate made me this jewelry set as a thank you gift for my message, and let me know it harnesses powerful protection and healing magic.

"Upon accepting her gift, I had seen myself in the far future handing them to someone else with the potent feeling of importance and certainty, and, well, here we are. I believe that these have always been destined for you, and I am just the placeholder through time," she murmurs, her voice growing wistful as she slides her gaze across the glittering shop. "Many of the items I've collected over the centuries have come into my possession that way, and I find fulfillment in successfully seeing them to their rightful owners."

My guard immediately drops and I glance at Kyran, finding him watching me carefully, his gaze lingering on the necklace for a moment before he turns to Stjarna. "Where were you a few days ago? I had come by your shop and found it closed for the first time in, well, *ever.* I could feel that you were far away. Out of respect I left you alone, but I am curious, what would pull you away from your home?" he asks lightly, sliding his hands into his pockets as he waits for her response.

As if on cue, the front door chimes as it opens. Stjarna whips her head around with a wild gleam in her eye.

"My star, are you in here? I found the berries you'd requested for the—oh, hello!" A dignified elder Englishman steps through the beaded curtain, holding a small basket in his dark, weathered hands.

He smiles kindly at Kyran and me before grinning brightly at Stjarna. He rushes over to her, planting a kiss to her temple affectionately. Kyran's sharp intake of breath has me swinging my gaze to him, and he wipes a hand over his mouth before a laugh of astonishment bursts free.

"No way," he whispers, his hand still pressed to his mouth as he shakes his head in disbelief.

"Yes way," Stjarna responds with a chuckle, nodding enthusiastically.

"*No way!*" Kyran leaps forward and wraps his arm around her, her silver braid flying free with her laughter as he spins them in a circle.

A grin pulls at my lips as I watch them, and I slide my gaze to the newcomer, finding him looking at Stjarna adoringly in a way that could only mean they are mates. My heart swells with the realization that *she* must have been the woman Kyran had mentioned a while ago when telling me about werewolves, how he knew of someone over seven hundred years old who never met their mate. Emotion chokes me and I smile at the gentleman when his gaze meets mine. The pure joy in his eyes pushes a tear to leak from mine.

"Congratulations! This is the best news ever, I am so happy for you!" Kyran carefully places Stjarna on her feet and takes her hands in his, grinning.

"Kyran, this is my long-lost mate, Wolcen," she announces proudly and beams at her mate as he extends his hand out to Kyran.

"Pleasure to meet you, Kyran," he says warmly as they shake hands, his Old English accent giving his words a proper tone.

"Wolcen, this is Kyran. He is the Alpha of my pack and one of the dearest people in my heart." Stjarna finishes her introduction with a wide smile.

Wolcen's steely gray eyes widen at her words, and he winces perceptibly, pinching the bridge of his nose on an exhale.

"Please excuse my indifference, *Alpha.*" He stresses the title and shoots Stjarna a pained look before addressing Kyran once more. "I was unaware—"

"It's alright," Kyran says with a chuckle, clapping the older man on the shoulder. "Stjarna is known to be...*troublesome* when it comes to rules and social normalities. She may be my elder, but she has a young and mischievous heart that rivals many of the pups running around."

They laugh and the old man nods dramatically.

"Don't I know it already," he mumbles sarcastically, giving Stjarna a warm smile.

She crinkles her eyes with a devilish grin.

Before she says anything, I hastily grab hold of Wolcen's hand, shaking it. "Hi, I'm Selene, Kyran's mate. It's so nice to meet you, and congratulations on your bond! I hate to cut this short, but we really must be going. Busy pack things to attend to! Have a wonderful day!" I ramble in a tight voice, not wanting to endure the awkwardness of another *royal* revelation.

I turn over my shoulder and scrunch my nose at a still-grinning Stjarna. She scrunches hers right back. Kyran coughs a laugh and glides his hand around my waist, pulling me to his side.

Stjarna gives the earrings to Kyran before she takes the basket from Wolcen, replacing it with one of her hands. She murmurs in his ear as she pulls him toward the back of the shop. When she glances at us over her shoulder, I wave goodbye with a watery smile and mouth a silent *thank you*. Stjarna just winks as they disappear through a doorway, and we turn to leave the shop.

"I am so happy for them," I say lightly as Kyran closes the door behind us. "Hopefully we can meet with them again this evening, I'd like to hear how they met."

Kyran dips his chin in agreement, holding out his hand for me to take the earrings. I quickly remove the ones I'm wearing and deposit them in my small purse before donning the magical set. The enchantment pulses as the second earring hangs in place, the trio of gems forming a triangle, and the slight hum of energy radiates from them for a few moments before it dissipates within me.

"I'll have to ask Hekate about these," I mumble, taking Kyran's outstretched hand.

We cross the street and I follow his lead, walking through a few blocks of shops before coming to a stop outside of a dark-windowed cafe. I notice the sign at the door is flipped to 'closed' and I squeeze Kyran's hand with a small smile. He just shrugs nonchalantly and his stomach growls, making me laugh at the betrayal of his disappointment.

"How about we go back to your house and I'll make us some lunch, since you took care of breakfast?" I offer, swinging our clasped hands.

Kyran gives me a sidelong glance, and his lips pull up at the corner. "Yeah, I'm sure I could choke your cooking down," he intones sarcastically and I narrow my gaze at him.

"Just for that," I threaten quickly, poking my finger in his solid chest. "I won't be gentle."

I harshly summon my shadow magic around the both of us, infusing *extra* power into it as I transport us onto the front yard of his house. Kyran stumbles dizzily onto his ass, and I throw my head back with a laugh, flipping my hair over my shoulder.

At the rumble of his growl, I hastily take the steps up to his front door and push through it hurriedly, squeaking as I barely close it in time.

The door rattles from the heavy *thump* of his body.

*"That was a dirty trick,"* he mumbles from the other side of the thick wood panel.

I laugh mirthfully as I cross into his kitchen to see what I have to work with.

# CHAPTER TWENTY-NINE

## ADMIRATION

### KYRAN

Selene's unexpected use of her power is impressive. I haven't asked her about it since reuniting, and I've been curious if everything feels the way it was for her long ago, after receiving her memories back.

I push through my front door with a grin and press it closed behind me, watching Selene walk into the kitchen. My smile grows wider as I think of Stjarna and her mate, how unbelievable it is for her to have found him this late in life. I am overjoyed for her and look forward to celebrating tonight with them.

Noticing how Selene is preoccupied with searching the cabinets, I silently sneak across the kitchen and duck into the pantry with the childish idea to scare her. My heart feels so light today, I want to run carefree like the pups do with their playful laughter, making mischief.

Pressing my back against the wall beside the open door, I breathe shallowly to remain undetected and listen for Selene's movements. I hear the rattle of some pans being placed on the countertop and her soft humming beneath the movements before the *clack* of her heels grows louder as she nears.

My muscles bunch in anticipation to jump, and I calculate how many steps she'll take before crossing into the pantry. *Five more to go,* I measure based on the echo and bend my knees. I smirk at how stupid this is, but I can't resist the desire to play with her the way she did with me moments ago.

*Three...two...one...*

I spring into a twist with a loud yell, slapping my palms against the door frame, only to be met with empty air. My brow pinches in confusion. I *know* she was right here. Leaning forward on my hands, I peer into the vacant kitchen and my mouth turns down at the corner.

*Where the hell—*

"Boo," a whisper grazes my ear and my body goes rigid at the sudden sound.

Whipping around, I find Selene perched on a shelf beside me and I can't stop my mouth from opening with astonishment at the sight of her. Her laughter rings out mirthfully, and she wipes at an eye from the force of it.

"You...you should see your face!" she says between giggled breaths.

She mocks my expression and starts laughing all over again.

My lips curl upward as her amusement fills me, even though I'm both shocked and embarrassed. I let out a chuckle.

"*How?*" I mumble, tilting my head curiously at her.

She gives me a wolfish grin and her eyes shine in the dim light as she lazily kicks her feet.

"How as in, *how did I get in here?* Or, *how did I know what you were doing?*" She raises an eyebrow, pursing her lips.

"Both," I mutter, grinning in return.

Narrowing her eyes with a smirk, she responds slyly, "*Magic.*"

I laugh at her playfulness and step between her legs, sliding my hands up her bare thighs to grasp her waist. She drapes her arms around my neck as I lift her, carrying her back into the kitchen and sit her on the island.

I kiss her forehead before asking, "What else can you do? The way you control your power is impressive. I have met witches who can't do what you do. Could you show me?" I take a step back, sliding my palms beneath hers.

An easy smile spreads across her beautiful face.

"Sure, though there's one thing I can't do during daylight. I'll show you that tonight, beneath the full moon. *It's so cool,*" she whispers dramatically, leaning forward with a grin.

"But for now, I can show you everything else. I have the ability to teleport, as you have experienced, though I call it shadow-walking. I can control shadows, wield them the same way you would with say, a knife, rope, or arrows, for example."

She releases my hands, swirling her wrists. Inky, writhing shadows appear and coil around her outstretched arms.

I stare openly dumbfounded at the sight.

Never in my life have I seen anything this… "*Amazing,*" I breathe, carefully reaching a hand toward her. "Can I touch it?" I ask, extremely curious about how something like this would feel.

Selene laughs with a nod, holding her hand out, and a shadow snake stretches toward me. I hesitate only for a heartbeat before gliding my fingers through the obsidian smoke. It is cool the way fog feels, and it leaves a slight tingle on my skin as my hand passes through it a second time.

I grin at Selene who grins back before narrowing her eyes a fraction, the only warning I get before the shadow coils around my wrist and hardens like steel. I glance down at it, giving my arm a slight tug, feeling absolutely no give with the binding. Peering up at Selene, I raise my eyebrows and pull harder, seeing the tension in her arm as a result, but feeling no change in the hold she has on me.

Her grin grows wider at my attempt and she shakes her head with a laugh. "Try all you want, you will not break free unless I choose to let you. These shadows are as fluid or solid as I need them to be, and believe me when I tell you, I am adept at wielding them."

She smirks as she releases her hold on my wrist and turns to look around the kitchen. "Is there anything you don't particularly care for in here, if it gets damaged?" she asks, turning back to face me.

"Everything except you," I answer automatically, and she barks a laugh. "I'm serious," I add, pulling my brow in.

Pushing off the counter, Selene grasps my hand and walks out of the kitchen toward the back door. Outside in the gardens, she points at the nearby forest and says flatly, "Name three things, and make them small. Then name something as big as you, and something that you could hold in your hand."

I take a brisk look around without questioning her, pointing as I rattle off a list. "The white mushroom on that tree, the patch of moss on the rock over there, and that little purple flower in the middle of the clovers." She nods. "The large oak log on the ground and…this rock." I gesture at a large river stone resting in a nearby flower bed.

Without a word, Selene winks over her shoulder at me, and flicks her hand out in three rapid successions, followed by three simultaneous quiet *thumps*. Glancing at the mushroom, moss, and flower, I find each impaled with a dart of shadow directly in their centers. My eyebrows raise at her skill and I silently watch as she whips her hand toward the stone.

A thin, wispy black rope flings outward before she yanks it back harshly, and the rock flies through the air to land in her awaiting palm. Without hesitation, Selene turns on her heel and throws her arms out in front of her, thick bands of shadows billowing out to encompass the fallen tree and forms a ring around the wide trunk. Her fingers bend inward and the resounding *crack* that echoes around us is astounding as the log crumples beneath her power.

When she releases the shadows, a pile of splintered wood remains between the severed halves of the tree, and I slowly drag my gaze to hers. Selene's chest rises and falls from the effort and she gives me a haughty smile. I just laugh in astonishment. With that sort of power, she is nearly unstoppable. I shake my head at the realization and consider what else there is to learn about her.

"That was *incredible*," I murmur with wide eyes. "I am beyond impressed. I've never seen anything like this."

"Thank you. It really is an effective force, especially in combat." My back stiffens at the thought. "Though, I can use it in other ways than with a fight. For instance, I can place my shadows like tangible objects, as you saw with the darts. They will remain there until I intentionally call them back to me. It does drain my energy, though, depending on the size or amount of shadow to keep them in place. Through them, I can hear and see things if I focus on it, although the visual aspect is grainy at best. I used to do this to play spy with Ria when we were young."

She smiles wistfully at the thought for a moment before blinking the memory away.

"Using the shadow magic is much like anything else you wield physically. It strains my body and takes a lot of stamina to uphold. It will deplete me if I am not careful, and that can put me in a predicament of being too exhausted to call it forward. The only replenishment I know of is sleeping and eating, just as anyone else would after a rigorous exercise," she explains, brushing her hands against her white skirt and smiling at me.

"That's honestly fucking awesome, and I'm kind of jealous." I grin at her, running my hand through my hair at the admission.

Selene laughs with a shake of her head and walks toward the house. I follow her back into the kitchen as she crosses over to the pantry, nodding her head for me to come in with her. She stands before the walls of shelving, her gaze searching for something before coming to a stop. Shaking out her hands, she briefly glances at me before turning her attention to the shelf once more.

"Okay, so besides the shadows and the teleporting, I also have the ability of telekinesis. It is nowhere near as strong as the shadows, and I'm honestly not that great with it. It's the least-used of my abilities, mostly *because* I have the shadows. The telekinesis came with the telepathy," she says offhandedly, and I gape at her.

"Wait, *what?*" I ask incredulously. "Telepathy? As in, mind reading?"

"Yes, and I can also push my thoughts into someone else's mind as well, make them see or hear what I want them to. Kind of like a vision or hallucination of sorts," she says softly, watching me over her shoulder. "It's not something I've ever really used. I don't like the idea of taking away someone's free will, even in combat."

I nod in understanding, recalling Vala's skill with her psychic magic and mention, "The only other person I've met with an ability like that was Vala, and I know it was strong, as I'd told you a while ago. Though hers wasn't technically quite the same as you, I don't believe. Is yours detectable?"

Selene just shakes her head slightly, eyes narrowed. "It isn't, unless I use it on Hekate or one of the elven," she mumbles. "Both are impossible to get anything past them magically."

"Elven?" I ask curiously, unsure of what she means.

She scoffs a laugh and rolls her eyes. "The *fae*. They despise the term, and refer to themselves as elves."

"The fae, as in faeries?" I clarify just to be sure, and she nods her head once. "We have a lot to talk about," I mutter, dragging a hand over my face.

Selene just laughs and turns back to the shelf, raising a hand. A bag of flour slides forward and topples off the shelf, landing in her hands with a poof of white dust. She giggles and blows the cloud away from her, turning to me with a grin and steps out of the pantry. In awe of Selene's abilities, my gaze flicks to the empty spot on the shelf and back to the doorway when I hear her voice call out to me.

"Could you get the sugars, some chocolate, and—actually, just bring me all of your baking ingredients, it'll be easier. *Please,*" she adds in a singsong voice, and a wide smile pulls my lips up in response.

"Yes, sweetheart," I call back to her, already filling my arms with her request.

After lunch, Selene adamantly refuses my offered help with making the cookies, and I concede by washing the dishes while she gets to work. We talk about her journey to unlocking her memories, and I feel some guilt about not being there to help her, even though she's clearly more than capable of handling herself.

It doesn't feel good to hear how volatile things were for her, especially with the condition she was in. I wish that there was something I could have done. She explains that her pain was her own to overcome. I understand that—hell, I respect it, even—since I'd essentially felt the same way with myself most of my life.

Sitting at the island, I watch Selene while she scoops the chilled dough onto a couple of trays. She has an easy smile as she goes, and I can't help but imagine her doing this with little fingers reaching for a taste, our children running around the kitchen in delight. I smile at the image and notice her glance at me with rosy cheeks, her smile growing wide as she undoubtedly sees my imagined scene.

Popping a bite of cookie dough into her mouth, she tosses me a small lump. I catch it effortlessly, taking a bite and groan at the flavor when the front door creaks open.

"This is easily the best I've ever had, and I'm not saying that as your mate," I say around the mouthful.

Selene laughs with a shake of her head.

"Whoa, whoa, easy there, we have company. I hope you're decent," Trey boasts sarcastically, and I laugh as he walks into the kitchen ahead of Castian and Mira.

After closing the oven, Selene lets out a soft sound of endearment at the sight of little Eudora cradled in Mira's arms, swathed in a soft yellow blanket, her big brown eyes blinking owlishly. I smile at them and nod my head in greeting as they enter. Mira carefully gives her baby to Castian and clasps her hands together, walking eagerly over to Selene.

"You must be Selene, I am so happy to meet you! I'm Mira, Alpha Castian's mate, and we just heard the news! Congrats!" She bounces on her toes and Selene smiles warmly at her.

"Thank you. Your baby is beautiful, what is her name?" she responds softly, her eyes sliding back to the little bundle.

"Eudora, it means—"

"Good gift," Selene murmurs with a wistful look in her eyes. "Yes, that is very fitting. All babies are a gift." She clears her throat lightly, blinking a couple of times. "Congratulations on her birth. By the looks of her sweet face, she must have been born recently?"

"Yes, just a few days ago," Mira says with a smile as she glances back at her child. "Thank the stars that Eir was here to assist with her birth. I fear things wouldn't have gone well without her help."

Selene's mouth turns up at the corner. "Ah, yes, of course. I couldn't think of anyone more suited than her. I'm glad you're well, and I am grateful for Eudora's presence."

As Mira talks with Selene, I get lost in thought over how she addressed the mention of Eir. As far as I'm aware, Selene doesn't fully remember being treated by her after ingesting venom. Hell, I don't even know for sure if I've even spoken about her besides that incident.

Narrowing my eyes at Selene, I mindlink, *Why did you speak of Eir as if you know her?*

She doesn't respond, a sly smirk appearing at the corner of her mouth as she listens to what Mira says.

I'm about to push it further when her voice whispers through my mind, *Tonight, Ky. It'll make sense later.*

She glances at me briefly before giving Mira a quick hug.

"I completely understand if I don't see you tonight, so do not fret over the matter. A raucous celebration is no place for a newborn, and I hope she sleeps well for you." She waves her hand with a grin as Mira and Castian make their way upstairs.

"Speaking of which," Trey announces as he slides his phone into his pocket, moving toward the garage. "Kira is back and has a carload of things for the ceremony. I'll be with her if you need anything," he calls over his shoulder before the door closes behind him.

"Okay," I call out to nothing and Selene chuckles as the oven dings.

She grabs an oven mitt and pulls out the trays, the mouthwatering aroma filling the kitchen as she places them on the counter. The door clicks open and Trey dashes across the kitchen, snatching a couple of cookies and garbling his thanks over a mouthful as he quickly leaves again.

We both laugh, shaking our heads, our gazes meeting across the room. Selene picks up a cookie and shadows swirl around her, transferring her to my lap. My arms snake around her waist and she takes a bite before holding it up for me to eat. I take it from her and push the entire cookie into my mouth, laughing at the way she scrunches her nose in disappointment.

Wrapping her arms around my neck, she presses her forehead to mine and rubs our noses together, sending little tingles down my back and over my arms.

"I'm excited for tonight," she whispers, her icy eyes shining brightly.

"As am I," I whisper back, brushing a kiss against her lips. "But I'm even more excited for tomorrow night, and the night after, and after."

Her giggles make me laugh and she squeezes me tightly.

"I love you," we say at the same time and grin widely, kissing through our laughter.

For the first time in my life, my heart is full and content, and I cherish the feeling of having my entire world in my arms.

# SELENE

Kyran and I spend the rest of the afternoon lounging around, talking about anything and everything that we could think of. He asks me many more questions regarding my powers, and I even go as far as projecting the idea of a beach into his mind to prove to him my ability with telepathy. His reaction is priceless as he walks around the kitchen gawking at the walls and commenting about the sand and waves.

I have a little bit of fun by abruptly shifting the vision to a precarious cliff top overlooking the ocean and imagine tumbling over the edge. I cry from laughter as Kyran falls to the floor claiming the dizziness felt real. With a growl, he throws me over his shoulder, carrying me toward the stairs.

When he takes the first step, a knock echoes at the front door and Kyran gently places me on my feet before crossing to the entryway. The moment he opens the door, Asteria's tell-tale squeal peals through the room, and I grin at the sight of her black gossamer dress.

She bustles past Kyran with her arms outstretched toward me and hurries across the floor, her thick black boots clomping noisily with each step. We collide in a tight hug for a few moments before she claps her hands together with excitement, her auburn hair flowing wildly around her in an invisible breeze.

"I could *puke* from how thrilled I've been since you left," she gushes, her lavender eyes flashing with her smile.

"Hekate," Kyran's surprised voice announces, and I peer over Asteria's bare shoulder to watch as he pulls the door open wider. "Welcome, please come in."

He steps aside with a hesitant smile before glancing over at me.

I sense his trepidation at being unprepared to host Hekate in his home and I cross the floor to stand by his side, smiling warmly at him as she enters. My eyebrows pull together when I notice how done-up she has made herself, and my smile turns watery as I look her over.

Her onyx hair is pulled back into an elegant twisted bun adorned with glittering jeweled pins, and she wears a deep purple dress with a billowing black chiffon shawl. In her hands she holds a small bouquet of fresh white flowers picked from her garden and my eyes flick up to her smoky lined ones.

She watches me carefully as she gives me a soft smile. I don't hesitate to throw my arms around her, taking care to not squash the flowers in the embrace. Before the stasis, it would have felt out of place to hold Hekate in this way. Our relationship had been more of a strong friendship than familial. After the loss of my memories, however, she was nothing but a fantastic mother toward me, and that feeling of love didn't just vanish when I unlocked my past life.

Though our relationship has changed and grown closer, it does feel weird to refer to her as Mother now that I am whole, but part of me sees her in a different light than before.

"I'm so glad you're here," I say quietly as I pull back with a warm smile. "I'd have thought you'd refrain from immersing yourself in such a large group of wolves. Would they even recognize you, though?" I wonder out loud.

Her wine colored lips part to reply, but Kyran's bark of a laugh pulls my attention to him.

He widens his eyes and scoffs. "Oh, yeah. They *definitely* would."

*What the hell does that mean?* I turn my narrowed gaze back to Hekate who has a sheepish look on her face.

"What did you do?" I accuse, placing my hands on my hips and trying not to smile.

She clears her throat, scrunching her nose. Her voice pitches a bit higher than usual as she replies nonchalantly, "I *may have* turned a few of them into dogs a while ago."

I gape at her admission, and Ria's cackle bounces off the walls throughout the house. Kyran just snorts in amusement.

"You *what?*" I ask incredulously. "Why? When?"

Hekate rolls her violet eyes with a scoff. *"Tch,* it was a couple hundred years ago, and they didn't respect my boundaries. They needed to learn a lesson," she murmurs as she brushes off invisible, non-existent lint from her dress.

Kyran huffs another amused laugh and explains, "It was my first time hosting the Convocation as Alpha, and you shifted over a thousand wolves from all the packs *into chihuahuas.*"

His laughter bubbles up at the memory before he continues. "Your spell lasted for an entire *year.* Do you know how difficult it was to manage shoe-size canines with the temperament of a pissed-off wolf? Images of your likeness were posted everywhere throughout the pack lands as a reminder not to cross you. All because some young wolves were running through your woods under the full moon." He shakes his head with crinkled eyes, and I can't help the grin that spreads across my face.

My laugh escapes me as I look back at Hekate, and she lets out a light chuckle.

"Okay, that's a valid reason for them to recognize you. Are you sure you want to be here tonight?" I ask jokingly, and she nods quickly.

"Of course, I wouldn't miss this for anything." She smiles widely at that and waves her hand toward me. "Now, let us get you fixed up for the evening, *hmm?*"

"*Ugh,* yes. I've gotta do something about that hair," Ria mocks and I glare at her.

"You really are the worst, you know that?" I snark back, unable to rein in the smirk that pulls at my lips.

Ignoring me, Ria just flutters her hands at Kyran and chastises him. "You need to clean up, you're a mess."

I notice the teasing gleam in her eyes as she places a hand on her hip.

He just glances down at himself with a slight frown and raises an eyebrow at her.

Nothing is wrong with him, and we all know it.

I roll my lips between my teeth, enjoying how comfortable Asteria is to treat him the same as me. I observe them with amusement as Kyran pretends to look at a watch that doesn't exist.

"Huh, would you look at that, it's five-thirty. Sundown isn't for another three hours," he says flatly and a snort escapes me at his dry tone.

"Exactly" Ria rolls her eyes. "Go…bond with your brother or whatever. We'll meet you in the Hall." She smiles devilishly and Kyran smirks at her before rolling his eyes to me.

*I don't know how you live with her,* his joking tone floats through my mind.

I bite back my grin and Hekate coughs a laugh beside me. Kyran shoots a grin at her as Ria smacks his arm and we laugh lightheartedly. He pulls me into a warm embrace, kissing the top of my head.

"I don't know what you said, but the feeling is mutual." Ria childishly pokes her tongue out at him before cracking a smile.

Kyran gently lifts my chin to look into my eyes, murmuring, "I'll be helping Trey and Kira with preparations. If you need me, you know how to find me." He tenderly kisses my forehead, hugging me tight.

"See you soon," I whisper with a smile and press up onto my tiptoes to peck his lips.

He leans forward for more, but cool wind whisks me away as Ria transports us into Kyran's bedroom, his grumbling growl following through the ether. His indignation make me chuckle.

Wincing at Asteria's gasp, I immediately freeze in place.

She'd marched straight into the bathroom and found the chaotic scene left from Kyran's destructive outburst.

Hekate peers through the archway with a shake of her head, mumbling under her breath about men and emotions, and whirls her hand around.

A puff of wind tickles me and Kyran appears, stumbling a bit from the sudden teleport. "Fuck, you've *really* gotta stop doing that," he growls, pressing a hand to his head and glares at Hekate.

She just cocks an eyebrow at him and crosses her arms, nodding her head over her shoulder at the destroyed bathroom. Kyran twists his mouth to the side and slides his hand behind his neck with a sigh.

"It was a lapse of control. I intend on renovating as soon as I can. It'll be a bit tough with the Convocation this week, but I will—"

"Show me," Hekate interrupts, dropping her arms and stepping in front of Kyran.

"What?" he asks blankly, taking an involuntary step away from her.

"What you intend to do, with the bathing room," she clarifies, coming to a stop before him and holding her hand up to his forehead. "Come now, we haven't got all day."

His gaze narrows slightly before he takes a step forward and presses his head into her awaiting palm. The amber in his eyes flashes brightly for a few moments and she draws her hand back, her mouth pulling down at the corners as she nods.

"You've got good taste," Hekate mumbles, eyeing him for a moment before waving her hand through the air. "Now, off with you. We have work to do." She smirks and whisks Kyran away once more.

His gravelly growl echoes around us and Ria's cackle emits from the bathroom. A giggle bubbles from my chest with amusement.

"I love how you both treat him so casually. I'm glad you like him," I say softly, knowing that they can hear me.

Hekate smiles warmly at me. "He really is a wonderful man, and I couldn't imagine a more perfect fit for you. Shall we?" She lifts her eyebrows and gestures toward the bathroom.

"*Mmm*, I'll admit I envy you, but only *slightly*. His brother *is* single, after all," Asteria drawls as she saunters over, shards of broken glass crunching beneath her boots.

I laugh openly at that with a shake of my head. "We never did talk about that first night at Howler's. I saw you flirting with him at the bar, though at the time, I couldn't place where I knew him because *somebody* fucked with my memories. *Again.*" I raise an eyebrow, staring pointedly at her.

"Oh, *that* was so fun. He was absolutely terrified of me after our little meeting at the park, and I couldn't help myself with teasing him at the club. He's just *so damn cute.*" Her lavender eyes sparkle as she talks about Treyvar, and I smile knowingly at her.

"What? Don't look at me like that. He is a wolf, after all." She rolls her eyes, but I don't miss the way her lips pinch with the flush of her cheeks.

Hekate's movements catch my attention and I turn to watch as she swirls her arms around, closing her eyes and murmuring a spell under her breath. The broken glass raises off the floor, the pieces floating through the air toward the shower, molding back into a solid pane and settling into the door frame. The cracked tiles in the shower solidify, transforming into a mosaic of black, white, and iridescent aqua tiles as a second shower head shimmers onto the bare side of the new wall.

I stare in awe while her magic effortlessly transfigures the bathroom, replacing the broken sink with a solid slab of black marble carved with dual basins and bright white cabinetry. An expansive mirror adorned by a wood frame carved with ivy spreads across the wall over the wide sinks. My smile grows wide, noticing how the details match the woodwork from Kyran's bar.

The floor shimmers for a moment, settling into elegant white marble tiles, accented by black tiles with aqua filigree designs. Fluffy white towels with black and aqua embroidery drape over new matte black bars, and matching floor mats appear by the shower and sinks, tying the room together nicely.

"This is gorgeous," I breathe, complimenting Hekate when she lowers her arms, looking around satisfactorily.

"It was Kyran's vision, I just did the magic," she says offhandedly and I laugh, turning to give her a tight hug.

*"Thank you.* Not just for me, but for him as well. This means a lot," I murmur into her shoulder, and she pats the back of my head affectionately.

"It's the least I can do, truly. Now," she pushes me back by the shoulders, "get out of these clothes so we can ready you for your ceremony."

I do as she commands and strip off my clothing, handing them to Asteria as she waves me toward the new soaking tub in the corner filled with steaming water, turning away to undoubtedly alter my outfit for the evening. I oblige, letting the heat of the water soothe me as I envision my future living here with Kyran.

An easy, relaxed smile rests on my lips while I daydream. I'm eager to see him tonight, waiting to meet me beneath the rising full moon, surrounded by thousands of our people excited to celebrate with us.

# Chapter Thirty

## CELEBRATION

### SELENE

I stand in awe before the intricate floor length mirror that Hekate conjured into Kyran's bedroom. *Well, our bedroom now, I suppose,* I wonder as I stare at my impeccable reflection. Hekate and Asteria took their time with me, drying and styling my hair traditionally rather than using magic, and I savored the intimate time spent with them.

Our conversations trailed from inconsequential things to heavier, more emotional topics, and the three of us had a few moments of wiping each other's tears away. It was really nice to spend time with them like that after everything that has transpired recently. I am immeasurably grateful to have these two strong women beside me in life, women I can undoubtedly count on for anything.

Thoughts of the past few weeks cause tears to well in my eyes, and I look toward the ceiling in an attempt to not ruin Ria's handiwork with my makeup.

After taking on the responsibilities required of me when I grew into adulthood, the chance of finding a soulmate was just a small dream that I'd let go of a long, *long* time ago. The role I upheld superseded my own personal desires as I focused on protecting and defending my race from the volatile nature of the vampires.

Now, with Kyran by my side, I am confident that we will prevail against Caedes, regardless of his reasons for wanting me dead.

As the thought crosses my mind, I pull on my bond with Kyran and ask, *Hey, Ky, have you spoken with the other Alphas about the Guardian blood magic and the changes they'll be undertaking?*

I focus on my reflection once more, staring into my bright blue eyes.

His warm, husky voice immediately trails through my mind, making me smile. *Yes, I have, and they all have a mix of eagerness and disbelief about it, as do most of the people here tonight.*

*Are you ready? How do you feel?* I ask quietly, running my hands over the bodice of my dress.

I sense his trepid laugh as he murmurs, *Just about as ready as I can be. Is it weird that I'm kind of nervous? Even though you've already accepted me and were bonded, my heart feels jittery again, as if I'm waiting to hear your decision once more.*

Closing my eyes, I focus on our bond and peek through his vision. He's standing before a mirror as well, in what looks to be a woman's bedroom. His sister steps up beside him and rests her head on his shoulder, smiling at his reflection. Kyran runs a hand over his freshly cut hair and blows out a breath as he drags his hand down his neatly trimmed jaw. I watch with a lazy smile as he straightens the cuffs of his black suit and adjusts the tie at his throat.

His movements portray his nerves.

I can't help commenting on his *sinfully* good looks.

*You are devilishly handsome. I'm liking this dark, mafia boss look,* I whisper in his mind, amused at the way his reflection shows his confusion.

He leans close to the mirror, his brow furrowing. *You can see me? How?*

I push my magic through our bond just enough to let a flicker of my icy eyes flash within his warm amber irises. I laugh as his gaze rounds widely at the sight.

Kyran narrows his eyes with a smirk. The moment I feel him push back, I lock down my end of the bond with another laugh.

*Nuh-uh, you have to wait. I want to watch your reaction,* I tease, sensing the frustrated growl he sends my way in return.

*See you soon!* I chirp, returning my attention back to my mirror.

Hekate steps up beside me with a watery smile and I grin at her, knowing she most likely watched everything transpire between us. I run my gaze one last time over my reflection with admiration. Asteria kept the same theme of my earlier clothes and drew them out into a more elegant, formal gown, one fit for a queen.

My dress has a sweetheart neckline, and it is fitted to my hips with sparkling diamonds intricately embedded in swirling patterns across the satin fabric. Thin gossamer straps cap my shoulders and trail behind me in billowing sheets, falling to the hem of my flowing skirts just above my ankle. The front of the skirt is pleated on one hip and drapes dramatically, parting with a slit that allows for room to move freely. Asteria explained how the dress has a simple zipper in the back for easy removal with shifting, and I appreciate her attention to detail.

I run my hands over my hair, pulling a couple curls free from the half-back style Ria did, and brush my fingers over the necklace that Stjarna gifted me. Satisfied with how I look, I smile at myself as I turn to take the shoes Ria holds out for me, sliding on the strappy white satin heels.

Hekate offers me her beautiful bouquet and I accept it with a grin. "I'm ready now. Let me know when to arrive," I say softly, inhaling the sweet scents of jasmine and gardenia.

She nods silently and gives me a wide smile before vanishing. Ria turns away from the mirror and gives me a tight hug. "You look magnificent, Sel. You're going to take his breath away," she whispers.

I laugh and nod in agreement. Ria disappears with a wink, leaving me to admire my reflection once more, waiting impatiently.

## KYRAN

I shake my head with a chuckle as Selene slips away in my mind. My chest is tight with unexpected nerves, but I'm anxious to see her again, to take her into my arms and never let her go.

I'm honored that she agreed to this ceremony. Not many wolves choose to hold one anymore as the tradition fades with the elders' passings. I am more than proud to have her as my soulmate, and dammit, I want to show her off to anyone that looks our way.

Kira eyeballs me in the mirror. She lifts her head, narrowing her eyes at me before crossing her arms.

"I want one," she pouts, and a smile pulls at her glossy pink mouth. "I'm *so jealous* right now, but I really am happy for you, Kyran. You deserve this, the happiness and the love. Mom would be in tears right about now," she says softly as she swipes at her eyes, then turns quickly toward the mirror to fix her makeup.

"Thank you." I smile genuinely at her and let out a sigh. "Goddess bless the man who gets fated to be bonded to you," I say mockingly, and she whips around to shove at my shoulder. "I'm kidding, you know I love you." I laugh at her sour look, stepping back to check myself over once more.

I feel slightly uncomfortable wearing clothes like this. I've never worn anything formal, and have never had the reason to until now. I want to look my best for Selene, though. Now that we are an extension of one another, I do not want to hinder her in any way. It is completely impossible for her to ever *not* look good, so I know I've got to step up my efforts as best I can.

I appreciate the suit Asteria gave me, knowing damn well I wouldn't have come close to this on my own. Kira even complimented me for it as well. Wearing all black, I find the look to be formidable, and I stand straighter because of it. Selene's comment replays in my mind, lifting the corner of my mouth.

"Are you ready?" Kira murmurs as she smiles warmly at me, slinging her arm through mine.

Smiling at myself, I nod as I let out a nervous breath, and turn to make my way to the Great Hall to have the love of my life declare our bond before all of our people.

My knee shakes back and forth as I clasp my hands in front of me, waiting on the dais in the filled Hall, listening to the buzzing murmurs of the crowd before me. My sister did an amazing job with redecorating the area, stringing warm lights over the rafters and trailing jasmine flowers throughout the flowing streams of white and black draped fabric adorning the walls. She placed a sprig of the little white stars in the breast pocket of my suit and I inhale the sweet, familiar scent, calming my nerves a bit.

Hekate manifests beside me, her wind sending stray petals flying. The crowd goes deathly silent at her unexpected arrival before erupting in a clamor of hissed whispers and gasps. Turning to meet her gaze, I find humor in her sharp eyes. I breathe a laugh when she cracks a smile on her usually stoic face.

She leans closer to whisper in my ear.

"I'm going to say a few words, if that's okay with you? I figure they might take this more seriously hearing it directly from *me.*" She pulls back, meeting my gaze with raised eyebrows, and I nod in agreement.

"By all means," I agree, sweeping my arm out and taking a step back for her to address the crowd.

Hekate clears her throat, and it only takes a second for the mass of people filling the Hall and spilling out into the surrounding fields to hush. Magically amplified, her voice carries her announcement across the air.

"Tonight, you are all gathered here to witness a beautiful ceremony to celebrate the bonding of a special pair of souls. The whispers of Alpha Kyran's mate being the legendary white wolf are true, and I am here to confirm it to those of you that still hold suspicions. Your Queen lives, and it is because of Alpha Kyran that she is able to walk among you once more. Selene holds great remorse for the suffering you all have felt by the hands of the vampires, and she will stand strong by you in the face of adversity." Hekate pauses her speech to let the noises of surprise fade.

"It saddens me that so much time has passed from when she last lived among her people, and it is with a heavy heart that I acknowledge the loss you all have felt. I ask that you not hold blame against Selene for the misfortune that has befallen your race. If anything, it is *my responsibility* that she has been gone for so long. Believe me when I say that if it had been up to her, she would have never left her people to fight alone."

Louder murmurs bubble out of the crowd, and Hekate raises her voice above them.

"Tonight, celebrate not only her return, but also the blessed gift of bonding with her soulmate. May the moon goddess bless many of you tonight, and all the nights to come, with the gift of your own bonds." Hekate tilts her head and smiles up at the night sky through the wide open doors, toward the full moon peeking over the treetops.

Many people clap and cheer when she steps back, the energy in the room heightening around me. I swallow thickly, my nerves coiling.

I reach up to loosen the tie at my throat and accidentally tear it free, swearing under my breath as I hold the fabric in my hand. Hekate chuckles and I flick my gaze to her. She leans toward me, undoing the buttons at the top of my dress shirt and lightly pats my shoulders.

"This suits you better anyhow," she mumbles with a smirk, and I huff a laugh.

She takes the torn tie from me and it combusts in her hand, the ashes disintegrating into dust that blows away on a gentle breeze. Hekate winks at me before vanishing from the dais as effortlessly as she arrived, reappearing in the front of the crowd with Asteria, Kira, and Treyvar.

Beside my brother stands Felagi, who is giving me a toothy grin as he holds up a mug of frothy beer, and I laugh as my eyes continue roaming. Castian and Luric are beside Felagi, both dipping their heads in greeting with genuine happiness. I nod and grin back at them until I notice the men keeping a distance from the others, and my smile slides away as my gaze meets Daine's.

He and Marx have matching sneers as they talk with each other, clearly being part of the few who don't believe Selene's existence to be real. It would be *so damned satisfying* to see the looks on their faces when she arrives, but I know I won't be able to tear my eyes off of her to see it.

Looking away dismissively, I let my gaze wander the rest of the crowd, finding the majority of them to be in high spirits. People congratulate me as our eyes meet. I smile genuinely at the gestures, and my heartbeat relaxes until a hush sweeps through the Great Hall.

At the warm tug in my chest, my gaze flies across the room and lands on Selene standing in the large open doorway. Moonlight illuminates her ethereally, her elegant white dress floating around her in the wind like clouds caressing a star. Her beauty is unrivaled, and

# LUNAR SHADOWS: AWAKEN

I forget to breathe as I drown in the sight of her. She looks every bit like the white wolf Queen depicted in our lore, and everyone in this room goes stalk-still as they gaze upon her.

I have to resist the urge tensing my legs to leap off this dais and run to her, swallowing thickly past the dry lump that has taken residence in my throat. My heart thunders in my chest when her brilliant gaze meets mine, her full lips curling into a warm smile. I grin like an idiot back at her, and her soft chuckle drifts across the Hall before she scrunches her nose at me.

Absently rubbing a hand across my aching chest, I force myself to take a tight breath before black splotches start forming in my vision. A soft melody floats through the air from some violins and a cello. The music is gentle and pretty, reminding me of how Selene feels when she is in my arms.

As she takes her first step toward me, I think about everything she's been through, about what we have prevailed together, and I'm in awe of her spirit and resilience.

She's taught me that it's okay to have flaws, to learn to love myself because of them. That I deserve love *because* of how I've chosen to handle my hardships, to not let them define me. It is *she* who gives me my strength and holds my heart in return.

I don't brush away the tear that streams down my face as I watch her walk to me.

It is unbelievable how this stunning, *magnificent* woman is fated to entwine her soul with mine. I silently thank the moon goddess for this divine gift. Glancing up at the full moon, I *swear* it pulses with a white light, and I grin at the sign as I drop my gaze back to Selene, finding an equally wide grin on her face as well. She's almost halfway across the Hall.

I shiver as her soft voice glides through my mind.

*That was really beautiful and touching, Ky.* She smirks, and my eyebrows pinch upward.

Knowing she heard my thoughts has me losing control over my body. I bound off the dais, the parted crowd giving out whoops and whistles as I rush through them to take my laughing mate into my arms. I lift her off her feet in my embrace and twirl us around before sliding an arm beneath her knees, carrying her to the dais.

Leaping onto the platform, I gaze adoringly down at her and murmur, "Hey, sweetheart. You are absolutely stunning."

I don't hesitate to lean in and kiss her, except my mouth is met with the soft petals of her bouquet. Chuckles wave throughout the spectators as Selene blocks me with a giggle.

*"Not yet,"* she whispers with a scrunched smile and I growl lightly, grinning.

Setting her gently on her feet, I can finally take a full breath. I close my eyes at her intoxicating scent mingled with mine, my chest relaxing in her presence. I wait for her to take the lead, keeping my eyes on hers as she takes a slow breath. With a slight nod, she turns toward the hushed crowd.

Many sets of eyes are rounded as they watch her, some people are already crying, and more than a few have expectant expressions as they wait to hear her speak. I slide my hand into hers and rub my thumb over her soft knuckles before raising it to my mouth for a kiss.

Selene smiles at me warmly before addressing our people with a firm, yet gentle voice.

"I want to thank each of you for taking time out of the Convocation to celebrate our bonding with us. Your presence is much appreciated, and I look forward to meeting with many of you tonight. As Hekate announced, the rumors *are* true. I am the white wolf you'd all believed to be a fable, as it has been nearly a millennia since I'd last walked freely among you. Some of your Elders may have spoken of my existence as if they'd known me, and I can guarantee you that *most* of them weren't lying." She raises an eyebrow with a smirk, and murmured laughter ripples throughout the Hall.

"I want to sincerely apologize for the suffering and tribulations that many of you have faced in my absence. It was *not* intended for me to be gone for as long as I have been, and I feel great sorrow for the losses that have occurred at the hands of Caedes and his followers." She swallows thickly, her jaw clenching, and I squeeze her hand in silent support.

*"Why were you gone?"* a voice echoes from across the Hall.

*"What happened?"* another calls out, and a few more jumble together in the broken silence.

Selene raises the hand holding her flowers and glances down at them with a frown. She tosses the bouquet to Asteria, and lifts her open palm up to the crowd, hushing their voices.

"Please, let me explain. I am more than happy to answer questions after the ceremony as well. Long ago, tension with the vampires had risen perilously to the point of a grave war between our races. Caedes sought to capture me for his control, maybe even to end my existence, marking him as the most superior made-being beneath the gods at the time. My *only* role was—and still is—to protect the werewolf race, to ensure our blood isn't squandered by vampire venom, ending our lineage.

"Hekate brought it upon herself to prevent this from happening. Knowing of the mortal danger a fight with Caedes would bring, and with my creation magic tying me to all of you, the best option was to put me into stasis. Her intention was to deter the vampires from pursuing chaos with our race and let time pass until my existence was slowly forgotten. There were some complications with the stasis magic, however, and I didn't have access to my wolf upon emerging from stasis later than expected. Caedes also devised a plan to hunt for me over the centuries, and this is the reason many of our young women have been abducted. It was not for nothing, and it angers me deeply that this has gone on for so long. If it wasn't for my disappearance, most of your losses would not have happened—at least not in this way—and for that I am truly, *deeply* sorry."

Selene takes a measured breath for a moment, letting her gaze sweep across the Hall.

After the hushed whispers subside, she clears her throat. "I am eager to meet with your Alphas and teach them the ways of the Guardians."

Collective murmurs flit throughout the Hall, and Selene raises her voice. "Their abilities will further strengthen our packs in defense against the vampires, especially in solidarity with one another. I look forw—"

"*Bullshit.*" Marx's interruption is harsh, and I narrow my eyes at him with a low growl.

Selene flicks her gaze toward him and coolly asks, "What is bullshit?"

Her eyes glide over him, narrowing slightly. "Who are you? An Alpha, I presume?" she adds dryly, noticing the way his arms are crossed and the cocky look on his face.

*"Tch."* He scoffs, turning his head to the crowd behind him. *"Our queen* must not be known for her intelligence," he mocks with a laugh, and the majority of the crowd around him shuffle away at the comment.

The only people to breathe a laugh with him are members of his pack, and even they seem hesitant at the remark. A low growl emanates from Selene. It sends electricity down my spine and my muscles respond automatically, tensing to defend my mate.

"His name is Marx, and he's the only alpha here *not* of bloodline," I state flatly, the insinuation intended to be the insult it is known for.

I smile wickedly at him, my ire at his disrespect toward Selene pushing its way through me, wanting to provoke him. When he bares his teeth at me in response, my smile just widens, exposing my teeth as well.

"What is bullshit?" Selene repeats herself sharply this time, releasing my hand and turning to face him directly.

When he doesn't remove his glare from mine, she raises her voice in a commanding tone. *"Alpha Marx."*

He tears his eyes from mine to look at her.

*"What is bullshit?* Please, enlighten me. I'd love to clarify any *misunderstanding."* Selene's words are formal, but her tone is cold.

She's clearly taken offense to his blatant disrespect, and the power radiating from her pulses like a heartbeat.

I raise my eyebrow at him when he glances at me again.

Marx rolls his eyes and scoffs. "It's hard to believe that—"

Luna's indignation rises viciously through our bond.

Selene's shoulders bristle, her voice cutting when she hisses, *"He did not ask you, so why are you answering to him? If you deign to speak with me respectfully, I have no problem putting you in your fucking place like an insolent pup."* Her shadows ripple down her arms in response, and everyone collectively gasps at the sight.

Asteria cackles in amusement, and I openly smirk at Marx as his wide eyes flicker between Selene and me. His gaze finally lands on her, and her posture relaxes a bit.

Until he opens his mouth.

"Your display of power doesn't prove *shit*. For all we know, you're just a powerful *witch* paid to fool us into believing—*ack!*"

His spiteful words are abruptly cut off from a rope of shadow coiled around his neck.

Selene looks enraged as she yanks her arm back, dragging Marx up over the edge of the dais to hold him suspended before her. Her eyes glow more than any I've seen before.

I cross my arms as his bulging gaze searches me pleadingly.

Selene grips his jaw in her slender hand, wrenching his gaze forward and peers closely into his eyes. A few silent moments pass before she shakes her head with a scoff of disgust. Releasing Marx with a rough shove, she removes her shoes and hands them to me silently before reaching for the zipper at her back.

As she drags it down, I watch in complete awe when she shifts into her wolf form for the first time. Everyone releases exclaims of excitement and disbelief.

Luna shakes out her luminescent fur before baring her teeth in a snarl at Marx. The shadows dissipate from his throat, dropping him onto his hands and knees before her. When he looks up at her, she growls savagely and snaps her jaws inches from his face. Luna dominantly presses her forehead down against his.

Her voice is undoubtedly heard throughout the Hall and fields, the crowd remaining silent as they listen.

*You are a cruel and vile wolf. You do not hold the Guardian blood, and therefore I couldn't care less for your life. Your pack is better off without you. You do not deserve to hold the title as an Alpha just because you are a brute who rules with fear. There are always others better than you, others who can best you, yet you walk around like an arrogant king.* Her savage growl reverberates through the air, sending chills down my spine.

*There is no king, only your Queen, and I find you to be a disgrace to all of werewolf kind. You have caused enough unrest to last many lifetimes. I deem you unworthy to call yourself one of ours.* Her growling intensifies as an eerie white glow blooms around her and envelopes Marx.

A deep, pained howling yell tears from him as his back arches intensely.

The Hall goes deathly still when a black wolf spirits out from his human form.

The ghostly apparition wavers for a moment before fading like smoke.

Marx groans a hoarse cry.

A wave of shock rolls over me, realizing that I just watched my mate *tear the wolf soul out of his body.* I never knew that was even *possible.*

Swallowing thickly in the face of her immense power, I flick my gaze from the keening man to my mate, and my skin heats at the sight of the powerful, radiant wolf before me.

Valdr proudly rises to the surface. *She is spectacular,* he murmurs, and her icy gaze meets ours for a breath before locking on Marx once more.

Luna's voice rings out with a savage clarity for all to hear.

*Since it is my bonding ceremony, I don't wish to spoil the night by bloodying myself in your filth. Your punishment for your abhorrent rule as an alpha will be spending the rest of your pathetic life as a human. Do not show yourself again, unless you wish to die. Now get out of my sight.* She snaps her jaws in finality and he cowers away from her, scrambling back on his ass with fear.

I watch with both astonishment and amusement as Marx flops over the edge of the dais and hurries through the parted crowd. Luna stamps her paw and shakes her head, lifting it regally as she looks out over the hundreds of stunned faces staring up at her.

*Whoever belonged to his pack now has the choice to collectively decide who becomes Alpha and how. I suggest using this opportunity to start anew. Seeing how there is no Guardian blood within your pack, at some point in time, someone must have deviated from the traditions and created their own pack away from the original five. Perhaps now is the time to begin a new tradition. Regardless of the structure you decide upon, your pack members shall have a choice of participation, admitting any willing wolf who desires it. Set your own rules, and adhere to them. Any wolf who wishes to join one of the other five packs has freedom to do so now.*

Her voice echoes around the eerily silent Hall, and she sweeps her gaze across the four remaining alphas standing ramrod straight at the front of the crowd.

*Are there any objections to this, Alphas?* Luna addresses them directly.

Daine immediately shakes his head with an adamant *'No'.* Luric and Castian also silently deny, and Felagi just grins wildly at Luna with a slight shake of his bushy hair.

*Good. I am glad we are in agreement. I look forward to speaking with you all further.* She lets out a huff of breath before shifting back to her human form.

Hushed murmurs float around the crowd from the spectacle that had just taken place. I bristle as Selene stands before them—*my naked mate*—waiting for everyone to collect themselves. It is *extremely* difficult for me to swallow back the hot discontentment at other males ogling her, and I have to force myself not to block her from view.

*It* is *a power move, though,* Valdr mumbles with an easy tone, and I growl lowly with disdain.

Selene's mouth twitches at the corner upon hearing his voice and she takes a measured breath. Before she speaks, however, many people begin to lower to their knees as they show their reverence for her, with some even bowing their heads. The crowd as a whole silently descends, and my gaze flickers to Selene, watching with a swelling heart as she raises a hand to swipe away a tear.

She holds out her arms to everyone with a small shake of her head.

"Please rise," she calls out in a gentle tone thick with emotion. "I do not see you as beneath me, so please do not kneel. My purpose is to hold power *with* you, not *for* you or use it as a show of status to hold over your heads. My only desire is to protect and defend our kind, not to be groveled at like some pompous *bitch*. Though I do hold the title as Queen, I only expect respect when I have shown it firstly. I will say, however, that I have no qualms with using my power to correct the *misguided ways* that some wolves succumb to. Believe me when I tell you that you *do not* want to be on the side of my wrath, as you have witnessed tonight." She flicks her gaze toward the doors Marx scurried through.

"I may appear pretty and soft like a flower, but be warned that I am a thorn bush adorned with roses, one whose sting is lethal, and I do not take kindly to threats of *any* sort against my people or myself." Her strong, clear voice echoes off the silent walls and into the balmy night.

It takes a moment for anyone to move. Once the alphas push to their feet, the rest of the crowd follows suit.

An admirable cheer billows from them as everyone applauds Selene in support. Howls and whistles ring out, and Selene grins widely as she turns to look at me.

I can't stop myself from stepping beside her, crouching to lift the dress pooled at her feet. Her laughter tinkles around me as I help her slide her arms through the thin straps. After she steps into her shoes, I zip the back of the dress for her. Gliding my hands over her waist, I lean forward and kiss the side of her bare neck before I replace her jewelry and turn her around, gently taking her hands in mine.

Once our eyes meet, I lower to my knees before my soulmate.

The crowd hushes, watching us intently.

"Kyran," Selene whispers with a pinched brow.

I hold her bright gaze and smile like a fool up at her, swallowing against the lump in my throat.

"Selene, I couldn't dream of a better woman to bond with, and I am *honored* to share my soul with yours. I vow to make you feel every bit of love, joy, and care that you have given me for every single moment of every day that I have with you. I will treat you like a queen, *even if you weren't one already,"* I whisper loudly, chuckling as laughter trickles out from the crowd. "I have loved you since before I even knew who you *really* were. I love the woman I met climbing the shelves at the store like a squirrel searching for her stash of nuts."

I grin as more laughter rings out, and Selene giggles with tears spilling from her eyes.

"I love the woman before me now, the most strong, selfless, and gentle person I have ever known. The woman I have the privilege to not only call my Queen, but my *soulmate*. You are far greater than I ever imagined I could deserve, and I promise to cherish you forever. You don't just hold my heart, Selene, you *are* my heart. I will love you forever, sweetheart," I murmur, smiling through the tears that have sprung, letting them fall freely as I hold her gaze.

A small sob escapes Selene as she smiles warmly at me.

Her eyes are filled with the love I feel radiating within me, and she pulls a hand away to swipe at her face. "Well," she sniffles, "I don't know what I can say to compete with *that.*"

She giggles through her tears and the crowd around us echoes her laughter. Meeting my gaze once more, she whispers my name and lowers herself to her knees before me.

"Selene," I start to protest, but she just shakes her head.

She pulls my hands to her lips, kissing the tips of my fingers before lifting our hands and rising to her feet. I stand with her, smiling adoringly at her as she slides her arms up over my shoulders and winds them around my neck. Crouching, I scoop her into my arms once more.

She presses her forehead to mine.

"Kyran, *you are a good man,* and I am *proud* to have you as my soulmate. *I love you,"* she whispers, her voice passionately firm, and my heart gives a weighted *thump* at what she said.

Her words mean more to me than an entire speech. She and I know that, making this moment all the more powerful because of it. I tenderly brush my hand across her face. Lifting her chin, I kiss her passionately and the crowd erupts with raucous, jovial cheering. We deepen our kiss, my chest filling with the warmth of our entwined love, and I laugh against her lips with the euphoric feeling. Selene laughs along with me and rubs our noses together lovingly before leaning back in my arms.

"May the moon goddess bless you all as she has done for us! Let us take to the woods and celebrate!" she bellows with a wide grin, throwing her head back to release a wild howl.

*Everyone* in the Hall returns the howl, and many even shift with the rising energy, taking off through the open doorways and into the night. I lower my head with laughter and meet Hekate's gaze amongst the writhing crowd. She grins up at me with a wink, and transforms into a swirling mass of ravens. The black birds soar overhead, whisking around us for a couple of passes before flying away with echoing caws.

Selene smiles widely as they disappear and brushes her hand over my face.

"Let's go party with our people," she murmurs with a chuckle, pulling me in for another kiss.

I sigh mockingly. "If I must," I drawl and smirk, kissing her nose before leaping off the dais with her cradled in my arms.

## SELENE

Elation doesn't even come close to how I feel as Kyran carries me through the ecstatic crowd. With the way these people have openly accepted me and Kyran's declaration of his love for me, my heart is ready to explode.

I can't stop the tears from falling as joy overflows within me.

Wiping a hand over my cheeks, I glimpse Ria pop her head around Kyran's shoulder with a wide grin.

"This has been *the* best night in a long time, and it's barely even started!" she shrills over the undulating cheers around us.

I laugh at her excitement and waggle my eyebrows at her. "Yeah? And why's that? I saw where you were standing," I insinuate and she smacks my shoulder in return.

Kyran's chest rumbles defensively, and I laugh because I know he'd never actually act upon it...*I hope.*

"Careful, or I'll sic my mate on you." I narrow my eyes at Ria and she glances earnestly up at Kyran before rolling her eyes at me.

"*Ha-ha.* He doesn't have anything to worry about. After your little display, I'm sure everyone here is far more terrified of *you* than him." She sticks her tongue out at me and I snort a laugh.

"Damn right," Kyran mutters with a chuckle as we approach a freshly lit bonfire. "She's fucking *badass.* Is it weird that it kind of turned me on?" He grins lopsided at me, making both Ria and I bark a laugh.

"Nope," Treyvar's voice drawls before he claps his hand to Kyran's shoulder. "Not weird at all, and you're *definitely* not the only one to think that." He grins widely.

We all laugh except for Kyran, whose gaze narrows on Trey. His eyes flash hotly at his brother, growling deeply, and Trey's palms fly up.

"Whoa, kidding, kidding! Totally just messing with you." He turns over his shoulder and dramatically winks at me with a devilish grin.

Ria snorts a laugh, and I slide out of Kyran's hold before he shoves at Trey. He just laughs and ducks out of Kyran's reach, evading a headlock. I roll my eyes at their boyish behavior and glance at Asteria, watching her watch them.

I give her a sly look.

Before I get the chance to poke fun at her, Kira arrives with an armful of full glasses and a wide, bright smile.

"Hey, love-pups! I come bearing gifts," she announces and bends forward for Ria and I to take a couple of drinks before whistling sharply at her brothers. "Boys! Take these before I drop them," she demands.

They obey her immediately, taking the glasses.

I grin at their dynamic, and Kira tosses her light blonde hair over her shoulder—a move *scarily* similar to Ria—and I stifle a snort as I take a sip of my drink. The bright pink and orange liquid is both sweet and sour as it coats my tongue, and it almost fizzles with an electric feeling when swallowed. Furrowing my brow at the drink, I hold it up to the moonlight, peering at the glass.

"Is this infused with magic?" I ask, noticing the swirling movement of the drink.

"Yep! Ria's very own brew," Kira chirps as she winks at my sister.

I smile at them, glad that they have formed a connection.

"I made it strong enough to withstand the wolves' healing ability, at least for a short while, so people could let *extra* loose tonight." Ria grins at me, raising her brows a few times.

"So, that means I probably *shouldn't* have downed it, I'm guessing?" Trey says sheepishly, holding up his empty glass.

Kira gawks at him.

*"Trey!"* she breathes incredulously. "I let Ria test it on me to get it right, and let me tell you, after a few *sips* you'll feel its effects, let alone the entire glass!"

Treyvar's laughter bubbles out of him uncontrollably, and all of us burst out with our own as he careens to the left a couple steps. Kyran reaches out to steady him, his face creased with amusement.

"Well, *shhhit,"* Trey drawls with another loose laugh, and Kira rubs at her forehead with a groan.

Ria chuckles and ducks under his shoulder, wrapping her arm around his waist. "I'll keep watch over him, you guys have a good night. I'll let him ride this out for a little while, then I'll give him something to clear it away in a bit. I need a good laugh." She grins wickedly as Trey sways on the spot and pets her hair with a hooded gaze.

She vanishes with him into the wind and Kira blinks at where they stood, glancing down at her drink for a moment before shrugging and taking another swig.

She turns and places a kiss on my cheek. "I'm really glad for you to enter our lives. You've no idea the impact you've already made." Her eyes glisten as they flicker to her brother, and she smiles warmly at the both of us. "Enjoy your night! I've got a mate to find," she says with determination, grinning at Kyran's mock sound of disgust and saunters away into the dense crowd.

"Kira!" Kyran calls out to her, trotting to catch up to her as she turns around. "Your bracelet, where is it?" he asks tightly, worry etched onto his face.

Kira rolls her eyes, and she holds out her hand with a thin, pretty leather bracelet dangling between her fingers. "I was just getting it on, relax. It's not like I *need* it tonight." She sticks her tongue out at him before disappearing between groups of people dancing wildly.

"*Fuck,*" Kyran growls, running a hand over his face. "I forgot yours in my study," he grumbles as he makes his way back to where I stand.

I turn to Kyran and take a small sip of my drink, watching him over the rim of my glass. Someone catches my gaze behind him in the crowd. My stomach clenches for a moment and I lower the cup, narrowing my eyes as I peer around his arm.

*No, it couldn't be,* I deny, searching the small groups of people clustered nearby. Kyran's warm hand grasps my bare shoulder and I pull my attention back to him.

His eyes are hard, sharply focused.

"What is it? What did you see?" he asks immediately, gently rubbing his hand along my arm.

I just shake my head with a small wince and mutter, "I thought I just saw B—"

"Selene," an old, worn and familiar voice greets me from my left. "It's been quite some time."

I quickly turn with a wide smile, finding Eirene and Chrestotes waiting with soft smiles on their weathered faces.

"Oh my *stars!*" I breathe with a laugh and throw my arms around Eirene in a warm embrace. "How are you? I am so glad to see you both! I hope things have been well since we last met." I smile broadly at them and they both chuckle as they nod in unison.

"We are well, thanks to you. It was difficult not to speak of you to Kyran, though I'd wanted to so badly," Eirene says quietly, wiping a tear away. "It is because of you we were able to escape that wretched place and live long, happy lives together here. Both of us have been eternally grateful for you, my dear." She places a soft hand against my cheek and I sniffle, nodding with a watery smile.

"I love love," I say with a shrug, "and I'd do anything to help it along." We both laugh at the brushed off weight of the situation.

I'll never forget aiding in their escape from their warring imprisonment camps, and by the looks in their eyes, they have not either. Kyran slides his arm around my shoulder and squeezes lightly, giving me a small smile.

"Elder Eirene was the one who pushed me to trust my instinct on following my pull to you," he murmurs, and I smile widely at her.

She just winks as her mate takes her hand in his and kisses her knuckles. They murmur their well-wishes before lowering their heads in respect, and I follow suit as they take their leave. I rest my head against Kyran's chest, watching them leisurely make their way through the boisterous crowd.

My heart is content as I glance up at Kyran. Smirking, I murmur, "Wanna go find Ria and Trey?"

Kyran laughs with a nod, taking a swig of his drink, and I focus on Asteria's power signature for a moment. Locating roughly where she is, I summon my shadows. The cool ether swirls around us for a heartbeat, gently depositing us in a small grassy clearing near another bonfire, and a few people holler out in excitement at the sudden sight of us. Kyran's grip on my shoulder eases as our feet solidly press into the earth, and he glances sideways at me.

"So you *can* be easy with it," he mumbles and I laugh, knowing how disgruntled he gets with the shadow-walking.

"You'll get used to it," I tease, pecking a kiss to his stubbly cheek.

Ria lets out a whoop of joy. "Look who's joined the fun!" She grins, her face rosy, and throws her arms up into the air. "Let's *really* get this party started!" she yells enthusiastically as loud club music booms across the fields from her magic.

Cheers echo hers as people start to dance wildly.

I laugh and sway along to the beat. Ria twirls around Trey and he watches her intently, grinning wide. Kyran chuckles with a shake of his head, but his eyes are light and carefree.

Just as I'm about to pull him over to dance with us, I notice Kira approaching behind him with a wary look on her face.

I scrunch my brow and easily find her connection through my bond with Kyran.

*Kira, what is it? You look troubled,* I mindlink her quickly.

Her light green eyes find mine immediately, and she looks a bit relieved, blowing out a sigh. *I, um, found my mate,* she hedges, and I can't help the grin that spreads across my face. Her eyes scrunch with a smile, then pinch as she winces. *I think Kyran should know now rather than later. I have a strong feeling he is not going to like this.*

I'm about to ask why that is, until I notice the man who slides his hand over her shoulder and smiles down at her adoringly.

*Oh my goddess,* I breathe, immediately understanding her trepidation.

Hearing my thought, Kyran's gaze whips to mine and instantly turns to follow my line of sight, landing on his sister and Daine standing a few steps away. A rumbling growl rolls from his chest as he notices where Daine's hand is. Kyran stalks toward him. Kira jumps between the two of them, placing her palms against her brother's chest. If it was *anyone else,* I would have had my own irritated growl tearing free at the sight.

"Kyran, stop, *stop,*" she insists and pushes against him, getting his attention. "He's my mate!" Kira blurts without preamble, and Kyran's head snaps down to glare at her.

"What? *Him?*" He groans loudly, tipping his head back at the sky. *"Why?"* he mutters, dragging a hand over his face.

I press my hand to my mouth to stifle the laugh that wants to escape. Kira cracks a smile as her brother lets out a heavy sigh, glaring at Daine. *"If you ever hurt her, in any way, I'll—"*

"I would never," Daine says solemnly, stopping Kyran's words.

They hold each other's gazes for a long moment before Kyran nods once.

I'm sure something has transpired between the two of them from the way he lets it go so easily. He turns to Kira again with a small smile and pulls her in for a one-armed hug.

"I am happy for you. Although, I'm sorry you're fated to bond with such a sack of shit," he grumbles, and Daine growls lowly at the comment.

My instinct to protect my mate overrides my common sense, and I smile coolly at Daine. I step into his line of sight and glare at him, cutting off his growl immediately. Asteria calls Kira over in a singsong voice, and I follow as she passes by.

"Congratulations!" I chirp and she squeaks in response, bouncing on her toes a little. I chuckle at her elation.

"It totally happened by chance. I was just passing by his group of packmates when someone accidentally bumped into me, and he caught my elbow to keep me from falling. I didn't realize *who* it was until I could focus after the bond magic settled over me. I was in disbelief for a few moments. I haven't officially accepted him yet, *obviously.*" She rolls her eyes dramatically, and we laugh as we come to a stop near Ria and Trey bouncing along to the music.

"Do you think you will?" I ask, swaying to the rhythm beating around us.

Kira takes a sip of her drink and sways as well, peering back to where Kyran and Daine stand talking a few paces away from each other.

"I don't know yet. I want to give him an honest chance before I decide," she murmurs, and I nod in understanding.

"I think that's a great idea," I say lightly. "You never truly know who someone is unless you give them the opportunity to show you themselves, without biased opinions clouding your judgment."

Kira nods, pulling her gaze away. "You're absolutely right, *sis,*" she says with a wink, and we giggle as Ria takes both our free hands in hers.

I do as Ria had said and let loose, finally allowing myself to let go of the restraint and allow my happiness to take me over. The heady feeling that's filled me since I accepted Kyran bubbles over, and my laughter trickles out into the night sky as we dance freely, letting our conjoined joy mingle with the stars.

Asteria catches me around the waist as we bump and spin to the music of her magic. Her fingers glitter, wiggling around me, and she transforms my gown into a sleek, silky sheath that hugs me to my mid-thigh. Kira lets out a whistle of approval, and Ria grins widely, twirling me around and around.

Through a spin, I catch Kyran's heated gaze as he watches me over the rim of his glass, and I beckon him to join us. He shakes his head, so I pout. Kyran tilts his head to the side with a smirk and makes his way toward me. I grin widely, reaching to pull him closely when he is only a few steps away.

He slides his hand over my waist and down to my lower back, drawing me in for a kiss. Just as his lips graze mine, he tilts me back into a low dip and kisses me passionately, stealing the breath from my lungs.

The girls holler around us and I laugh against his smile. Kyran straightens before he sends me into a twirl, pulling my hand lightly and spinning me so my back lands against his chest. He wraps his arms around my waist and rests his head on my shoulder, kissing the crook of my neck. My heart swells at his touch and I lean into him as he sways us to the music.

Daine, Felagi, and the other alphas join us, and Trey lets out a raucous shout that turns into a howl, triggering a domino effect throughout the surrounding crowd. I laugh loudly and Kyran's chest shakes against my back from his laughter at his brother's antics.

A willowy, stunning red-haired woman appears before us and offers me a small wave in greeting. I squeal at the sight of my *very old* friend. Kyran's grip releases me as soon as I pull away, and I launch myself at her with elation.

"*Eir!* I was hoping I'd see you tonight!" I trill as I push her shoulders back to look into her golden eyes.

She laughs melodically. "So did I. It is good to see you, *ithildin,*" she says softly with a wide grin.

Kyran sighs as he steps up beside me, eyeing the both of us. "I take it you two know each other?" he says flatly, and we laugh in response.

"Oh, yes. I met Eir *quite* a long time ago. Have you lived here since?" I turn to her, raising a brow.

"*Mhm.* After our little...*trade*, I sought these mountains as my home, and have remained here ever since. The pack formed a while after I arrived, and they had accepted my previous residence without qualms since I offered healing services in exchange for my privacy." She smiles at Kyran knowingly.

He squints at her before turning his narrowed gaze on me. "Trade?" he asks hesitantly.

I laugh and Eir nods her head toward me. "Do you still have it? I didn't get the chance to check when I healed you," she murmurs, and my brow furrows.

"I'm not sure. I hope so," I say, glancing down at my bare hand.

Kyran flicks his eyes between us with an odd look on his face. "*What* are you two talking about?"

Eir grabs my left hand in hers and waves her fingers over the back of it, a silver-glowing rune appearing on my skin for a moment before fading away. She nods with a grin.

"Yup, still there. Good. I would've replaced it anyway, if it had somehow disappeared," she says offhandedly.

Kyran's gaze darts from my hand, to Eir, stopping on my eyes. "Selene, what was that? Will one of you *please explain?*" he grumbles, glancing at Eir again.

She and I laugh, and I rub my palm against his thick chest, soothing his tension. "It is an elvish rune of protection. It prevents an elf from glamouring me or deceiving me with their magic. Eir traded it with me for the ability to shift into a wolf," I inform him quietly.

I roll my lips between my teeth, biting back the giggles that threaten to escape me at his bewildered expression.

Eir quickly sweeps her arm out and snags Kyran's hand, pressing a glowing palm over his. His lips part to object, but a flash of silvery light silences him, and his eyes flicker to the rune fading on his tan skin. She just winks at him before giving me a warm smile.

"I'm not *supposed* to do that, but I'll make an exception for your mate," she whispers with a twinkle in her gilded eyes, and I whisper my gratitude in return.

Treyvar stutters a few curses before staggering into our little group with rounded eyes. He clearly overheard what I'd just said. He opens his mouth and Kyran slaps his palm against it, wheeling his gaze back to Eir.

"So you're *not* a werewolf." Kyran narrows his eyes at her, and she shakes her head with a playful smile. "*Or* a witch," he says flatly, clearly having his own curiosity about her finally being answered.

Eir's golden eyes brighten, her smile spreading wider when she shakes her head again, and Kyran lets out a small sigh. "You really are fae. How did I not know? So *that's* where my father got the blood…" His voice trails off, shaking his head in disbelief.

Trey slaps Kyran's hand away with a squeaky inhale and whirls around to face Eir.

"*You're a fucking faerie?*" he shouts incredulously, his eyes nearly bugging out.

Many heads turn at his outburst, and wide, curious eyes glance our way. I burst out laughing at the flat look on Eir's face as she crosses her arms.

I nod as I laugh and wipe my eye, answering, "Yes, though she—and the *rest* of her people—prefer if you'd call them elves."

Stunned silence hovers for a few moments before Treyvar throws his head back and bellows a laugh, holding his abdomen. "That's fucking *awesome!* Do you have the ears, like in the stories? *Please* tell me it's true." He grins like an idiot, and Eir glares at him as if she's contemplating turning him into a toadstool.

Kyran and I snort at the imagery. She just rolls her eyes, brushing back her coppery hair. Her ears appear normal like anyone else's, until she waves a hand over one and the air shimmers for a moment, revealing the elongated pointy tip. Trey whoops with a laugh and Eir smirks at his antics, letting her hair fall back into place. She smiles warmly at me.

"I am very happy for you, Selene. May you both live long, joyous lives. I look forward to ushering your babies into this world one day," she adds with a wink and grins before vanishing on a shimmery cloud of dust.

Asteria cackles and throws a fistful of magical glitter into the air. It explodes around us like a firework, inciting hollers and cheers from the crowd. She sends more higher into the sky with glee. I grin up at Kyran as I wind my arm around his waist. He presses a kiss to my head and I snuggle into his embrace.

"Magic is fucking awesome!" Trey exclaims, the joy on his face childlike in his drunkenness.

I slide out from beneath Kyran's arm, giving him a sly smile. "Wanna see the last of my abilities?"

He nods eagerly and I take a step away, glancing up at the moon high overhead. "I can only do this with moonlight," I murmur, dropping my gaze back to him.

The other alphas watch me curiously, the four of them hovering behind Kyran, and I flicker my gaze over each of them. "One of you will be able to do this, too. Should be fun figuring out who gets which of my abilities," I tell them brightly, smiling wide.

When my eyes meet Kyran's again, I wink before imbuing my magic and everyone gasps as I disappear. Kyran looks immediately concerned, whirling around in search of me. I can't help the giggle that escapes me and he faces forward, his eyes not quite focusing on where I stand. Reaching out, I brush my fingers over his arm and he flinches, his eyes darting to the empty air beside him.

"Selene?" he calls out, his nostrils flaring. "I can smell you. Where are you?"

I let my magic slip away for a moment, displaying myself in a flash only to vanish again just as quickly. Everyone around us exclaims with excitement and disbelief, and Kyran's mouth lifts at the corner, focusing on where I was. I silently creep around him, my steps undetected with the noise of the celebration. Lifting my hand, I quickly tap his shoulder and dart away when his arms sweep out to grab me.

My laughter floats away as he lunges and I dance out of his reach again. Kyran growls, his smile showing he enjoys this game. He turns his head away from me, scenting the air where I just stood. I back track, trying to trick him into expecting where I will go, but he suddenly lashes his hands out, snatching my waist. He lifts me off my feet and my laughter erupts as I release my magic, coming back into view.

Kyran grins triumphantly, setting me down gently and gives me a quick kiss. "You can't hide from me, I'd find you anywhere with that scent," he murmurs in my ear, sending tingles throughout my body.

Daine steps forward with wide eyes, his gaze flitting away from mine. "You become invisible? What else can you do?" he asks with astonishment, glancing toward Kyran before meeting my gaze once more.

I grin, sliding my fingers through Kyran's. "A few things, which each of you will be able to do. I'd like to meet with you all tomorrow so we can discuss what it means to be a Guardian." I meet each man's gaze individually. "Training will become a lot more interesting for you all," I say with a laugh, glancing up into Kyran's warm gaze.

He glides his hand across my jaw, tipping my face towards his and kisses me slowly. Trey hollers another incoherent cheer, and Ria sends more sparks into the sky.

I couldn't be happier as the night goes on, surrounded by my new family.

We party for hours, mingling with strangers who quickly become friends until the full moon creeps toward the trees. Many of the party goers have drunk their fill, with plenty of people running wildly through the fields and woods, both naked and in their wolf forms. Masses of people dance endlessly with everyone in the highest of spirits.

On my way back from a trip to the house with the girls, I pass by a tightly clustered group of people at the outskirts of the fields. A sickeningly familiar scent burns my nose. The same smell of tobacco and cheap cologne, but the new hint of rusted metal hits me hard. My stomach clenches as I whip my head around, locking eyes with Bolvi's scarlet glare.

My mind *wasn't* deceiving me earlier. I *had* seen him.

I tear my gaze from his for a fleeting moment to scour the massive group he stepped away from, noticing that *all* of their eyes are blood red. The mass of bodies is a mixture of berserk wolves and...

*No, no. It can't be.*

I exhale harshly in astonishment and dismay.

*Vampires.*

# CHAPTER THIRTY-ONE

## DEVASTATION

### KYRAN

*Kyran!* Selene's panicked voice cuts through my mind, and I immediately crane my neck above the undulating crowd in search of her.

*Berserkers and vampires, at the edge of the field, hundreds of them! Alert everyone immediately! I'll hold them off as best I can!* Her tone is cold and angry without a trace of fear, and my heart leaps into my throat as I take off towards the woods, shoving people out of the way with a savage growl.

*Jeger!* I mindlink him with a shout, *Hundreds of infiltrators, how did they get here?* I seethe, my blood pumping painfully as I snarl in my effort to get to my mate.

*I'm being ambushed! They're coming in droves, out of fucking nowhere!* His gruff voice strains in response.

My fury spikes violently.

*"Fuck!"* I hiss through clenched teeth.

Screams peal throughout the crowd.

A hazy smoke drifts upward from the ground. It becomes impossible to see through the rapidly growing chaos, and I suppress the urge to start throwing bodies out of my way as my desperation increases in search of Selene.

*We're under attack! Shift now and take out any red eyes you find,* I command the other alphas at once.

All of them send outraged responses, immediately followed by distant sounds of agony tearing through the air.

Valdr pushes forward and I shift, multiple wolves falling into step behind me as I cut my way through the melee, releasing a harsh howl into the cacophony of screams and terror. Many howls instantly respond. I know my pack is working cohesively, they are well trained to fight in units and I trust them to hold their own.

My paws slam into the grass as I cross paths with a hoard of vampires. Their razor tipped fangs are exposed in bloody grins, and I bare my teeth at them as I charge.

At the last moment, I feint to the left and leap onto the closest vamp to my right, clamping my jaws around his neck and tearing his head free in one swift movement. A few wolves tag team the vampires, one taking them down at the knees as another crushes their skulls in one fell swoop.

A harsh whine emits behind me and I glance over my shoulder as I run, finding a wolf not of my pack collapse beneath a vampire, their throat torn out and lifeless eyes staring at the sky. The sight enrages me and I search for Selene with haste, fearing the worst with her being the one to have uncovered them.

*Where are you?!* I yell out to her as I run.

Cutting through a small cluster of berserk wolves, I latch onto their throats and thrash their bodies to the ground, letting the wolves behind me finish them off as I keep moving.

*In the woods, not far from the Hall.* Her reply is brisk and tight, and I curse as I bank hard to my left, picking up speed.

A witch manifests in my path and snarls at me, throwing up her hands to raise sharp, craggy rocks from the ground. I am nearly impaled by one and leap clumsily to the side. A wet *crunch* echoes with another cut-off yelp of pain, knowing without looking that two of my wolves have met their end. Their loss rips through me and I clench my jaw as I circle around the distracted witch, stepping carefully to not alert her of my presence.

*Hybrids! Clear out the smoke and put markers in the air above any enemy you can find!* I call out to my pack.

Within seconds, bright floating stars begin popping up and dart around the writhing mass of chaos. A dark movement to the right of the witch catches my attention. Felagi hunts her as well.

Our eyes meet in silent acknowledgment for a moment before we simultaneously attack.

Just as I leap with parted jaws, Selene's spike of emotion causes me to falter. The witch whips her head around, hurling a mass of rocks like meteors. They slam into me painfully, knocking me off my feet.

## SELENE

The throng of berserk wolves and vampires break off into clusters, surrounding me. I summon my shadows to encompass my entire body. A drove of wolves pours through the forming wall and blood flies around me as bodies tear one another apart.

My eyes lock onto Bolvi's. He grins wickedly, the manic gleam in his red eyes portraying the loss of his human mind. I bare my teeth in a snarl, all of my emotions and memories of him pooling into one solid pit of rage as I lower my stance, tensing my muscles in preparation to fight.

This piece of shit *deserves to die,* and I am more than glad for it to be at my hands. He doesn't get the gift of healing his disease. Not when I know the true monster that lies within him, regardless of the vampire venom poisoning his wolf's soul.

I match his steps as he circles me, his crazed laughter echoing above the cacophony of death and despair. He just points a finger at me and numerous vampires dive in my direction. A few of them are ripped out of the air by wolves, and many of them are torn to pieces the moment their feet hit the ground. At least two dozen make it past the protective circle the wolves have formed around me, and I lash out with my power.

Sweeping my arms in an arc, shadows billow out widely and latch onto most of the vampires darting for me.

Clenching my fists, I harshly slam my arms downward and the resounding *cracks* of their bones shattering pulls a satisfied smirk to my face.

The few vampires who evaded me dash over their fallen brethren in a frenzied pursuit. I shadow-walk to vanish and reappear behind them, their rapid steps skittering to a halt in confusion. One whips around with a hiss and I smile wickedly, slicing a thin ribbon of shadow through the air, effectively beheading all seven of them at once.

My chest heaves from the exertion. I wheel my gaze around to find Bolvi baring his teeth at me with anger. He throws his head back, letting out a garbled howl and charges at me. His speed is unexpected and I leap back into my shadows, transporting myself to the other side of the small make-shift clearing.

I laugh dryly as he pulls himself short and whips around, glaring at me. He shifts, his dirt colored wolf baring his teeth, growling viciously.

A savage roar rips through the air, Kyran's pain and rage rolling through me, causing me to stagger a step.

Bolvi uses my distraction to leap.

# KYRAN

Felagi is successful with the witch's distraction, clamping his jaws around her middle and thrashing her side to side like a ragdoll. It gives me enough time to heal from her attack and I launch myself at her, snapping my jaws over her skull, crushing it without hesitation. Her putrid blood tastes like tar in my mouth and I cringe, shaking my head in an attempt to fling the bits of flesh from my teeth.

Bounding away, Felagi falls into step beside me and we cut through the slowly diminishing crowd as the fighting spreads out over my lands. The Great Hall crests into view through the hazy mist, and a beam of moonlight illuminates in the distance.

*Selene, it has to be.* I focus on the light and charge toward it.

A blast from a fireball rockets into Felagi, a pained snarl tearing from his chest at the impact. I whip my head to its wielder, finding a smirking, familiar witch holding up a flaming hand. She waves her fingers tauntingly.

She's one of the witches that was responsible for poisoning Selene that night at my bar.

I snarl at her as I skid to a stop.

She doesn't hesitate to throw fire at me, the burning balls coming in rapid succession. A couple singe my fur as I dodge my way toward her. She snaps her fingers, releasing a thin whip of flame along her side and lashes it toward me. It burns my flank as I dart forward and I growl from the impact. Leaping away as she strikes for me again, the fire flares around the ground, nearly missing my face.

*Kyran!* Trey's alarmed voice rings out, and his tawny wolf rushes up behind the witch with Asteria at his side.

The look of fury on her face as she rips her gaze toward me matches how I feel inside.

*"I've got this, go to her!"* she yells out over the din of fighting.

I don't waste a breath as I turn, bounding toward the glowing area where Selene must be.

I'm blindsided by a vampire, their arms wrapping around my ribs like steel as we collide, cracking my bones and dragging me to the ground. A savage roar leaves me as I slam into the dirt.

I catch sight of Selene surrounded by vampires, her shadows swirling around her. Gritting my teeth against the pain, I shift in the vampire's hold and drive my elbow *hard* into his head, his iron grip releasing me on impact. Rolling quickly to my feet, I wrap my hands around his throat and tear his head off with an angry yell, hurling his skull into another vampire lunging toward me.

It slams into her face, careening her backward, and I turn to run toward Selene.

Fire incinerates my skin as I collide with a wall of flames.

A scream of agony tears free as I throw myself backward. My blistered skin heals slower than usual.

I clench my jaw, scrambling painfully to my feet. The witch bitch's twin sister is standing at her back, grinning wickedly at me. I shift in my rage at the sight of her. My burns heal with my shift and I launch myself at the witch, my swift movement startling her, causing her to miss the hastily thrown fireball.

Trey darts out beside her. He clamps his jaw around her leg, dragging it with him as he passes, the *snap* of her bones echoing with her scream. She collapses and I lunge forward, but my jaws snap through the air as she vanishes with a shriek. My growl reverberates loudly, drawing the attention of her sister.

Asteria's black and white eyes glow brightly, raising her hands in the air. Lightning skitters around her fingers before shooting toward the witch, caging her body in a searing net of deadly power. Her agonized screams grow haggard as she burns alive, and I turn to race toward Selene without a glance back.

The wretched screaming abruptly chokes off, and a few sets of heavy paws pound the earth on either side of me.

I sense the other alphas' presence as we break off to encircle the hoard of vampires and berserk wolves surrounding Selene. The five of us tear through the writhing clusters, taking care to avoid each other's packmates as we thin the enemy masses in synchrony.

## SELENE

I manage to evade Bolvi's attack as I wrap my shadows around him, lifting his wolf off the ground and slamming his body down hard. He yelps as two of his legs break, but he heals *ridiculously* fast and charges at me again. I bare my teeth with a savage snarl, waiting until he leaps to shadow-walk behind him, lashing out a stream of shadows around his neck. I clench my fist and send him flying into the writhing mass of vampires.

*"You fucking bastard!"* I seethe with all my pain and fury at this monster who haunted me for too long.

I yank my arm back harshly, dragging his wolf across the ground.

*"Shift,"* I command powerfully, glaring into Bolvi's crimson eyes.

He shifts, pinned on his hands and knees before me.

Losing control, I hurl my fist into his jaw as hard as I can, his blood flying from his mouth on impact. I scream my rage with another blow, and another, before driving my knee into his chin. Thrusting my hand out with another furious yell, I slam my splayed palm against his awful face and blinding white light emanates around me.

Tears pour from the searing rage as I viciously rip the wolf's soul from his body. The agonized screams pouring out of him makes me grin savagely.

I clamp my hand around his throat, *hard.*

"I hope this fucking *hurts*, you piece of shit," I grit through clenched teeth, only inches from his face. "I hope you feel every ounce of pain you put me through. Let this agony be the last thing you feel as you *die by my hands,*" I hiss the words, glaring into his fearful eyes.

I raise my other hand, razor-sharp claws growing from the shadows coating my fingers. With a vicious snarl, I cleave into his chest. His eyes bulge when I grip his racing heart in a vice. Without hesitation, I crush it within my fist, tearing it free from his body as it still thumps its last beats.

My chest heaves as I watch the life leave his bloodshot eyes, slowly releasing my hold on his corpse with a sneer. I lift my gaze to the surrounding writhing mass, many eyes staring at me with either horror or pride, but I cannot find my warm, amber glow amidst the chaos.

# KYRAN

A bright white light catches all of our attention for a few heartbeats, and I shift to see Selene slam her hand against Bolvi's face.

*That fucking bastard,* I seethe, my rage boiling over at the sight of him. My agitation distracts me and I growl with frustration as I am tackled to the ground.

A vampire sinks his fangs into the side of my bare neck.

His venom burns into my blood and I rip him off of me, rolling on top of the parasite as I shove my hands into his mouth. I tear his bottom jaw free and another leaps onto my back, biting into the other side of my neck. I bellow out in fury and reach over my shoulder to drag it off of me, when another and another piles on, each venomous bite forcing me to my knees.

I watch Selene as she rips the soul out of Bolvi's body, and part of me is proud of her for being able to seek vengeance for what he'd done to her. The other part of me wants to be the one to do it.

I feel myself weakening with the venom coursing through my veins, their sharp nails clawing away at my skin, and all I can do is watch Selene. On my hands and knees, my gaze follows her as she slams her hand into his chest and gouges out his heart, his cries of agony dying with his body.

*I'm glad you could be the one to do it. I'm proud of you,* I murmur to her through our bond as my vision starts to blacken.

I shake my head to clear my sight and find her eyes locked onto mine through the writhing chaos around us.

I vaguely hear her cry out my name.

The weight of the vampires fly off of me. I shove hard against the ground with effort, twisting to grip the bloodsucker clung to my back and hurl him into the crowd. My blood seeps fast, streaming onto the churned earth in rivulets as I drag my gaze to Daine. He just nods once before diving back into the melee.

Whirling around, my vision narrows to a pinpoint on Selene's glowing body as she lets out a sob and stumbles toward me, her chest heaving from exhaustion. I curse against the thick throng of bodies in my way.

My stomach hits the ground, my breath turning to concrete in my lungs as a swirl of smoke billows out behind her.

Caedes manifests with the witch who evaded me, his eyes boring into mine.

The bastard's mouth pulls into a wicked grin.

*"Selene!"* I hoarsely scream in terror, ripping everyone away from me in my panicked desperation to get to her.

*"Fuck! Selene!"* I helplessly bellow out into the air.

Haunting screams screech through the night. I watch in absolute horror as my worst fucking nightmare comes to life before my eyes.

It happens so fast.

Selene doesn't even finish turning to react when Caedes wrenches her head to the side, tearing her throat out with his fangs.

# SELENE

I drop the warm, slick heart to the ground, frowning at Bolvi's prone body. Kyran's trepidation waves through me. I whirl around in search of him, my heart in a vice. I'd seen him fending off vampires and my gut clenches when I find him on his knees entirely covered with them.

His blood coats his torn skin, eyes burning into me as he tells me how proud he is of me.

A sob escapes me at the awful sight.

"*Kyran!*" I cry out, reaching a shaky hand toward him, pulling my shadows to me once more.

My chest heaves with exhaustion and my body feels pushed to the limit, but I'd fight to my last breath to keep him alive. Alarm courses through me at the sight of the numerous puncture wounds on his body.

Luna's voice flows through me, easing my worry.

*He is our Guardian, he will be unaffected,* she speaks reassuringly, her voice firm.

Another sob wracks my chest and I stumble forward on weak legs, cursing my body for not being in proper shape. I breathe a sigh of relief when Daine appears beside Kyran, tearing the vampires off of him and he pushes to his feet.

Kyran's eyes blaze with fury as he meets my gaze again, shoving his way aggressively through the mass of bloodied, fighting bodies.

Time seems to falter as his eyes widen with terror, screaming my name. His husky voice is thick with rage and fear as he punches and tears his way toward me.

The chilling air at the back of my neck warns me too late of my demise. A hot tear streams down my face as Kyran bellows my name again, his pain roaring through both his voice and our bond. I turn too late to defend myself, my gaze ripping from his when my head violently snaps to the side.

Searing agony courses through me as Caedes's dark chuckle fills my ears, his sharp, metallic scent roiling my stomach before my blood spills from my torn throat.

White light bursts from me in thick beams, arcing through the air and slamming into Kyran's chest, ripping a savage roar from him.

Several equally bestial cries echo from the other alphas as the Guardian form takes over their bodies.

Collapsing to the blood soaked earth in a heap, my vision flickers. The last thing my conscious can focus on is Kyran.

*I love you,* I whisper to him with my last breath.

# KYRAN

My world slams to an excruciating halt when Selene's blood pours from her torn throat. Her body radiates blindingly, her power crashing into me with such force that it drags me to my knees. The intensity of it sears through my body, ripping a roar filled with every ounce of fury, pain, and despair within me.

The other alphas emit the same sounds around her.

Icy, raging energy tears through me and my limbs lengthen with hardened muscles as I shift into the lycan form of the Guardians.

Selene collapses to the ground.

Her gentle voice caresses my wild, seething mind. The purest, gut wrenching pain I have ever felt eviscerates me when I hear her whisper.

*I love you.*

My heart freezes solid when Caedes's wicked gaze meets mine the moment before he vanishes with Selene's body.

A blast of lightning engulfs the now-empty ground, charring it black. Asteria's horrified screams rake over me.

Blindly tearing through the people before me, I stumble to my knees and slam my elongated claws into the burnt earth coated in Selene's blood. Over and over I shatter my hands with the force of my blows, my agonized screams of rage and despair ripping through me.

My heart fractures and disintegrates with the torturous devastation coursing like fire in my veins. Raging shadows burst from my body in lashing ribbons, writhing around with my fury and agony at losing the love of my life.

I thrash the ground with my rage and distress that Selene is dead, my throat repeatedly bleeding and healing from the screams of agony ripping their way through me.

The darkness is consuming, swallowing me whole as shadows writhe viciously around the air in my unending despair. Collapsing forward, my claws gouge the bloodied earth. I'm overcome with wracking sobs, my pain unbearable, and my cries grow hoarse from the heavy emotion drowning me.

*"She's gone, she's fucking gone!"* I scream incessantly, *"I just had her and she's fucking gone!"*

My raw voice shakes the earth beneath my bloodied body.

Pressure at my shoulder causes me to lash out on instinct, a savage roar leaving me as I throw my body back. Fury blinds me as I swipe my claws through the intruder. Cries of fear and dismay echo around me as I search for the victim.

My stomach bottoms out when my bleary eyes clear enough for me to see.

I am sickened, *horrified,* falling to my knees when I find my brother lying listlessly on the ground before me, his chest gouged open from my strike.

*"No! No no no! Trey!"* I scream haggardly, scrambling forward and pressing my monstrous hands over the river of blood streaming from his shredded body.

*"Eir! Eir I need you! Please!"* I bellow, both into the night and mentally through my pack bond.

Treyvar's mangled chest rises and falls in a shallow, staggered pattern, wet breaths gurgling from his bloodied mouth. His wound isn't healing.

*Why isn't he healing?!*

Panic rises as guilt and shame eat me alive. I press into his wounds in a pathetic attempt to staunch the endless bleeding. I stare in horror at my foreign hands, at the elongated palms and fingers of the lycan form.

The hands of a Guardian.

*Some fucking Guardian I am!* I clench my hands into fists, sharp nails stabbing through my skin, and the searing pain does absolutely nothing to lessen the agonized fire raging inside of me.

A light, feeble touch grazes my fist and I jerk my head down to see Trey's colorless hand over mine. His arm shakes violently as he tries to say something.

"Treyvar, I am so sorry, I didn't know—I didn't mean to, I—" Pain radiates deeply throughout me, my voice cracking with the surge.

I grit my teeth against the keening wail that escapes me.

*"Please don't die, Trey, I need you,"* I whisper raggedly through my never-ending tears.

His fingers faintly squeeze mine before his hand slowly slides away, hitting the ground with a soft *thump*.

My breath falters.

A loud curse sounds beside me with a blinding golden light. I belatedly realize Eir has arrived, covered in dirt and blood, sobbing as she shoves her hands into my brother's chest, imbuing him with her healing magic. My gaze drags up his prone body, his faded green eyes staring blankly past me.

My chest constricts into a vice at the sight and I lurch to my feet, staggering a few steps away, shaking my head in denial. My mind reels when I realize he isn't moving.

*No, no, no. He…he can't…I…I killed my brother.*

Every seething emotion boils over and I throw my body back, screaming my agony into the night sky. I blindly turn and carve through the quickly parting crowd that surrounds us, running ceaselessly to nowhere, just running and running, never once turning back.

Not when there's nothing to turn back to.

# COULD THIS TRULY BE THE END FOR KYRAN AND SELENE?

## FIND OUT BY READING

## BOOK 2 COMING SOON!

# ABOUT THE AUTHOR

## D. M. MALONEY

is a veteran, a full-time stay-at-home mom, and part-time overlord of fictional realms. When she's not wrangling her minions or conquering Mt. Laundry, she's busy consulting her Chief of Staff Meowth, a Maine Coon cat who graciously oversees her work.

She enjoys crafting, nurturing her family, and dreaming up stories that delve into the dark and beautiful corners of love, where every heartbeat is a step into the unknown.